30119 027 856 38 6

Even
Angels
Fall

D1612858

By

F L Darbyshire

Grosvenor House
Publishing Limited

All rights reserved
Copyright © F L Darbyshire, 2014

The right of F L Darbyshire to be identified as the author of this
work has been asserted by her in accordance with Section 78
of the Copyright, Designs and Patents Act 1988

The book cover picture is copyright to Yan Stav

This book is published by
Grosvenor House Publishing Ltd
28-30 High Street, Guildford, Surrey, GU1 3EL.
www.grosvenorhousepublishing.co.uk

This book is sold subject to the conditions that it shall not, by way of
trade or otherwise, be lent, resold, hired out or otherwise circulated
without the author's or publisher's prior consent in any form of binding or
cover other than that in which it is published and
without a similar condition including this condition being imposed
on the subsequent purchaser.

A CIP record for this book
is available from the British Library

ISBN 978-1-78148-733-4

LONDON BOROUGH OF SUTTON LIBRARY SERVICE (SUT)	
30119 027 856 38 6	
Askews & Holts	Feb-2016
AF	

ACKNOWLEDGEMENTS

A huge thank you to my truly amazing family and friends for all of your constant and unwavering love and support over the years. I appreciate just how lucky I am to be surrounded by such an incredible group of people and I love you with all my heart.

The biggest thank you however, must go to my wonderful grandparents, who are still loved and missed every single day. My Grandma Rose, my Grandfather Robert but most of all my beautiful Nana Mona, who actively encouraged my writing and creativity from a very young age. She was my greatest supporter, my biggest fan and my best friend.

There are honestly no words to describe, just how much I miss her.

dedication

**In Loving Memory
of**

Samantha Rhodes

and

Johnny Duckett

There is always hope in the depths of despair.

"It Can't Rain All The Time…"

ଓଃ ————— ଃ୦

CONTENTS

PROLOGUE

REFLECTION

The bright, mid-afternoon sun pours through the open window, as the soft, summer breeze makes the trees outside sway together in a gentle dance. Abbey Miller turns her face towards the sunlight and closes her eyes, feeling the warmth on her skin. As the birds sing and the leaves rustle softly in the wind, she allows her thoughts to slowly drift away from her.

"Abbey...?"

She reluctantly opens her eyes and returns to the present moment. Sitting across from her is Dr Morris, with a pen resting in her right hand and a clip board balanced in her lap. She watches Abbey curiously.

"Writing about your experiences, actually putting them down on paper... it has been proven to be an effective tool when coping with trauma. I feel you might benefit from this... you may find it an easier way to communicate?"

Abbey shifts uncomfortably in the large leather armchair. How can she be blamed for not wanting to 'communicate' when she is so aware of Dr Morris assessing her every movement, enthusiastically scribbling down more notes because she rubbed her head or cleared her throat. It's not that Abbey doesn't trust her. She is clearly good at her job. The many certificates of achievement and qualifications that are framed and mounted neatly on the wall speak for themselves. She is patient and understanding, as all therapists ought to be. She just doesn't get the point in being here. What difference is it really going to make? Everything that has happened to Abbey in the past 18 months can't be changed or altered in any way. She can't take back all the bad decisions she has made.

No, there is no point. In Abbey's opinion, no amount of 'communication' is going to make the slightest bit of difference what so ever.

"Would you at least be willing to give it a try? You could write in the form of a story, or perhaps a diary... whatever you find easiest. And then in our sessions we can go through what you have written and discuss it together. Does that sound fair?" Abbey sighs quietly, nodding in response as Dr Morris flashes a brief, reassuring smile and seemingly satisfied, once again begins to add to her notes.

As the sun sets over the beautifully landscaped gardens outside, Abbey sits in her room, staring in frustration at the computer in front of her. It is dark - the only light coming from a small desk lamp that is balanced precariously on a pile of books and CD's. She watches the cursor flashing at the top of the screen, her mind completely blank. Why on earth did she agree to this? How is she supposed to put her tragic, dysfunctional life into words? She exhales the smoke from her cigarette and twists it into the ash tray, running her hands through her long auburn hair. She looks older than her years. Only 19, yet her pale green eyes reflect the maturity of someone much older, someone who has been through more than the average teenager. Someone, in fact, that has been through more than the average person ever will.

Eventually, she reaches for the keyboard, hesitating for a moment before she begins to type...

'Have you ever taken a step back and looked at your life?

Are you where you expected to be? Or do you often find yourself wondering 'how the hell did I end up here?'

I seem to be asking that question a lot these days - and as I reflect on the circumstances that led me to this point I still find it hard to believe.

Trinity and All Saints Rehabilitation Centre is somewhere I never expected to end up.'

CHAPTER ONE

THE NEW GIRL

The small, dark alleyway at the back of Labyrinth nightclub is littered with rubbish and drug paraphernalia. Situated on the outskirts of Leeds city centre amongst various lock-ups and storage units, it perhaps isn't the first place you would expect to find a bustling venue that is full to capacity. However, Labyrinth's popularity amongst the student crowd is obvious, and at 2am, many of them are spilling out into the street, staggering drunkenly arm in arm and falling into the back of waiting taxis.

Away from the vibrant scene in the shadow of the alleyway a young couple lean against a wall, kissing passionately as the dull beat of the music pounds through the air, but their stolen moment is quickly interrupted as the nightclubs service door flies open, slamming loudly and startling them into breaking apart. They turn and run towards the high street without stopping to look back, as a group of men come crashing outside.

Alex Matthews pulls himself to his feet and throws another punch at the baby faced skin head he is fighting, hitting him hard in the jaw and knocking him to the ground. The young thug struggles to get up and Alex kneels over him, grabbing him by the collar and pulling his face menacingly close as he shouts in a strong Irish accent.

"If you ever, EVER cross me again... you will be fucking sorry, do you understand me?" The skin head nods fearfully and Alex head butts him, knocking him out cold.

This isn't the first violent altercation Alex Matthews has ever had; far from it. In his early 20's the buzz he would get from a good fight would last for days after. That initial charge of adrenaline as the tension built between him and his opponent... the excitement, that feeling of being alive when so close to harm, it was what he lived for. But that was then - and even though Alex is only 28 years old, he feels like he has already lived a lifetime. The problem with that much violence is you soon become immune to its affects, the good and the bad. It becomes a regular occurrence, an everyday event, and the thrill soon fades. Although his anger still drives him, there is now a stronger, underlying feeling of inconvenience whenever he is forced to take action against someone who has wronged him. Despite his irritation, the option of walking away or letting it go would never even cross his mind. He will never be weak.

Alex can't help feeling a little envious towards his close friend Liam Dobson, as he undeniably still relishes the thrill of the fight. Only being 18 years old, it is to be expected. Liam, a dark haired, almost angelic looking boy, slams the man he is fighting head first into the wall and watches with a smile as he drops to the floor. He dusts himself off, wiping the blood from his nose with the back of his hand as he turns to witness his best friend, Nathan James, collapse to the ground, shielding himself as another of the skinheads over powers him. Without hesitation, Liam reaches down and picks up a large plank of wood, smashing it over the back of the man's head. There is a sickening crunch and he slumps to his knees.

"Are you alright man?" Liam holds his hand out to Nathan, pulling him to his feet.

"Yeah... cheers..." Nathan coughs in response, as he leans forward and spits a mouthful of blood onto the floor. As they steady themselves against the tall wire fence, a pretty, blonde haired girl appears at the end of the alley, holding a cigarette in one hand and her shoes in the other.

"GUYS... COPS!"

"Shit..." The three of them quickly sprint towards the opposite end of the secluded alleyway and jump the fence into an empty business park, doubling back towards the road and hiding in the shadows, as distant police sirens get louder and closer.

"Jesus, there's gonna be police all over the fucking street, there's no way we won't be seen..." Liam always manages to think the worst in any situation; perhaps that is down to his age as well? Alex however, knows it can always be worse and he knows that from personal experience.

"Well we can't exactly double back..." He states, calmly. "I doubt our skin head friends will be too happy to see us and I bet more of them will have shown up by now..." He casually lights a cigarette and leans against the wall.

"So what do we do?" Nathan, easily the quietest of the group, always keeps it together, at least on the outside. Alex likes him a lot - he is a good friend - but there are times when he can't help feeling that he doesn't quite fit in with their chosen lifestyle. He is shy with those who don't know him, articulate, well-spoken and incredibly smart. Alex always felt that he would have done more with his life had he been blessed academically, but maybe intellect isn't always enough? Not if you'd got a crappy start in life. Nathan is definitely the rational one, and even though he too is only 18, he is wise beyond his years. He and Liam have known each other since they were kids and they are definitely an unlikely fit for best friends, but then that is probably why it works so well. Liam's hot-headed nature is in stark contrast to Nathan's maturity, which seems to create a balance between them. Whatever the reason, they are incredibly close.

The loud, piercing screech of a speeding car startles Alex and he is instantly on guard, reacting before Liam and Nathan have even acknowledged the sound. They begin to back away as a black Vauxhall flies through the entrance of the car park and comes to an abrupt halt in front of them. Leaning out of the smashed, driver side window is Tom Warner. He too is in his late 20's, but could easily pass for older. He is stocky, well-built with dark spikey hair and a far too confident attitude. Alex always felt that he could be the poster boy for what a stereotypical cockney lad should look like. They had originally met in London, where Alex first settled after he moved over from Ireland with his Uncle, and on his move up to Leeds a few years later, Tom quit his job and came with him. Alex didn't ask him to, but he certainly didn't complain either. Tom is the closest person to him, his best friend who he trusts completely; even if he does drive him crazy at times.

"Care for a ride ladies?" The drunken passenger, 25 year old Darren Blake, stands up and leans out of the sun roof, with a cigarette hanging out of his mouth and a bottle of vodka in his right hand. He pushes his shoulder length brown hair back in one swift movement and rests his heavily tattooed arm on the roof of the car. Darren is the one person who hardly ever fails to make Alex laugh, but he ignores his question and marches towards them, pointing at Tom, accusingly.

"Where the fuck have you been?"

"Nice to see you too, sweetheart, are you getting in or what?" Tom looks incredibly pleased with himself as he smiles up at Alex, and he winks, knowingly antagonising him for his own amusement. It is something he does quite often, but he is the only person who can. He is the only person who can get away with annoying Alex Matthews and escaping unharmed, or with a dead arm at the most.

Liam climbs straight into the back seat, laughing at Darren as he loses his footing and drops back into the car, miraculously without spilling a single drop of vodka, despite how drunk he is. Nathan, ever cautious, follows a little more reluctantly.

"Where did you find this piece of shit?"

"A couple of streets down…" Tom taps his hand on the steering wheel, impatiently.

"Well who's is it?" Alex laughs at Nathan's question, as he walks over to the front passenger door.

"Jesus Nate I don't know, I didn't stop to fucking ask did I?! Come on!" Nathan shakes his head but dutifully climbs into the back seat next to Darren and Liam, and as the door slams shut, Tom floors the accelerator speeding off into the night.

Janet Miller stands with her hands on her hips, trying hard to remain calm as she assesses the chaos around her. Boxes and furniture are piled high in every corner of the bright, open hallway and removal men stagger through the door in turn, carrying even more of her family's belongings.

The large, semi-detached house in Meanwood stands in a leafy cul-de-sac, aligned on both sides with beautiful, weeping willow trees. Built from Yorkshire Stone with pale blue windows and a pale blue door, it is picture perfect, exactly what Janet had hoped she would find when she started looking for a new place to live. She had been so excited about the move, counting down the days in anticipation, but now, standing in the overcrowded hallway not knowing where to start, the excitement has all but vanished and the reality has very much 'hit home'.

"Where do you want this to go love?"

"Oh... that needs to be in the kitchen please..." She calls after the removal man, but he is out of sight before she barely has time to answer. Why did she think this was a good idea? As if she hasn't been through enough lately, the added stress of moving house surely isn't going to help. She rubs her tired eyes and glances at her reflection in the grand, iron mirror that is hanging on the wall to her right. She is tall and slim, with cropped blonde hair, perfectly styled. She is incredibly attractive for her age, yet she certainly doesn't feel it. 'Looking old girl', she thinks to herself. 'No wonder he left'. Her dejected train of thought is suddenly broken as her

24 year old son saunters into the house, casually surveying the hive of activity around him.

"Nice to see you helping out Peter..." She remarks, sarcastically.

"Don't blame me. Every time I try and help I'm told I'm getting in the way! So I thought I'd just wonder about, casually observe and you know..."

"Get in the way?!" Janet raises her eyebrow knowingly, with a half-smile on her face.

"I was going to say help if I'm needed...!" He laughs.

Although his cheekiness is infuriating at times, Janet adores her son. The way his light brown hair sweeps across his green eyes and his huge smile. He got away with murder when he was little, all he had to do was flash her that smile. But he is a grown man now and has matured so much lately. What with their family going through the most difficult thing imaginable and then some, he has really stepped up and supported her, helped her through the worst of the pain and stood by her. She will be forever grateful to him for that. Perhaps more than he will ever know.

"How are you holding up?" Peter asks - and once again Janet's thoughts are interrupted as she notes his look of concern.

"I'm fine. Really I am. I'd just forgotten how much work was involved in moving house. I mean look at this place... there's so much to do..." Her voice trails off as she stares anxiously at the pile of brown boxes that seem to have doubled in size in the last 5 minutes alone.

"Don't worry, it might be a bit overwhelming but we'll get it done..." Peter steps forward and puts a reassuring arm around Janet's shoulders.

"What on earth would I do without you...?" She asks.

"You don't ever have to worry about that!" He smiles in return, kissing her lightly on the head before lifting two boxes that are on the floor by his feet, "See... witness me... helping!"

He staggers over towards the kitchen, struggling a little under the weight, and as he reaches the door another removal man comes charging through it, almost crashing straight into him.

"Watch out of the way mate..." The man shouts in frustration and as he pushes his way past, Peter turns towards Janet with an exasperated look on his face. 'See!' he mouths, and Janet breaks out into laughter.

There was a time when she had almost forgotten what it felt like to laugh, but lately she has found herself smiling a lot more. It is still hard, but she doesn't feel quite as guilty as she once did. Things are definitely improving and Peter is right, no matter how huge a task it might seem they will get the house sorted, then they can start their new life together, a new beginning for the whole family.

As she shakes her head in amusement at her hopeless son, Janet's attention is drawn to two more boxes stacked over by the front door. They have 'Abbey' scrawled across them in bold, black marker and her smile falters a little as she takes a breath, and with a slight reluctance but a strong feeling of hope for the future, picks them up and climbs the stairs.

The pale cream walls and bare laminate floor make Abbey's new bedroom look cold and uninviting. Besides a bed, a wardrobe and a small chest of drawers, the room is empty and unfamiliar. Abbey stands by the window, trying to imagine living in this house and calling this room her own. Surely once she has all her belongings unpacked and organised around her she will feel much more at home? At least that's what she is hoping, because right now, everything feels totally alien. There is a light knock on the door and Janet peers round.

"Can I come in?" Abbey nods, but Janet is already in the room and walking over to her regardless.

"These are yours... " She places the boxes on the floor by the foot of the bed.

"Thank you. I'm almost done in here for now... I'll come and help downstairs when I'm finished..." Abbey's voice sounds unnatural and far too formal - as if she is talking to a complete stranger - but it is something she has become more than accustomed to. She can barely remember talking to her mum with a natural ease, just the two of them having a friendly conversation without a care in the world. That feels like a different life.

"There's no rush, I have your brother doing all the heavy lifting. Proof that there are actually odd occasions when he can be quite useful if he wants to be...!" Abbey manages a half-hearted smile at Janet, who is clearly trying hard to break the tension between them, but she isn't in the mood for jokes. All she wants to do is try and make this shell of a room even slightly resemble the bedroom she once loved. The bedroom she was forced to leave behind. She doesn't respond, and a moment passes in awkward silence.

"Well... I'll leave you to it then... " As Janet turns toward the door, Abbey feels a strong pang of guilt, but not enough to speak. This is all so new to her. She is in a strange house in a strange neighbourhood, where the family have moved because apparently it was in 'everyone's best interests' to do so. Abbey doesn't agree. She was much happier staying put in the house she grew up in. She wanted to stay at the school she knew with the friends she loved, but no. Apparently her opinion hadn't counted. Her feelings were a moot point. Everyone else had agreed and she was left with no other option.

"Abbey..." Janet turns hesitantly, "I know that we can be happy here. We can be a family again. It will just take a bit of time to get used to all the change, but I know this will be good for us... I'm sure of it..."

"It'll be great Mum..." Abbey isn't sure whether she is trying to convince Janet or herself that it is all going to work out, but either way, her words barely sound convincing at all.

As Janet returns to the madness downstairs, Abbey is once again left alone with her thoughts. She carefully lifts one of the boxes onto the bed and opens it, pulling out the contents one by one; a clock, a cuddly toy, and a photo album. She gently runs her hand over the cover of the album before opening it to the first page. Two smiling 5 year olds grin at the camera, a cake with lit candles sits on a table in front of them and there are others stood around them, adults and children alike, all singing happy birthday. It is a typical carefree scene that most experience at some point in their childhood, but instead of smiling at the memory, Abbey feels a stab of sadness, like a knife through her heart.

On the following page is a picture of a young man in his teens. He too is smiling widely at the camera, looking relaxed and happy. He has dark blonde hair with just a hint of red and bears a striking resemblance to Abbey. Written beneath the photo are the words 'Ryan on our 16th birthday'. Abbey traces her finger lightly over the picture and swallows hard as she feels the familiar sting of tears in her eyes. She loves this picture, but hates it at the same time. She hates how it makes her feel; looking down at her brother's smiling face from a time when he was happy and well, and still here. It is difficult to believe that it all went so wrong... thinking back to how it used to be and the person he was. She misses him so much, every single moment of every single day. Yet there is absolutely nothing she can do about it. There is nothing she can do to help him now.

Abbey's eyelids feel heavy, and after a long and hectic day of lifting, carrying and unpacking, she is completely exhausted. She has a million and one things racing through her mind; mainly her worries about the future and her regrets about the past. Everything has changed so much in such a short space of time and looking at the picture of Ryan that she treasures so much only makes her feel all the more lost. It is like she can't catch her breath. No matter how hard she tries, she can't wake up from this living nightmare. Lying on the bed in a room she doesn't recognize, she clutches the photo album tightly to her chest and lets her tears fall, breaking down and allowing the complete and utter despair take hold of her without trying to fight it any longer. Before she even realises, her exhaustion pulls her under and she falls into a deep but disturbed sleep.

It barely feels like 5 minutes have passed when the high pitched shrill of Abbey's alarm clock jerks her awake. She hits the snooze button - perhaps a little more aggressively than needed - and rubs her eyes as they adjust to the light. It never turns out to be a bad dream. In that initial moment after waking, when the real world comes rushing back, she always gets that hollow, sinking feeling without fail. Looking around her new bedroom she feels that sense of dread even more than usual. It's her second year of sixth form studying her A-levels and she has had the upheaval of moving house and transferring to a new school. The butterflies in her stomach make her feel nauseous as she wonders what the day will bring, her first day at Eden Comprehensive.

Abbey reluctantly climbs out of bed and gets ready in a daze, hoping that by taking her time she can somehow avoid the inevitable. 'I hate this' she thinks to herself. When the idea of moving house was brought up, Abbey had made her feelings clear from the start. They were of course ignored. Being the youngest and always considered the baby of the family her opinion never seemed to hold much of an impact. Even on this occasion, when she thought her feelings would at least be considered, she was wrong.

Her older sister Anna had moved to Leeds several years ago with her husband Dom. They originally met at university and loved the city so much, they stayed. When it was decided that the whole family needed to be together to get through the difficult times ahead, there was no question of Anna and Dom moving to them. They had just bought their first house, Dom had recently received a promotion at the I.T Company he works for and Anna is now, just over 4 months pregnant.

Her brother Peter is a plumber by trade and being self-employed, the move hasn't really fazed him at all. He will be able to find work and build up a client base in whatever city he finds himself in, which means it is only a minor setback.

And then of course there is her Mum. Janet works for a firm of solicitors as a P.A but for almost a year now she has been on a leave of absence. It started with bereavement leave, before quickly turning into sick leave as her state of mind deteriorated and she was struggling at her lowest. Although things have improved and she is more or less back on track, the whole family are constantly on edge, hoping that she doesn't fall back into the deep depression that completely took hold of her. Despite everything she has been through, Janet is still well regarded within her company. She has been a near perfect employee for the past 20 years and everyone still thinks very highly of her. For that reason, when the house is finished and things have settled down, she will be starting a new job at the Northern office of the firm.

It is only Abbey who has to start again from scratch. It wouldn't be so bad if she had Ryan with her to help her through it all. They would joke about their new teacher's, moan about how rubbish the uniform looks and laugh at all the kids who laugh and make fun of them. They always faced everything together; the two of them against the world, but Ryan isn't here anymore. Although he is part of the reason she is.

Abbey straightens her tie and stares at her reflection in the mirror. 'It could be worse' she thinks. At least the uniform is black and navy and not a ridiculous colour like you find at some schools. She hopes to blend in as much as humanly possible. In an ideal world she would have powers of invisibility and wouldn't be noticed at all. Or better still, in an ideal world, she wouldn't even be here.

"Abbey come on you're going to be late...!" Janet shouts from downstairs and suddenly the moment at hand seems very real. New school, new people, no friends. Abbey tries hard to focus and think positive. Maybe this will be a good thing? Maybe it will go great and she'll really like it? As she tries her best to convince herself, she is hit by another wave of nerves that cause her stomach to flip uncontrollably. Positive thinking never was her strong point.

It is a 20 minute bus journey to Eden Comprehensive from Abbey's new house but seen as it's her first day, Janet has offered to take her. Time is passing far too quickly, and whenever Abbey glances at the clock on the dashboard it appears to have jumped forward 5 minutes in what seems like 30 seconds. Her nerves are getting worse and she is starting to feel sick.

"Here we are!" Janet announces their arrival in an annoyingly enthusiastic manner, clearly trying her best to be encouraging. She pulls up outside a large, modern building that has 2 flights of stairs leading up to a walkway and the front doors to the school.

"You'll be fine darling, you'll do great...!" She adds, checking her watch distractedly.

Abbey takes a deep breath and climbs out of the car, glancing around at the mass of students - all in their matching uniforms - talking and laughing together as they make their way inside. The sudden desire to be back at her old school overwhelms Abbey. Her friends will be sat on the wall by the side of the gym right now, in their usual spot, chatting excitedly about what they did at the weekend and exchanging as much gossip as possible before the first bell rings, announcing the start of class.

She wonders if they are missing her as she slowly climbs the steps towards the main entrance, trying hard to ignore the stares and whispers coming at her from every direction. If only the ground would open up and swallow her. She should be so lucky. There is no going back now, as of today she is officially a pupil here and all she can do is accept it – and with that resignation, she opens the main door and nervously walks inside.

Abbey manages to find reception easily enough by following the various signs with their colourful little arrows pointing the way and she cautiously approaches the large oak desk that stands in the middle of the room. It is littered with stationery, fliers, in trays and post-it notes, and is occupied by a woman who is wearing far too much make-up and a perfume so sickly sweet it almost burns Abbey's throat.

"Excuse me?" The woman looks up from her computer with a vacant expression.

"Can I help you?"

"I'm new here... I was wondering if you could tell me where I need to be?"

"Name?" The woman speaks in a chirpy, pleasant voice but somehow still manages to come across as rude.

"Abbey Miller..."

"If you would like to come through..." She stands and walks over to the far side of the room and Abbey follows her obediently. She taps twice on the door in front of them before opening it and gesturing inside.

"Principal Grant? Our newest pupil to see you..." The man behind the desk doesn't look up from the letter he is drafting, but raises his hand and beckons Abbey into the room. She sits down quietly as the receptionist returns to her post and waits for him to finish writing. He finally screws the lid back onto his expensive fountain pen, puts his notepad away in the drawer and - rather abruptly - gets straight to the point.

Principal Grant is quite possibly the most stereotypical looking head master Abbey has ever seen. He speaks in a stern, well pronounced voice, his short grey hair and sharp features make him look hard faced and unapproachable and his glasses balance on the very tip of his nose, as if even they are trying to escape him. She hates him already. 'Good start'.

"Here is your class schedule, your book list for the term and a map of the school..." Principal Grant reaches across his perfectly arranged desk and hands Abbey an envelope. As he pulls his arm back, he accidently knocks his name plate, which he straightens immediately, making sure everything in front of him is in a neat, tidy line.

"So Abigail, is there anything you wish to ask me? Any questions you may have?"

"Erm... no, I can't think of any at the moment..." She replies, "And it's just Abbey... no one really calls me Abigail..." She smiles warmly at Principal Grant but his expression doesn't change. He simply stares at her for a moment, before continuing his well-rehearsed speech with little enthusiasm.

"Well, I am sure you will fit in well here at Eden. Of course if any questions do arise, you can come and find me or ask one of your teachers for help..." As Abbey is making another mental note of how much she hates her new principal, there is a light knock on the door and a young male teacher enters the room.

"Ah Mr Harper, this is Abigail Miller..."

"Abbey..." She mutters under her breath, too quietly for Principal Grant to hear, but by the look on Mr Harper's face he heard her just fine and sensed her irritation. As Abbey worries that she might be in trouble already, Mr Harper catches her eye and smirks mischievously.

"Very nice to meet you...*Abbey*..." He exaggerates her name as his smile widens - lighting up his whole face - and Abbey can't help but smile back. He is tall, slim, with ruffled brown hair and deep brown eyes. They definitely didn't have teacher's this attractive at her old school.

"Mr Harper will be taking you for A-Level English. He has offered to show you to your first class..."

"All part of the service..." Mr Harper gestures towards the door and Abbey stands, picking up her bag and her envelope of information before following him out of the room. Once they leave the reception area her nerves return, stronger than ever. She scans the busy corridor, trying her best to blend into her surroundings and remain unnoticed as they walk together down the long, crowded hallway.

"How are you feeling?" The genuine concern in Mr Harper's voice catches Abbey off guard.

"Pretty nervous..."

"Ah don't be... I was the same on my first day working here, but it soon becomes the norm. Give it a couple of weeks and you'll wonder what all the fuss was about..." The bell rings and there is a sudden burst of activity. Lockers slam to a chorus of laughter, shouts and screams, before the commotion quickly trails off into silence and the students make their way into their various classrooms, "I'm sure you'll be fine..." He continues, "But if you do need any help or you have any questions that need answering, don't hesitate to come and find me. I am you're teacher but I'm also..."

"... my friend?!" Abbey finishes Mr Harper's sentence with more than a hint of cynicism in her voice.

"I was actually going to go with 'head of sixth form'..." He stops walking and turns to face Abbey, amused and slightly curious at the same time. Abbey senses that he is trying to figure her out, and she likes it. Her nerves seem to have vanished, at least for the moment, "That's why I offered to walk you to your first lesson this morning. It's my job to know all the sixth form students and make sure they're doing OK. This is your class..."

Abbey peers through the door at the room full of students, all sitting together in their tight knit groups, laughing and talking, leaning back in their chairs and playfully reaching across their desks. She can already predict the hush that will fall across the room as she walks in. The new girl.

"Thank you..." She smiles up at Mr Harper.

"I mean it though. If you need to, do come and find me... even if it's just to talk. About school, course work, anything... home life... anything, anything at all. It really isn't a problem..." The concern that litters Mr Harper's voice suddenly makes complete sense to Abbey as she stares up at his sympathetic expression. It doesn't take a genius to spot how quickly he rushed over the words 'home life' either. He knows.

"Thanks..." Abbey's tone is a little cooler and she hopes that he senses it. She appreciates that he is only being kind, but if there is one thing she hates more than anything else, it is feeling like a charity case. She doesn't need or want pity. Pushing her thoughts to one side Abbey mentally composes herself as she opens the classroom door, trying in vain to ignore the hushed silence and obvious whispering, as she sits down at a desk at the front of the room.

The first part of the day passes by in something of a haze for Abbey. Her morning classes seem to be over in the blink of an eye, yet she finds herself struggling to keep her head above water. Everything is so new; there are so many names to remember and corridors and classrooms to memorize. The school is huge; at least it feels that way, and she is late to almost all of her lessons after getting lost using the so-called 'map' that Principal Grant gave to her. This doesn't help with her plan to go unnoticed. Instead of keeping her head down and blending into the background she had burst into almost every room in a state of blind panic, much to the amusement of the other students - and some of her teachers.

Lunchtime doesn't bring any sense of relief either, quite the opposite in fact. Apart from a few people who made polite conversation during her first few classes, she hasn't really spoken to anyone and she certainly hasn't made any friends. She doesn't know anybody, doesn't fit in anywhere, and for that reason she avoids the cafeteria like the plague.

She can't stand the thought of sitting at a table by herself amongst all the staring and pointing, so instead she finds an empty classroom and eats her lunch while going over the homework she has already been given. Abbey knew that starting from scratch was always going to be like this, but the sense of loneliness she feels is affecting her more than she thought it would. In the darkened classroom it is easy for her to give in and wallow in self-pity. Her first morning had been even worse than she could have predicted, and having an hour to sit and think about it all means she is on the verge of sinking into despair again. Breaking down in private is one thing, but she can't afford to do it here.

Luckily she is able to keep it together until the bell rings, signalling the end of lunch. She collects her books together and heads back towards her form room, rushing slightly so that she isn't late for the hundredth time today. As she charges around the corner - unsure whether she is even heading in the right direction – she is far too preoccupied with her thoughts to notice the small group of people that have suddenly appeared in front of her. Before she has time to react and to her absolute horror, Abbey collides with someone, and everything from that point on seems to happen in slow motion.

The breath is knocked out of her, there is a loud clatter as her books fall to the floor and she staggers back, unable to keep her balance. As Abbey hits the ground she can already feel the heat rising to her face in sheer, mortified embarrassment and she wishes more than anything that a cold, dark rock would appear in front of her so she could crawl under it and never come out. She can hear laughter erupting from the people around her, but when Abbey looks up at the girl she has just charged into at full speed, she sees no amusement on her face, only anger.

"What the fuck are you doing?!" She barks.

"I'm really sorry, I didn't see you..." As Abbey stands and regains her balance, she suddenly feels a sharp, piercing pain in the back of her head. After a moment of initial shock, she realises that she has been slammed violently into the lockers behind her and the girls hands are clenched tightly around the collar of her shirt.

"Wh... what are you...?" Abbey can barely get the words out - and her head and heart are pounding as the girl slams her into the lockers again.

"You don't barge into me bitch..."

"I said I was sorry... " Abbey can feel a lump beginning to form in her throat as tears build behind her eyes, but she is determined not to cry. A crowd of people gather to watch the confrontation unfold - staring in anticipation as they wait to see what will happen - and the girl eventually let's go of Abbey's shirt, laughing menacingly.

"Just stay out of my way freak..." She threatens, smiling at her friends as they saunter away.

Abbey quickly straightens her uniform and reaches down to gather her things from the floor, her breathing fast and her hands shaking. The sound of casual chatter once again fills the hallway and the scene instantly returns to normal, almost as if nothing has happened at all. Abbey can still feel the heat in her face and she hides behind her hair, not daring to look up in case she is still being started at, or worse, pitied by the people who have just witnessed her violent and very public humiliation. 'What the hell is that girl's problem?' Abbey thinks to herself. 'It was an accident'. A strong feeling of anger and resentment starts to build in Abbey as the hatred for her new school intensifies. It wasn't even her choice to be here yet she is the one suffering. Completely alone, totally alienated and now apparently she has made a brand new enemy... oh and no friends. All in all an incredibly successful first day. Honestly, of all the people she could have bumped into it had to be the crazy psychopath... typical! 'I knew I would hate this place'.

Abbey's furious, internal rant is interrupted as a hand appears in front of her, holding out one of her books. She looks up from behind her hair and sees a girl, crouching on one knee, smiling kindly.

"You missed this one..."

"Thanks..." Abbey takes the book and stands quickly, trying to act as casual as possible. The overwhelming urge to cry returns but she manages to control it.

"Are you OK?"

"I'm fine, thank you..." She always was a dreadful liar.

"Listen, don't worry about her, she's got a major problem with pretty much everyone..."

"Well, at least it's not just me, that's something I guess..." Abbey tries her best to laugh it off but she can feel her hands and voice still shaking and the girl smiles again. She is very pretty - small, petite, with wavy blonde hair and brown eyes. She is dressed in quite an eccentric way which is surprising to Abbey, seen as Principal Grant had drilled into her on their first meeting how much he values smart uniform at all times. 'Self-presentation is everything' were the exact words he had used. But this girl seems to openly flout that rule. She is wearing a skirt but it is short, her black boots are studded and her shirt is un-tucked. Her tie hangs loose around her neck and Abbey can see that she has a lot of jewellery on, at least 4 or 5 different chains and a ring on every finger. She is wearing the standard blue blazer but it is adorned with badges that have the names of numerous rock bands printed on them, and she has a scruffy looking green bag thrown over her shoulder.

"You're new here right?"

"Yeah, it's my first day..." Abbey sighs, regretfully, "I'm Abbey... Abbey Miller..."

"Nice to meet you Abbey Miller, I'm Lucy..." She chimes, sweetly, "Bit of friendly advice? Maybe try and watch where you're walking, especially when you're around dickheads like her...!"

"Yeah, I think it's safe to say I've learnt that lesson the hard way!" Abbey laughs, before their brief exchange is interrupted when Lucy's name is called from the other end of the corridor. Liam and Nathan are standing by the fire exit that leads outside into the courtyard and down to the back entrance of the school. As Liam raises his arms up, asking a silent question, Nathan checks back and forth, making sure that they haven't been seen.

"Sorry Abbey, I have to go... but I'll see you around..." With a friendly smile and a quick wave, Lucy races off to join the two boys and Abbey stands, watching curiously as the three of them disappear out of view. She lingers in the empty hallway, running over the last 15 minutes in her mind, trying to make sense of it all, when the bell rings, breaking the silence and causing her to almost jump out of her skin.

'OH SHIT!' Late again for the hundredth time today.

The rest of the week follows more or less the same pattern for Abbey, although her time keeping improves considerably. She keeps her head down in lesson and spends most of her lunch hour hiding herself away in whatever empty classroom she can find; a welcome break in the middle of the day where she can escape her new surroundings and the strange faces that aren't getting any familiar. She knows that she isn't helping herself and she should probably make more of an effort, but she just doesn't care enough to try. Everyday Janet asks her how school has gone and 'fine' is the only response she gives. There isn't an awful lot of point in telling Janet the truth. She wouldn't be able to do anything about it anyway and even if she could, she has always known Abbey's feelings about moving school. If she didn't listen to her before, why on earth would she now? The fact is, as much as Abbey may hate it, this is her reality.

On the plus side though, she has thankfully managed to avoid another run in with the crazed psychopath who she has since discovered to be a Miss Natalie Alder. She is, unsurprisingly, the resident bully. Abbey is constantly alert in between classes and especially at break times, forever looking over her shoulder and checking that she is nowhere in sight. Ridiculous that she should be made to feel this way by one girl, but the memory of Natalie slamming her into the lockers is still fresh in her mind and she certainly doesn't want anything like a repeat performance. Finally, after what seems like the longest, most nightmarish week of her life, Abbey makes it to Friday afternoon, relatively unscathed and still in one piece.

CHAPTER TWO

FRIENDSHIP

Abbey rubs her tired eyes and blinks hard as little patches of coloured light dance in her vision. She shuts the book she is reading and stretches out on her bed, staring up at the ceiling. 'Why do weekends always go so fast?' She wonders.

Abbey had never been so happy to see a Saturday before, and despite the weather being quite nice for this time of year she had spent most of the weekend locked away in her room. It still doesn't feel like hers yet, but she is working on it - hanging pictures and posters on the walls and arranging then re-arranging the furniture until she is relatively happy with how it looks. She has plenty of framed photos - most of which are of her friends back home - but she hasn't put them out yet. Although they will no doubt make the room feel much more personal, looking at them only brings on a feeling of deep depression, so for now they remain hidden away in a box in her wardrobe.

She had spent the majority of her Sunday tackling the mountain of homework she was given in her first week. Her entire class had been told about the amount of work they would be expected to produce in their final A-Level year, but it is still a shock to the system. What they should have been warned about was the fact they would have to kiss goodbye to their social life, as in between the studying, coursework and almost constant revision, there is hardly any 'down time' left at all. Not that it matters to Abbey now of course. She doesn't have anything that even remotely resembles a social life at the moment.

The alarm clock next to her bed beeps once, marking the hour. It is 8pm on a Sunday night, easily the worst time of the week. Abbey lets out a groan; that hollow feeling of dread has already started to creep up on her. Soon it will be Monday morning and the start of another fun filled week.

The house is quiet and has been for most of the day. Peter is out running various work related errands and Janet has spent the afternoon fighting her way through the remaining boxes that were stacked up in the garage. Almost everything is unpacked now apart from those few, and Abbey has to admit that it is starting to look and feel a lot more like home... but not enough for her to feel completely comfortable. She still can't shake the notion that this is all just a temporary solution. It hasn't really sunk in yet.

Abbey makes her way downstairs and shuffles into the kitchen wearily. She isn't exactly tired, but the thought of what might be in store for her at school tomorrow is enough to drain her energy and make her feel completely deflated. As she stares out of the window, absentmindedly making a drink, a familiar voice catches her attention and snaps her out of her daydream. She strains to hear, not sure whether she had simply imagined the sound that is all too recognizable to her. A moment passes and there is nothing but silence. Concluding that it must have been her mind playing tricks, she turns off the kitchen light, but as she is about to retreat back up to her bedroom Abbey hears the sound again. It is clearer this time, and it makes her stomach lurch and her heart drop in her chest... the careless laughter that she has missed so much and not heard in so long. Ryan.

It is then that she notices the dim glow from under the living room door, and Abbey knows exactly what she will find behind it. She has seen it so many times in the last year that she has lost count. It is extremely difficult to get through to her mum when she is like this, but what is she supposed to do? A big part of her wants to go back upstairs and pretend that she hasn't seen or heard anything, but that wouldn't exactly be fair. Despite how distant and cut off she feels from her family, particularly her Mum, she isn't cruel enough to walk away and ignore her when she is in pain and she is obviously having a difficult night.

Abbey places her drink on the side and carefully pushes the door ajar. Janet is sitting on the floor leaning against the arm of the sofa, with a large glass of wine in her hand. There is half a bottle on the table in front of her and she reaches forward, topping up her drink before resting her head back and wiping the sleeve of her cardigan across her tear stained face.

"Mum?" Janet looks up in surprise and opens her mouth as if to say something, but stops herself, "Are you OK?"

"Abbey..." Her voice is breathless when she finally speaks. "I thought you were in bed..."

"It's only 8pm. I was just getting a drink..."

"Oh."

Abbey waits patiently for Janet to speak again, but she simply stares at the glass in her hand before taking another large, comforting sip.

"Are you...?"

"I'm fine..." Janet sighs, cutting Abbey off mid-sentence while forcing a fake smile, "I've just had a bit too much to drink... you know how I get..."

"It's alright to miss him Mum." Abbey states, softly.

Although Janet has behaved this way before, it has been a while since she turned to alcohol to help her cope. She is getting much better at dealing with her grief, but she has never truly opened up to Abbey. Never spoken to her about what happened or how it affected her. She has never even asked Abbey how she is, at least not in so many words, as it is a topic that is more or less avoided altogether, and deep down, Abbey knows exactly the reason why.

"I know it's OK to miss him. It's just hard to miss him..." Janet finally responds.

"So talk to me..." Abbey pleads. She moves further into the room, and Janet flinches. Although only a slight movement, it doesn't escape Abbey's attention and she stops.

"Not now... I'm tired...." Janet whispers, resting her head on the arm of the sofa and closing her eyes. It is a typical reaction, one that Abbey was expecting, but it still hurts. Janet sighs again deeply, as she looks back at the TV screen and at the old family movie that is playing, "There's still so much I don't understand. He was fine. When he was little, growing up... he was your average, sweet, happy little boy. How could I have known? There were no warning signs, nothing, so how could I have known?" Her voice breaks and she lifts her hand to her mouth, forcing back her tears.

"You couldn't have known, none of us did…"

"No, well, he made his choice…" Janet's face crumples in pain, "I just wish I could have done something…" She begins to cry; thick, heavy sobs and Abbey moves quickly but cautiously to her side. She takes the wine from her hand, placing it on the coffee table before turning back and circling her arm around Janet in an attempt to comfort her. Again she flinches, pushing Abbey away as she climbs up off the floor and perches on the edge of the sofa, resting her elbows on her knees and her head in her hands.

"Hello? Anyone home?" The front door slams and Anna's cheerful voice sounds completely out of place as she calls from the hallway, "I had a late night ante-natal class so thought I'd swing by…. Hello?"

"We're in here Anna…" Abbey calls, flatly.

"Oh there you are, I was just…" Anna comes to a sudden halt in the doorway and her face drops as she asses the scene she has walked in on, "What's the matter?"

"Mum needs you…" Abbey shows no emotion as she steps aside and let's Anna pass, her face completely blank. She is well aware that she must seem uncaring and cold, but she can't help it. It is her best way of coping. Block it all out, don't react, just walk away. If Abbey ever sat and allowed herself to think for too long about how her own mother treats her, she would most likely have an emotional breakdown. Instead she has chosen to take an objective view, almost as if she is on the outside looking in at somebody else's life. It is scary how good she is these days at exercising complete emotional detachment. But maybe that's just what happens when the people you love the most push you away and shut you out? You become detached.

Abbey watches silently as Anna sits down on the sofa next to Janet and places her arms around her. Janet doesn't flinch or back away, instead she rests her head on Anna's shoulder and holds her hand. Eventually, her crying begins to slow and her breathing returns to normal as she regains control of her emotions.

"You know you shouldn't drink, Mum. What on earth made you put these videos on?"

"I found them when I was going through the last of the boxes. I thought I could handle it... stupid I know..."

"It's not stupid. You've been doing so well lately, but you can't rush it. It's not going to get better overnight, it will take time, but you will get there Mum, I promise..." Anna has a special gift of making people feel like everything is going to be OK, even when it isn't. She has been that way ever since she was little. She is the oldest of four so it is perhaps only natural for her to mother her younger siblings. She always looked out for Peter and Ryan, but she completely doted on Abbey. They were incredibly close despite the 9 year age gap and Abbey grew up idolising her sister in every way. When Anna left home to go to University, Abbey was devastated. She was only 10 years old at the time and she cried for weeks after. Anna came home often though, and their relationship if anything became stronger due to the distance. She would always visit as much as she could no matter how much she had going on in her life. Anna has always been a real family person, kind, caring, and a lot of fun to be around. Beautiful on the outside as well, with soft features and a heart shaped face, framed by her long, light brown hair. She is going to make an incredible mum.

Yet despite their closeness in the past, Abbey still can't help sensing a change in their relationship. The alienation she feels towards Anna might be nothing compared to what she feels towards the rest of her family, but it is still there, that slight difference. 'It shouldn't be surprising really', Abbey muses to herself, 'nothing's the same anymore', and with a lingering sadness, she turns and slips quietly out of the room, unable to watch the bond between Anna and her Mum any longer without feeling the crippling loneliness that she tries so hard to bury. She can't resist one last glance at the TV screen as she leaves, but instantly regrets her decision as she sees a 16 year old Ryan waving and laughing at the camera. A few weeks after that footage was filmed, he was gone.

Abbey's second and third week at school are much more successful than the first, and as the days pass her time at Eden Comprehensive seems to be gradually improving. After almost a month spent hiding away in empty classrooms during her lunch hour, she finally decides that enough is enough. She is being pathetic, deep down she knows it, and it is about time she gets over her constant sulking and starts trying to make the best of her current situation.

The sun is shining today and Abbey finds it strange how a change in the weather can make such a difference to her mood. Things are strained at home; in fact it's the worst it has been since her family moved to Leeds. Abbey and Janet aren't talking, mostly because Abbey is avoiding her. Peter is making minimal effort, which is usually the case, and Anna and Dom are busy transforming their spare room into a nursery as well as making various other preparations ready for the new addition. All of them are occupied with their own lives but Abbey isn't overly bothered, these days she prefers being left alone to deal with things in her own way. It is, at the very least, a nice day, and despite her current problems at home, she finds herself humming along to her ipod on the bus as she makes her way to school.

Her first few lessons are productive, even enjoyable. Now that Abbey has settled into her routine and caught up with the work she has missed, she finds that she is very much on top of her A-Level courses. She knows and likes all of her teacher's and has even started talking quite regularly with a few people in each of her classes. Still only polite conversation, but it is better than nothing. The horror of her first week is waning slightly, and although she is a long way off from liking Eden Comprehensive, it is starting to become more tolerable. It is these positive changes that make Abbey all the more determined to finally venture out of her self-imposed, solitary confinement.

Her class is one of the first to be dismissed for lunch, which she is thankful for. It means that she can beat the rush and discreetly find a seat before the crowds descend. She walks quickly outside, across the courtyard and over to the picnic tables opposite the cafeteria. She chooses the table furthest away from the building and sits down. Her new found bravery has definitely affected her appetite and she doesn't feel much like eating, so instead she pulls out the book that her class are studying in English and makes notes in the margin as she reads. It doesn't take long before the picnic tables and the surrounding fields are full of students and Abbey finds herself distracted, watching the various people come and go. Some she recognizes, a lot she doesn't.

Not thinking about anything in particular as she idly scans the courtyard; her thoughts are suddenly pulled into sharp focus as she makes eye contact with someone. Abbey turns cold and her stomach drops, when she realizes Natalie Alder is staring over in her direction. She is stood in the centre of a group of people on the other side of the lawn and they are clearly talking about her, laughing and pointing in the most obvious way imaginable. Abbey can feel her breath quickening. If she gets up and walks away now, will they follow her? But what if she stays and they come over to her table? The complete humiliation she suffered on her first day would feel like nothing if she is ridiculed in front of this many people; she will be the talk of the school. Abbey begins to panic. Any minute now Natalie will make her move and it will be too late to escape, too embarrassing for her to just turn and run away. 'Why the hell didn't I stay inside?' she scolds herself.

Concentrating on her book, Abbey tries hard to ignore the group of bullies and Natalie in particular. If she keeps her head down and doesn't acknowledge them, maybe they will get bored and let it go? Abbey's good mood from this morning has all but vanished and she counts down the seconds, praying for the bell to ring so that she can escape this horrible girl who for some unknown reason has it in for her. But there is half an hour left until the end of lunch break, half an hour to endure the dreaded possibility that at any moment she might find herself in another frightening confrontation. Abbey can sense someone approaching her table and her heart beats fast as her breath quickens even more.

"Abbey, hi..." The voice is friendly- not the one Abbey is expecting – and she glances up cautiously to see Lucy standing in front of her table, thankfully blocking Natalie from view. The two boys who interrupted their first meeting are standing behind her.

"Hi Lucy, how are you?" Abbey tries to compose herself, speaking as calmly as possible.

"Great! Do you mind if we sit?"

"No go ahead..."

"This is Liam and my boyfriend Nathan..." The three of them join Abbey at the table and she waves timidly in response. Liam is good looking in an unconventional way, fairly small, but lean, with short dark hair, a slightly crooked smile and an air of confidence about him. Abbey is obviously assessing him a little too closely as he catches her staring and winks, laughing under his breath.

The other boy, Nathan, is good looking in a *very* conventional way. He is tall and slim, quite muscular, with messy brown hair that sticks out at every angle. He seems a strange match for Lucy, given that his uniform is almost pristine. They are both equally attractive but look like polar opposites in terms of presentation, yet he sits with his arm draped protectively across her shoulders, obviously smitten, as he smiles warmly at Abbey.

"So, how have you been? Has this place got any more bearable yet?" Lucy asks.

"I'm not sure... it was starting to..."

"What changed?"

Abbey sighs and looks directly over Lucy's shoulder. The three of them all follow her gaze over to Natalie's table, where she is sat looking less than impressed that her intended target suddenly has allies.

"Jesus Christ, Natalie Alder is giving you grief already? She doesn't waste any fucking time does she?!" Liam rolls his eyes with a look of irritation on his face.

"We met on my first day, it was definitely an experience. She slammed me into the lockers…"

"Seriously…?"

"Yeah, Lucy came to my rescue…" Abbey smiles, gratefully.

"I wouldn't say that. I saw the aftermath…"

"Still, I never said thank you…"

"Don't mention it…"

Abbey starts to relax as the four of them chat together in the blazing sunshine and she listens intently as Liam recalls numerous horror stories of Natalie and some of her poor unsuspecting victims. By the sounds of it, she got off lightly. It does make her worry even more though, knowing what Natalie is capable of.

The half an hour that Abbey had at first been wishing away, comes to an end all too soon. It has been so nice talking to people her own age without the shadow of her past hanging over her. She hadn't realized until now how much she has missed this sort of interaction. She has clearly gotten too used to being on her own.

The courtyard is almost empty with only a few stragglers left behind and Abbey can't put it off any longer; she has to head back to class or she will be late. She hopes it won't be the first and last time that she gets to spend lunch with Lucy, Nathan and Liam. She really likes them, and they give her a sense of hope that things might finally start to improve.

"We're headed down to the arcade in the park, if you fancy it?" Lucy's question catches Abbey off guard. She wasn't aware of any free periods. In the hours you don't have lesson you are expected to attend study sessions in the library.

"Oh... I can't... I have class..." She stutters.

"Come on Abbey, live a little..." Liam winks at her again.

"It's far too nice a day to be stuck inside..." Nathan adds.

Abbey hesitates. Nathan is right, it is a gorgeous day and she is already ahead in her French class. She is good at languages, and a lot of what they are learning at the moment she has already covered in her first year of sixth form back at her old school. She finds herself seriously considering it, but she is still reluctant. Abbey has never skipped class before. Ever.

"Plus, you could end up running into your best friend again. She didn't look too happy earlier..." Lucy smiles innocently, knowing full well that if anything is going to convince her to ditch, that is it. The three of them begin to edge away as Abbey looks back at the school, still uncertain, "Come on Abbey, it'll be fun!" Lucy shouts, gesturing for her to follow, and after another brief moment of hesitation, she does.

The last thing she wants is another run in with Natalie and from her behaviour over lunch she is obviously gunning for her. Plus it is only one afternoon, what harm can it do? Abbey is clearly trying to convince herself. Trying to come up with whatever reason she can to justify what she is doing when really, there is only one reason she is skipping school... because she wants to. It has been a long time since she did something for herself - and she can't even remember the last time she'd had 'fun'.

After a 15 minute walk they reach the outskirts of Hall Park, a large expanse of grass that contains within it a cricket green, a skate park and a children's play area. Situated on the very edge of the park - with a walkway that leads back out onto the main road - is a modern café with an adjoining arcade. Outdoor tables and chairs are scattered over a large paved area at the front of the building, most of which are taken up by mothers with prams, gossiping over coffee. They receive a few judgmental looks as they sit down. It is after all the middle of the day and they are in school uniform, but it doesn't seem to bother the others; it is almost as if they are totally oblivious to the reaction, either that or they are immune to it after skipping school so many times before? It makes Abbey uncomfortable though, any minute they could get caught.

Nathan orders drinks with the waitress as Liam leans back in his chair, kicking his feet up on the table. He puts a pair of aviator shades on and rests his hands behind his head.

"I fucking love this weather..." He sighs.

Lucy rolls a cigarette and offers one to Abbey but she politely declines.

"So what's your story then, how come you moved here?" Lucy flicks her lighter and holds the flame to the end of her roll up before snapping it shut again.

"I came up with my family just over a month ago, well, with my mum and my brother... my sister and her husband already lived in Leeds..."

"Just fancied a change of scenery?"

"Yeah, something like that..." Abbey can sense immediately where the conversation is heading but she isn't ready to tell anyone the full reason behind the move. She has only just met Lucy, Nathan and Liam, and the last thing she wants to do is scare them off with her depressing history. It would make the conversation awkward, and she certainly doesn't know them well enough yet.

"My parents separated. My Dad left, he met someone else... so we came here..." It is a half-truth. Abbey's parents have separated. Losing Ryan was too much for them and their relationship broke down over time as her dad found it too hard to cope with his own grief while trying to support her mum. Abbey can understand that part of their break-up at least. Janet was almost sectioned several months after Ryan died and there was a point when no one expected her to get better. It was a horrible time and her dad was suffering too, although that seemed to get overlooked quite a lot. In the end, the only way he could move on was in the literal sense - with a total brain dead bimbo about half his age. Abbey hated him for abandoning his family at the most horrendous time possible, what he did was selfish beyond belief, but these days she finds herself relating to him a little bit more, maybe even understanding his choice. It was just too painful for him to carry on as they were and he was suffocating, trying to hold everything together. He had to get out.

"My parents split up too, when I was little, so I know how shit it can be..." Lucy makes her personal statement in a very casual way, which gives Abbey the impression that it clearly doesn't bother her anymore, and she wonders if she will ever be as accepting of her own family situation.

"Yeah... it wasn't easy..." She agrees.

"Do you still see your Dad?"

"Not really, we speak sometimes... but not so much anymore..." Another sad fact of life that Abbey has simply become accustomed to.

"I don't see either of my parents these days, they're a total nightmare. It's just me and my brother Darren now..." Nathan puts his arm around Lucy and squeezes her shoulder, "... and this one too of course!" She smiles, leaning in for a kiss.

"How long have you guys been together?"

"Just over 3 years..." Nathan answers before Lucy has chance to and he smiles at the ground, looking a little embarrassed, "God knows how she's put up with me for that long...!"

"I do ask myself that question a lot... I guess I'm just a saint!" Nathan pulls Lucy closer and kisses her forehead.

"Well, I'm glad you do put up with me that's for sure..."

"Of course we all know I was his first true love..." Liam interrupts, "it took him a while to get over me but Lucy helped!" He grins and Nathan rolls his eyes, throwing the lighter at him from across the table. Liam catches it but nearly falls off his chair in the process.

"You should meet my brother, Abbey..." Lucy adds as an afterthought, "and the rest of our group..."

"Sure..." Abbey feels a flare of excitement. "Do they go to our school?"

"No, they're all older than us. Next time we're out, you should come..."

"I'd like that..." Abbey is so grateful to Lucy. She wants to tell her how much her kindness means to her but she isn't about to come on too strong. 'Play it cool' she thinks to herself.

As Abbey leans forward to take a sip of her drink she notices Nathan and Liam - who had been fighting across the table during this exchange - have gone oddly quiet. Abbey glances at Liam and spots the look he is giving Lucy. It only lasts for a moment and Lucy barely acknowledges it, but he was definitely frowning, with his expression almost portraying alarm, though Abbey can't imagine why? Maybe she will ask Lucy about it later, but for the time being she chooses to ignore it.

At 3pm, Abbey reluctantly leaves the others and heads back home. She knows she could always stay out longer and tell her mum that she had met up with friends after school, but that would no doubt lead to questions being asked and Janet would see right through her. Lying convincingly is a skill Abbey has never possessed.

The following morning she bounds out of bed in a ridiculously good mood feeling nervously excited, wondering whether she will see the three of them again. Maybe they wouldn't be bothered today? Maybe they were just being kind because they felt sorry for her? Liam might have said something to Lucy? The look he gave her might have been because she invited Abbey out again and he didn't want that? Abbey shakes her head and snaps herself out of her deep rooted paranoia. It is getting to be a nasty habit, always thinking the worst.

She rushes her breakfast down in three bites and races out of the door, managing to catch the bus with only seconds to spare. When she arrives at school she makes her way down the side of the playing field and straight over towards the cafeteria, and as the crowd parts and the picnic tables come into view, she instantly relaxes, as sat at one of the benches waiting for her are Lucy, Nathan and Liam.

"We were starting to think you'd stood us up?" Liam throws his arm around Abbey as she reaches the table and she laughs to herself quietly, feeling stupid for getting so worked up earlier. She clearly had nothing to worry about. In fact it soon becomes a familiar routine. Every morning and every lunch time the four of them meet at the same bench. They don't always skip school, but most days they cut out early or ditch the study sessions that are supposed to be mandatory. The way Abbey sees it, she is only missing a few of her proper classes and she is keeping on top of her work... mostly. When the weather is good they head down to the park and relax on the grass in the sun, or they go to the café and play on the arcades. The looks they get from judgemental eyes have stopped bothering Abbey too. What the hell is it to them if she skips school?

As time goes on, Abbey is amazed at how comfortable she feels in her new friends company. It's as if she has known them for so much longer than she actually has, but then it isn't difficult to feel at ease around Lucy. She is an open book, totally honest and a little bit crazy in the best way possible. She talks animatedly about almost everything, getting louder and faster the more excited she becomes. She discusses the books and films she loves, her family life and her childhood... and music. The conversation always comes round to music. In between her constant chatter she questions Abbey relentlessly about her life; about her favourite this and favourite that, listening intently as she answers. Abbey responds as truthfully as possible while managing to avoid the one topic she isn't keen to bring up. Lucy's attitude is infectious. She lives by her own rules and isn't afraid to be herself. All she seems to care about is having fun, and Abbey loves that about her... about all three of them.

The more she gets to know Nathan, the more she understands why he and Lucy are together. They are a perfect match. Forever finishing each other's sentences and laughing at the same things. He was very quiet when they first met but he has definitely come out of his shell. He is a great conversationalist and Abbey can chat with him easily. Despite his relative shyness, Nathan is at his loudest when he and Liam are messing around. They are like a little double act, cracking jokes and play fighting, constantly throwing insults and banter at each other. Abbey can't remember a time when she had laughed so much or so often... and she feels free. As if all her troubles have been forgotten, pushed to the back of her mind and locked away. She still misses Ryan, just as much as always, but she is starting to feel like she has a life again. She has something positive to focus on, a genuine friendship, with people she likes... and it feels great.

Abbey kicks off her shoes and stretches out on the grass, closing her eyes, contentedly. It is another gorgeous day - not a single cloud in the clear blue sky - and best of all, it is a Saturday. No school to worry about, just an entire afternoon of sunbathing and relaxing in the park. 'Bliss'.

Lucy sits cross legged at Abbey's side, mindlessly flicking through the pages of a gossip magazine as her portable radio plays the latest chart music. Nathan and Liam are in the arcade - battling it out on the air hockey table - and every now and then Abbey can hear one of them swear or shout something indecipherable, making her smile. It is clearly getting competitive.

"The usual load of crap..." Lucy sighs as she throws away the magazine. She untangles her sunglasses from her wild, mess of hair and leans her head back to face the sun. "Abbey...?"

"Yeah?"

"Do you miss your old life?" Abbey turns towards Lucy, who is staring at her pensively.

"A little, there are certain things I miss... certain people... but I'm happy enough..."

"It must be strange, having to start all over again..."

"It was... but things have definitely got better lately..."

"Because you met three totally awesome people...?!" Lucy laughs.

Although she is only joking, Abbey can't help but answer her seriously. It is after all, the truth.

"Yeah actually... that's pretty much the reason..." She feels as though she wants to elaborate further but the look on Lucy's face tells her she doesn't need to. Instead they simply smile at each other in acknowledgement. They have become friends, very good friends; and the feeling is clearly mutual on both sides. It doesn't need to be discussed.

"You are such a bad loser..." Abbey and Lucy turn at the sound of Liam's voice and see both him and Nathan striding across the grass towards them.

"You fucking cheated..." Nathan shouts, shoving Liam playfully.

"Bollocks, you're just shit... It's not my fault..."

"You were covering the goal thing with your hands!"

"Now, now boys..." Lucy moves so that Nathan can sit in front of her and he leans back in her lap as Liam reaches down and takes a bottle of beer out of his bag, opening it with his teeth.

"If you can't play together nicely..." Abbey adds, mockingly.

"Tell him, he's the one that's sulking...!" Liam exclaims, lighting a cigarette.

"I'm not sulking... I'm just stating the fact that you only won because you cheated!"

"Whatever! I had you beaten from the word go! It was all over before it even started..."

"Oh, I know that feeling..." Lucy smirks mischievously and Liam bursts out laughing, nearly choking on his beer as Nathan half turns towards her, "Just kidding...!" She adds, sweetly.

"You little..." Nathan spins around and pins Lucy to the ground, and she thrashes about, half laughing, half screaming as he tickles her manically.

"Say sorry and I'll stop..." Nathan grins.

"Oh my god, I'm sorry, I'm sorry, I'm sorry..." She shrieks.

"Now say 'My boyfriend's the best and he's amazing in bed'...!"

"Don't make her into a fucking liar mate" Liam laughs.

"I'M SORRY... I didn't mean it, I was joking... I'm sorry!!!" Lucy can hardly breathe from laughing as Nathan finally lets her go, pulling her upright and onto his lap.

"Am I forgiven?!" She asks, still giggling.

"I suppose so...!" Nathan kisses Lucy gently, tickling her once more as she wriggles in protest. Their laughter subsides and Liam and Nathan's bickering continues on a quieter level, as the sound of the radio creeps back into the foreground. Abbey instantly recognizes the song that is playing and she feels a sickening jolt of pain at the sound of the lyrics and the quiet strum of the acoustic guitar. 'Wonderwall' by Oasis.

She couldn't hear it at first over Lucy's laughter but she can hear it clearly now and her face drops as she struggles to keep her composure. She always hated how a piece of music can instantly bring up memories that you would rather keep buried. Music can provoke emotion like nothing else and this song effects Abbey in a way she can't control. Without thinking, she instinctively rocks forward and flicks the radio onto another station, causing all three of them to turn and look at her.

"Abbey are you OK?" She had hoped they wouldn't notice, but Lucy looks concerned.

"Yeah. Fine..." Is all she can manage.

"You don't look so good, Abs..." Nathan sits upright and Lucy climbs off his knee, as Liam reaches across and gently puts his hand on Abbey's shoulder.

"What's up?" He asks.

There is no hiding the truth anymore. She will have to tell them the reason for her strange behaviour and explain why she has suddenly gone from laughing and joking to looking drip white and stone faced.

"I just don't really like that song..." She says quietly. "It reminds me of... it was played at my brother's funeral..." The three of them stare at Abbey in silence for what seems like forever.

"But I thought you said you moved here with your brother?" Lucy asks, almost reluctantly, unsure whether she should push Abbey on the subject considering her suddenly fragile state.

"That's my older brother, Peter. I have... I had... another brother, Ryan. He was my twin brother actually..." Abbey takes a long, deep breath; it always requires a lot of strength to say these words out loud,

"He killed himself last year. A few weeks before our 17th birthday..." Silence again.

"God, I am so sorry Abbey..." Lucy whispers, sadly. It is the reaction that Abbey usually struggles with, the shock and the pity that people show towards her when they find out about Ryan; it is hard for her to bear and it normally makes her feel incredibly self-conscious, causing her to shut herself off... but this time feels different.

"I'm sorry I didn't tell you before now... I just... it was nice, to not have to think about it all the time, you know? To pretend for a while..." Abbey speaks fast while looking down at the floor, almost embarrassed at causing such an awkward atmosphere, "But that's why my parents split up, and the real reason, well, the main reason why we moved to Leeds, to start over..."

"That's really awful mate, I'm sorry..." Liam states.

"So it's nothing personal against the Gallagher's..." She jokes, "It's just pretty hard to listen to that song, you know...?" Another moment passes and the three of them smile at Abbey sympathetically. No body speaks, almost as if they are taking a minute to digest the information she has shared with them, and when it becomes apparent that Abbey has nothing else to say, Nathan is the one to break the tension.

"I think they're overrated anyway to be honest..." Lucy turns to face him in an overly dramatic fashion before he has even finished his statement.

"Are you kidding me?!" She asks, incensed, "They're one of the best bands the UK has ever produced...!"

"I'm entitled to my opinion..." He laughs, "no matter how misinformed you think it is..." He sticks his tongue out at Lucy and she shakes her head in mock disbelief.

"Ah now this…" Liam points at the radio excitedly as another song kicks in with an electric guitar blasting out a heavy, rock riff. "THIS is a tune…!"

Abbey doesn't recognize the song, but she is grateful for the change in topic. It hadn't escaped her attention that it was Nathan who lightened the mood and she catches his eye, smiling appreciatively. He nods and smiles back, before joining in the lively debate that has suddenly erupted between Lucy and Liam. Abbey voices her opinion and watches in amusement as Lucy excitedly agrees with her, pointing out to the boys that they clearly have no idea what they are talking about when it comes to the Oasis back catalogue.

She sits quietly, listening to their animated discussion as relief floods through her. They know the truth. Her secret is out. And instead of being met with a barrage of awkward and uncomfortable questions, they simply listened. Abbey is so used to people shying away from her because they don't know how to act or what to say, but they had just let her talk - and had made sure that she was alright without prying or asking for any of the morbid details. It is something she has never experienced before. Even her oldest friends back home had changed around her after it happened, but not Lucy, or Nathan or Liam. It's as if they understand her better than anyone, and she suddenly feels like a huge weight has been lifted. For the first time in a long time… she feels happy.

CHAPTER THREE

THE PARTY

Abbey's life at home and her life away from it couldn't be more different. They are complete polar opposites. Two totally separate worlds occupied by the same person. Her relationship with her family has broken down even more than she ever thought possible and there is hardly any interaction at all with her mum. She is far too immersed in the new house and making a good impression with the neighbours, concentrating on her new job, and proving to everyone that she is 'fine' after her minor relapse a month ago. Needless to say there has been no more wine kept in the house after that episode. Janet may ask Abbey how her day has been and how school is going, but she never really listens to the answer- far too busy focusing on more important things than her teenage daughter. At least that's how it seems. Peter is the same, so wrapped up in his own life that he shows minimal interest in Abbey or how she is, and Anna and Dom are only slightly better. The fact they live on the other side of the city means they don't visit all that often and even when they do Janet monopolises their time, bombarding them with never ending questions about her future grandchild, who she can't wait to meet. It is getting increasingly claustrophobic, living in that house, with the endless small talk and constant silences... and Abbey hates it. She feels completely cut off, almost as if she is ceasing to exist.

She is well aware that she should probably care more, but even Abbey is surprised at how little she feels towards her less than perfect situation. She isn't overly upset or worried about the deteriorating relationship with her family; in fact it barely affects her at all, because when she is with Lucy, Nathan and Liam, she can escape that world. She can find a release and forget about everything else. Being with them is like a breath of fresh air and all the doubt and hurt that she is so used to just don't touch her anymore. She may feel as though she is disappearing at home but with her friends she feels completely herself and more content than she ever has before. It's like a paradox, both lives running alongside one another at the same time; the good and the bad.

It is a Thursday afternoon when Abbey's two worlds eventually collide. It is strange to see Lucy in her kitchen; she has never been over before and Abbey is so used to their friendship being totally separate from the misery of her home life. It feels odd to have her at the house, but here she is, perched on the breakfast counter swinging her legs, as she chats away in her usual excitable tone. Nathan and Liam had stayed behind at school to play football with friends and the weather was far too cold and overcast to make them want to stay and watch. The arcade was quiet - and a little boring without the boys - so before she knew it and without properly thinking it through, Abbey had extended her invitation. Janet is still at work and Peter is rarely home through the day, so Lucy probably won't even get to meet them, yet the possibility makes Abbey feel nervous and on edge despite not being entirely sure why?

The afternoon passes quickly as it always does in Lucy's company. It amazes Abbey how she never seems to run out of things to say... there are never any awkward silences or breaks in conversation. Her carefree attitude always puts Abbey in a good mood and Lucy makes her laugh with all the random things she brings up and talks about. It had been nice, just the two of them for a change... but as Lucy is getting ready to leave, the front door slams and Abbey turns to look at the clock. It is only 5:00pm. Her mum isn't normally home this early.

"Abbey?!" Janet calls out - her voice stern and slightly panicked. She rushes into the kitchen and takes a sharp breath as if she is about to speak, but stops when she sees Lucy, eyeing her suspiciously.

"Mum, this is Lucy; she's a friend from school..."

"Nice to meet you Mrs Miller..." Lucy smiles politely but gets no response. Janet simply nods once and turns abruptly back to Abbey.

"I need to talk to you... now please..."

"Mum!"

"That's OK... I should get going anyway..." Lucy throws her bag over her shoulder and Abbey flushes with embarrassment as she follows her to the door.

"I'm sorry I don't know what's wrong with her..."

"Don't worry about it... I'll see you tomorrow!"

As Lucy leaves, Abbey's irritation quickly boils over into full blown anger. It is the first time her mum has met any of her new friends and she behaves in such a rude, obnoxious way. It is totally uncalled for. She turns furiously, ready to storm back into the kitchen to confront Janet, but she is already in the hallway, standing with her arms crossed and her eyebrows raised. The look on her face irritates Abbey even more.

"What the hell is your problem?!" She yells.

"My problem?!" Janet shouts back, "My problem is I got a call from your school today. They told me that you've been missing your lessons! Now do you want to tell to me what the hell is going on or do I need to ring them back for some sort of explanation?!" She scowls, her face red with anger, "WELL?!"

Abbey quickly weighs up her options and runs through various excuses in her mind. There aren't any. It is obvious that Janet knows everything and there is no point even trying to convince her that the school have got it wrong.

"What do you want me to say?" She asks, still annoyed "I hate it... I never wanted to move there in the first place, I told you that, repeatedly..."

"So you just decided not to go?!" Janet cries with exasperation.

"It's not like I could talk to you about it... you don't care, you wouldn't have even noticed anything was wrong if they hadn't called..." Janet's angered expression falters for a moment and it suddenly becomes obvious to Abbey that she knows exactly how she is behaving; shutting her own daughter out, keeping her at arm's length. In that split second it is written all over her face.

"Well thank god they did..." Her voice is calmer, but just as firm, "This stops now. You're grounded. You are not to see your new friends, not until you get your school work back on track...."

"WHAT?" Abbey is astounded. She has never been grounded before in her life and the thought of being stuck in this house unable to see her friends is horrifying. She shakes her head at Janet, infuriated, "You just don't get it do you?!"

"You are not in a position to argue young lady that is final! Now go to your room...!" Abbey storms past her mum and races up the stairs, slamming her bedroom door so hard the force of it shakes the house. Janet holds her head in her hands and sighs wearily. She knew things weren't great, but she never expected this. The call she received earlier from Abbey's headmaster had truly shocked her. Maybe it is her fault? Maybe she should have paid more attention? She will be watching much more closely from now on, that's for sure. She isn't about to let Abbey throw away her whole future no matter how much she is struggling and she is determined to try harder, because if one thing is clear, things seriously need to improve.

Abbey may be grounded, but through the week between the hours of 8:30am and 3pm, her mum has no control over who she spends her time with. The following day at school she lacks the usual 'Friday feeling' due to her impending house arrest, but is grateful that she gets to see Lucy and explain to her exactly what happened after she left. Abbey is obviously less than thrilled about the situation and the fact she has been caught, but at least it explains Janet's rude behaviour and partly excuses her attitude from the previous night. Not that Lucy seems to care. It has been so long since she has had to deal with her own parents, other peoples certainly don't faze her.

Abbey goes straight home that afternoon despite how much she wants to stay out. She knows it would be stupid to push Janet to her limit so soon after their argument. She will be at work until after 5:30pm, but Abbey's gut instinct tells her not to take the risk and she is right to be wary. She has hardly made it through the front door when the phone starts ringing. Janet is short and to the point, she didn't call for a lengthy conversation... just to make sure that Abbey is following the rules of her curfew. This weekend is going to be difficult.

Although it pains her to admit it, Abbey has fallen behind in some of her lessons. Saturday is slow, but she ploughs through the mountain of homework and revision that has stacked up due to the days she was 'inexplicably' absent. She stays in her room for the best part, only occasionally venturing downstairs for food or to make herself another drink. Being grounded is her worst nightmare and she is miserable. It doesn't help that it has come at a time when Abbey wants to be out of the house as much as humanly possible. She already feels trapped by all the grief and pain that lingers from the recent past. Now with the added anger and disappointment that practically radiates off her mum in waves, the atmosphere is horribly oppressive and it makes her feel restless.

Luckily, Janet hasn't gone as far as to confiscate her phone, so Abbey spends the day texting Lucy and Liam, staving off the boredom with light hearted conversation, asking them what they are up to and what their plans are for the weekend... although she immediately regrets asking, knowing that she can't be a part of what ever fun they have in mind. Talking to them does make her feel better though and helps her boring day pass a little easier.

It is early evening when Abbey's phone beeps again. A couple of hours have gone by since Lucy's last text and she wasn't expecting to receive another. She opens her phone and reads the message with an overwhelming sense of disappointment and frustration.

'Any chance at all you can break out tonight? x'. She so badly wants to say yes, but deep down she knows it isn't realistic. Even if she could get out of the house without her mum noticing, how would she get back in? And if she was caught, well, the repercussions aren't even worth thinking about. The temptation is there, but Abbey isn't about to go and make life any harder for herself.

'Afraid not... have fun tonight. x' Is all she replies. Abbey knows that they have plans to go to a party later as Liam had mentioned it in passing when they had been texting earlier. They will most likely be out with the rest of their friends who Abbey has yet to meet. She had been looking forward to the prospect of expanding her social life and getting to know the group that Lucy, Nathan and Liam talk about constantly. Although the four of them have become incredibly close, there are still times when Abbey doesn't quite feel included. She is still the new girl and they have known each other for years, plus she doesn't move in the same circles outside of school as they do. She tries her best to ignore it, whenever she feels left out, but it bothers her. Abbey had hoped that would all change once she finally got to meet the group of friends they speak so highly of. How typical that the opportunity should finally arise when she is locked up against her will.

Just as Abbey is thinking how things can't possibly get any worse, her bedroom door bursts open and Peter charges into the room with his hands clenched angrily by his sides. His demeanour isn't subtle and Abbey can tell instantly that he is ready for an argument. She can feel herself shift into defensive mode as he walks forward three paces and stops abruptly.

"Don't you knock?" She asks, sharply.

"What the hell are you playing at Abbey?"

"Excuse me…?"

"I've just been speaking to Mum and…"

"And what…?" Abbey snaps. She looks up at her brother and fumes at the disapproving look on his face. Peter annoys her at the best of times, but she hates him when he patronizes her like a child. When Ryan died and her dad left he suddenly started acting like the newly appointed head of the family. It makes Abbey's blood boil and she can't stand his superior attitude, "What the hell has it got to do with you…?" She demands.

"It's got everything to do with me when I get home and see how much you've upset Mum. Seriously, what were you thinking? You're in your last year at school, you've got exams coming up and you're skipping lessons, hanging around with a bunch of losers?"

"They are not losers…" Abbey seethes, "and you have absolutely no room to talk. You skipped school; you were almost expelled for god sake!" Peter's mouth snaps shut. Abbey knows it is a different situation entirely, but she can't resist the satisfaction of wiping the smug look off his face. Peter had fallen in with the 'wrong' crowd when he was much younger, around 14 years old. He was never badly behaved and never got into any real trouble, but the one time he had agreed - out of peer pressure more than anything - to skip class, they had been caught. Unfortunately one of them was spray painting graffiti on the side of the school fence at the time and all of them were punished. It was only after an extensive amount of grovelling from their parents that he was allowed a second chance. She knows Peter still feels terrible and that's why Abbey is so quick to mention it whenever he climbs up on his high horse. He wasn't always the perfect, golden boy he makes himself out to be.

"I was stupid..." He admits through gritted teeth. "...but luckily I was younger and I learnt from it. If you mess up now during you're A-levels, you could be paying for it for the rest of your life..." Abbey knows he has a point but her stubbornness makes her reluctant to acknowledge it out loud. She had worked so hard in her first year up until Ryan's suicide. And then even afterwards - when she had returned to school - she found her studies were a pleasant distraction from the devastating loss she felt. It took her mind away from it all and as a result, even in the immediate aftermath of her twin brother's death, Abbey's work didn't really suffer. To make it through all that trauma and heartache with good grades only to throw it away now doesn't make a great deal of sense even to her. But things have changed. In fact everything has changed, and her priorities have shifted considerably.

Peter might be incredibly condescending with his advice - if you can even call it that - but it seems as though he genuinely cares about Abbey and doesn't want her damaging her future prospects. She is still irritated, but her defensive attitude softens slightly due to her brother's apparent concern. She sighs grudgingly, almost ready to admit defeat, but before she can speak he interrupts her in the same antagonistic tone, "... I'm serious Abbey, how the hell do you think Mum would cope if you messed everything up now?!"

It takes a brief moment for Abbey to process his words before anger swells inside her. How could she be so stupid? How could she mistakenly believe that Peter actually gives a damn about her? It is all about Janet. It is *always* about Janet and Abbey is still totally and utterly insignificant. Her life, her pain, her grief... none of it matters to him. He is only there to lay on the guilt. To fight Janet's corner like he always does. She should have known better.

"Oh what a fucking surprise...!" Abbey slams her hands on her desk and jumps up, shoving her chair out behind her, "I should have seen that one coming...!" The volume of her voice takes Peter by surprise and he rocks back on his heels, "It's always about her isn't it? As if the rest of us aren't suffering too..."

"Can you hear yourself?" His voice is breathless with disbelief, "Mum has enough to deal with right now without you acting like a spoilt little kid! Sort it out...!" Peter storms out of the room and Abbey tries to shout after him but her words get stuck in her throat. She is so angry. How dare he speak to her in such a condescending way... he isn't her father for god sake, it's none of his business. What right does he have? What right do any of them have? Both Peter and Janet have spent the last few months practically ignoring her, acting as though she doesn't even exist - and now they think they can tell her how to behave and dictate her life? It is so hypocritical.

Abbey snatches her phone from her desk and slumps onto her bed. She struggles to hit the buttons as her hands are shaking so badly, but after a few attempts she manages to type out a message to Lucy and without any hesitation, hits send.

'What time and where tonight? X'

Abbey is genuinely surprised at how easy it is to sneak out of the new house. She goes downstairs in her pyjamas to set up her alibi and make it seem as though she is getting an early night, being careful not to make too much of a show and rouse suspicion. Once she is back in her bedroom, she gets ready as quickly and as quietly as possible - occasionally creeping over to the door to listen out for approaching footsteps while doing her hair and make-up. There are a few brief moments of doubt when her conscience almost gets the better of her, but she is still so angry with Janet and Peter that those moments don't last long. Her window opens fully and is more than big enough for her to climb out of and her bedroom is thankfully on the side of the house that adjoins to the garage, the roof of which is only a metre and a half below. If that wasn't the case, her mission might have failed.

Abbey throws her bag as gently as possible into the bushes below, before sitting on the windowsill and swinging her legs round so that she is facing outside. She carefully lowers herself down as far as she possibly can - and with a quick glance back - let's go of the window frame. There is a dull thud as she lands and she waits a moment, listening intently for any movement inside the house. Satisfied that she hasn't been heard, she stands on her tiptoes and pushes the window to, so that it is only open an inch. There is a drain pipe next to it that she can use to climb back in, but she will worry about that part later.

Abbey hurries across the garage roof, climbs down onto the garden wall and drops onto the driveway, looking back at the house one last time as she dusts herself off and dashes out into the street. There is still a part of her that can't believe what she is doing but she won't turn back now.

Lucy, Nathan and Liam are waiting for her outside the co-op down the road and their expressions flit between shock and admiration as she approaches.

"We didn't know if you'd make it...!" Lucy shouts, as Abbey crosses the road towards them.

"I said I was coming didn't I?!" She greets Lucy with a hug; followed by Liam and Nathan - instantly forgetting about her worries and the huge amount of trouble she could potentially be in.

"I got some booze already... you like vodka right?"

"Sure, vodka's fine..." Abbey isn't much of a drinker so she can't really say what alcohol she does like. She had turned 18 in February - two weeks before the move to Leeds - and needless to say there wasn't much celebration involved. It was a milestone birthday but it was also a stark reminder of what Ryan would never experience. He would never drink, never drive, never vote. He had died 4 days shy of their 17th birthday, so the last two have passed by with no real festivities at all. They have become a more sombre occasion, and in a way Abbey feels as though she is betraying Ryan by getting older, almost as if she is leaving him behind. She is moving forward, while he is frozen... forever sweet sixteen.

After a 15 minute taxi drive through Leeds, past the train station and out towards the bottom end of town, they stop at a modern, high rise building on the outskirts of the city next to the water of the Leeds-Liverpool Canal. They pay the driver and approach the main door, where Liam presses a button for flat 38. There is a pause, then a click.

"Yeah...?"

Liam leans forward, putting his mouth right up to the speaker as he shouts in a stupid voice.

"EASY BRUVVAAAA...!" Whoever's on the other end of the intercom responds in exactly the same way, and the buzzer sounds, releasing the door. Lucy rolls her eyes as the four of them make their way inside.

They ride the elevator up to the 9th floor and walk down a long narrow corridor that is painted and carpeted in neutral colours. Various pieces of modern art hang on the walls and large free standing vases are placed sporadically along the passage way.

"Wow, this is really nice..." Abbey wasn't sure what she was expecting, but it definitely wasn't something this up market.

"Yeah, Alex has a pretty high paying job..." Liam laughs and the three of them glance at each other as if sharing a private joke. Once again Abbey feels a little left out, but at least she is here with them. They have included her by bringing her along tonight and she reminds herself that she should be grateful for that. As the four friends approach the very end of the hallway and flat number 38, Lucy reaches up to knock, but before she has a chance, the handle turns and the door swings open unexpectedly. Abbey stares, wide eyed and breathless, as everything around her fades into the back ground. Time seems to stand still and in that fraction of a second, her whole entire universe shifts. "What time do you call this...?!" The man standing in the doorway asks his question in a deep Irish accent that flows so beautifully, it is almost surreal. He is tall, with dark brown hair that is styled into a slight quiff at the front. He is wearing faded jeans, a grey v neck t-shirt and a set of silver rosary beads that hang just past his chest. He is incredibly lean and toned, with the muscles in his arms standing out in stark contrast to his slender frame. He has incredibly chiselled features with a few days' worth of stubble and the most piercing, electric blue eyes that Abbey has ever seen.

"We're not that late! We just had to go pick Abbey up...!" Lucy kisses him on the cheek as she enters the flat and Abbey follows behind, smiling timidly. Her heart is beating so fast it feels as though it is going to explode out of her rib cage. She had never really given any thought to what Alex or the others looked like... she had never asked. So it is a complete shock seeing first-hand how unbelievably good looking he is.

Liam enters the flat and Alex shakes his hand, slapping him on the back in greeting. Abbey can't resist glancing back over her shoulder but she quickly looks away when she sees that he is still watching her. He greets Nathan in exactly the same manner, before shutting the door without once taking his eyes from Abbey's face. She begins to feel uncomfortable under his constant stare and turns away shyly, desperately trying to control her blushing.

"Lucy! You're here!" An incredibly attractive, glamorous looking girl bursts into the room and dashes over to Lucy, hugging her tightly. Following calmly behind her is another girl of a similar age. She has strawberry blonde hair and freckles, and is very pretty in a much more natural, girl next door sort of way.

"Guys this is Abbey... Abbey this is Gemma Sanders and Sophie Richardson..."

"Hi Abbey, it's so nice to finally meet you!" Gemma, the first and more flamboyant of the two, hugs Abbey in greeting and passes her a drink, "We've heard a lot about you..."

"Thanks. All good I hope?!"

"Of course all good...!" Lucy smiles encouragingly.

"Yeah, she's alright is our Abs...!" Liam winks, cracking open a can of lager and casually draping his arm around Abbey's shoulders, "Where are tweedle dum and tweedle dee?!"

"I thought that was you and Nathan?!" Gemma teases, but before Liam has chance to retaliate two more men enter the room.

"EASY BRUV! Took your time didn't you... you sort me out?!" The first makes a bee line straight for Liam and they slap hands. He has a broad build, short dark spikey hair and is obviously from London, as he speaks in a strong cockney accent.

"Yeah mate, your beers are in the fridge. This is Abbey. Abbey this is Tom..." Tom nods and winks as he steps forward, pulling Abbey into a huge bear hug.

"You alright darlin'? It's good to meet you...!"

"Yeah, you too...!" Abbey smiles back. He has a cheeky, mischievous look about him and comes across as extremely approachable. She likes him instantly. Lucy skips excitedly across the room, pulling on the hand of the other man who Abbey has yet to meet. He has long shoulder length brown hair and a full sleeve tattoo on both arms. It instantly becomes apparent that this is Lucy's brother, Darren, as they look scarily alike.

She introduces them in her usual flamboyant manner and Abbey holds out her hand.

"Hi Darren, it's nice to meet you..."

"Yeah you too love, heard plenty about you. Good to have you out..." He gives Abbey a warm smile before helping himself to another beer out of the fridge and Abbey gradually starts to feel at ease as she sits and chats with the girls around the kitchen table. They go out of their way to include her in the conversation and her nerves begin to fade slightly as they all laugh and joke together. Everyone is incredibly friendly and welcoming. All but one.

Abbey tries her hardest not to look round as she can still feel Alex's eyes burning into her. Why is he staring at her so much? And why hasn't he said two words to her since she walked through the door? Is this normal behaviour for him? Abbey blocks it out of her mind and tries to focus on the others and the conversation they are having, but she can't help feeling constantly on edge due to the incredibly beautiful, unwelcoming man, assessing her intently from across the room.

As the night goes on the atmosphere remains the same and Alex's attitude doesn't improve. Every time there is a lull in conversation, Abbey becomes hyper aware of his presence, and in an attempt to ignore his hostility she tries to focus her attention on absolutely anything other than him... including her surroundings.

Abbey can't deny that Alex's flat is seriously impressive. It is large and incredibly modern; the walls are a light cream and the laminate floor a deep, rich mahogany. The front door opens straight into the kitchen with its black gloss work tops and light grey units and the adjoining breakfast area is a large space, that has a long glass table stood in the centre with 8 tall, leather seats arranged neatly around it. The light décor and black furnishings make it look crisp and clean – and very contemporary. Out of the kitchen diner is an L shaped hallway with four more rooms leading off it. The first two are bedrooms, the master room which is Alex's and the other large double which belongs to Tom. In the middle of the two bedrooms is a door leading into a monochrome bathroom, with a large free standing bath and a corner shower. The final door at the very end of the hallway opens out into a spacious living area. It has 3 black leather sofas with chocolate brown cushions, arranged around a matching brown rug in the middle of the floor. On the rug stands a glass coffee table, similar in design to the larger table in the kitchen.

At one end of the room there is a massive plasma TV mounted on the wall and a black HIFI unit underneath that houses all sorts of technology, from a DVD player and a XBOX to a very futuristic looking sound system. At the opposite side of the room there is a double door that opens out onto a small balcony. Again the walls are plain cream, except for the main feature wall, which has an enormous black and white image of the London skyline printed on it. Abbey finds herself wondering what Alex must do for a living in order to afford a place like this and she remembers the exchange between Liam, Nathan and Lucy in the corridor outside. The look they gave each other suggested Alex's job is something of a secret and she can think of only one reason why that would be the case.

After a few drinks the party moves into the living room, where the girls sit gossiping as the boys play against each other on the games console. The music is blasting out of Alex's impressive sound system and Abbey is feeling much more relaxed - which probably has a lot to do with the several glasses of vodka and coke she has drunk. She is actually, for once, enjoying herself and has almost completely forgotten that she has to somehow climb stealthily back into her house through her bedroom window, far too busy having fun like a normal teenager to start panicking about that.

Needless to say she finally understands why Lucy, Nathan and Liam speak so highly of their group of friends. They are all incredibly close - more like a family unit - and they are all really lovely people... except perhaps for the one exception.

Gemma is hilarious; she is very loud and has an incredibly dry sense of humour. Abbey has never come across anyone with such an immaculate appearance before. She has long glossy brown hair, a gorgeous complexion, the longest eyelashes and a figure any model would die for. Yet she doesn't show any sign of an inflated ego – she is very down to earth and incredibly easy to get on with, just like Lucy had been when she and Abbey first met. Sophie is very friendly too but in a far less extravagant way. She is quite shy and softly spoken, but still very funny and great to talk to. She and Darren have been a couple for over 7 years and it is clear to see how much they love each other.

Abbey's first impression of Tom couldn't have been more on the money. He is very funny and full of banter, constantly telling ridiculous tales and stupid stories, and it is hysterical the way he and Gemma bounce off each other's sarcasm. There is clearly something between them as they flirt outrageously, but Sophie assures

Abbey that they aren't a couple, which she genuinely finds a shame.

The one thing Abbey really can't get over is how alike Darren and Lucy are. They have exactly the same laugh and the same quirkiness about them; they have the same expressions and mannerisms and the same taste in music. It is almost spooky... but also understandable. Since their parents left it has been just the two of them and they were forced to learn how to take care of themselves. To share that experience and to endure such a difficult childhood, was undoubtedly going to make them close -and evidently - very similar.

Despite how long they have all been friends, Abbey doesn't feel at all like she is intruding. They interact with her the same way that they interact with each other, making her feel like part of the group almost instantly. It is only Alex that seems to have a problem with her. He has spent most of the night in the kitchen, but whenever he re-joins the party the intense staring continues. Instead of it being unsettling like it was at first, he is starting to get on Abbey's nerves and she wants to know what the hell his problem is, but she certainly isn't about to ask him. Even though his behaviour is annoying her, every time she glances up and catches his eye her stomach twists with anticipation and she feels a rush of adrenaline. He is so incredibly attractive, dark - and if her intuition is correct - a little dangerous too.

"OH FUCK OFF...!" Tom chucks the control pad on the floor as Darren throws his arms up in celebration, "That is pure fucking fluke... I can't believe you pulled that back and won..."

"What can I say? I'm a natural...! Dobs you're up!" Liam takes his place next to Darren for the next round of FIFA and Tom perches on the corner of the sofa - sulking as he swigs his beer and rummages through his pockets.

"I can't actually believe you beat me... you used to be utter shite at this game..." Tom carries on ranting as he opens up a little bag of white powder and tips a pile of it out onto the glass table in front of him. He licks the residue off his fingers and opens his wallet, taking out one of his bank cards, "How many am I racking up... 2 each, yeah? Abbey, you want some?"

Abbey shakes her head and smiles awkwardly, staring down at her feet. Darren and Liam are completely engrossed in their game and Sophie and Gemma are too busy talking to notice her reaction, but Lucy glances worryingly at Nathan, sensing how uncomfortable Abbey has become.

It isn't that she disapproves or is angry in any way; she just hasn't ever been openly exposed to drugs before. She has been told so many times in various awareness classes at school how dangerous and harmful they are and her old friends would never have touched any type of illegal drug in a million years. She has never really thought about it at all, as they simply weren't on her radar. Until now.

"Nice cheeky little pick me up... don't mind if I do..." Tom rolls up a twenty pound note and leans forward; placing the note inside one nostril as he covers the other with his finger before inhaling sharply. He does one line, then the other, and passes the note to Gemma, who kneels on the floor next to him, pulls her hair back and does the same. Abbey looks on curiously, so morbidly fascinated with what she is seeing that she doesn't notice Alex standing in the doorway until he speaks.

"So, Abbey..." A mixture of emotions shoot through her at lightning speed as Alex says her name out loud for the first time, in his incredibly seductive accent. Shock, delight, excitement... then overwhelming nerves as the sullen, unsociable stranger, finally - after almost 3 hours - directly acknowledges her, "What are your feelings on drugs?" He asks, "Are you game? Or are you one of these self-righteous, sanctimonious do-gooders who believe that they're a black mark on society... responsible for the high crime rate and the poor choices made by the fucked up youth of today?"

Abbey realises she is holding her breath and exhales, slowly. The room has gone quiet and she pauses for a moment – carefully processing Alex's outburst - before deciding to answer him truthfully.

"I've never really thought about it..."

"Of course you haven't..." He smirks.

"Give it a rest Al..." Lucy frowns and he shrugs at her indifferently.

"I'm just asking our guest a question..."

"As you can probably tell he doesn't have a strong opinion on the subject..." Tom quips, sarcastically, laughing to himself as he follows Alex out of the room.

"Don't worry about him... he's a little touchy with people he doesn't know..." Lucy smiles reassuringly, as she sits down next to Abbey.

"It's OK. I am in his house; he can say what he likes..."

"I'm sorry..."

"For what...?" Abbey frowns, she wasn't expecting an apology.

"I probably should have told you, you know... about the drugs...we just weren't sure how you'd react and we wanted you to meet everyone first, without it being the only thing you knew about them..."

"I would never judge anyone I didn't know. Especially over something I have no clue about. It might not be my thing but, you know, each to their own..." Abbey tries her best to sound casual and unaffected, and it seems to work.

"I'm so glad you came tonight...!" Lucy beams.

"Me too...!" And despite the last 10 minutes being a bit of an eye opener, Abbey means it. She has really enjoyed herself and it feels great to be part of a group of friends again – to spend time with people who just want to hang out, get drunk and have a laugh together. It hadn't exactly gone great with Alex but she feels better after Lucy's explanation... 'he's a little touchy with people he doesn't know'. At least that implies she isn't the only person who has received a frosty reception.

An hour or so later and the double vodka and cokes have definitely started to take effect. Abbey feels seriously light headed as she leans on the sink for support, running her hands through her hair and taking a deep breath as she asses her appearance in the mirror. 'Maybe it's time to slow down' she thinks to herself. She can hear the others shouting and laughing in the living room over the thudding beat of the music and after checking her hair and make-up one last time, she turns back to re-join the party.

As Abbey unlocks the bathroom door and opens it rather clumsily, she stops dead in her tracks – freezing on the spot, totally shell-shocked – as leaning casually on the doorframe in front of her, is Alex.

"Having fun...?" He isn't being polite. Abbey can sense the underlying tone in his question.

"Yes thanks..." She answers, quietly. He is so intimidating, but Abbey can feel the excitement pulsing through her as they stand just inches apart.

"Listen, I get that you're Lucy's friend an all, but I'm not exactly a fan of people I don't know hanging around. I don't want you involving yourself in business that doesn't concern you. Whatever you see or hear, you best be able to keep to yourself..." Alex's body language is assertive and his words are a warning, but surprisingly Abbey doesn't feel threatened. In fact, standing face to face with him in the darkened hallway she sees through his defensiveness and instead, glimpses a brief flicker of vulnerability. She doesn't know this man at all and he has been nothing but rude to her all night, yet she finds herself drawn to him in a way she can't explain. There is no denying that she is physically attracted to him – he is breathtakingly gorgeous – but it is more than that. He is so guarded, brooding and mysterious... and he fascinates her.

"I'm sorry that me being here bothers you. I only came because Lucy invited me..." She explains, cautiously.

"I know that. It's nothing personal – and I know it might seem like I'm being paranoid, but if you'd been through half the shit I have you'd be wary of people too..." Abbey is taken aback by Alex's honesty but also irritated by his assumption that she hasn't been through shit of her own. He obviously has an issue with her being in his home, amongst his friends, but for some strange reason, she really doesn't want him to feel that way. With a sudden, new found bravery - probably due to the alcohol in her system - Abbey steps forward and stares directly into Alex's eyes, trying to match his intensity. They are so dark and penetrating that it almost feels as though he can read her mind.

"I know I'm a complete stranger to you and there is no reason why you should trust me..." She whispers, sincerely, "But for what it's worth... you really don't have to be wary of me..."

They hold each other's gaze in a heated silence until the living room door bursts open and Gemma stumbles over, immediately sensing the tension between them.

"Oh... sorry... have you finished...?" She stutters, pointing to the bathroom.

"Sure..." Abbey smiles and lets Gemma pass before crossing the hallway towards the living room. She pauses outside the door, turning back to face Alex who is watching her closely, with a mixture of curiosity and confusion on his face.

"And for the record..." Abbey states, defiantly, "... You have no idea what I've been through..." And with an unusual amount of confidence, she leaves Alex standing in the dark behind her, shocked but also impressed at the fact she stood her ground. This is obviously going to be far more interesting than he first anticipated.

Chapter Four

Choices

Abbey knows she is drunk, but as soon as she steps outside Alex's flat into the cold, morning air, it really hits her. It is an unfamiliar sensation. Her head is spinning and she can barely remain upright as she waits in the doorway of the apartment block with Lucy and Nathan. It is 3:00am and they have only just ordered a taxi. The reality of sneaking out is starting to dawn on her and Abbey has no clue how she is going to climb back through her bedroom window in the state she is in… let alone quietly.

The taxi stops at the top of Abbey's street and Nathan insists that they get out too and walk her home. The rational part of Abbey knows this isn't the greatest idea, but she is so drunk and on such a high after the party that she doesn't care enough to object. The three of them stagger along arm in arm, leaning on each other for support and as they reach Abbey's driveway Nathan trips over the curb, falling into the gate and almost pulling it off one of its hinges. They burst into hysterical laughter while drunkenly urging each other to be quiet and after finally calming down and saying goodnight, Abbey watches fondly as Nathan and Lucy stumble off down the road. As they get further away in the distance a familiar sense of gloom slowly creeps back in, like a black cloud hanging over Abbey's head. The fun is over and it is back to reality.

She smiles as Nathan picks Lucy up and swings her around, kissing her passionately under the street light. They stagger backwards into a parked car and the alarm sounds; shattering the eerie silence and making them both jump as they burst into laughter again, before racing hand in hand, around the corner out of sight.

Abbey ducks into the front garden and carefully creeps down the side of the garage. 'How the hell am I going to do this?!' She muses. After 5 minutes of trying to calculate the best way to clamber up the side of the house without falling on her face or alarming the neighbours, Abbey concludes that she is simply going to have to hope for the best.

She throws her bag over her shoulder, climbs onto the garden wall and hoists herself up onto the garage roof... so far so good. She crawls across the garage on her hands and knees, quietly laughing to herself, amused at how ridiculous she must look and how funny it would be if someone saw her at this precise moment. The window isn't as high as she had thought and about half way up the drainpipe there is a bit of plastic fastening it to the side of the house, which sticks out just enough to act as a good footing.

Abbey opens her window as slowly and gently as possible and holding onto the window ledge she pushes herself up, swinging her right leg over and through in the same movement. Using all of her strength she manages to twist her body and lift her other leg inside until she is hanging out of the window head first. She starts to laugh again, partly due to the level of alcohol in her system and partly because of the head rush from being upside down. She rocks backwards -and ever so gently - slumps onto her bedroom floor, highly impressed at herself for not only managing such an athletic feat but for doing it rather stealthily. Abbey sits there for a moment, catching her breath, before slowly standing up and dusting herself off. She throws her bag onto the bed and pushes the window shut triumphantly, but as she turns around, the lamp in the corner of her room clicks on. Peter is sat in the chair by Abbey's work desk. His face is blank and his eyes are full of anger, as he folds his arms and purses his lips. 'Busted'.

"Jesus... could you be any more dramatic?!" She quips.

"Where have you been?" Peter's answering tone is cold and abrupt.

Abbey knows she is in big trouble and that she should be careful, but her brother has an uncanny ability to get under her skin and as a result - despite the situation - she immediately goes on the defensive.

"Out..." Abbey mirrors Peter's tone.

"Did you have fun?"

"Yeah, I did actually..." She smiles to herself as she thinks back to the party and Peter's temper suddenly flares. He hurls himself out of the chair and strides towards Abbey, looming over her as he spits his words out furiously.

"What the hell do you think you're doing?! Is this some pathetic little crusade to get attention or are you trying to impress that set of losers you call friends?!"

"You. Don't. Know. Them...." Abbey pronounces each word slowly through gritted teeth.

"I know that they've changed you. I know they've got you doing stupid stuff like skipping school..."

"They are NOT the reason I've changed..." Abbey shouts, forgetting for a moment that it is almost 4am. The risk of waking Janet is the only thing stopping Abbey from launching at her brother and screaming at the top of her lungs out of sheer frustration, "I changed because my twin brother died! It happened, whether you admit it or not... it happened, and I can't do this anymore..."

"Do what?!"

"THIS..." Abbey shrieks... "This fake life, pretending everything's fine when it's not fine...! Acting like nothing happened isn't going to make it all magically go away, it will only make things worse..."

"I don't act like it didn't happen..." Peter gasps, disgusted at the accusation.

"Yes you do. You all do..." Abbey argues, "you can't move on properly if you don't grieve and the best way to do that is to talk about him, but you don't... ever. When was the last time we talked about something good or funny Ryan did?!" Abbey can feel her voice falter as she battles with her angry tears.

"You think it's that easy?!" Peter snaps, "You think we can all sit down at the table and have a laugh and a joke about the good old days and how great he was?!"

"I'm not saying it's easy, but it has to be better than this. Not talking about him, or even acknowledging him... you act like he never even existed..."

"That is not true..." Peter tries to keep his voice stern but he can't face Abbey any longer. He turns away and drops back down into the chair, holding his head in his hands.

"Yes you do..." She disagrees, kneeling down in front of him, "...and I know why you do, because sometimes I feel it too. It's like when you think about him and how he used to be, it's too hard... because we failed him. It wasn't an illness, it wasn't an accident, it was his choice and we should have known he needed help..." Abbey can no longer stop her tears from falling and Peter forces himself to look up. He too is crying, but his demeanour is still aggressive, his anger palpable.

"You honestly believe that he isn't on my mind every single day? He is my brother and he will always be a part of this family, but constantly bringing him up and talking about what happened will only make it harder to let go. It doesn't mean I don't love him..." Peter stands, wiping the tears from his face as he moves wearily towards the door and he stops when Abbey speaks again.

"If everything I just said is wrong...?" She asks in a pained whisper, "Why can't you bring yourself to say his name...?" She waits for Peter to respond and he eventually turns to face her, with the same blank expression fixed in place once more.

"I don't know what you're trying to achieve by behaving this way..." He states, flatly. "But you need to grow up and stop being so selfish... for everybody's sake..." And with that parting shot, he leaves, quietly closing the door behind him.

Abbey drops exhausted onto her bed and sobs into her pillow, pulling the covers tightly around her in an attempt to block out the pain. She never believed it was possible to feel such crippling loss. If only her family would open up and be honest with their grief, but Abbey knows that isn't going to happen. They won't talk about Ryan, what he did or why... especially not with her. No matter how much she wishes they would. She is completely on her own - totally lost - and more scared than she ever has been before.

The following few days are excruciating. Abbey is constantly tense, waiting for Janet to come charging into her room at any moment, shouting the odds and no doubt threatening to ground her for the rest of her natural life. But Sunday passes by with no confrontation. In fact, Janet is in a strangely pleasant mood as she potters about the house, cleaning and running errands. Abbey is far less cheerful due to her horrendous hang over. She feels sick enough without the added nausea in the pit of her stomach caused by the knowledge that there will most definitely be repercussions from her late night 'jail break'. At least that's what she is expecting... but as the days go by, Abbey starts to feel even more anxious. What is Peter waiting for? Why hasn't he told Janet? Is this some form of punishment, is he dragging it out to make her sweat? It doesn't make any sense.

Abbey can no longer take the anticipation and she decides to confront Peter. They haven't spoken a word to each other or even made eye contact since their huge argument, but she can't take the not knowing any longer. If she is going to be in serious trouble she wants it over and done with.

It is Friday afternoon and has now been a week since she was caught red handed by her brother... but still nothing. As she throws her keys onto the side and hooks her school bag over the banister, she strains to hear the low murmur of voices coming from the kitchen. Janet is ranting and she sounds fairly pissed off. 'Here we go'. Abbey thinks, as she takes a deep breath and enters the room. Peter is sat at the breakfast table reading a paper. He doesn't look up or even acknowledge her presence as she walks in, but Janet turns, and to Abbey's surprise, she is smiling.

"Oh Abbey, there you are..."

"Is everything OK?" She asks, cautiously.

"Oh, yes its fine darling... a slight problem with the conference room we have booked for tomorrow but nothing that can't be fixed...."

"Tomorrow?"

"I'm away this weekend I thought I told you...?"

"No, I don't think you mentioned it..." Abbey manages to refrain from rolling her eyes. 'Why the hell would she mention a little thing like that?'

"Well, I leave tonight and I get back late on Sunday. Peter is in charge while I'm gone and there's plenty of food in the fridge for you both. I'll be on my mobile if you need me for anything..."

"OK..."

"Listen..." Janet stands in front of Abbey and puts her hands firmly on her shoulders, holding her in place... "I know it's been difficult recently, and I want you to know that I like it about as much as you do. I don't want us falling out all the time. You've been really good these past few weeks and your school work is back on track... so... I don't see any reason for you to be grounded anymore..." It's a good job that Janet is gripping Abbey so firmly, as she can feel herself rock backwards, almost passing out with shock. Is this really happening? Surely Peter isn't going to just sit there and let this go?

"Thanks, Mum..." She stutters.

"You're welcome… but I still want you on your best behaviour alright? No slacking off at school. I'm trusting you here Abbey, I'm giving you a chance…"

"I know. So… if I'm not grounded, does that mean I can see my friends this weekend?" Janet hesitates and Abbey almost regrets pushing her luck.

"I suppose so…" She replies with a degree of uncertainty, "But I want your coursework done first and you need to be home when your brother says so – no arguments…" Abbey can live with that. Peter isn't here half the time anyway. Janet collects her laptop and a stack of folders off the table and rushes upstairs to pack. She is being picked up in an hour by one of her colleagues and then she will be gone for a whole weekend. An entire 48 hours. And to top it off - Abbey has her freedom back. As her excitement starts to build, Peter clears his throat and leans back in his chair. Abbey still can't figure out what game he is playing but that was the perfect opportunity for him to drop her right in it… and he didn't.

"You haven't told her?" She states the obvious.

"No."

"Why not?"

"Don't think for one second that I'm OK with what you did, or that I'm going to let it go…" He scoffs. "But Mum has been in a really good place recently and she's been looking forward to this trip for weeks…" Oh, so Janet had known for 'weeks' about this business trip and still Abbey knew nothing. Great, "She is doing really well and there's no way I'm going to let you upset her and bring her down…" There it is again, that overwhelming urge to punch her brother square in the face.

"Are you done…?" Abbey stares at him.

"You've got some nerve... don't think this is over. Mum is giving you a chance and you better not blow it. If you do I won't hesitate to tell her exactly what's been going on..."

Peter's snide, bitter words linger in the back of Abbey's mind as she gets ready in her room. She isn't in the greatest of moods, but she is determined to shrug it off and enjoy herself tonight, no matter what it takes. She is no longer grounded and that is definitely a cause for celebration. She rings Lucy straight away and she is over the moon that Abbey can join them on their night out without having to conduct a covert operation in order to get there. She gasps in amazement as Abbey tells her in detail about what had transpired that afternoon. Of course Lucy, Nathan and Liam knew all about Peter catching her as she snuck back into the house - she had filled them in the following Monday at school - so they are all as shocked as Abbey when she tells them that her curfew has been lifted.

The plan is to meet at Alex's flat for a few drinks before heading into town. A brand new club opened up the previous week at the bottom of Call Lane and they are all eager to try it out. Abbey struggles to control the butterflies in her stomach, knowing that she will see Alex again. The way they had left their last encounter means this time round it could go either way. He might be even more standoffish and aloof than before, or maybe he will start warming to her? One thing is for certain – if he is going to stare at her as much as he did last Saturday, she is going to give him something to stare at. Abbey is under no illusions. She knows deep down that there is no way someone as breathtakingly good-looking as Alex would ever be interested in her. She has always been told how beautiful she is but she doesn't think herself as anything special and Alex is way out of her league. This time though, she is prepared, and determined to make herself look as appealing as she possibly can, regardless of her chances.

After applying her make-up Abbey dries her long, red hair and curls it into soft waves that fall just past her shoulders, styling her fringe so that it sweeps softly over her left eye. She knows exactly which outfit to wear to achieve the effect she desires. A pair of black shorts with gold buttons down the front, her favourite cream, sleeveless crop-top and her cream stiletto heels. She finishes her outfit with a set of gold bangles on her right wrist and a pair of gold drop earrings.

Abbey gathers her phone, money and most importantly, her I.D and shoves it all into a cream and gold clutch as she checks her reflection in the mirror one last time. She looks good... and she feels it too. A car horn beeps as her taxi pulls outside... 'perfect timing'. She skips downstairs and is almost out of the front door when Peter appears behind her.

"Where are you going?" He snaps.

"Out with friends... Mum said I could remember...?"

"Dressed like that?"

"We're going out Pete... I'm 18..."

"Don't be back any later than 11:30pm..." Abbey bursts into laughter before she can stop herself.

"Half 11?! You were out every single weekend when you turned 18 and you were rarely ever home before 2:00am!"

"Maybe not... but I wasn't taking the piss by sneaking out and playing truant from school like a complete idiot either, was I?!"

There is so much that Abbey wants to say, but it would be a complete waste of time trying to get her brother to listen and she is so sick of arguing with him. The taxi beeps again.

"Don't wait up..." She smirks, racing out of the door and down the driveway before Peter can stop her.

As Abbey approaches the apartment block she begins to regret not meeting Lucy beforehand. Her nerves are kicking into over drive and she is one step away from hyperventilating. 'For god sake get a grip' she scolds herself. She presses the button for flat 38 and the door buzzes immediately. As she exits the lift on the 9th floor she has to keep reminding herself how to put one foot in front of the other. She is really eager to see Alex, but he is so unpredictable and so completely uninterested in her. Why she is getting her hopes up and allowing herself to get excited about something that is clearly never going to happen, she has no idea. As Abbey approaches the door to the flat she can hear music playing and what sounds like Gemma laughing. She takes a deep breath, composes herself, and knocks loudly. The door swings open and Tom's eyes widen in surprise. He takes the joint he is smoking out of his mouth and looks Abbey up and down.

"Fucking hell girl... you scrub up alright don't you...?!"

"Thanks... I think!" She laughs. Tom hugs her as she enters the flat and she quickly scans the kitchen, trying not to make it obvious exactly who she is looking for. Sophie and Gemma are sitting at the table and Darren is leaning by the fridge... but no Alex. Abbey makes her way over, hugging them all in greeting.

"You look great babe..." Gemma smiles.

"Thank you, so do you..." Abbey replies, blushing at the compliment.

Sophie pours Abbey a glass of wine and the five of them move into the living room to join Lucy, Nathan and Liam. As they pass through the hallway Abbey prepares herself, knowing that she could bump into Alex at any second, but rather disappointingly, he is nowhere to be seen.

Lucy jumps up excitedly and squeals with delight as she races over to Abbey, hugging her tightly - and Nathan and Liam glance up from dividing out numerous lines of cocaine on the coffee table.

"Christ Abs... you look like walking Viagra...!" Liam winks.

"How charming... thanks Liam..." She quips, hugging them both as she sits down.

"You do look amazing..." Lucy agrees... "Those shoes look pretty high though, I hope they aren't going to stop you dancing because it is on tonight...!" She laughs, shaking her arms from side to side.

Abbey giggles at Lucy as she launches into one of her super excited outbursts, chatting about how great the night is going to be and how much fun they will have at this new club, which she describes as 'like the best club ever'. The only time she stops talking is when she takes a sip of her drink or has another line.

Just like the previous weekend they all make Abbey feel completely welcome and her nerves soon vanish. She finds herself marvelling again at what a close knit group they are and she feels incredibly lucky to be a part of it. She is beyond grateful that they have welcomed her into the fold so willingly. It is just what she needs; a fun night out with no drama, to let loose and enjoy herself with friends, but no matter how hard she tries she can't seem to switch off completely or forget about her problems at home. The resentment she feels towards Peter and the detachment she feels from her mum is slowly starting to eat away at her. Things have gotten so much worse recently and she is constantly playing it over and over in her mind - wishing there was a way to resolve the tension, but knowing there is nothing she can do as long as her family refuse to face up to their pain and acknowledge their grief. Until they open up about Ryan and remember him the way that he deserves to be remembered, they are never going to see eye to eye.

"Just got off the phone to a mate, he says the club is packed..." Tom returns from the kitchen with his phone in his hand... "It's gonna be mint...!"

"I hope we don't have to queue for ages..." Sophie muses.

"Course not, Alex got us guest list...!" Tom laughs, incensed at the thought.

As Darren changes CD, the others gather around the coffee table, preparing to play what sounds like a rather complicated drinking game. When the music kicks in, they cheer in approval at Darren's choice and start singing along to the track, albeit loudly and rather out of tune. Abbey uses the opportunity to lean towards Lucy, ensuring that only she can hear.

"Where is Alex...?" She asks, as casually as she can manage.

"Work... but he should be back anytime soon..." Lucy doesn't bat an eyelid at Abbey's question and she is left wondering again what Alex does for a living that causes him to be out so late.

Another hour or so passes and the several Sambuca shots that Abbey has drunk start to take effect. It turns out she isn't very good at drinking games. Feeling tipsy she begins to lighten up a little, but the buzz she is feeling still isn't enough to completely dispel her worries and her brain is working overtime. Why can't she just relax and enjoy herself?

"Here he is...!" Tom shouts over the music... "Busy night son?!" Abbey looks up from the CD case she is studying and sees Alex standing in the doorway; their eyes meet for a brief moment before he steps forward and slaps hands with the lads. He looks even more appealing than the first time she laid eyes on him – if that is even possible.

He is wearing dark blue jeans and a black shirt that fits his frame perfectly. The sleeves are rolled up to his elbows and the top two buttons are undone, showing a slight glimpse of his sculpted chest and the chain of his rosary beads. 'Don't go bright red, don't go bright red...' Abbey chants, over and over in her mind. The butterflies in her stomach return and a rush of adrenaline shoots through her body. She can't believe that just been in the same room as him affects her in this way.

She takes a sip of her drink – glancing nonchalantly over to where the lads are sitting – and her heart leaps. He is staring at her again. This time though it isn't threatening in the slightest, instead he looks more intrigued, with only a slight, underlying hint of irritation. It is a definite improvement from last time.

Abbey jumps as her phone vibrates in her pocket and she reaches for it grudgingly, pressing the message icon in the top corner of the screen. '1 New Voicemail'. She hadn't heard her phone ringing over the music but she can already guess who the missed call is from. She walks out onto the balcony where it is quieter and calls through to her message bank.

'Where are you? You need to be back no later than midnight Abbey, I mean it. Don't be late.' Peter is obviously still furious with her. Why can't he just leave her the hell alone instead of involving himself in her life? He obviously gets a kick out of lording it over her and acting all superior. She wishes he would just back off.

"Hey, are you OK?" Lucy joins Abbey on the balcony, hugging her arms to her chest, "It's freezing out here..."

"Yeah... sorry, I was just checking my phone. I have a voicemail from Pete..."

"And what did he have to say?" Lucy raises an eyebrow and tilts her head disapprovingly.

"Oh the usual, just barking orders at me. He says I have to be back by midnight..."

"What?!" Lucy pouts... "But we aren't even leaving the flat until 11pm and you can't skip the club it's going to be great..."

"I know. But he won't budge..."

"So just pretend you haven't got the message! Come on Abbey... he clearly doesn't understand what's going on with you. What you need right now is to have a laugh and get your life back! Just because he isn't dealing with it, don't let him drag you down as well..."

Abbey breathes in the cold night air and stares down at the lights of the city that are sparkling below. Lucy has a point. She seems to understand Abbey better than anyone and always knows exactly what she needs. But it doesn't change how terrible she feels about how strained her relationship with her family has become and she knows that she is making it worse by acting out. She should be on her best behaviour instead of making things more difficult for her mum, but she isn't doing it on purpose. She just can't bring herself to carry on as normal like they do, pretending as though everything is fine. Her sorrow, her anger and her grief, they are always there - a constant ache in her heart which there is no escape from, and it is far too strong to ignore.

"I just wish I could run away from it all, you know...?"Abbey whispers, "This last year has been the worst year of my life and I'm so sick of feeling this way... hurting all the time. I want to grieve, I want to remember Ryan and celebrate him and move on but I can't because of them. The way they act, like it didn't happen, like Ryan was never here... It makes me so angry. He doesn't deserve that..."

"Maybe they act that way because they find it easier to block it all out rather than deal with it...?" Lucy suggests, hesitantly.

"Yeah. That's exactly it. I know that it's their way of 'coping', but I just don't understand how they can turn their back on him like that..."

"You really miss him don't you?" Lucy asks, and tears spring behind Abbey's eyes. She isn't used to talking about Ryan this way as her family hardly ever mention him at all, and it is strange, openly admitting her feelings.

"Every single day..." she sighs, turning to face Lucy, "Have you ever felt like you wanted to escape your own life and be someone else...?" she asks, shaking her head, sadly, "I wish I could make it all just disappear... even for one night..."

"Maybe you can...?" Lucy's tone is quietly cautious.

"What do you mean?"

"Look, I know you said it isn't your thing and you've never done it before. But it sounds to me like you're in serious need of a release, and... well... maybe a little pick me up will help?" Lucy nods once towards the living room and to the coffee table in particular, where Nathan, Liam, Sophie and Darren sit, sharing line after line of cocaine.

"I don't know Lucy... I've always been told drugs are bad news..."

"The only people who say that are the ones who've never tried them. There are risks, yeah, but there are risks involved in everything you do... as long as you're careful and you don't get stupid with them, you'll be fine..." She states, convincingly, "It sets you free Abs... makes all your troubles just melt away and for one night you can forget about all the bullshit and enjoy life. You can be whoever you want to be..."

Abbey has to hand it to Lucy; she has one hell of a sales pitch, but she is still incredibly wary. She had always been told about the horror stories regarding drug use and she is certain she doesn't want to go down that road - or does she? The others are all doing it, and it doesn't seem to be affecting them in a negative way at all. They are happy, laughing and joking, enjoying themselves. They look so relaxed and care free... exactly how Abbey wants to feel more than anything. She desperately wants that escape.

"Hey, no pressure, but think about it..." Lucy puts her arm around Abbey and pulls her back inside. They join the others around the table just as Nathan finishes cutting up several more lines and after inhaling his he passes the rolled up note to Lucy, but she only does one, looking at Abbey inquisitively. She holds the note out to her and without stopping to think or over analyse, Abbey leans forward and quickly does the line of cocaine in front of her, before she has chance to change her mind. She passes the note to Darren and sits back on the sofa.

Her nose burns and her eyes sting as she feels a strong, dizzying sensation. She blinks hard, trying to get her blurred vision back into focus and after a brief moment of discomfort, she starts to feel a swell of excitement, giddiness even, and much to her surprise it instantly lifts her mood.

As Liam, Nathan, Darren and Tom carry on with the drinking game from earlier, the girls dance together in the middle of the room. The music is turned up full and Abbey throws her head back and forth in time to the beat, relishing her new found energy and feel good frame of mind. Lucy was right, it really is a release.

Abbey spins around with Gemma and Sophie, laughing as they struggle to keep their balance. As she staggers slightly she reaches for Lucy's hand, but quickly realises that she is no longer by her side. Alex is marching her over towards the balcony with his hand tucked under her arm, pulling her along carefully but firmly. 'What is his problem now?'

Alex comes to a halt just inside the balcony door and Lucy shakes her spilt drink off her hand, holding her glass at arm's length so as not to get any on her outfit.

"What's wrong...?!" She asks, irritated by Alex's man handling.

"It doesn't exactly take a genius to figure out this is Abbey's first time with drugs..." He answers sharply, under his breath.

"Of course it is... she hardly even drinks!" Lucy laughs.

"In that case just watch her will you? For fuck sake Lucy she's new to this, she's not like us. The last thing I need is some naïve little rich girl collapsing in my fucking living room!" Alex pinches the bridge of his nose and breathes calmly, trying to get his anger under control.

"Ok, Ok... I'll take care of her, of course I will... chill out Al...!" She smiles, standing on her tiptoes and reaching up to kiss his forehead. He warms to her immediately and his angry demeanour softens. Lucy can always wrap him around her little finger. She is just as much a little sister to him as she is to Darren.

As Lucy skips back over to join the girls for the next dance, Tom quietly takes her place next to Alex, passing him another beer. They stand in silence for a moment as Tom struggles to hide his amusement. Alex is staring at Abbey... again, something which hadn't escaped Tom's attention last week either.

"She's pretty isn't she?" He asks, innocently.

"Who?"

"You know who...!"

"She's alright..." Alex shrugs.

"Alright?!" Tom laughs, "Is that why you haven't stopped fucking gawping at her all night...?" Alex turns and looks directly at Tom, whose face is amused and expectant, and he can't help smirking in response.

"Don't you have someone else to irritate?"

"Struck a nerve did I?" He teases, "She's a sweet girl...!"

"Shut the fuck up...!" Alex laughs, shaking his head, "She won't be sweet for long if she gets involved with me...!"

Alex is incredibly grateful to have a friend like Tom who always has his back. But sometimes he wishes he couldn't read his thoughts quite so well, as it makes it almost impossible to keep things from him. He always knows what Alex is thinking – sometimes before Alex even knows himself - and he has obviously noticed the tension he feels in Abbey's presence. What is it about this girl that he can't figure out? She is quiet and unassuming, yet when he confronted her she confidently stood her ground. And the way she looks at him, it's as if she knows him, like she sees right through the bullshit. She is inexperienced and naïve, yet she seems to fit into the group with ease and is clearly up for having a good time. And she is beautiful... funny but sweet natured. He has figured out that much about her at least and it has totally thrown him.

Women and the complications they bring are the reason Alex has spent the majority of his 20's completely single, with only the occasional 'casual fling'. He isn't used to feeling this way about someone. He isn't used to feeling drawn to a girl so strongly, but Tom is right... she is more than OK, much more than pretty and he can't take his eyes off her.

That is why he had gotten so agitated the previous week when she turned up at his door with Lucy, Nathan and Liam. He doesn't like strangers in his house, that much is true, but as the night went on it became much more than that. He could feel his interest peaking, his fascination and attraction to her growing and he didn't like it. He doesn't want that distraction, that utter inconvenience in his life, but much to his annoyance he can't seem to fight it. That is why he lashed out... self-preservation. Truth be told it has been so long since he has felt these sort of emotions, it scares him a bit. Fucking ridiculous, Alex Matthews scared by a prim and proper 18 year old, middle class girl who is worlds apart from the life he leads. What a joke.

"Taxi's here in 5 minutes!" Liam shouts from the kitchen, and Lucy downs her drink before quickly racking up two more lines of cocaine to share with Abbey. The fear and reluctance that had consumed her earlier is completely gone and she loves the effect the cocaine has on her... that happy drunk feeling, like everything is great. She is alert and aware of everyone around her, totally content and completely self-confident. The only problem is, the effects fade after a little while and to get that feeling back she has to do more. But she is having an amazing night so far and she doesn't want it to end. She finishes her vodka and coke as Lucy does two more lines, then quickly follows suit. Leaning forward with the note in place, she breathes in slowly, dragging it along the line of cocaine until it is gone. She glances at her phone; 12:15am. She is quarter of an hour late. There is no point in rushing home now as she will already be in deep trouble.

After a short journey to the bottom end of town, their taxi pulls up outside the new nightclub and Alex jumps out first. He wastes no time in striding past the long queue of people and approaches the door, greeting the bouncers like old friends. After a minute or two of conversation they shake hands and he turns to the others, gesturing inside. Tom, Darren and Sophie lead the way with Liam, Gemma and Nathan just behind. Abbey links arms with Lucy as they follow last and there are loud, expletive filled shouts of protest from the angry revellers who have been forced to queue outside in the cold. Abbey can't help but get the impression that Alex is used to getting his own way. He is so cool, calm and under control... and it is so attractive.

The club itself is fairly small. Through the entrance there are three flights of stairs to walk down which lead into a main room, with two smaller rooms at either side. The walls are thick stone, the décor dark, and there are mirrors everywhere, giving the illusion that the space is much bigger than it actually is. The main room has a dance floor in the centre, a DJ booth at the very far end and a large bar on the right hand side, which is absolutely packed, the crowd waiting to be served around four people deep.

A sign hanging over the entrance way to the smaller room on the left, advertises that it is the 'VIP AREA' and it is obvious to Abbey straight away that they are heading over in that direction. The way the bouncers had acknowledged Alex, 'VIP' is a fairly apt way of describing him. It is like this is his domain and he is in charge.

In the VIP area there is another bar - this one thankfully a lot quieter than in the main part of the club - and on the far side of the room are several large, red booths, one of which has a 'reserved' sign on the table next to a complimentary ice bucket stacked with beer and champagne. It is of course, their table. Abbey has never experienced anything like this before. She has never really been clubbing, so she certainly hasn't been given the 'celebrity' treatment. It is amazing and even though the buzz from the last two lines she did back at the flat is starting to wear off, she is still on a massive high.

"So what do you think?" Nathan asks, amused at her awe struck expression.

"It's great..." Abbey smiles as Lucy passes her a glass of champagne, but her good mood fades as she catches sight of the clock above the bar. 1:00am. As fun as this is, that little voice in the back of her mind has started nagging away again and she is beginning to worry about what she might have to face tomorrow. She glances at her phone. No signal. They are obviously far enough underground so that none of Peter's calls or messages will get through. She wonders how many times he has tried already.

"Hey come on you... toilet trip...!" Lucy grabs Abbey's hand and Sophie and Gemma follow behind. They head into the VIP restroom and cram into one of the cubicles as Lucy gets the cocaine out of her bag, gently placing the toilet seat down before she kneels in front of it.

"What if we get caught?" Abbey whispers, panicked.

"Don't worry about it; it's not gonna happen..." Gemma states, calmly.

"Even if it did they wouldn't do anything... not to us!" Sophie adds.

"What do you mean...?" Abbey is totally confused. She knows that drugs are illegal and she is pretty sure clubs, bars and pubs can get into serious trouble if people are caught doing them on the premises. Why should they be an exception to the rule?

"We might get a slap on the wrist..." Sophie continues... "but they wouldn't take it any further. Not only are we Alex's friends but we're here with him so it's all good!"

"Um..." Abbey is unsure whether to ask, but she has to know, "Is there something I'm missing... about Alex I mean? He seems to be pretty well connected and now you're telling me we won't get into trouble just by being with him?!" Lucy does her two lines then swaps places with Sophie as she rubs a few drops of cocaine into her gums.

"Not when it comes to drugs we won't..." Lucy smirks.

"She doesn't know yet?" Gemma asks.

"Know what...?" Abbey can no longer hide her intrigue. She is dying to get as much info on Alex as she possibly can. She is so into him it's embarrassing.

"Alex is one of the biggest dealer's in Leeds..." Gemma declares... "That's how he earns such good money and it's why he knows so many bouncers and bar owners around the city. Well, the ones who are interested in making a few back handers and aren't all that bothered about staying on the right side of the law, if you know what I mean...?"

"So the two bouncers outside...?" Abbey asks.

"Friends of his..." Lucy replies, "Just like the owner of this place. He has two more bars in Leeds that Alex works at supplying to the clientele, and he gives him a cut of the profit. That's why they all bend over backwards for him; he's the man to know in these circles..." Lucy winks... "And he has his eye on you, you lucky girl...!" All three of them burst out laughing and Abbey looks on in shock, completely gobsmacked and unable to process Lucy's last statement.

"What?!" She gasps, as Gemma stands up and passes the rolled up note to her.

"Not to rush you babe, but the longer we're in here the bigger the chance we actually will get caught!"

Abbey kneels down in front of the toilet and does her two lines in a complete daze. She can't believe what

Lucy has just said and now that they are chatting away about other things the moment has gone for Abbey to get more out of them. Does Alex really like her? If so... why? She couldn't be more different to him if she tried. She is well aware that this newly acquired information about him should probably scare her off, but it doesn't. Her first instincts were bang on the money though. He is dangerous.

The night quickly turns into the most fun Abbey can ever remember having. The alcohol flows and in between the frequent trips to the toilet to 'powder their noses' as Darren puts it, they hit the dance floor; messing around, play fighting and throwing down the worst, cheesiest, most humiliating dance moves they can possibly think of in order to make each other laugh. Occasionally Sophie and Lucy cuddle up to Darren and Nathan, leaving Abbey and Gemma to ditch the couples and find their own fun, which mainly consists of flirting outrageously with the bar men. Gemma has it down to a fine art, much to the annoyance of Tom, who clearly likes her much more than a friend.

For the majority of the night, Alex is nowhere to be seen. He occasionally comes back to sit in the booth and have a quick beer, but it isn't long before he disappears again. According to Lucy he is working the club, mingling with the crowds and figuring out the layout of the place. He has to familiarise himself with his surroundings and get to know the staff if he wants to run drugs here as well. An interesting occupation to say the least and Abbey is unnerved at how readily she accepts it and how little it seems to bother her.

She dries her hands on the harsh paper towel and straightens her top, checking her appearance in the bathroom mirror. Despite being drunk she still looks pretty good. It is 3:30am and the club is nowhere near winding down. It is open until 5am and by the looks of things the others aren't about to leave any time soon. Peter will be going crazy but it is far too late to let that trouble her now. She has ignored him and his pathetically early curfew and as a result is, oh... only 3 and a half hours late. She is going to pay for it tomorrow, so she might as well have fun for as long as she can.

As Abbey leaves the toilet and walks around the edge of the bar, a rough hand grabs hold of her arm. Thinking it will be one of the lads she turns expectantly, but her smile quickly vanishes as she asses the stranger in front of her.

"Can I help you...?" She asks, confused.

"Let me buy you a drink gorgeous..." His words come out in a slurred mess as he leers towards her suggestively.

"No thank you, I have a drink at my table..." She turns to walk away but he pulls her back.

"No, I want to buy you a drink..."

"I don't want a drink, let go of my arm..." The disgusting man smells of stale beer and cigarette smoke and he tightens his grip as he slides his other hand around Abbey's waist, and she tries in vain to push him off, "I said I'm not interested..."

"Why are you playing hard to get? I just want to buy you a drink, that's all don't be such a bitch..." He leans in closer still and Abbey realises with absolute horror that he is attempting to kiss her. She squirms, trying to break out of his grasp, but she can't move. She can see the others across the room but none of them are looking her way and the music is too loud for her to shout over.

As he edges her towards a dark corner she contemplates kneeing him as hard as she can in the groin, if only she can get the right angle. She shifts, but he moves with her, anticipating her move. As she truly begins to panic someone slams into them out of nowhere and a pair of hands grab the creep around his throat, throwing him backwards into a table. He falls to the floor and several half empty glasses smash around him, as he clumsily pulls himself to his feet. He staggers back towards Abbey but she no longer feels frightened, as standing between them is Alex.

"She said no..." He states, forcefully.

"And what the hell has it got to do with you? We were having a private conversation it's none of your damn business..."

Alex steps forward and towers over the drunken idiot who clearly has no idea who he is dealing with. His face and voice are calm on the surface but impossibly threatening at the same time and it sends a shiver down Abbey's spine.

"You lay a hand on her and it becomes my fucking business... She said no. Now you've got five seconds to get the fuck out of my sight..."

The man sneers at Alex as he rocks back on his heel, and, rather stupidly, throws a punch at him. Alex's face remains impassive as he catches the man's fist in mid-air, spins his arm around his back and slams his face, hard into the table.

"Apologise to her...." The man struggles in pain as he tries and fails to get out from under Alex's grip, "I said apologise..." He demands again.

"I'm... S... sorry..." He manages to force out, despite the agony he is in, and Alex lets go of his arm as one of the bouncers rushes over.

"Problem...?" He asks.

"He's ready to go home..." Alex points at the man who is now crumpled in a heap on the floor and without hesitation the bouncer grabs hold of him and frog marches him across the room. Abbey rubs her arm mindlessly as she stares after them in shock and Alex's expression softens.

"Are you alright...?" He asks, and Abbey looks directly at him for the first time, still a little bit shaken.

"Yeah, I'm OK. Thank you..."

Alex edges forward in silence and takes Abbey's arm in his hands, carefully checking it over. The sensation of his fingertips brushing against her skin makes it spark and tingle and she glances up to see him staring down at her beguilingly.

"Come on..." He commands, and as he begins to walk away he gently slides his arm down Abbey's back, guiding her forward before casually reaching for her hand and interlocking their fingers. A bolt of lightning shoots through her and she almost gasps out loud. 'Can this really be happening?' A smile slowly spreads across Abbey's face as Alex pulls her gently through the crowd and back over towards the booth. He is the most attractive, confident, self-assured, enigmatic guy Abbey has ever met... and he is holding her hand. And for this one shining moment, she allows herself to pretend that he is hers.

CHAPTER FIVE

THE DEBT

Abbey is trying her hardest not to look insolent and the last thing she wants to do is add fuel to the fire by yawning in her mother's face, but her lecture has been going on for almost half an hour now and she is starting to lose focus.

Peter had of course gone ballistic with her when she finally staggered in at around 6:30am on Saturday morning and she knew that this time there was no way he would let it pass without telling Janet. He laid it on thick, explaining dramatically how worried he had been and how he thought something terrible had happened to her.

Abbey knows it's a load of crap. He is just annoyed that she laughed in his face, completely ignored him and didn't do as she was told. This is payback for making him look like an idiot.

"I un-ground you and this is how you behave? This is the thanks I get?" Janet has at least stopped shouting, but her anger is still visibly bubbling under the surface and Abbey has to tread carefully.

"You said I could go out..." She replies meekly.

"Yes. And I also told you that you had to be home when you're brother said so..."

"Look I'm sorry... I just lost track of time..."

"For 6 and a half hours?!!" Janet's high pitched shriek makes Abbey flinch. It is Sunday night and despite spending all day Saturday in bed she still feels absolutely shocking. Hangovers are bad; but she is totally convinced that a hangover from drink *and* drugs must be as bad as it gets. She can't imagine it being any more painful than this. It isn't possible.

"We were in a club and we were just dancing, having a good time, I didn't think anything of it until I looked at my phone, I'd missed his calls because I had no signal..." Abbey tries in vain to justify her actions, but she can barely muster the energy. Her head is pounding and all she wants to do is go back to bed.

"It's not good enough Abbey. I told you specifically that Peter was in charge..." Janet and Peter both glare at Abbey and she can feel her face redden with anger.

"I'm not a child Mum, I'm 18 years old and I don't need babysitting. I just wanted to go out and have fun with my friends like every other normal teenager... like Pete and Anna did when they were my age. I'm sorry I got home late but you said I could go out..." Abbey knows she is pushing it with her last statement. She tries not to look directly at him but she can sense Peter raising his eyebrows in a 'you're really going to go there?' sort of way. He could easily get her grounded again in an instant, but seemingly, he still hasn't told Janet about her sneaking out, which in Abbey's book is quite frankly nothing short of a miracle.

"Peter, will you give us a minute?" He stands slowly, arms folded and strides arrogantly out of the room. 'Tosser' Abbey thinks.

"I feel like I don't recognize my own daughter anymore..." Janet's words are harsh and abrupt and they strike Abbey like a bolt out of the blue. She knows they have grown apart recently, but Janet acknowledging it out loud suddenly makes the situation very real, "Missing school, staying out late, drinking... it's so out of character for you. I just don't know what I'm supposed to do anymore..." Janet stares out of the window as if lost in a distant thought and Abbey looks on helplessly. She feels a sudden and desperate urge to reassure her but she has no idea what to say.

How on earth did it get to be like this? Abbey's childhood was a happy, stable one. They weren't exactly well off but they had a good life and didn't want for anything. With four kids and two loving parents, it was always a home full of joy and laughter. And they have lost it all. Abbey has only come to realize now how much she took it all for granted before. She never appreciated it as much as she should have done.

She wants to make things right with her mum, but she knows it isn't that simple. She can't just forget the past and behave as though the last year never happened. She can't get up every day and go through the motions. Ryan's absence is all around her. She feels it constantly, every minute of every day, and it baffles her that Janet and Peter - and even Anna and Dom to some extent - can carry on as before without a hint of grief, or any form of acknowledgement. Maybe she feels the loss more than they do? Maybe the bond that twins share is much deeper, therefore the hurt takes longer to heal? Whatever the reason, she isn't on the same wave length as the rest of her family and even if they did open up and talk about it, they still wouldn't talk to her.

The only people keeping Abbey's spirits up at the moment are her friends. They are the ones that are bringing her to life again. They make her feel like she can finally start to move on from this and it feels amazing to be part of a group who accept her for who she is without question. A group of friends who understand that life is shit sometimes, but you have to stick together and have a laugh anyway. That is where Abbey's head is at and that is the mentality that is helping her heal. She is so unbelievably grateful that she met Lucy Blake on her very first day at Eden Comprehensive, because she would be utterly lost without her... without all of them. But that is the problem. The very thing helping Abbey is the same thing causing the rift with her family to grow. The more Abbey sees her friends the more alive and happy she feels, but the more it angers Peter and worries Janet. As much as Abbey wishes she could make things right with her family, the thought of cutting her friends out of her life is a notion she can't even comprehend. They are the only people who she feels she can be herself with and even though walking away from them might prevent further arguments at home, Abbey knows all too well that as a result, she will feel even more isolated and alone... and she can't bear the thought.

So she is stuck. Catch 22. Be alone and miserable, or risk losing her family altogether. It is a completely heartbreaking situation, but if her mum still refuses to open up and let her in, then she is left with no other choice. So as Janet sits and stares sorrowfully out of the kitchen window, she says nothing.

After a long, exhausting weekend, Abbey is seriously struggling through Monday morning. She still doesn't feel 100% back to normal after the copious amount of drink and drugs she took the previous Friday and she feels depressed and hollow after the awful conversation with her mum. She can't forget the look on Janet's face as she told Abbey she didn't know her anymore. It was as if she had completely given up. Abbey can't do anything about it though and as a result she feels totally deflated and is not in the best of moods.

Lost in her troubled thoughts Abbey opens up her locker, completely oblivious to the fact that Lucy is bounding down the corridor towards her and she almost jumps out of her skin as she throws her arms around her neck, hugging her from behind.

"There you are!" Lucy chimes, "I've been looking everywhere for you! We're off to Alex's, are you coming?" Abbey's heart leaps at the mere mention of his name and the butterflies in her stomach make her feel faint, but after his knight in shining armour routine and the all too brief hand holding on Friday, he had disappeared again and she had barely seen him for the rest of the night. They had said goodbye when Abbey's taxi arrived but there was no further interaction other than that.

She can't figure him out at all and it is driving her insane; he is so hot and cold. She desperately wants to get to know him better and today would be the perfect opportunity, but she has already decided that she isn't going to skip school. She has made a conscious decision to try harder after what unfolded yesterday afternoon and seeing Janet's utter disappointment in her. It doesn't make sense for her to get into any more trouble and her conscience has finally started to kick in.

"I can't Luc, not today..." Abbey smiles, apologetically.

"Why not?"

"I just don't feel up to it that's all..." She closes her locker and turns toward Lucy, who has a sceptical look on her face.

"What happened?" She asks, mildly defensive.

"What do you mean?"

"Come on Miller, obviously something is bugging you; you look like your puppy just died! Where's the live for now Abbey from Friday night?!"

"She is still well and truly hung over...!" Abbey laughs... "I just don't think it's a good idea, sorry. I should get to class..."

"That sounds like your brother talking to me! He got to you didn't he? He grassed you in and now you're being all mopey about it?!"

"I am not being mopey!" Abbey snaps; and the two of them stare at each other for a moment before bursting into laughter. She is definitely moping, that much is obvious... "I'm sorry Luc, but I mean it... I just don't think I should risk it today..."

"Well, not to worry, that's fine..." Lucy nods slowly with a look of mock understanding on her face and smiles a little too innocently, "But I respectfully disagree! It seems to me you need cheering up and believe it or not, I had sort of predicted this, knowing your brother would probably bring you down and make you feel all guilty. So I guess I'll have to resort to plan B...!"

"What are you..." Abbey frowns, completely baffled, but she doesn't even have chance to finish her question as Lucy whistles loudly and on command, Nathan and Liam sprint around the corner. Nathan grabs hold of Abbey's bag and in one swift movement Liam picks her up, throwing her over his shoulder into a fireman's lift.

"Oh my god, what the hell are you doing?! Get off me!!!" Abbey shrieks as she kicks her legs furiously, but they have already reached the other end of the corridor. Lucy opens the door and they race outside, down the front steps and over to the corner of the road with Abbey shouting in protest the whole way. Liam finally lets go once they are clear of the school gate and the three of them practically fall about laughing, as the un-amused look on Abbey's face entertains them even more.

"It isn't funny guys..." She moans.

"Christ I think I'm having a fucking heart attack!" Liam gasps, pacing back and forth with his hands on his hips before leaning forward and resting on his knees.

"Oh charming!" Abbey smarts, "I told you I wasn't coming..."

"Well now you're here you might as well?!" Lucy flutters her eyelashes and Abbey smiles, shaking her head in dismay.

"Um, I think we better go..." Nathan is staring past Lucy over towards the front of the school and the others turn in unison to follow his gaze. One of their teachers has marched outside onto the top step and he looks less than impressed as he points over in their direction.

"You lot what are you doing? Lessons have started, get inside!"

Without a word the four of them turn and sprint towards the end of the road, and despite her best intentions Abbey can't keep from laughing. She feels alive... and totally free.

It isn't even midday yet, but the sun is already shining through a scattering of cloud and it is pleasantly warm as the four of them stroll along the canal. They jumped on the bus into Leeds and stopped off at the supermarket to pick up supplies on the way, mainly cigarettes and alcohol and a bit of food. Abbey is nervous, but much more excited and expectant than she has been before. It is like a game of roulette with Alex, she never knows what mood she will get him in, whether he will be pleased to see her, angry and stand offish or just completely indifferent.

Only Darren and Sophie will be there today as Gemma and Tom are at work. She had been surprised to learn that Tom has quite a high-paying job as a manager at a local art café, which is quite posh by all accounts. Abbey doesn't really know why it had shocked her; perhaps his party boy lifestyle and brass cockney attitude don't really fit the stereotype of what she imagines someone in that role to be like, but then he is incredibly funny and charming - and definitely has the confidence to interact with members of the public on a daily basis.

Gemma works in the city centre as part of the admin team at a firm of financial advisers, a job which she loves but is apparently quite stressful at times, hence the need to seriously unwind on a weekend with her friends.

Sophie is a hairdresser, which means she doesn't work Monday's and Darren's shifts at a local D.I.Y warehouse vary. They always spend what time they can together; a lot of it just the two of them but with the rest of the group as well. If they have no specific plans or a lack of money limits what they can do in their free time, they usually end up at the flat. It is only Alex and Tom who officially live there but unofficially, they all do in some respect. Coming and going as they please almost every day. It is very much their base and they all treat it like home.

As they enter the kitchen the mouth-watering smell of sizzling bacon hits them and it makes Abbey's stomach growl. Darren is dancing around the room, juggling various pans with a tea towel thrown casually over his shoulder. When he sees the four of them he stops and salutes.

"Just in time for breakfast kids! I don't suppose there's any point in me telling you, you should be at school?!" He frowns at Lucy.

"Monday's are so overrated..." She smiles, "Besides I got the brains of the family remember, no point wasting my time studying when I could be spending the day with my intellectually challenged big brother!" Darren throws the tea towel at Lucy's head and rolls his eyes.

"It'll be 5 minutes... you hungry?!"

"Starving mate...!" Liam exclaims, hovering over his shoulder to see what's on offer.

"Back off, back off, give the master space!" He states, pushing Liam away playfully and slapping hands with Nathan as his winks at Abbey.

"You wanting some, Abs...?"

"Yeah please, if there's enough to go around. It smells great..."

"Cheers. It's a talent of mine, one of my many talents in fact, don't listen to my irritating little sister I am incredibly intelligent... and skilled with a frying pan!"

Lucy and Liam sit at the table rolling cigarettes as Nathan puts their shopping away in the fridge, and Abbey leans on the counter watching Darren cook up his masterpiece, laughing as he spins and jumps around the kitchen with a childlike enthusiasm. He is obviously in his element and his enjoyment is contagious as he talks animatedly about how he went to Cookery College before enrolment fees forced him to drop out. Abbey is so involved in the conversation that she hardly even notices the kitchen door open, but as she turns, her heart drops through her chest right down to her feet. Standing in front of her is a half-naked Alex. He has a towel hanging around his neck which he is using to dry his damp hair, there are water droplets scattered across his unbelievably toned body and he smells absolutely divine, a mixture of aftershave and shower gel. He is wearing a pair of dark grey joggers that hang enticingly low and if her mouth wasn't watering before, it certainly is now.

As Alex greets the others he strolls over to the fridge, eyeing up Darren suspiciously.

"How long does it take to cook a fucking breakfast?!" He jokes.

"This my friend, is more than a breakfast, it's a work of art!"

Alex laughs as he takes a carton of orange juice out of the fridge, turning to face Abbey as he looks her directly in the eye.

"Hello..." The word sounds like velvet as it rolls off his tongue.

"Hi..." Abbey smiles, shyly. It doesn't escape her attention that this is the first time Alex has ever directly acknowledged her in front of the others; apart from the time he rather aggressively challenged her opinion on drugs across the crowded living room. She cringes slightly at the memory.

Darren's breakfast is as delicious as expected, and they all eat together sat around the long, glass table in the dining area. Sophie arrives an hour or so later after running a few errands and the rest of the day passes by in the same relaxed manner. They laze about, watching TV, talking and listening to music and the boys find plenty of time to play on the Xbox, especially Liam and Darren who apparently have a score to settle. Abbey's spirits have definitely lifted and she is feeling perfectly content, if not a little surprised. She had been wondering earlier what to expect from Alex and she finds that she is seeing a side of him today that she hasn't witnessed before. He is clearly at his happiest and most comfortable in this environment, at home surrounded by his friends. He is very talkative, funny and engaging, and when he laughs he seems so much younger and far less troubled than he usually does. He always seems so serious, as if he has a lot on his mind, yet he shows none of that now. He is calm and happy... almost playful.

The clouds from earlier have completely cleared and Abbey can feel the sun burning down on her as she sits with her feet up on the balcony. Nathan, Sophie and Alex are sitting next to her and the double doors are pushed wide open, allowing the sunlight to pour into the living room. Nathan passes the joint he is smoking to Sophie and makes his way inside, cuddling up with Lucy on the sofa. Abbey has obviously never smoked marijuana before, but seen as it is a step down from a class A drug like cocaine she doesn't really see the harm in trying. She likes it, it has a calming effect and her limbs feel heavy, as if she has been sedated. It feels a bit like floating and definitely suits her current mood. Much like the effect of the cocaine, but in a different sort of way, it seems to make all her worries temporarily disappear.

Abbey takes the joint from Sophie and walks over to the edge of the balcony, leaning her arms on the railing and looking down at the bustling city life below. It's like they are in their own little bubble high up on the 9th floor. No one knows they are here and nothing can touch them. It makes her feel giddy, or maybe that is just the weed kicking in?

Abbey anxiously takes another drag as she realises Sophie has gone back inside, leaving her alone with Alex. Too nervous to look around, she stands in silence and carries on gazing out across Leeds City Centre, trying to ignore the tension that is building between them. As it becomes almost unbearable she considers retreating back inside, but stops suddenly when she feels Alex's arm brush lightly against hers. He is standing right next to her, their skin touching, and it sends a warm shiver through her body. It is like electricity, being so close to him, and although she is trying to keep her cool she struggles to get the image of his unbelievable physique out of her mind, playing the memory of this morning in the kitchen, over and over. He is complete perfection and she wants him more than ever.

"So..." He purrs, "Skipping school, taking drugs, hanging around with trouble makers like us...? And to think I had you down as a good girl!" Abbey glances up to see a flicker of mischief in Alex's deep blue eyes.

"Not all the time..." She smiles, impressed at how calm and unaffected she manages to sound.

"So how are you liking Leeds?"

"It's starting to grow on me I guess. It's just different..." A slightly less confident response but she is still managing to hold it together, despite the fact that

Alex is staring at her again. It is incredibly off putting, she could easily get lost in those eyes.

"Different? To how your life used to be? I'll bet we're not much like your old friends either...?" Alex smirks.

"No you could say that. I don't think they would approve of my recent lifestyle choices..." she jokes, darkly.

"What would they say if they could see you now I wonder?!"

Abbey's smile fades as she fights an unexpected pang of sadness. It has been months since she has seen her old group of friends, or even spoken to them. She does still miss them sometimes and how it used to be. Alex clearly senses the change in mood and he moves his hand towards Abbey - as if to comfort her - hesitating for a moment before quickly resting it back on the railing.

"Lucy told me, about what happened with your brother..." He says after a moment's pause, "I was sorry to hear about that..."

It is rare for someone to bring the subject up so bluntly and Abbey finds Alex's honesty incredibly refreshing. She turns towards him, and noticing the look of cautious concern on his face she can't help but smile. She doesn't want their first proper conversation to be so depressing and she suddenly feels a strong desire to lighten the mood.

"Is this your hidden, sweet and sensitive side coming out?" She asks, mockingly, and he frowns at her for a split second before a huge, unguarded smile spreads across his face.

"Fuck off..." He laughs.

"Well, I was just wondering if you were likely to start crying on me because you know, I would probably find that a bit awkward..." It suddenly registers with Abbey how much she enjoys seeing Alex laugh, to see the constant tension and worry in his face vanish, if only briefly.

"Nah, that isn't gonna happen..." Alex takes the joint and Abbey watches the end blaze alight as he breathes in before exhaling slowly, "but you know, I just figured I should say something..."

"Thank you. I appreciate that..." She answers, sincerely.

Abbey really is touched that he cares enough to mention anything at all, and he clearly knows a lot more about her than she had first realized. Has he been asking questions? Getting information about her as she has about him? It hardly seems plausible. It still seems completely unlikely that this beautiful man would ever be in anyway interested in her, but then what was Friday night all about?

"So does this mean I'm not the unwanted stranger anymore?!" She asks, sarcastically, "I'm not going to be thrown out of your flat at any second...?" Alex smiles again but there is a hint of sadness behind it.

"Yeah, sorry about that... years of being screwed over by people kinda takes its toll. I'm not too good with strangers, but I suppose I know you well enough now... although I'm sure I could know you better..." He flashes Abbey a mischievous grin and she blushes furiously.

"I suppose you could..." She gulps. Alex passes the joint back to her and she takes another drag, coughing slightly as she takes too much back. She starts to giggle, and for some reason she feels like she can't stop as Alex shakes his head and rolls his eyes at her. This is a new sensation. Clearly weed doesn't just make you calm and drowsy it makes you hysterical as well. She eventually manages to calm herself down and Alex reaches across, trying to take the joint from her hand.

"I think you've had enough of that…" He laughs.

"No, no I haven't…" Abbey is enjoying herself too much to pass it back.

"Yes you have… anymore and you'll be sick…"

"No I won't I promise…"

"Oh what so you're a fucking expert now?!" Alex reaches for the joint again but Abbey hides her hands behind her back, "Give it here…" He laughs as he wraps his arms around her waist and she wriggles, trying to break free. He grabs hold of her wrists but she pulls away and they stagger backwards to the far side of the balcony, both of them now giggling hysterically.

"You're laughing too, maybe you've had enough…" Abbey gasps, barely able to get her words out. She turns her back on Alex and he wraps his arms around her again, playfully pinning her hands by her sides as he tickles her. She shrieks in response, spinning around so quickly that they are suddenly face to face, so close that she can feel Alex's breath on her lips. They lean back on the railing as their laughter subsides while staring at one another, standing only inches apart. Abbey can feel the electricity surging through her entire body and her breathing becomes ragged as Alex runs his hand down her arm and round her back, pulling her closer. With his other hand he slowly brushes her hair away and holds the side of her face, tracing his thumb softly across her bottom lip. The anticipation is killing her and her mind is racing at a hundred miles an hour. Is this really happening? Is he seriously going to kiss her? She had imagined this moment since the first time she laid eyes on him and it is almost perfect... but what if she isn't any good? She isn't exactly inexperienced but she has never been with an older guy before, never one as confident as Alex. What if she ruins it? All these thoughts flash through her mind in the fraction of a second it takes for him to move one step closer. She closes her eyes and leans into him, her stomach in knots as their lips almost touch.

"ALEX..." Nathan shouts urgently from the living room and Alex takes a large step backwards, shoving his hands in his pockets as he turns away from Abbey. She is left leaning against the railing, completely dissatisfied.

"What's up?" He asks, casually. Nathan has a phone in his hand and he is covering the speaker.

"It's Marcus..." He states, solemnly.

In an instant Alex's entire demeanour shifts and he stands bolt upright and alert, with a deep frown etched into his brow. A look of anger washes over him and just like that the happy, smiling, carefree Alex from two minutes ago is gone - the Alex that she was laughing and play fighting with... and very nearly kissing. He takes the phone from Nathan and marches inside without so much as a glance back. Abbey follows behind, joining the others on the sofa where they are all sitting quietly, looking noticeably worried. 'Who the hell is Marcus?'

Alex hates this part of the city. It is such a dive. It reminds him of the backstreets of Dublin where all the drug addicts and prostitutes hang out. It is full of late night bars, gambling venues and strip clubs, the most popular of which is 'The Red Lounge', belonging to Marcus Holt.

Alex makes his way to the back of the club and bangs loudly on the large, rusting metal door. It slides open and a surly bouncer assesses him closely before stepping aside, allowing him to pass.

He stands in the entrance way as his eyes adjust to the dark, murky room, which is a sharp contrast to the bright sunlight outside. Once the hazy patches of green fade from his vision, he hesitantly makes his way across the empty club and up the flight of stairs that lead to Marcus' office. His skulking friend isn't far behind, following silently.

Alex is nervous, although he doesn't show it. He is so used to being in control these days that it is an alien feeling to him, being unsure of himself. He doesn't like not knowing what to expect and he has absolutely no clue why Marcus has summoned him here.

Alex knocks once and enters without waiting for a response. The office is a large, seventies style room with wood panelled walls that are covered with various sports pictures and memorabilia. There is a plush, mahogany desk in the centre of the room and sitting in a large leather chair behind it, is Marcus. He is dressed in a sharp pinstripe suit, his usual ensemble, which is reminiscent of a 1930's gangster. Marcus is definitely 'old school'. He is a good 20 years older than Alex, his dark grey hair is neatly slicked back and he has a prominent scar under his left eye that he wears with pride, like a soldier would display a medal. He isn't overly tall but he is stocky, solid, and strong, and he has one hell of a presence.

"Mr Matthews, there you are!" Marcus greets Alex with a friendly smile, throwing his arms open wide as he enters the room. It is all just for show of course, a form of intimidation that Alex has witnessed many times before, "I was starting to think you were going to stand me up for a moment there…" He adds.

"What do you want?" Alex doesn't care for pleasantries or for playing games. He hates Marcus and the feeling is mutual, there is no point in pretending.

"I'll get straight to the point then shall I?" Marcus' fake smile is gone in a flash and he stands, straightening his jacket as he walks round to the front of his desk which he leans on, nonchalantly, "You owe me money Alex. Now I know we've already discussed this and worked it out like the civilized business men we are. You asked for a bit of time to pay me back and I showed you some courtesy and gave you that time. However, it seems there has been a slight change in our circumstance…" Alex frowns, unsure of what he could possibly mean. He hasn't seen or spoken to Marcus since they made that arrangement, how can it suddenly be no good?

"You'll still get your money. Nothing's changed…"

"I'm afraid that's where you're wrong…" Marcus gently folds his hands in his lap and although only a slight movement, it still manages to be incredibly menacing. Marcus' whole appearance and attitude is a threatening one, hidden behind a facade of pleasantness. He always conducts himself properly, adamant that manners should never be over looked. It makes him even more unpredictable… and frightening, "A little birdie told me that a few weeks back you made a deal with Chris Moorland? That apparently you'll be running for him up in this neck of the woods? Now Mr Moorland and I have always had a mutual respect for one another and although he owes me no favours, that deal should have been mine. That is until some cocky little fucker from Ireland swooped in and stole it from me…" Alex can't believe what he is hearing, it is so unexpected and completely out of the blue.

"Moorland never mentioned any potential deal with you…" That is the truth, but clearly it doesn't matter much to Marcus.

" Perhaps not…" He sneers, "But that isn't really the point is it? Surely you see my predicament Alex? Now not only do you owe me the money I lent you, but you have also taken business away from me that would have left a nice tidy sum in my bank account. I was going to take the missus on a cruise and as you can imagine, she's very upset…" He shakes his head in dismay as he stands up straight and strolls over to where Alex is standing. They square up to each other face to face and Marcus leans into him, making his point perfectly clear as he speaks calmly through gritted teeth, "I have wasted too much fucking time, energy and money on you kid… game's up. I want what you owe me, all of it, by the end of the month…" Alex has to stop himself from laughing out loud in sheer disbelief. He owes Marcus twelve grand, and the end of the month leaves him less than three weeks to get it for him.

"There is no way! How the fuck am I meant to get that kind of money together by then?!" He gasps.

"That isn't really my problem is it?" He takes a step closer to Alex, "But just make sure you do son… or you will be very, very sorry…"

Alex's head is spinning as he walks back outside into the warm, sunny afternoon. How on earth have so many separate, completely unrelated events crashed together in such a way that he is now in deep shit?! It is almost impossible for him to get his head around and there is no way he could have foreseen it.

Twelve thousand pounds is a lot of money and it is money that Alex doesn't have, at least not all of it. He had been on track to pay Marcus back on time but now that he has moved the goal posts, he is stuck with no way out. His time is up, just like Marcus had said, and he is short by almost half. Alex's first instinct is to go to Moorland and explain the situation. He is the only person that Alex knows who has that sort of money at his disposal and who can get it for him that quickly, but he dismisses the idea. There is no way he can lose face with him, not now.

Moorland had taken an interest in Alex when their paths had crossed a few months back. Chris Moorland is big news in London. He owns a string of restaurants and take-aways and is a highly successful businessman, with it all being entirely legal and above board. However, he is into making extra money on the side as well, which led him into the world of drug dealing and supplying. He has a lot of contacts and connections down south that he has built up through the years and he is the ultimate top dog, not to be messed with.

His new venture, a restaurant which recently opened in Brewery Wharf, is the reason he headed up to Leeds and onto Alex's radar. It wasn't a permanent arrangement; he only come up North to oversee the opening before returning to the capital, but during that time Alex was introduced to him by a mutual friend.

The owner of one of the bars that Alex runs drugs at knows Moorland from his days in London. It was a chance meeting, a pure fluke, but Alex happened to be in the club on the same night that they decided to meet up for a drink. It turned out Moorland had been told quite a lot about Alex from various people in their line of work and he was impressed with what he heard. Now that he had a restaurant in Leeds it made sense to expand on his other 'business ventures' up here as well and that is how the proposition came about.

Alex is Moorland's new dealer up North. Moorland sends the drugs to Leeds every six weeks where they are held at a safe house - a very expensive, upmarket property that won't come under suspicion - and Alex 'distributes' them, keeping all his old contacts as well as supplying to any new ones cleared by Moorland. The clubs that allow them to run their operation, Moorland and of course Alex all get a cut of the profits... everyone's a winner.

That is until Marcus decided to take it as a personal slight, which in all honesty Alex doesn't find surprising. The thing that attracted him to the deal with Moorland is his level headedness and straightforward, no mess attitude. It is a business arrangement and Moorland treats it as such, even telling Alex that if the agreement doesn't work out and he wants to call it quits, he will be willing to discuss it.

It is an operation that has been planned to the finest detail and so far it has run smoothly, mainly due to Moorland's professionalism. Marcus' attitude however, couldn't be more different. He takes pleasure in violence and he revels in the drama that this lifestyle brings with it. He likes to think of himself as a shrewd businessman but he is nothing more than a bully, a control freak and a thug who loves to scare, intimidate and throw his weight around. He is in no way as professional or as polished as Moorland; in fact compared to him he is practically a loose cannon, much more interested in the gangster connotations and the notoriety than actually running a successful business venture. Although making money is of course high on his list of priorities.

In short, Marcus is a nasty bastard who is used to getting his own way - and whether he meant to or not - Alex has embarrassed him by stepping on his toes. Plus he is more than likely irritated by the fact that Alex has entered into an arrangement with somebody else. Even though they hate each other now, Alex was once Marcus' golden boy and he always resented him for walking away.

Moorland approached Alex after being impressed with his initiative and the way he can handle himself in a difficult situation. Therefore, asking him for a lend so early on in their partnership would no doubt do more harm than good. Alex has to prove to him that his first impression was right. That he can deal with any issues himself and be trusted to hold down the operation while Moorland is in London; so asking for his help is out of the question.

Alex walks home in a daze, trying to think of any way possible that he can miraculously get his hands on thousands of pounds in just over a fortnight. The money he earns is good, very good, but he can't make that kind of cash in that sort of time frame and he knows what it will mean for him if he doesn't pay up. Marcus Holt isn't scared of getting his hands dirty and he certainly isn't scared to act out his threats. There is a reason he has such a frightening reputation... and a reason why he has a 3 inch scar, sitting proudly underneath his left eye.

CHAPTER SIX

FALLING

"Right I've gotta go..." Tom balances a roll up in the corner of his mouth and shoves his tobacco tin, phone and wallet into the back pocket of his jeans. Abbey has spent the last hour listening to his highly entertaining stories about the group and their various exploits - drunken nights out, failed relationships and even brushes with the law - and she could easily spend the rest of the afternoon the same way. But unfortunately Tom has work, which he is already running late for.

It is early Saturday afternoon and the others are spending their day elsewhere. Liam is playing football, Nathan and Lucy are having some alone time, and Darren, Sophie and Gemma are also at work, at least for the next few hours. Had Abbey known this she probably wouldn't have ventured over to the flat, but she couldn't stand the thought of being at home all day. You can cut the tension with a knife and she seriously needed to escape. It is becoming more and more excruciating, living under that roof.

Tom leans over and gives Abbey a quick kiss on the cheek before he dashes out of the door, struggling to put his jacket on without dropping his keys. It is strangely quiet once he has gone and she stares blankly at the TV screen, completely unaware of what she is watching as her mind is totally preoccupied. Alex was on the phone in the kitchen when she arrived and Tom had immediately ushered her into the living room. It was obvious why, as the almost permanent frown and stress lines on Alex's face were even more apparent than usual. He was talking into the handset in a low, agitated voice while pacing up and down, clearly trying to remain calm.

It is clear that there is a problem and she wonders if it has anything to do with the phone call he received last Monday and the mysterious Marcus? Nothing has been said about it since, but she can tell that something isn't right.

After internally debating with herself for a good 20 minutes about whether or not she should disturb Alex, she finally caves in to her boredom and curiosity and makes her way down the hall towards the kitchen. She gently pushes the door open and loiters by the glass table, suddenly unsure of what to do or say. Alex is leaning over the counter top resting his elbows on the side and holding his head in his hands. He has numerous sheets of paper strewn out in front of him along with his phone and a packet of cigarettes.

"Hey…" She finally musters up the courage to speak, but Alex doesn't respond, "Are you OK?"

"Fine" He forces the word out and Abbey can hear the warning in his tone.

"OK… It's just… you don't seem fine, and I was…"

"You were WHAT, Abbey?" Alex turns on the spot so fast he is almost a blur, "What exactly is it that you want…?"

"Just... to help..." She stutters.

Alex's demeanour is aggressive and Abbey suddenly feels incredibly uneasy around him. He can be so unbelievably intimidating.

"You want to help?! Well unless you have a spare six grand lying around that you can lend me by the end of next week I don't think you can fucking help, can you?"

"I'm sorry I asked..." Abbey can feel her face redden and she looks down at the floor, defeated and embarrassed.

"I told you not to get involved didn't I?! God you have no idea what you're doing, you're just a kid..."

Abbey's head snaps up and she retaliates before she even has chance to think about what she is saying. It probably isn't wise to anger Alex further, but his remark is so patronising it makes her blood boil. She has to deal with her mum and her brother sharing that opinion, she isn't about to take it from him as well.

"I am not a fucking child..." She yells, louder than she means to, "And I am sick to death of people treating me like one..."

"You have no fucking clue do you...?"

"You don't know anything about me..."

Alex strides across the room and they stand just inches apart as he bears down on her, but Abbey doesn't back away.

"Why the hell are you here, Abbey?" He snaps, "What do you want?"

Abbey stares him out, determined not to whimper like a coward and give in, to prove to him that she isn't just some stupid kid and that she can stand up for herself when she needs to. After a few seconds - and just as Abbey's nerve is starting to fail her - Alex's expression shifts and the tension between them suddenly alters. His anger and irritation fade and he has a different look in his eyes, a look of determination and desire. Abbey's breathing quickens and she feels Alex's change too, the physical closeness between them is suddenly obvious and that charge of electricity is back stronger than it was on the balcony... stronger than Abbey has ever felt it before.

Their eyes are locked on one another and when the longing between them becomes almost intolerable Alex reaches up and grabs hold of Abbey's face with gentle force, moving his hands through her hair and pulling it tightly as he presses his lips to her mouth. They stagger backwards from the force of the kiss and slam into the fridge, their lips and bodies locking together with an intensity and sense of desperation, as if nothing and no one else matters.

Alex slides his hands down the back of Abbey's thighs and lifts her up, causing her to instinctively wrap her legs around his waist. She is running on pure instinct, without thinking or analysing anything. She is just there in the moment, completely losing herself in Alex like he is in her. All their worries and problems, the drama and stress... it is all forgotten as Alex carries her into his room and they collapse onto the bed.

A patch of sunlight breaks through a crack in the curtains and falls across Abbey's face, steadily bringing her round from sleep. She props herself up on her elbow and glances drowsily around Alex's room, surveying it properly for the first time. It is modern and minimalist, very much in keeping with the rest of the flat. It has cream walls and a cream carpet, a large black leather sleigh bed takes up the majority of the room and there are two small bedside tables on either side of it. The only other piece of furniture is a huge, black gloss wardrobe with sliding doors stood directly opposite. The bedding she is wrapped up in is a dark maroon colour and there is a grey and black mural on the wall of another city skyline, although she doesn't recognize it. The toilet flushes and a few moments later Alex leaves the en suite in just his boxers. Abbey blushes as he smiles at her.

"Welcome back…" He laughs gently as he climbs back into bed. He turns onto his side and rests his arm across Abbey's chest, causing her heart to skip several beats. She was almost convinced it had been a dream, but here she is, lying in Alex's bed, feeling warm and content… and very satisfied. He tucks a strand of hair behind her ear and follows her gaze to the wall.

"It's Dublin…" He says, answering her unspoken question. "A little piece of home…"

Abbey rolls onto her side to face Alex and he pulls the covers closer, wrapping his arm tightly around her waist.

"Are you from Dublin?" She asks.

"No, I lived there for a couple of years but I'm originally from North Antrim. I was born in a little town called Ballycastle…"

"Do you miss it?"

"Not really…" He muses, "I don't have many happy memories from my time there. My Ma died when I was seven and my Dad wasn't exactly father of the year, if you know what I mean? He was into his drinking and gambling, never really had much time for me. I got out of there as soon as I turned sixteen…"

"On your own?"

"With my Uncle Graham. We were always close so when he told me he was leaving I wasn't about to let him go without me. We moved to Dublin, then London two years later..."

"And you met Tom..." Abbey smiles.

"Yeah, and I haven't been able to get rid of him since..." Alex laughs affectionately.

"Where's your Uncle now?" He blanches at Abbey's question before quickly composing himself.

"He died."

Abbey reaches up and places her hand on Alex's cheek and he holds it in place, turning his head slightly to kiss her palm.

"I'm sorry..." There is a brief moment of silence and Abbey can hear the soft hum of the traffic outside. It is strange to think that the world is still turning below them; she is so completely engrossed in Alex that it is easy to pretend that there is nothing outside the four walls surrounding her, like they really are the only two people in existence, locked away in their own little bubble.

"So how did you end up in Leeds?" Abbey asks with quiet curiosity. The silence between them isn't in anyway awkward but she desperately wants to keep Alex talking. She wants to get to know him, to learn about his life, his past, his likes and dislikes... plus she could happily listen to his soft, honeyed accent all day long. It is like a lullaby when he speaks.

"It was time for a change..." He shrugs, "Probably the best decision I ever made to be honest. Me and Tom got this place and we met this bunch of mad heads..." Abbey can see the affection on Alex's face every time he mentions his friends. For all his front and tough guy attitude, it is plain to see how much he loves them.

"How did you guys meet?" Abbey is genuinely intrigued by the back story. She had heard a lot of tales from the past -most of them from Tom earlier that morning - but she had never been told how they all became friends in the first place, she just knows they have been together for a long time.

"Well, Tom met Gemma on a night out when we first moved here. They were texting and meeting up for a while and through Gemma we met Soph and Darren..." Abbey knew there must be some sort of history between Tom and Gemma, as it is obvious - on Tom's part at least - that it isn't completely over, "Then as Lucy got older she'd come round here and hang out. It drove Darren fucking crazy at first, but in the end it became normal for her to show up at the door with Nathan and Liam in tow. And then you..." He smiles, casually tracing his fingers up and down Abbey's back as he talks, sending shivers through her whole body. She wants to lean forward and kiss him, but despite the past few hours, she still isn't sure if she is brave enough to make such a bold move.

"You're all so close... I've never really known that before. I mean I had friends at my old school but, not like the type of friendship you all have..."

Alex appraises Abbey with a half-smile on his face, his electric blue eyes soft and curious, and she can feel herself blushing again under his stare. It's as though she can't look at him for long without her thoughts and feelings showing all over her face. He is so beautiful, lying in front of her with his dark hair all messy and ruffled, and his toned, muscular arms snaked around her. Abbey can't believe her luck; it seems far too good to be true.

"You talk about the group as if you're not a part of it..." Alex notes and Abbey frowns slightly. She wasn't really aware that she spoke in that way, but then being the new girl, it is to be expected. She has only known them for such a short amount of time in comparison to their ten plus years, "You're very much a part of the group..." He adds, shyly.

Abbey's heart swells and she almost has to stop herself from crying. She can't believe that this is the same person who made her feel so unwelcome just a short time ago. Alex 'isn't good with strangers' and he had his guard up at first - he explained that to her - but this is still such a huge turn around. To go from complete hostility to ending up in bed together; it is everything Abbey had hoped for and more. To have Alex in this way is something she has secretly craved from the very first moment she saw him.

"We are close..." He continues, "We've been through a lot together and some of us, mainly Tom, Daz, Lucy and myself... we don't have anyone else. Apart from my Uncle I never really had any family as such so I've spent a fair bit of time on my own... I know how it feels. That all changed when I met these guys. They are my family..." Alex looks so lost and vulnerable it makes Abbey want to reach out and take his pain away. She understands exactly how he feels and wants him to know that he never has to be on his own again. She leans forward and plants a soft, tender kiss on the corner of his mouth and smiling in response, he rolls over onto his elbows so that he is looking down at her, running his thumb gently across her cheek, "Are we done with the interrogation now?!" He asks, and she laughs, nodding in anticipation, as he kisses her again.

In the days that follow, Abbey feels as if she is floating along with her feet barely touching the ground. She is still in her warm, contented little bubble after her perfect afternoon with Alex - excluding of course the very heated argument in the kitchen - but that feels like a distant memory now compared to what transpired afterwards.

She sits in her English lesson and stares blankly at the whiteboard as her mind constantly drifts away into a glorious daydream. Mr Harper is scribbling down notes about Shakespeare's Othello while dictating over his shoulder to the class, and despite trying hard to focus, all Abbey can think about is him. The image of Alex is such a distraction, his eyes, his smile, his voice, the way he makes her feel... it sends an ache right through her and she longs to be with him. She replays that afternoon over and over in her head. The way he picked her up and carried her so effortlessly, the way she ran her hands across his flawless chest as he kissed her. She wants to do it again, right now, and she wishes more than anything that she could be back in his room, curled up in his arms instead of being stuck here at school.

Abbey swallows hard and shakes her head, trying to dispel her thoughts and focus on her work. She picks up Othello and starts flicking through the chapters, looking for some inspiration that will help her answer the practice exam question that Mr Harper has set them. As she is about to continue writing, a slight movement at the classroom door catches her eye and she sees Liam and Lucy standing in the window, grinning like idiots and waving at her before they quickly duck out of sight.

'What the hell are they doing?' Abbey thinks to herself, confused and more than a little concerned.

She sits up straight in her chair and cautiously looks over towards Mr Harper's desk. He has his head down and is concentrating on marking the pile of exam papers stacked up in front of him. Thankfully he seems completely oblivious to Lucy and Liam outside in the corridor. If they get caught they will be in so much trouble, but then that has never really bothered them before.

Abbey looks back towards the classroom door and her mouth drops open in disbelief as a small, dog hand puppet suddenly appears in the corner of the window, with a sticker on its chest that has her name scrawled across it. She stares in shock as it waves at her before dropping back out of sight again. She runs her hand through her hair and glances over her shoulder as inconspicuously as possible, trying her best not to draw any attention to herself as she scans the room. It appears that everyone else is oblivious too, hunched over with their heads down, feverishly writing away or sat with their noses buried in their battered copies of Othello.

"Abbey…" She whips round and looks over at Mr Harper who is eyeing her suspiciously, "Is there a problem?" She smiles and shakes her head in response, picking up her book and pretending to be utterly engrossed in Shakespeare's tragedy.

After another minute or two, she senses that Mr Harper is no longer watching her and after finally plucking up the courage to check, she very cautiously glances back over at the door. The puppet re-appears, but this time another one pops up beside it, with a sticker on its front that reads 'Alex'.

'Oh for god sake' Abbey shakes her head as both puppets wave in unison and drop out of sight. She knows exactly where this is heading.

Why are they doing this to her? Not only is she in class she is sat in a mock exam, in absolute silence. Harper is already sulking with her for missing some of his lessons. Sulking wouldn't normally be the right word to use but in this case she can't think of any other way to describe it. He definitely isn't happy with her and Abbey doesn't need this tipping him over the edge. As the two puppets re-appear again, Abbey bites her lip and tries with all her strength not to laugh as they start bumping and grinding erotically against one another, slowly at first, but getting faster and faster as they simulate rampant sex.

Abbey can feel herself going bright red as she laughs under her breath. She covers her mouth with the sleeve of her jumper and stares down at her desk, with her shoulders shaking as she desperately tries to bring her hysterics under control. The puppets quickly drop out of sight and Abbey turns back to the front of the room to see Mr Harper staring at her with a disapproving look on his face. He frowns, and looks over at the window where Lucy and Liam had been performing their warped, puppet porn only moments ago. He pushes his chair back very slowly and approaches the door as Abbey looks on in horror, unable to warn her friends. Unbeknownst to her, Lucy and Liam can see both of them clearly through the keyhole and as Mr Harper makes his way towards them, they scramble over one another - still laughing at their hilarious prank - and race down the corridor where they dive into an abandoned cloakroom. Mr Harper opens the door expectantly and Abbey breathes a sigh of relief as he steps out into the empty corridor.

When the bell finally rings for lunch Abbey packs her books away, still smiling but also mentally preparing herself for the barrage of questions, jokes and innuendo that she is about to face from her friends. She knew this was bound to happen. Abbey had spent all day with Alex on Saturday - in fact she had spent almost the entire weekend at the flat - and when the others had joined them they had picked up on the change in their body language straight away.

It is unsurprising really. Even a blind man probably would have noticed. They had been acting like love sick idiots, stealing little looks and smiles, sitting together constantly and holding hands when they thought no one was watching. It certainly wasn't subtle. How ridiculous that it has only been a few days, yet she can't imagine it any other way. She misses him already and can't wait to see him again. As Abbey reaches the door with her thoughts a million miles away, Mr Harper holds out his arm, abruptly snapping her out of her loved up daydream.

"Can I have a word please?" His tone isn't angry but it's clear that he isn't impressed. She follows him reluctantly back inside the classroom and sits in the empty seat beside his desk.

"What's this about?" She asks.

"I just wanted to see how you were doing. You've been with us, what almost 3 months now?"

"That's right..." Abbey nods.

"I just wanted to see how you were getting on really..."

"I'm fine."

"Anything you want to talk to me about?"

"Nothing I can think of…" Abbey tries hard to keep the petulant tone from her voice but doesn't quite manage it. Mr Harper is wearing his concerned, pity face again and she would rather him be angry at her.

"OK, Abbey…" He leans forward, resting his forearms on his knees and clasping his hands, "I'm obviously aware of the fact that you've been missing quite a lot of lessons lately and not just in this subject either…" He waits for Abbey to react, but she says nothing, "I notice that you've become quite good friends with Lucy Blake?" Abbey rolls her eyes and shifts in her seat, folding her arms defensively.

"I suppose you're another person who's going to tell me she's a bad influence'? Nathan and Liam too?"

"They aren't exactly model students but I'm not here to tell you who to be friends with…" Abbey is thrown for a moment. She had been mentally preparing herself for a lecture because anyone would be completely within their rights to have that opinion. They are a bad influence.

In the few months she has known them they have convinced her to skip school, got her grounded and introduced her to the world of hard partying and mild substance abuse. They are at least partly to blame for 'leading her astray', but then Abbey also has to accept that she willingly made those choices for herself. Regardless, it doesn't matter either way, as they understand her better than anyone and are there for her, unconditionally. They are her best friends, and she will always stick up for them, despite other people's opinions.

"So, why exactly are we having this conversation?" Abbey asks. Something about Mr Harper's demeanour has stoked her curiosity. He is acting differently, almost as if he is worried about her. More than a teacher would usually worry about a troublesome student.

"When you arrived here we were made aware of what you and your family have been through recently…"

"That's not really any of your business…" Abbey instantly feels guilty for her abrupt response as she can tell Mr Harper is trying to approach the subject sensitively, but it is her usual knee-jerk reaction. Talking about her family situation with her friends is one thing, but it is a different story altogether talking about it with someone she barely knows. She feels very guarded and strangely protective of Ryan, even still.

"Maybe not, but you skipping class is my business…" He states with a little more authority in his voice, "Look, I understand how something like that happening can give you a new perspective, and school might not be on top of your list of priorities right now; but I don't want to see you making any decisions that could damage your future, decisions you could end up seriously regretting…" Mr Harper has hit the nail on the head. It has changed her. She does have a new perspective and outlook on life, but for some reason him figuring that out only annoys her further. She doesn't need him psycho analysing her or sticking his nose into her personal life.

"I don't think you have any idea how I feel…" She says, bluntly.

"No one can know exactly how you feel except you… but I do get it…" Mr Harper's voice drops to a whisper and there is a sorrowful look in his eyes, "My brother was killed. He was knocked down by a drunk driver outside his house…" Abbey stares in silence, shocked at his sudden and intimate confession, "For a long, long time, I wasn't willing to accept that. Why him, you know? His wife told me after the funeral that he left the house a few minutes earlier but he'd forgotten his keys, so he went back... and that one, simple decision cost him his life. He should have been on the other side of the road when that bastard turned the corner and I hated him for that; I became a different person because of it. Started acting out, doing stupid stuff because I didn't know how else to cope..."

"You think that's what I'm doing?" Abbey isn't quite so defensive now. In fact she is fairly sure she is wearing the same sympathetic, pity face that she resents Mr Harper using on her, but she can't help it. She really feels for him. She knows all too well what that crushing sadness and anger feels like, when the person you are closest to is suddenly gone from your life and there is absolutely nothing you can do about it.

"You tell me..." He asks, "Is you skipping school out of character?"

"Maybe... I mean, I guess it's out of character for the person I used to be..."

"That's understandable..." Mr Harper smiles and Abbey returns it. Who knew his past could so closely mirror her own situation? She sighs and stifles a laugh.

"What are you anyway, a teacher or a shrink?!"

"I'm a teacher who cares. We are rare but trust me we do exist!" He jokes, "Listen, I know you've been through a lot and I understand that you're figuring things out at the moment, but I mean it... I won't tolerate you missing my lessons without a legitimate reason..."

"Fair enough..." Abbey shrugs in defeat, and she stands, throwing her bag over her shoulder as she turns towards the door. Part of her wants to say something reassuring or helpful to Mr Harper, to make him feel better... but she has nothing. She knows no words can take the pain away.

"I appreciate you not wanting to talk to me today..." He adds, just as she is about to leave, "but if you ever get to the point where you do... you know where I am..."

Abbey nods appreciatively and walks out into the crowded hallway with her head buzzing from all the new information she has just acquired - highly personal information - about her tutor. Is he always so open with his students? There is something about their exchange that doesn't quite add up but Abbey can't put her finger on it. She replays the conversation over in her head as she reaches her locker, but she doesn't have time to dwell on it, as one of the puppets suddenly appears right in front of her.

"Hi Abbey! Did we learning anything fun in lesson today?" Liam talks in a childish, high pitched voice as he makes the puppet move just inches from Abbey's face. She punches it out of the way and he gasps in mock disgust.

"I worry about you, I really do..." Abbey shakes her head in dismay at Liam and Lucy who are smiling from ear to ear and looking very pleased with themselves.

"You have to admit that was pretty funny!"

"Hilarious...!"

"Where have you been anyway? Lesson finished 10 minutes ago!" Lucy asks.

"Harper wanted a heart to heart..."

"What...?"

"Never mind..." Abbey waves her hand and dismisses her last comment. She feels uncomfortable talking about her conversation with Mr Harper as what they discussed is so private. She quickly decides that it is best to keep this one to herself.

"Yeah never mind about that..." Liam thankfully changes the subject, "What about you and our Alex then, eh?" Or maybe not so thankfully.

"Yeah, we may have heard a few things..." Lucy smiles, innocently, "hence the impromptu puppet show!"

"You couldn't just ask like normal people?" Abbey frowns.

"Where's the fun in that?!" Lucy's tone is so genuine that Abbey can't help but smile. Everything has to be fun with Lucy; otherwise there's no point. There is never a dull moment.

"Yeah... puppet animals need to know the gossip too, you know!" Liam resumes his squeaky voice and holds the puppet just inches from Abbey's face again. She smacks it away, giving him her 'I'm warning you' look, but he is too busy pretending to be deeply offended by its mistreatment.

"You've become weirdly attached there Liam..." Lucy jokes.

"They'll never understand our love..." He turns to the puppet and caresses it's head.

"You're such an idiot..." Abbey laughs, shaking her head at the ridiculousness of the situation as Liam starts to back away down the corridor.

"I'm off to get Nathan... we'll see you at the flat later, or should that be... *lover boys*?!" He swoons, blowing a kiss to Abbey as he flutters his eyelashes.

"Just take your puppet whore and go!" She shouts after him – perhaps a little too loudly – as a group of people nearby turn and stare at them, as Liam sticks his middle finger up, grabbing his crotch with the puppet before disappearing into the crowd.

Abbey and Lucy make their way outside and walk slowly across the playing field, arm in arm. The lunchtime buzz is in the air and they weave in between the mass of students that are sitting on the grass, chatting in the sunshine, laughing, joking and flirting with each other.

Abbey can't help giggling at Lucy's excited ramblings and the fact that she hasn't paused for a breath in about 10 minutes. She is clearly thrilled at the recent developments and is getting more than a little bit carried away, constantly referring to Abbey and Alex's 'relationship', which is probably jumping the gun a bit. The weekend had been wonderful, perfect even, but it is still very early days. Even so, the way she casually says the word 'relationship' makes Abbey's stomach flip. She is so attracted to Alex on every level and she wants nothing more than for it to be true.

Lucy continues to discuss in detail the limitless potential of double dating and Abbey is so amused by the conversation that she has become almost oblivious to her surroundings, completely unaware that they are approaching the end of the playing field. The crowds have thinned considerably and they are almost at the back exit of the school, when out of nowhere someone barges past Abbey, slamming into her shoulder so hard that it knocks the breath out of her.

"Jesus, watch where you're going!" She snaps, irritated.

"Or what...?!"

Abbey rolls her eyes as she slowly turns around and comes face to face with Natalie. She is flanked by two friends and her expression is twisted into a bitter snarl. With everything that has happened in the last few months, Natalie and her little harem had almost become irrelevant. They backed off once Abbey made friends with Lucy, Nathan and Liam... probably because it is far less fun victimizing someone when they aren't quite so isolated and vulnerable. That is usually how bullies work.

"Have you got a fucking problem...?" Natalie hisses, rocking back on her heels in anticipation, while waiting for Abbey to respond. There was a time when she first arrived here that Abbey would have been utterly petrified by such a confrontation. She would have panicked, probably cried, and internally debated whether she should run away or try and talk her way out of trouble, but now, she feels nothing. Nothing but anger, intolerance and pity for the horrible, vindictive girl stood in front of her. She has been through too much shit in the last few years to let someone as pathetic as Natalie Alder get to her. She just isn't worth it.

"Whatever..." Abbey sighs, shaking her head and exchanging a look with Lucy as they turn away and carry on walking.

"God look at you, you think you're so fucking special don't you?!" Natalie shouts after them, and Abbey turns to face her again.

"I don't think that at all, I'm just not pathetic enough to get into an argument with you over nothing..."

"Oh and I am pathetic is that what you're saying?!"

Abbey simply shrugs and turns back to Lucy once more, but Natalie doesn't give up. She begins to follow them, shouting louder as her anger builds and she becomes more determined to frighten Abbey, or at least provoke a reaction.

"Everybody knows about you, you know? About your freak show of a family... The teachers were talking about it before you even came here!" Abbey's pace slows to a stop as she feels her face redden and an overwhelming anger rush through her. She knows she should rise above it and not be drawn in by Natalie's games, but her patience is severely limited.

"What the fuck did you say?" She snaps.

"Come on let's just get out of here..." Lucy's voice momentarily pulls Abbey out of her rage, bringing her back into focus and she takes a long deep breath, trying her hardest to remain calm. 'She's not worth it, she's not worth it' – she repeats the phrase over and over in her head with every step she takes but Natalie follows behind, reeling from her reaction and goading her even further.

"You heard! It's a running joke! How your Mum had a nervous breakdown. Who could blame her having you as a daughter? That would drive anyone crazy..."

Abbey keeps her head lowered and puts all her strength and self-control into placing one foot in front of the other. Her pulse has quickened, she can feel her breathing deepen and her fists clench tightly at her sides, as Lucy glances worryingly at her every few seconds. They are almost at the gate, almost off the school grounds, when Natalie shouts out five words that make Abbey stop dead in her tracks.

"No wonder he killed himself..."

It only takes a fraction of a second for the words to register before the pain hits Abbey like a lightning bolt through the stomach. Her blood runs cold and all the anger that was bubbling away beneath the surface moments ago suddenly explodes. Her frustration and her guilt, the heartache of losing Ryan and the anger towards her family... it all completely overwhelms her and she finally lets go. With no conscious thought about what she is doing or of the potential consequences, Abbey runs at Natalie, channelling all her fury as she swings her arm back and punches her hard across the face. As she falls to the floor Abbey doesn't hesitate, taking advantage of her shocked reaction by quickly striking her again. It takes a moment for Natalie to regain her composure, but when Abbey goes to hit her for a third time, she is ready, and the two of them begin fighting viciously in a tangled heap on the floor, spitting, scratching and lashing out as a crowd of students gather around them, cheering, and chanting loudly.

CHAPTER SEVEN

HOME IS WHERE
THE HEART IS

Abbey sits perfectly still and stares at a fixed point on the wall, as she waits patiently for Principal Grant to finish reading through Mrs Clarkson's account of what happened at lunch. She is the unlucky teacher that had come across the fight between Abbey and Natalie and had courageously fought her way through the chanting crowds to separate them, only to have to send another pupil for help when she failed to force them apart.

Abbey's head is throbbing from where Natalie had been swinging on her hair and a sharp pain shoots through her ribs every time she shifts in her seat. Other than that she is fine. Natalie on the other hand has a broken nose and a split lip, and looks much, much worse. Abbey takes more than a little pleasure in that. It is the first fight she has ever been involved in so the fact that she more or less won - or at least came away with fewer injuries - makes her feel rather smug. It is probably due to the sheer rage she felt coupled with the element of surprise. The last thing Natalie expected was meek little Abbey Miller to actually retaliate. Or perhaps it was just blind luck? Either way despite the gratification, it definitely isn't going to help her case.

Abbey cautiously glances to her left, mostly to check that Janet is actually still sitting beside her, as she hasn't moved in the slightest since they first entered the Principal's office. She too stares straight ahead, clearly trying to control herself and prevent her emotions from showing on her face. She is perfectly still, almost business like and as far as Abbey can tell, very, very angry.

Principal Grant finally looks up and carefully removes his glasses, while rubbing his forehead wearily.

"Well, Abigail..." Abbey bites down on her lip to stop herself from correcting him. There is clearly no point in asking for the millionth time to be called Abbey, and now isn't exactly the best moment, but it really irritates her, because she has an overwhelming suspicion that he is doing it on purpose. 'Fucking idiot', she thinks, wishing she could say it out loud, "We took into account your unfortunate situation when you arrived at this school...' He continues, 'and because of this we gave you the benefit of the doubt. Yet you have continued to miss numerous lessons, even after we contacted your mother about it..."

Janet snaps her head around, no longer a living statue, and glares at Abbey.

"What?! I didn't know about this...!" She protests. Shaking her head at Principal Grant and holding her hands up, mystified, almost acting as if she is the one on trial.

"No, you weren't immediately informed. We thought perhaps we should give her a bit more time to get back on track, but needless to say, she hasn't..." Janet closes her eyes in disbelief and shakes her head, as her cheeks flush a deep red. Abbey can't tell whether it's out of anger or embarrassment... probably both.

"Well, now that I know things will change, I assure you! Her life will consist of school and coursework... nothing else."

"Isn't anyone going to ask me what happened?" Abbey asks, defensively. It is starting to get on her nerves, sitting here with her mother and Principal Grant only to be talked about as if she isn't in the room. Janet's eyes look like they are about to burst out of her head and she almost chokes on her words.

"I don't think you are in any position to..."

"Mrs Miller..." Principal Grant cuts her off and gently raises his hand, with a slight smile playing on his lips as he turns to face Abbey. 'He's enjoying this, the little...' She curses to herself.

"If you feel you can justify your actions Abigail, then please go ahead..." Abbey sits up straight and takes a breath, ready to explain to them exactly what started this whole mess and that Natalie is nothing more than a bully who deserves everything she gets. But before she can recount her version of events, Principal Grant speaks again, "But may I remind you that no matter who started the argument or what it was regarding, we simply do not tolerate any form of violence at this school..."

Abbey can feel angry tears pricking in her eyes. It is so unfair, she hasn't caused any of this, she is the victim here but it obviously doesn't matter to either of them.

"Whatever..." She sighs, slumping back in her chair and folding her arms across her chest.

"Abbey!" Janet gasps, disgusted at her daughters rude behaviour, but Abbey couldn't care less. Even her own mother isn't willing to listen to her side of things and hear her out. So why should she care what she thinks?

"OK then... although I don't doubt that you will be keeping a close eye on your daughter from now on Mrs Miller I am afraid it isn't that simple. We have already given Abbey plenty of chances, chances the typical student most certainly wouldn't have been given. I have no choice but to suspend Abbey from school until further notice..."

"And Natalie?" Abbey snaps, her anger building once more, "What about her?"

"She will be dealt with also. We will organize work to be sent home on a weekly basis and if there are any problems or you need any assistance you can contact your teacher's via email..."

"How long will this suspension last?" Janet's asks quietly. Her voice is softer than before and it reveals more than a hint of shame and disappointment.

"That depends. After a fortnight I will have to review the case with the board, but with truancy and fighting on her record, it could go either way. She may be allowed straight back in under supervision..."

"And if not?"

"The worst case scenario would be Abbey being transferred to another school in the area..."

"You mean expelled?" Janet states, flatly.

"Yes."

"I see."

"Abigail is there anything you would like to add?"

Abbey stares at him with her arms still folded and shakes her head once.

"Very well. Mrs Miller I will contact you as soon as I have any more information..." He rises to his feet, buttoning up his suit jacket before holding out his hand. Janet takes it, shaking it abruptly.

"Thank you for your time." She says politely, before picking up her bag and coat and stalking towards the door. Abbey turns and follows at a slightly slower pace and by the time she reaches the corridor, Janet has already stormed out of the main entrance and down the steps outside.

Mr Harper is leaning casually against the doorway that leads to the main reception area with a cup of coffee in his hand. The top button of his shirt is undone and his tie hangs loose around his neck. Abbey catches his eye as she approaches and sees a genuine look of concern on his face.

"Are you alright?" He asks.

"Me? Never better…!" She retorts sarcastically, striding past him as she leaves Eden Comprehensive for quite possibly the last time.

When Abbey reaches the car park she half expects to find Janet has sped off and left her there, but she is sat perfectly still once again, gripping onto the wheel with her perfectly manicured hands. The journey home is awkwardness personified. They don't speak a single word to each other and as they pull up in the driveway, Janet has barely secured the hand brake before she storms dramatically into the house. This isn't going to be in any way pleasant but Abbey, to her own surprise, really doesn't care. She feels nothing; no remorse, no guilt, just agitated by the whole stupid, messed up situation. It has finally all come to a head with Natalie and with her family. She has tried so hard to fix things, tried to get her family to talk to her, to open up and let her in, but they have fought her back every time.

They have distanced themselves from her, but then they still feel as though they can wade into her life and throw around judgement whenever they feel like it? She is sick of it and as a result she has absolutely no fight left in her anymore.

"Get upstairs..." Janet commands, without even looking at Abbey, and she doesn't argue. She trudges wearily up to her room and throws herself onto her bed, exhausted from her rather eventful day and wincing slightly at the pain in her ribs. She shuffles over to the mirror to assess her battered appearance and sees a dark purple bruise beginning to form under her left eye.

"Damn it..." She sighs, pressing her cheek bone with her finger to see how much it has swollen. As she reaches for her make up in a vague attempt to cover it up, her mobile rings.

"Hello?"

"Oh. My. GOD... Abbey are you OK? How are you feeling? Are you hurt?!" Lucy fires off her questions without waiting for Abbey to answer, her voice littered with worry.

"I'm fine, don't panic..." Abbey assures her.

"I can't BELIEVE you did that, I mean you just went for her!"

"I know Luc, I was there remember..." She laughs. There is a lot of background noise and Abbey strains to hear as the phone crackles with static, "Where are you? You keep breaking up..."

"We're at The Locke..."

"ABBEY YOU ABSOLUTE LEGEND!" Liam shouts down the phone cutting Lucy off mid-sentence and Abbey can hear her whack him while muttering something inaudible.

"Liam's so pissed that he left just before he's gutted he missed it! So are you coming to meet us?"

"Yeah sure. I'll be there in half an hour..."

"Cool, see you soon..."

Abbey hangs up the phone and throws it into her bag along with her keys and her purse. There is no way she is staying in her room and moping. It is starting to get old, this whole 'prisoner' routine.

She quickly changes into a black off the shoulder jumper, her tight blue jeans and black buckled ankle boots, but her make-up she unfortunately can't rush. It takes a bit more time than usual as she has to layer on her foundation to cover up the bruising, but once she has finished she doesn't look half bad, better than before at least. After pulling a brush through her hair and a quick spray of perfume, she grabs her bag and skips down the stairs, pausing briefly in the doorway.

"I'm going out..." She shouts and there is a loud clatter as a dish hits the kitchen floor and Janet appears in the hallway.

"I beg your pardon?!" She asks, slowly. Pronouncing each word with added emphasis.

"I'll be back late..." Abbey turns and closes the door swiftly behind her, but half way down the driveway she can still hear Janet cursing and shouting for her to get back inside. Worried that she might follow, Abbey breaks into a sprint, ducking into a cut through at the bottom of the road before running down a muddy path between two houses, checking behind her once more as she heads out onto the main road.

The Locke pub is absolutely packed and Abbey has to literally fight her way through the door, dodging people the best she can while trying to avoid knocking her increasingly sore ribs. A local rock band is playing on a small stage by the bar and the room is full of people crowding around to watch them, despite the nice weather outside.

After a quick scan of the room Abbey weaves her way to the back door and out into the beer garden where she spots her friends straight away. Liam is attempting to balance a pint glass on his forehead - most likely for a bet or in an attempt to prove Nathan wrong - and the others are goading him, throwing beer mats at his face and trying to make him laugh. As Abbey approaches the table, Darren glances over in her direction.

"Well, well here she is... the woman of the hour...!" He shouts, and Lucy is already on her feet, greeting Abbey with a gentle hug.

"Are you alright?"

"Yeah, I told you I'm fine, really..." Abbey smiles.

"I'm so glad you're here! We didn't think your Mum would let you out like, ever again...!" Abbey shrugs at Lucy's comment, not quite knowing what to say. Her mum does feel that way but she isn't about to be grounded again for something that isn't her fault - and especially not for something that she feels was perfectly justified.

"You are a complete fucking legend girl, she has had that coming for a long time!" Liam high fives Abbey as she reaches the table and she greets the others with a shy wave. It feels strange to be the centre of attention and it makes her a little uncomfortable.

"Too right..." Sophie agrees.

"She's fucking horrible; it's about time someone stood up to her. Who knew you had it in you Abs?!" Nathan smiles.

"Not me..." she answers, honestly.

"Jesus, that's a shiner..." Abbey's heart lurches in her chest and a warm shiver runs down the back of her neck, as her body reacts instinctively to Alex's voice. She turns to face him, blushing slightly.

"Hey..." She smiles as he tucks a strand of hair gently behind her ear, tracing his finger lightly under her swollen eye.

"Are you alright?" He asks, staring at her with concern.

"I'll live..." She sighs; wishing in that moment that it was just the two of them and that she could be alone with him. Content, safe and protected from everything.

"Natalie came off worse trust me...!" Lucy gloats, "You should have seen her face when Abbey went for her, it was priceless!"

"She sounds like a total bitch, I'm surprised no one has hit her before now..." Gemma adds, lighting a cigarette and looking as gorgeous as ever. She winks reassuringly at Abbey.

"Like I said she had it coming..." Liam reiterates.

"Well, maybe she'll be more careful who she pisses off in future...?" Tom declares, "what with our Abbey on the scene..." He drapes his arm over her shoulder and squeezes it affectionately, swaying slightly as he takes a swig of his pint.

"Can we drop it now?!" Abbey pleads, embarrassed by all the attention.

"Oh never..." Darren laughs, "We'll be talking about this for at least the rest of the night...!" Abbey rolls her eyes at him and Alex laughs quietly. Sensing her discomfort, he gently snakes his arm around her waist and pulls her closer to his side and Abbey's breath catches in her throat as she reacts to his touch.

"Would you like a drink?" He whispers in her ear.

"Yes. Please!" A drink is exactly what she needs after the stress of today, "Make it a double...!" She jokes.

"No problem..." Alex grins, "Anything for my 'Million Dollar Baby'..."

"Alex!" Abbey digs her elbow into his stomach as she frowns disapprovingly and the others burst out laughing.

"It's my round, what you drinking Rocky?!" Tom shouts across the table with that ever present mischievous glint in his eye.

"Guys... shut up!"

"Whoa, steady on boys..." Darren laughs, holding his hands up in a defensive gesture, "I wouldn't push it if I were you, you don't want to make her angry..."

"You wouldn't like her when she's angry..." Nathan quotes 'The Hulk' in a deep, throaty voice and the lads roar with laughter again as Liam suddenly slams his hands down on the table - drumming repeatedly while chanting the 'Rocky' theme tune. Sophie, Gemma and Lucy smile sympathetically at Abbey as Nathan and Darren join in and Tom jumps up onto the bench, knocking over a few empty beer glasses and staggering slightly as he starts ducking and weaving, punching the air in time to the tune. Abbey groans and turns towards Alex, disappearing under his arm in an attempt to hide herself away, but she is still unable to keep from smiling at her crazy, ridiculous friends.

A drunken night at the pub is exactly what Abbey needed. It is so easy to shut everything else away and completely switch off when she is with Alex and the others. There were of course endless comments and the odd joke thrown in her direction - and after Tom accidentally spilt his pint over her he spent the rest of the evening cowering dramatically every time she approached him - but a bit of banter was always to be expected.

Abbey had been enjoying herself so much that time has passed far too quickly and the landlord is soon rounding everybody up, collecting glasses and wiping down tables in a subtle attempt to get people out of the door. As much as she wants to stay here, laughing and joking with her friends while wrapped up in Alex's arms, she knows that it is time to face the music. She hopes that her family will be in bed seen as it is gone midnight, but deep down she knows that scenario is extremely unlikely. There is no way she can avoid this, she just has to get it over and done with.

As Abbey climbs out of the taxi at the bottom of her drive she wonders whether she assumed wrong, as the entire house is in complete darkness. She creeps up to the front door and carefully turns the key in the lock, slipping inside as quietly as possible, while taking off her boots and placing them at the foot of the stairs. There is nothing but silence as she tiptoes through the pitch black hallway and into the kitchen, reaching for a glass and filling it with water. She gulps it down; quenching her thirst. Drinking vodka always seems to make her dehydrated. She carefully places the glass by the sink and gets ready to sneak upstairs when a voice in the dark suddenly startles her, making her jump so badly she almost screams out loud.

"You're late..." Janet is sat in the far corner of the room at the head of the dining table with a half empty bottle of whiskey in front of her. She stares at the glass in her hand, swilling the last drop round and round before downing it in one mouthful. Abbey holds her hands to her chest, waiting for her breathing to return to normal.

"Shit... you scared me..." Janet tops up her glass and takes another large sip as Abbey assesses her closely, "You're drunk..." It isn't a question. Abbey has seen her mum in this state many times before, although admittedly not for a while. Janet looks up at Abbey and unexpectedly bursts out laughing, shaking her head and blinking rapidly, trying to get her eyes to focus.

"Very perceptive darling..." She slurs.

Abbey hates seeing her mum like this. It brings back too many painful memories of how she was when Ryan first died, drinking herself into oblivion every night before she completely lost her mind and was committed. It had been her way of coping when things got too difficult, a way to shut out the world and avoid reality. Abbey feels a wave of guilt, knowing that her behaviour has clearly pushed Janet to the brink again but she quickly dispels it. She is a grown woman, capable of making her own decisions. Abbey hasn't forced her to pick up that bottle, not physically at least.

"I'm going to bed..." She sighs, wearily.

"No. We need to talk..."

"I'm not wasting my time trying to have a conversation with you when you're like this..."

"We need to talk. So we are going to talk..." Janet speaks firmly through gritted teeth, as she tops up her glass again.

"I think you've had enough..." Abbey snaps.

"Oh you're right about that. I have had enough; I have most definitely had enough..." Janet's eyes are red raw and she runs her hands through her hair before holding her arms out to the side in exasperation, "I mean what the hell is going on Abbey. You're leaving the house at all hours, fighting, getting kicked out of school... where the hell has my daughter gone?!"

"Look, I'm trying OK?"

"Oh really?" Janet gasps, "You're trying? Because it seems to me like you aren't trying at all. It seems to me that you don't care about anyone or anything but yourself..."

"God... you just don't get it do you?" Abbey's whispered voice becomes much louder as she tries to fight back her anger without success.

"Oh here we go... you know what, why don't you explain it to me Abbey? Why don't you tell me what it is I'm NOT getting?" Janet leans across the table, waving her glass of whiskey around while gesturing dramatically.

"You don't see what's right in front of you, do you...?"

"Oh I should have known it would be my fault..."

"Of course it's your fault Mum, it's never Abbey's fault is it?" Both Janet and Abbey turn in unison towards the doorway where Peter has appeared. He is wearing a t-shirt and joggers and looks very tired, as if he has just woken up. He rubs his face with his hands and folds his arms across his chest, glaring at Abbey.

"Go back upstairs Peter this is between me and your sister..." Peter ignores Janet's request and Abbey starts to laugh cynically, throwing her head back while rolling her eyes at the ceiling.

"No it's OK let him stay, I mean you need more people to gang up on me don't you? Why don't we give Anna a call, get her involved too...? Because it's all my fault isn't it? It's all down to me and what a complete and utter failure I am..."

"Oh for god sake..." Peter scoffs.

"Why are you doing this? Why are you behaving so selfishly?"

"*I'm* being selfish?!" Abbey gasps, smarting at her mother's accusation, and Janet stands up, leaning on the table to steady herself.

"Just tell me... tell me why the hell you are acting this way?!"

"BECAUSE I FEEL LIKE I CAN'T BREATHE!" Abbey finally snaps, shouting at the top of her lungs, so angry that she can no longer hold back her pain or keep her frustrations at bay, "I feel like I'm suffocating living in this house..."

Usually Janet would try to calm the situation down, or at least respond in a quieter, muted voice while panicking about what the neighbours must think, but she is too drunk and too involved in the argument to care - and she shouts back, just as loud.

"Everyone is suffering Abbey... everyone in this family feels the way you do but nobody else is acting out because it is irresponsible. I mean what gives you the right to behave this way? As if you're suffering is worse..."

"It is worse..." Abbey yells in exasperation as her tears spill down her cheeks and she quickly wipes them away.

"Oh you think so do you?!" Janet asks, incredulous, "How the hell do you think I feel every day when I wake up? I lost a son for god sake..."

"AND HE WAS MY BROTHER..." Abbey screams
- and in one swift movement she picks up the glass from
the kitchen unit and throws it at the wall behind Janet.
It smashes into pieces and scatters the room with tiny
fragments of glass, causing both Peter and Janet to
shield themselves, "He was my twin brother, he was
everything to me. He was with me every single day of
my life and now he's gone and I can't do this anymore..."
An empty sob breaks out from Abbey's chest and she
places her hand over her mouth, trying desperately to
keep from collapsing.

"Abbey..." Peter gasps, instinctively reaching out as
he steps towards her but she backs away, holding up her
hand to stop him.

"Don't. Don't you dare, it's too late for that." She
snaps, with a distinct warning in her voice.

"Abbey please..." He begs, looking suddenly
frightened.

"I didn't just lose Ryan the day he died; I lost all of
you..." She states, as her voice breaks again. The truth
is finally coming out. The flood gates are wide open and
there is no way Abbey can prevent the words from
flowing, even if she wanted to.

"What are you talking about...?"

"I told you...! I told you before but you still wouldn't
listen!"

"Told me what?" Peters asks, confused, and Abbey
takes a long, deep breath, speaking as calmly as she can
manage, but her hands are still shaking wildly after her
aggressive outburst.

"I remind you too much of him... so you shut
me out...." There is a brief pause as both Peter
and Janet display a series of emotion on their faces.

First shock, horror, guilt and then a slow and painful realisation.

"That isn't true." Janet whispers, unconvincingly.

"You're lying..."

"We tried... we tried to..."

"No just STOP... STOP LYING TO ME..." Abbey screams and neither Peter nor Janet react this time. There is no come back remark or argument, no eye rolling. Both of them simply stare at Abbey as she speaks, "He was my twin. We were so much alike and I know that being around me only reminds you of Ryan and what you lost. It's too hard for you... so you shut me out. You pushed me away and put up a wall and you did it because it made things easier, for you. That's the truth..."

"Oh god Abbey... I didn't... we didn't mean..." Janet struggles to find the right words as Peter stands quietly with tears now falling, and Abbey blinks once, composing herself as her expression becomes eerily blank and she looks her mum square in the eyes.

"Now ask yourself who's selfish..."

Janet slumps back into her chair as Abbey pushes past a motionless Peter and races up the stairs. No longer able to hold herself together, she completely falls apart, sobbing uncontrollably as she bursts into her bedroom. Without pausing to think she grabs her travel bag from the top of her wardrobe and frantically throws in all the clothes she can get her hands on, struggling with the zip as she grabs her phone with her free hand and dials for a taxi.

Due to the nature of his profession and his typical 'office hours', Alex rarely sleeps. His internal body clock is so messed up from working late nights into early mornings that even when he isn't dealing, he usually stays awake until dawn, unable to completely unwind.

It is almost 1:30am. Tom is fast asleep, snoring loudly, and Alex is on the verge of going to bed in the vain hope of getting a few hours rest when he is startled by a loud banging on the front door.

Ever cautious, he picks up the baseball bat that is leaning against the side of his wardrobe and creeps carefully into the kitchen. He waits, listening in the dark, and after a few seconds he hears the banging again, much more frenzied than before. Very slowly, he turns the key and releases the latch, raising the bat above his head as he whips the door open. Abbey is standing in the doorway, her face stained with tears, and Alex drops his guard instantly, pulling her inside by the hand.

"I'm sorry... I didn't know where else to go..." She sobs, her voice muffled against Alex's shoulder as he hugs her tightly. Just being there, in his embrace, makes her feel instantly better.

"What happened?" Alex shuts the door and guides her over to the table, pulling out a chair and taking her bag from her shoulder as he kneels down in front of her.

"Nothing more than I expected really. It was worse this time though, the argument... I just had to get out of there..."

"You look exhausted..." Alex holds Abbey's face gently between his hands and she smiles half-heartedly. She is so glad to be with him, but she cringes at how much of a mess she must look right now. He doesn't seem to mind.

"Can I please stay here tonight?" She asks timidly.

"Of course you can, you can stay as long as you like... come on..."

Abbey drags her feet as she follows Alex into his room, and as he throws back the duvet she crawls into bed. The last time she was in here she had been on cloud nine. What a difference, compared to how she feels now. Only one thing is the same, and that is how her pulse quickens every time Alex looks at her or touches her, no matter how briefly. She wants so much to lay awake and talk to him - or just curl up in his arms and savour the moment - but she is so completely drained both physically and emotionally, that she falls into a deep sleep as soon as her head touches the pillow.

Abbey's dreams are vivid, and although it is late morning by the time she wakes, she doesn't feel at all rested. As she blinks hard her vision comes into focus, and it takes her a moment to realise where she is. Her heart skips a beat and she feels a rush of excitement as she registers the familiar walls of Alex's bedroom. Her excitement doesn't last long though, as the events of the previous day come rushing back to the forefront of her mind and she is pulled under by a deep depression.

She feels so hurt, alone and angry... but more than anything, she feels betrayed. She knew why her family had been acting so strangely towards her. It was only a few months after Ryan's death when she first noticed the change in them. How they would speak to her but never really say anything, and how they would spend time with her but always seemed distant and removed when they did. They put up their walls and in retaliation - whether it was a conscious decision or not - she did the same. The fact that she is a constant and painful reminder of Ryan is the only conclusion she arrived at when trying to understand their behaviour towards her. And as more time went on, she realised she was right.

Yet last night, after saying it out loud, after finally confronting the tension between them and acknowledging the problem for the first time, she thought they would at least attempt to deny it. She thought they would shout and swear and be incensed at such an accusation, or, if they did admit it, that they would grovel and apologise and beg for forgiveness... but they didn't. There was barely any reaction at all. They didn't admit it outright, but they certainly didn't deny it either and to Abbey it only validated further that she has been right all along. Not only is her theory correct, but deep down, her mum and her brother know exactly how they have been acting towards her. And that hurts more than she can stand.

Although a big part of Abbey wants to lie in bed all day and spiral into despair, she knows that it will serve no purpose. Staring up at the ceiling and wishing things were different certainly isn't going to change anything or make the situation any better.

She begrudgingly heaves herself out of bed and stumbles over to the en suite bathroom, rubbing her eyes as she flicks on the light. Considering her emotional meltdown last night she doesn't look half as bad as she was expecting. She must have rubbed most of her make-up off and her face isn't red and puffy like it usually appears after a major crying session. Her black eye on the other hand is definitely darker, casting a think purple shadow across her cheek bone. Not a great look.

After splashing cold water on her face, cleaning her teeth and brushing her hair, Abbey changes into her joggers and a vest top and makes her way, rather sheepishly, into the kitchen. Alex is sitting at the table reading a paper with a cup of coffee in his hand. He is dressed in a thin, black V neck jumper and his usual dark blue jeans that fit him perfectly. He looks wide eyed and awake, ready to take on the day, and it makes Abbey feel a little self-conscious. As she enters the room he smiles her favourite smile and folds his paper, placing his coffee mug down on top of it without taking his eyes from her face.

"Good morning..." He purrs.

"Hi..."

"How are you feeling?"

"OK, thanks... a little stupid actually..." She sighs, "I am so sorry for barging in on you like that Alex, I really didn't mean to dis..." Alex shakes his head stopping Abbey mid-sentence, and he leans forward, holding his hand out towards her. As she takes it he pulls her carefully into his lap and wraps his arms securely around her waist as he kisses her neck tenderly.

"Don't apologise. I'm glad you came here. It was horrible seeing you that upset I'm just glad I could help in some way..."

"You did..." Abbey smiles, "Thank you, for letting me stay..." Alex tilts his head back and Abbey automatically leans forward to kiss him. As their lips touch her stomach flips and her whole body tenses. She still can't get over how he makes her feel. Despite everything else that is going on in her life, she still can't suppress the elation that overcomes her every time she is with Alex. She slowly traces her finger down his cheek and across his perfectly square jaw, losing her train of thought as he stares up at her with his unfathomable blue eyes. He smirks and she smiles back coyly.

"What are you thinking?" He asks.

"I was actually thinking it should be illegal for someone to be this good looking..." She blushes furiously, instantly questioning what on earth possessed her to say that out loud. Alex laughs, and a fleeting hint of shyness and uncertainty flickers across his face. It makes Abbey melt and she automatically leans in to kiss him again.

"I could say the same about you..." He says softly as they break apart, "Do you know what I was thinking?" He asks, "I was thinking that it might be a good idea for you to ring your family..." Abbey's heart sinks and her insecurity kicks into overdrive as she quickly reaches the conclusion that he must be tired of her already. Yet before she can let the disappointment overwhelm her, he explains further, "They'll be worried, not knowing where you are and I don't want them sending a police search party out which will eventually lead them to my door. Tell them you're OK, tell them you need time... that is if you still aren't ready to go back? Tell them whatever you want, but just let them know that you're alright and that you're safe..."

"Are you sure I'm OK to stay here?" She asks, and Alex removes one arm from around Abbey's waist and places his hand on the side of her neck, softly stroking her cheek with his thumb as he smiles sweetly.

"I want you to be happy and I sincerely hope you sort things out with your family, I really do... but I'd be lying if I said waking up this morning with you sleeping next to me was in any way a bad thing. I could definitely get used to having you around on a more permanent basis, if that suits you...?" Abbey breaks into a huge smile and Alex pulls her down so that their lips meet again, this time with much more urgency. He stands with ease, still holding Abbey in his arms, and carries her back into the bedroom.

The emotional conflict that is raging inside Abbey has her head in a spin and she can't understand how it is possible to experience two completely different emotions at the exact same time. On one hand, she feels hollow and angry at the situation with her family, so much so that she is willing to move out to get away from them. She knows that things becoming so intolerable should be beyond upsetting, yet instead all she feels is a childlike excitement at the prospect of living with Alex. Waking up to him every day, being with her friends and getting to spend all her free time with the guy she is absolutely crazy about... it will be like her own little piece of heaven amongst all the turmoil in her life. Things just make sense when she is with him and she feels as though nothing can touch her, because Alex won't let it.

By the time she finally manages to tear herself away from him and get dressed it is mid-afternoon, which means she has to be quick. Usually both Peter and her mum would be at work at this time, but considering the circumstances, Abbey is almost expecting to turn the corner at the end of the road to see police cars all over the street. She doesn't quite know how to feel when she reaches the house and it stands locked up and empty like usual. At least she can get inside and pack without another horrible argument. She is grateful for that at least.

Abbey throws her holdall onto the bed and flings open her wardrobe. She has more time to pick through her clothes today than she had in her haste last night, and she folds them up neatly, careful not to waste any space by packing anything unnecessary.

It is a task that takes her less than half an hour, but as the time approaches 4pm she suddenly becomes eager to get out of the house while there is still no one there to stop her. Abbey reaches under her desk for her favourite photo album and throws it on top of her clothes before hastily zipping her bag shut. She is literally seconds away from leaving, when her bedroom door creaks open.

"Hi…" Anna enters the room cautiously - as if approaching a startled rabbit - and her body language instantly annoys Abbey. She isn't as fragile as her family make her out to be. She has dealt with a lot these past couple of years, most of it completely on her own, "What's going on…?" She asks, desperately trying to hide the alarm in her voice.

Despite her initial irritation Abbey feels a pang of guilt and the melancholy slowly starts to creep in. Her beautiful sister who she was once so close to, is standing in front of her with panic and concern in her eyes. It is seriously bad timing. Peter and Janet she can still be angry with but Anna is so calm, understanding and rational that it is hard not to be influenced by her, and she doesn't want her sister to talk her into staying by promising to fix everything… because she can't, not this time.

"I was just leaving…" She answers, firmly, "I'm going to stay with a friend for a while. I need some space…"

"Abbey, please don't do this…" Anna begs, "Look, I know that things got a bit out of hand last night but it isn't going to get sorted if you run away. Mum feels terrible…"

"Does she?" Abbey interrupts, "Did she tell you that?"

"Yes... she rang me in floods of tears, told me what had happened last night and how bad she felt about it, Pete too..."

"That's interesting... so why did she ring you and not me? If they both feel so terrible why didn't my phone ring last night Anna, or this morning? And how is it that they're both at work like nothing has happened at all?" Anna swallows slowly, desperately trying to find an adequate explanation, but she doesn't have one.

"Abbey, you can't just leave..."

"You can't stop me. I'm 18..."

"Please, please don't go. Let's just sit and have a coffee and talk..."

"That isn't going to work Anna..." She sighs, "I'm just exhausted. I can't be here anymore. I feel like I'm losing myself and I need time to figure a few things out. It's all been falling apart for a long time and nothing is getting better and I'm scared, I'm scared that one day I'm going to wake up and feel how Ryan felt before he..." Abbey trails off and tries to bring her rapid breathing under control. It is so hard, knowingly hurting Anna, but Abbey is determined not to go back on her decision.

"I'm so sorry that you feel that way Abs, I really am. I feel like it's partly my fault, that I should have been here more, I ..." Anna fights back tears as she struggles to process what is happening.

"Don't. It is how it is for a million different reasons Anna..." The last thing Abbey wants is to be guilt tripped, it will only make her more inclined to give in.

"Where will you stay?"

"At a flat in the city centre... it's safe, I'll be fine, don't worry..." Abbey desperately wants to reassure Anna and put her mind at ease but she knows that the more she gets drawn into a conversation the less likely she will be able to walk away, "I'll call..." She whispers, giving her a quick kiss on the cheek before hurrying out of the room.

"Wait... Abbey, wait..." Anna calls after her but she is already half way down the stairs, struggling with her bag as she ignores her sister's pleas.

She places her hand on the latch and has one foot out of the door when Anna shouts again, but this time, the sound is different. It sends Abbey's blood cold and she flinches at the guttural, pained scream – immediately dropping her bag as she turns and races back up to her room. Anna is on her knees at the top of the landing, leaning forward and clutching her stomach as a small pool of blood forms on her jeans.

"Something's wrong..." Anna sobs and Abbey rushes to her side, trying her best not to panic and to keep her sister calm as she frantically dials for an ambulance.

CHAPTER EIGHT

NEW ARRIVAL

Abbey stands perfectly still with her back against the wall of the hospital room as three nurses frantically rush around Anna, hooking her up to various machines and monitors. The eldest of the three and the one who seems to be in charge lifts Anna's jumper and gently presses the ultra sound equipment onto her stomach. There is a brief pause as everyone stares expectantly at the screen.

"There…" The nurse says, with more than a hint of relief, "The baby's heartbeat, she's doing fine…" Abbey exhales sharply - she hadn't even realised she was holding her breath.

"She?" Anna asks, her eyes filling with tears.

"Oh I'm so sorry, you didn't know?"

"No, but it's fine. More than fine… really…" Anna puts her hand to her face and half laughs, half sobs with a strange mixture of elation and relief.

"A mini Anna…" Abbey smiles, "Look out world!" She takes her sisters hand and perches on the chair at her bedside, waiting for her to calm down and for her breathing to steady.

"Dom will be thrilled…" She jokes.

"He's on his way, I'm sure he won't be long…"

"Thank you, for being here with me…"

"Of course… I wasn't going to leave you was I?"

"But you are leaving…" Abbey rolls her eyes. Trust Anna to be laid out on a hospital bed surrounded by scary medical equipment after going through something genuinely traumatic and still being able to carry on an argument.

"I told you. I just need space. It isn't working and I don't think it'll be healthy for any of us if I stay in that house…"

"But if you just talked it out…"

"We tried that, it didn't work. You aren't going to change my mind…"

Anna looks ready to launch into another pleading monologue, but instead she flinches, grabbing hold of the metal rail that runs the length of the bed as she shuts her eyes tightly.

"What is it, what's wrong?!"

"Contractions…" A voice answers from behind Abbey's shoulder, startling her. She hadn't noticed the nurse re-enter the room, "They'll be coming stronger and much more frequently now. She's almost 5cm's…" She moves skilfully around the bed - dodging the equipment with ease and passes Anna a breathing tube that provides the gas and air. She takes long, deep breaths and after a minute her body begins to relax again.

"I'm sorry Abbey…" She whispers.

"It's OK… it's not like you can help it, I'm just glad the baby…"

"No, not about this, for what you're feeling, what you're going through…"

"It's not your fault…"

"I haven't exactly been there for you though have I, like I should have been?"

"Anna you have a lot going on right now, I don't hold that against you…"

"It's no excuse though. We used to be able to talk about everything… I really miss that…" Abbey feels a wave of sadness as she nods in agreement. She misses it too; she misses the way things used to be so much more than she can bear. It is so hard without Ryan, but it isn't just his loss that she is grieving. She is in mourning for times gone by, much happier times, when things were simple and life was good.

It's as though Ryan created a black hole when he took his own life and that hole sucked everything in, pulled everything apart, and her world has been spiralling ever since. In the past 18 months, the only time she has felt grounded, safe and anchored is with her friends and with Alex.

"Please don't go…" The pain and longing in Anna's voice momentarily breaks Abbey's resolve and as she is about to speak up and state her case again, Dom interrupts her by charging into the room.

"I am SO sorry babe, I was across town and the traffic was a nightmare, then there was nowhere to park…" He gasps for breath as he kisses Anna's forehead, "Hey Abbey…"

"Hi…" Abbey smiles as she rises to her feet, gesturing towards the chair.

"Oh… no… it's OK… you stay…" He pants.

"Dom, you look like you're about to collapse, maybe you should sit for a minute…" Abbey can't keep from laughing as Anna rolls her eyes and shakes her head, affectionately. He gives her a grateful thumbs up as he slumps into the chair and tilts his head back, still wheezing.

"Is everything alright?" He asks, with sudden concern, "The nurse said you were fine but then she mentioned something about bleeding...?"

"Yeah, there was a bit of a scare but we're all good... thanks to Abbey."

"I didn't do much it's just lucky I was there..." Abbey feels uncomfortable as she waits for Anna to explain the full story to Dom. It is two against one now, if they both start guilt tripping her she might give into them and she already wavered slightly before Dom unintentionally saved her by breaking up the conversation. This isn't a decision she has made lightly, leaving home, but she truly feels that it is the right thing to do. She doesn't need them making it any harder for her, "I should probably go..."

"Oh no Abbey stay, please..."

"Yeah you don't have to go Abs, besides I might need you here, I have a feeling I'm going to be completely useless...!" Dom quips light heartedly, not fully understanding the situation and that Anna is trying to prevent her from leaving, not just the hospital but the family.

"Please..." Anna stares at Abbey with beseeching eyes and again she falters. She still finds it so difficult to knowingly upset her sister. She is far too kind and loving, the last person on earth anyone would want to disappoint.

After surrendering reluctantly to Anna's request, Abbey escapes out into the corridor to phone Alex. She tells him about the drama that has unfolded throughout the afternoon and he of course encourages her to stay at the hospital. She agrees it is the right thing to do but hearing his voice makes her pine for him badly and she longs to be back at the flat, safely in his arms, with all her worries and troubles forgotten.

A nurse sitting behind the admin desk eyes Abbey disapprovingly and she reluctantly finishes the call. She takes a seat in the waiting room, pausing for a moment to mentally prepare herself for the onslaught she is about to face as Anna will most definitely have filled Dom in during her momentary absence. After gathering all her inner strength ready for their emotional ambush, Abbey eventually makes her way back through the maternity ward and into the delivery room, freezing instantly as she opens the door and is unexpectedly confronted by her mum.

Abbey quickly realises that Anna must have called Janet behind her back and she glares at her sister, feeling utterly betrayed. She smiles back apologetically as Janet takes a cautious step forward but Abbey edges away, like a cornered animal ready to bolt.

"Abbey...?" Janet seems just a surprised.

"She was with me when I collapsed, she called the ambulance..." Anna answers the question in her mum's tone and she smiles.

"You came home?"

"Just to get some more stuff..."

"We need to talk about this..."

"We tried that remember..." Abbey snaps, "Only it didn't work out so well because you were blind drunk..." Janet shifts defensively but still tries to remain reasonable.

"We can't leave things like this..."

Abbey opens her mouth to respond but stops as Anna arches her back in pain, crying out. A nurse comes rushing in and straight over to her side, examining all her drips and monitors before finally checking under the bed sheet.

"It won't be long now…" She announces, "You'll be ready to push soon…"

A wave of panic washes over Anna and all the colour drains from her face as Dom and Janet hold her hands, soothing her gently. Abbey looks on, completely split in two and wrestling with her conscience as she tries to decide whether she should stay or go. After another brief moment of inner conflict she seizes the opportunity to escape, grabbing her bag and quickly hurrying out of the door.

Anna isn't alone; she is with Dom and her Mum, in hospital, surrounded by professionals. She will be fine, more than fine, in a short time she will have a brand new baby girl and she doesn't need the added stress of worrying about Abbey and watching her fight with Janet - and no doubt Peter too - once he arrives. It is for the best that she gets out of the way while she still can.

As she runs down the stairs, through the main entrance and out of the automatic doors, Abbey repeats her reasons over and over in her head, trying hard to convince herself that she is doing the right thing. It is so hard. Hard knowing that Anna is in pain and hard knowing that this should be a happy, joyful occasion. Her baby niece is been born and she can't stay and be a part of it. It makes her feel utterly helpless.

Abbey's mood only marginally improves once she is back at the flat. Even Lucy is struggling to cheer her up and it's something she can usually do with ease. She sits cross legged on the bed, sipping a glass of wine while watching Abbey carefully hang the last of her clothes in the limited space in Alex's wardrobe.

"You did the right thing you know. It would have gotten out of hand again and it really wasn't the time or place for another glass to be dramatically smashed against a wall..." Lucy winks and Abbey smiles at her sarcastically, shaking her head as she slides the wardrobe door shut.

"I know. It doesn't make me feel any better though, abandoning my sister in her hour of need..." She moves into the en suite with her toilet bag, finding space for her things wherever she can.

"You're unbelievable!" Lucy laughs scathingly, "I know Anna isn't as much of a villain as your mum and Pete in all this but she is right to feel guilty about not supporting you. She hasn't been there for you as much as she should have been, none of them have, yet you're the one who still feels guilty...!"

"I suppose so..." Abbey sighs as she joins Lucy on the bed, picking up her glass and taking a sip of wine, "Just when I think things can't possibly get any worse..."

"I've learnt that there's no such thing as 'can't get any worse', but it isn't all bad. You have us, and Alex... at least you're not on your own..."

"That's true..."

"You have an awesome group of friends, a super-hot boyfriend and a new glamorous, city centre flat. Life is actually pretty great if you think about it that way..." Lucy gestures, enthusiastically.

"It isn't my flat, and I'm not really sure what me and Alex are defining ourselves as yet..."

"Jesus you're determined to sulk aren't you Miller?"

"Sorry..." Abbey laughs, "You're right about the friends though..." Lucy smiles broadly and raises her glass, but Abbey's answering smile doesn't quite reach her eyes.

Lucy finally gives in trying to cheer her up and for once she stops cracking jokes in an attempt to lighten the mood. Instead, placing her wine on the bedside table, she reaches behind her neck and gently unfastens one of the many necklaces she is wearing before passing it to Abbey. It is a delicate silver chain with a small, teardrop shaped amber stone bound on the end.

"Here, you need this more than I do..." Abbey takes it, turning it around in her hand as she studies the gemstone closely, "It's Amber... it promotes good luck, happiness, inner peace... and... loads of other stuff, apparently! It probably doesn't work for shit seen as it was about a quid from the Market, but it's the thought that counts... or something..." Abbey leans forward and hugs Lucy. She is always so understanding, supporting her through drama after drama and listening to her endless problems, no matter what. She knows how lucky she is to have her, and the necklace - whether a cheap bit of market tat or not – is a reminder of that and she is deeply touched by the gesture.

"Thanks Luc, for everything. I don't know what I'd do without you..."

"I honestly don't know either...!" She grins, "Come on..." Lucy jumps up, grabbing her glass and the half empty bottle of Pinto Grigio as she skips towards the door, "Let's go put some music on and have a little pick me up, I think we both need it..."

"I think you're right..." Abbey agrees, as she follows Lucy into the hallway.

"Things have got a little too serious around here for my liking..." Lucy adds, and they both glance instinctively down the hall towards the kitchen. Abbey can hear the low, steady murmur of voices but they are too muffled for her to make out exactly what is being said.

The tension in the room is palpable and there is no way Alex can dispel it. He can't make light of the situation or what he is asking his friends to do for him, because what he is asking is huge, and he knows it. He has exhausted every avenue he can think of in order to get hold of the money he owes Marcus. Contacts, dealers, friends, all the people that owe him a favour... but he has come away with nothing. Time is running out. If he doesn't pay up, Marcus will kill him, or at the very least break his legs so that he never walks again. There is no doubting his threats.

One contact did have a semi-helpful suggestion but Alex had laughed it off at the time. Now, however, it seems like it might be the only option left and he is genuinely considering the idea. The only catch is he can't do it alone.

This person moves in dangerous circles and is heavily involved in crime - much more serious crime than he or any of his friends have ever been involved in - and in order to square a long standing debt with Alex he had promised to get him information about various businesses that are an easy target, for armed robbery.

Alex doesn't like it. He deals drugs, but other than that he keeps himself clean and has absolutely no desire to get dragged further into the criminal underworld. But it seems as though the choice is slipping away from him and the walls are closing in. He has to make a decision, which is why he has called the lads together to discuss the idea. So he can explain to them the general plan and ask, very reluctantly, if they will put themselves in a position that he doesn't even want to be in himself.

"That's pretty extreme mate..." Nathan is the first to break the stunned silence.

"I know, but it's the only choice I have. Believe me; I wouldn't be standing here asking you this if there was any other way... any fucking way at all..."

"What about Moorland, surely he'd want to help you out, this whole Marcus situation could damage the business you two have together?" Darren asks, confused.

"Exactly. It's far too early in the relationship to lose face with Moorland and bring trouble to his door, I can't risk upsetting him by bringing him into this. It might cause more problems than it solves." It is an option that Alex has thought about numerous times. He doesn't know Moorland well enough yet to be able to accurately predict his reaction. He might help, but it might go the other way and Alex can't afford to take that chance.

Liam leans back in his chair and locks his hands behind his head as Nathan rests his elbows on the glass table, both of them deep in thought. Darren perches on the kitchen counter, staring at the floor, while Tom stands directly opposite Alex on the other side of the room.

"What exactly are we talking?" Tom hasn't spoken a word since Alex put his plan across to them, but that isn't exactly surprising. He always takes a decent amount of time to think things through; if something is troubling him or there is something he needs to process, he works through it internally in his own way before he acts on it or voices his opinion. At least when he finally speaks it isn't a complete rebuff or a straight forward 'no'. Alex is grateful for that, as deep down, it is Tom's decision that means the most to him and the one that holds the biggest influence with the others.

"My guy says the shop we're looking to target has a collection from the safe the last Saturday of every month. So we'd hit it on the Friday night just before close. I have a warehouse space we can use before and after..."

"Armed?" Tom raises an eyebrow.

"Yeah. Not to use, obviously. Just to scare. We'll be in and out, no mess... just keeping it as quick and simple as possible..." There is silence again as Tom takes it all in, shaking his head.

"This is a lot mate... dealing drugs and boosting a couple of cars here and there is one thing, but it's a hell of a fucking jump to armed robbery..."

Alex sighs, running his hands though his hair as he leans back against the wall in anguish, struggling with his conscience at what he is asking his friends to sacrifice for him.

"I know. I'm sorry boys... I don't like this either and I fucking hate myself for having to ask. I know it's a massive risk and I understand if it's one you aren't willing to take. I just had to run it by you as a last resort, tell you where I'm at..."

"A one off?" Tom asks.

"Of course. I have about five grand, I just need to get the rest of it to pay off Holt and get him the fuck out of my life for good..."

"Alright..." Alex blinks twice as Tom's answer slowly registers. A huge part of him is beyond grateful but there is still another part of him that is incredibly apprehensive. He is reluctant for his friends to agree to this. He doesn't want trouble for them and he hates putting them in this situation.

"Are you sure?"

"Like you said there's no other way out of this fucking mess and I can't exactly stand back and do nothing while Marcus comes after you can I? You're my best mate..." Alex crosses the room in three quick strides and slaps hands with Tom, pulling him into a hug.

"Thank you brother..."

"I'm in..." Darren jumps down from the counter top, "But if were doing this it needs to be done right. I have a mate who can get us some wheels, blacked out, fake licence plates, untraceable..."

"That would be a big help man, get on to him..." Darren squeezes Alex's shoulder reassuringly, as he leaves the room with his phone in his hand.

"Were in as well, if this is what you need mate, we're there..." Liam and Nathan both stand and Alex nods, gratefully.

"You can drive us to the warehouse and wait for us to get back; we'll need to get away fast so you'll have to be ready..."

"What about the bust, you'll need back up?" Liam argues.

"No... I have Darren and Tom for that, any more than three of us will be too difficult to co-ordinate. It's not that I don't trust you mate, of course I do, but you're not even out of fucking high school yet.

How about you finish sixth form before you add armed robbery to your C.V..."

"Agreed..." Tom nods and Liam looks more than a little put out, but Nathan relaxes slightly. He doesn't feel right about any of this, so the less he is involved the better. Liam is obviously disgruntled that he will be missing out on the excitement but that is his impulsive, hot-headedness coming into play. Once he has thought it through and Nathan has talked him down he will understand that it's for the best.

"Don't worry mate..." Nathan jokes, "If you're really that keen to break the law we'll still be accessories, driving the getaway car..."

"Nate..." Alex approaches him solemnly and holds out his hand, "Thank you for doing this mate; It means a lot... and you know I really am sorry..."

"Don't worry about it man; I'm only messing. I can't say I'm thrilled with the idea but I know you wouldn't ask and it's what we do isn't it. We're family...."

There are no words that can express how much Alex appreciates his friends and the lengths they are willing to go to in order to help him. If they had said no he would be well and truly stuck and in deep trouble, with absolutely no way out. It is hard to believe how everything has got so complicated and out of hand with Marcus, but at least now there is a slight hope that he may be able to pay him off and cut all ties with him once and for all. If everything goes to plan he will never have to see Holt again, and Alex is praying to god that it does go right, because if they fail, there will be consequences. Not just for him, but for all of them.

Abbey rolls over in the large, double bed and stretches her arm out, searching for Alex. Her eyes flicker open in confusion when she is met by a cold, empty space where he should be sleeping and she sits up, feeling a little disorientated. It is obviously still early as it is pitch black outside and she can hear nothing but the soft hum of the occasional passing car from the road below. She flicks on the lamp and rubs her eyes, gathering one of Alex's shirts from the floor and hastily throwing it over her shoulders. She fastens the middle three buttons and tiptoes across the hallway, mindful of Tom asleep in the next room as she carefully opens the living room door.

Bursts of colour illuminate the darkness, as scenes from an old martial arts film flash across the TV screen. Alex sits alone, resting a bottle of beer in his lap as he stares at the muted movie, unable to switch off and stop himself from thinking about the earlier conversation and the impending raid. It had broken his heart to ask his friends to stoop so low, and the feelings of guilt and self-loathing are beginning to surface. Abbey stifles a yawn as she approaches the back of the sofa and gently runs her fingers through Alex's hair.

"What time is it?" She asks.

"A little after 3am..." He takes a sip of his drink and looks down at the floor. It isn't unusual for Alex to be up so late but Abbey can see that something is clearly troubling him and after the events of earlier that day, it doesn't take a genius to figure out what. She moves round to the front of the sofa and sits down by his side, tucking her legs beneath her as she strokes his face lightly. He closes his eyes at her touch and sighs.

"You're worried..."

"There'd be something seriously wrong if I wasn't..." He states, leaning his head back and staring up at the ceiling, "I just don't know if this is right, dragging them into my fucking problems, asking them to get involved… what kind of friend does that make me?"

"When you're in trouble you're friends are the people you turn to…" Abbey reaches up and twists Alex's hair between her fingers as she speaks, trying her best to comfort him without getting too close. It is still hard for her to judge his moods and she isn't sure if all the walls between them have been knocked down yet.

"But asking them to do this…?" Alex looks at her with a pained expression as the movie flashes brightly again, "This isn't what we do. We're far from fucking perfect and I know I'm no exception, but to go this far…? I'm a dealer, not a thief. I know what I do isn't exactly heroic but the people I supply to make that choice for themselves; it's their decision to take drugs, I just provide them. But taking money that isn't mine to take, involving the boys…" Alex shakes his head, disgusted at himself, as he reaches up and takes Abbey's hand.

"They have a choice too. They could have said no but they didn't. They want to help you out Alex; you aren't forcing them into anything…"

"I've still put them in this position…"

"Well, it's a one off…" Abbey doesn't know what else to say. She wants to reassure him but it is almost impossible for her to sit there and condone what they are planning to do. She can't bring herself to openly encourage armed robbery.

This whole situation is worlds apart from the life she is used to and it frightens her, but Marcus is a genuine threat to Alex's safety and the thought of someone hurting him, or worse, the thought of losing him altogether, is something that she just can't handle.

"I keep telling myself that. It's a one off, the shop we hit will be insured…" Alex laughs once without humour, "As if that will make a blind bit of fucking difference to the guy who owns it…" He looks up at Abbey again, searching her face, "I can't imagine what you think of me? I can't actually believe you're still here…" Disarmed by his vulnerability, Abbey takes the bottle of beer from Alex's grasp and places it on the coffee table, turning and shifting in his lap as she rests her head on his shoulder, still holding his gaze.

"I think you're a good man, who's trying to make the best of the hand he's been dealt. You're loyal; you love and protect your friends, and it's obvious how much they love you…"

"Armed robbery isn't exactly a character trait of a good man, Abbey…"

"If you weren't a good man you wouldn't care either way and you certainly wouldn't be beating yourself up over it. I know you wish you had another choice. I wish I could change this for you…" Alex stares down at her, mystified.

"How do you always see the good in people?"

"I see it when it's there to see…" Abbey smiles and she reaches up, gently touching her lips to Alex's. He exhales slowly, almost with reluctance, but as their mouths lock together with more force he lets go of any worries and distractions and desire takes over. He runs his hand across Abbey's chest and down to her waist, twisting his body so that she is on the sofa beneath him. As he holds her face to his with one hand, he unbuttons the shirt she is wearing with the other.

"It's fucking ridiculous how good you look in this…" He whispers breathlessly. Abbey giggles as he throws the shirt to the floor and trails kisses all over her body, before stopping suddenly and shifting so that they are face to face again.

"I'm so glad you're here..."

"Me too..." Abbey locks her arms around Alex's neck and pulls him down into another lingering kiss. She slides his t-shirt off in one swift movement, tracing her hands across his perfectly toned chest and back up over his shoulders. She can feel the strength in his arms as he lifts her on top of him and her hands pull hungrily at his hair as they get lost in one another, and for a time, everything else just slips away.

Emotionally, Abbey has never felt so tired, but for some reason her body refuses to give in to the exhaustion. It is strange to see Alex looking so content and peaceful. As he sleeps his face is completely relaxed and it no longer holds the almost constant frown lines that Abbey is so used to seeing. She has been staring at him for a while now - marvelling yet again at how inconceivably gorgeous he is while thinking over everything she has learnt about him. On the surface Alex Matthews is one thing, but underneath all the bravado there is a mess of contradictions that hold more questions than answers.

He is a drug dealer. A fact that probably should have shocked Abbey when it was first revealed to her but it didn't. To people that know him through his line of work he is strong, powerful, respected... and potentially dangerous. Although she had been greatly intimidated at first, Abbey no longer feels that way towards him. If anything, he makes her feel safer than ever. And although he is about to involve himself in an incredibly serious and dangerous crime, he doesn't enjoy or relish that fact in any way. He is completely cut up and emotionally tormented, knowing how wrong it is and hating himself for involving the people he loves.

Abbey understands all too well, that as first impressions go, Alex is extremely bad news, but there are so many different layers to him that run much deeper than the image he projects on the surface. They have so much in common, much more than she initially thought, and although their lives have been completely different prior to this point, she understands the pain of being alone, to be disconnected from your family and to suffer loss. It is something that Alex has dealt with from a very young age. Despite rarely talking about his difficult upbringing and never using it as an excuse for his actions, his troubled past set him on this road and he simply adapted and found a way to survive, any way he could. So is it really his fault? Did he choose this life, or were the circumstances that led him to this point out of his control? Abbey can definitely relate to that notion. Her own life has spiralled so much in recent months and it has brought her here, a place she never expected to be. So who is she to judge?

It is getting increasingly difficult for her to reconcile between right and wrong these days and things aren't quite as black and white as they used to be. The world that Alex and her friends belong to has serious moral flaws which she can't deny or ignore, but they are good, caring people... just struggling, lost and a little messed up. Like her. And in the several months she has known them they have supported her far more than her real family ever have. When she hit rock bottom, the person who held her as she cried and gave her a place to stay, was Alex and she can see, unmistakably, that deep down he is a good person; conflicted and troubled, but with a strong conscience and a good heart. He will do anything for the people he cares about and now, by some miracle, that includes her.

Abbey's head is aching from a severe lack sleep and from wrestling with her mess of conflicting thoughts. The sun is beginning to rise over the city and she sneaks out onto the balcony, breathing in the cold morning air in an attempt to clear her mind. Deep down, she knows that she is exactly where she needs to be and doesn't regret her decision in the slightest, but she still can't cut herself off completely from what and who she has left behind, particularly now that there is a brand new member of the family who she has yet to meet.

Anna had text Abbey to let her know that her baby niece was born at 8:05pm weighing 6lb 11oz. She desperately wants to reply, but has no idea what to say. Even typing out a message several times without hitting send. She feels as though she has no right to share in Anna and Dom's excitement after walking away. It seems far too hypocritical. Anna of course doesn't see it that way at all and wishes more than anything that Abbey would get in touch.

"She'll come round. Just give her time…" Dom whispers softly, as he stares in awe at his baby daughter. She curls her tiny hand around his finger and he smiles in doe eyed amazement. The hospital room is quiet, apart from the constant, low beep of the monitor and the light rain tapping on the window.

"I don't know. I get that she's upset but she seemed different somehow; I'm really worried about her, Dom…"

"Have you tried calling her again?"

"I've left loads of messages but she hasn't been in touch..." Anna confesses, sadly.

"She will when she's ready. You can't force this, love. I know you want to help but she is pretty vulnerable right now and if you pressure her into coming home it might have the opposite effect..."

"Maybe... we just don't know where she's staying or anything about the people she's staying with. Doesn't that bother you?"

"Of course it does, but we have to wait for her to come to us. You've called; you've let her know that we're here for her, that's all you can do, the balls in her court now. She knows where we are when she's ready to talk..."Anna shrugs in half-hearted agreement, frustrated that her hands are tied and that she is unable to do anything more.

Despite her concern, she still can't fight the urge to smile as she watches Dom melt when their baby daughter wriggles and yawns in his arms, stretching out her fingers as she briefly opens her eyes to look at him.

"God she is so perfect..." He beams, adoringly.

"I was thinking..." Anna muses, "I was thinking, maybe it would be nice if we named her after Abbey? Her middle name I mean. She really helped me out today, and I don't know what I would have done if she hadn't been there. Plus it might make her feel a bit more included, you know?"

"I think that's a great idea babe..."

"You do?"

"Sure, I think it's a beautiful name. Amelia Abigail Murray..." He announces proudly, gazing down at her, "welcome to the world kid..."

"I wish she would call, so I can tell her…"

"She will. I promise…" Dom leans forward and places a tender kiss on Anna's forehead, but straightens quickly as the movement disturbs Amelia and she squirms uncomfortably in his arms. He paces slowly across the room and over to the window, rocking her gently as he looks out over the early morning sunrise. Anna watches her husband and new born daughter with a strong feeling of contentment, but her happiness is tainted with the underlying anxiety that is nagging away at her. Abbey has practically disappeared. Her little sister is hurt and struggling, and she has absolutely no idea what to do to or how to help her.

CHAPTER NINE

THE RAID

"In here mate…" Darren points to the entrance of an old abandoned scrap yard and Liam swings the van around; with the beam of the headlights flashing across the dark, empty space as they pull up outside a deserted building.

The atmosphere is tense and nobody speaks as Darren jumps out of the passenger side and approaches the large iron gate, unlocking the padlock and pushing it open in one swift movement. Liam drives inside and parks by the far wall of the warehouse, turning the engine off and climbing out to slide open the transit door.

Tom and Nathan leap down from the back of the van and make their way over to a huge pile of dust sheets in the opposite corner of the room. They throw them to one side, revealing a black 2005 ford Mondeo. It has tinted windows and fake licence plates, just as Darren had promised. He had met with his contact the previous night and took delivery of the car, which is to be collected again in three days' time as long as everything goes to plan.

Tom slides in, revving the engine loudly and the noise reverberates off the damp, stone walls, echoing around the warehouse. He is eager to get going - to get this over and done with as soon as possible - as the anticipation is beginning to make him edgy when he needs to be calm and completely focused.

"So you know what to do?" Alex asks, gravely.

"Sure…" Liam's answering tone is far more upbeat, "Three blasts of the horn mean all's good, we open up and help you load the van as quickly as possible…"

"We should be an hour max, if we get held up or don't make it back by half 11, wait for us at the flat…" Alex grabs a black gym bag from the driver's side foot well and slams the van door, striding purposefully over to the waiting car before throwing himself into the passenger seat. With a quick nod, Darren climbs into the back and Tom floors the accelerator as they speed off into the night.

"I really don't like this…" Nathan muses. There is nothing but silence as he and Liam stare out into the blackness, with the roar of the car engine fading into the distance.

"I know… But what else can we fucking do? How many times has Alex had our backs? How many times has he got us out of shit and put himself on the line for us? He's never asked for any help, not before now so I say he's earned it…" Liam snaps.

"I'm not saying I don't want to help him mate, I want this fucking mess sorted too, but this could go badly wrong… have you even thought about that?"

"They'll get the money…"

"Yeah, maybe… if they manage to get into the safe, past the shopkeeper and any customers that might be in there… then there's the CCTV, plus a good chance there'll be a panic button installed seen as money is kept on the premises. It isn't that simple Liam, this is seriously fucking dangerous…"

"They'll be fine…" He states again, with less certainty in his voice.

"Yeah, I fucking hope so… but they've got to get in and out of there as fast as they can. If there's even a slight complication, it could all be over in a second. Then it won't matter how much money Alex owes Marcus, because he'll be too busy serving time for armed robbery to worry about paying his debts …" Nathan lights a cigarette and climbs back into the van, winding the window partially down as he rests his foot on the dashboard in front of him. Liam follows a minute or two later and quietly starts the engine, turning the heating up and rubbing his hands together as he stares at the clock in a suddenly nervous and pensive mood.

Alex is nervous too; nervous to the point of almost backing out. He has never done anything like this before. It is completely unknown territory and he hates going in blind, not knowing what to expect. The numerous scenarios he has imagined over and over in the last week all end in a variety of different ways. The one where everything goes perfectly to plan seems the most unlikely but then he always did have a nasty habit of preparing for the worst. Regardless of his doubts, they have come this far and there is no turning back now.

Tom and Darren sit in silence, reflecting quietly on the task they are about to undertake. The shop is getting closer and Alex stares down at the black holdall in his lap, the contents of which signify an act that he has been forced into. An act that makes him question who he is.

He has never lived a straight life. Never quite walked on the right side of the track, but he isn't entirely on the wrong side either.

He tries to be a good person, despite it being a constant struggle between knowing right from wrong and fighting to survive. He needs money to live and although drug dealing isn't exactly a respectable profession, he has never really felt guilty about supplying. He has certainly never felt guilt like this before.

"We're here..." Tom snaps Alex out of his internal self- loathing and back into the present moment.

"What time are we on?" Darren asks.

"It's 10:45pm, they'll be shutting up in the next 15 minutes so we need to move fast... Al? What do you reckon?"

Alex takes a deep breath and pulls his thoughts into focus. He doesn't like being here, but it is happening now, and he just needs to get through it. He can live with regret... but he will never be weak.

"Get ready..." He unzips the holdall and throws them both a pair of gloves and a balaclava each, "We'll wait until the last possible moment. Once were inside you two cover my back and I'll go straight for the cash. I want this done fast, no hassle..."

"OK..."

"We'll be right behind you mate..." Darren reassures him.

Tom reverses the car into an alleyway directly across from the shop and turns off the headlights, leaving the keys in the ignition. The street is deserted and eerily quiet as they sit and wait, counting down the seconds. They each hold a shot gun in their hands, but only Alex's is loaded.

"They're pulling the shutters down, now's our chance…" Alex pulls the balaclava over his head and with a determined resolve, he flings open the car door and races across the road as Darren and Tom follow immediately behind.

As they reach the entrance to the shop the manager is seconds away from locking the deadbolt when Alex boots the door with all his strength. The force of the blow sends the shop keeper flying backwards and toppling into a newspaper stand which crashes to the floor on top of him. A female employee starts to scream and the young male student behind the counter eyes the alarm, calculating whether or not he can reach it.

"Don't fucking move…" Tom orders, calmly, as he cocks his gun and points it at the two of them. They both hold their hands up and the girl bursts into a hysterical fit of tears.

Darren deadbolts the door and pulls the last shutter down as Tom keeps watch; scanning the empty isles and checking for CCTV cameras while keeping the two terrified staff members in his line of sight. Alex grabs hold of the manager's arm and pulls him to his feet, shoving him forward.

"Open the till… NOW…" He shouts.

The manager stumbles slightly as he makes his way behind the counter and with shaking hands, types in the code that opens the cash register.

"Fill it up…" Alex commands as he throws an empty bag at him.

The man does as he is told as quickly as he can without protest, then hands the bag full of money back to Alex. He snatches it away and throws it over to Darren, who is still keeping watch by the door.

"Now the safe..." The man shakes his head, looking dazed and uncertain, and Alex cocks his gun, pointing it closer to his face, "Don't waste my fucking time, I know there's more... in the office... move, now..."

Without further argument the manager staggers through the door to the right of the counter and into a tiny back room. Alex follows and waits in silence, watching the man's every move as he clumsily types in a pin number on an electronic keypad and turns a dial on the front of the safe. It clicks open and Alex throws another bag at his feet.

"Fill it..." He demands.

The manager once again does as he is told, stuffing the neatly bound wads of cash into the empty holdall. Alex is running on pure adrenaline and he is elated that everything seems to be going to plan. He quickly glances over his shoulder, checking that Tom and Darren are still in position and that everything is OK on the shop floor. The woman employee has calmed down and she stands with her arms wrapped around her waist, crying quietly. The young man stands beside her, his free arm draped awkwardly over her tense shoulders and his other hand still in the air. The notion of being a hero was clearly forgotten as soon as Tom waved a shot gun in his face.

"Th... that's it. That's everything..." The manager stutters and he hands over the second, larger bag of money as his breath catches in his throat. He swallows hard, staring, wide eyed and fearful, and Alex is momentarily thrown off guard as he observes the man properly for the first time. He must be in his late 50's, quite tall but with a slim, unassuming build. The weathered name tag pinned to his shirt reads 'Bob', his grey hair is thinning at the front and there is a wedding ring on his finger. He must have someone to go home to tonight. Someone he is no doubt hoping he will get to walk out of here and see again.

The overwhelming feeling of disgust that Alex has been suppressing all week, suddenly resurfaces, stronger than ever. This man is innocent. He doesn't deserve this. All he did was come to work just like any other day, to earn an honest living and he has been threatened with his life. Threatened by Alex. This isn't who he is, this isn't what he is about, and he feels a sudden, uncontrollable urge to explain himself to Bob. To apologise for his actions and tell him that he has no other choice.

"Everything OK...?" Tom shouts, with an edge of concern in his voice.

Alex breaks away from his train of thought and slowly composes himself, trying to get back into the same cold, detached frame of mind that he was in before but he can feel his resolve slipping. 'Pull it together'.

"Move..." He commands, trying to remain as threatening as possible. He gestures back through to the shop with his gun and Bob stumbles out of the office and over to his two terrified employees.

"We good to go...?" Alex shouts over his shoulder at Darren, who is peering through the window with one hand resting on the deadbolt.

"One second..."

"Don't even think about moving, shouting, or pressing that alarm..." Tom threatens, as he marches the three of them to the back of the store and makes them face the wall with their hands on their heads.

Alex rocks back and forth impatiently as he waits for Darren to give the all clear and his inner turmoil from moments ago begins to subside as relief slowly creeps in. It is almost over; they have what they came for, now all they have to do is get back to the car and drive away.

"LET'S GO..." Darren lifts the deadbolt and kicks open the door, swinging the holdall he is carrying over his shoulder as he darts out of the shop and across the road. Tom follows just seconds later, backing away with his gun still pointed at the three cowering shop workers before he turns and runs at the very last moment.

Clutching the shotgun and the bag full of money in his right hand, Alex stops in front of the counter and trashes a large flower stand, throwing it over so that the mess blocks the path to the panic alarm. As an afterthought, he quickly grabs a bouquet of roses from the floor and sprints out across the road which is thankfully still deserted. As Tom pulls up alongside him, barely slowing down, Alex dives into the passenger seat and removes his balaclava.

"Nice flowers..." Darren comments, dryly.

"A little something for my girl..."

"We're they on offer?" Tom can barely contain the humour in his voice.

"As a matter of fact they were..." Alex smirks, and as they drive out onto the ring road further away from the scene, the tension ebbs away and all three of them burst into laughter, elated, thrilled and above all relieved that they have managed to pull it off. Alex rests his head back and closes his eyes, exhaling slowly. They did it.

The car horn beeps three times and Nathan and Liam exchange a look of surprise. They slide open the warehouse door and Tom swerves past them, parking up in the same corner of the room where the car was hidden less than an hour before.

"That was quick..." Nathan states as Alex throws him the bags of money, "Everything go OK?"

"It was almost too easy..." He smiles.

"Nate, give me a hand with this..." Nathan throws the money into the back of the van before helping Darren re-cover the car with the dust sheets. They push a few large crates and cardboard boxes in front to partially hide it from view - not that anyone will have access to the warehouse - but it is better to be safe than sorry.

"Holy shit...!" Liam exclaims, loudly. He is crouched in front of the two open bags, holding a wad of cash in each hand, "How much did you get?!"

"It's enough..." Alex states, "As soon as I get that fucker paid off the better..."

"We should get going..." Darren states and Liam tosses him the keys as Nathan jumps into the back of the van. Before Tom can join him, Alex holds his arm out and turns towards him.

"Thank you..." He nods, sincerely, and Tom grasps his shoulder supportively.

"No worries mate..."

They are quiet on the drive back to the flat, all of them reflective and lost in their own thoughts. Liam is eager to know what happened and is dying to ask but instead he keeps quiet. It is clear even to him that it isn't the right time. Alex rubs his eyes, feeling suddenly exhausted. It has been a long, draining night and he just wants to get home and back to normality. Back to Abbey. It feels like he hasn't seen her in so long and he is anxious to be alone with her again. Her innocence, along with her ability to make him feel like everything is going to be OK, is exactly what he needs right now. He smiles down at the bunch of flowers at his feet as he thinks about surprising her, but his pleasant thoughts are quickly interrupted as the image of Bob returning home to his worried wife, springs unwelcome into his mind.

"What time is it?" Abbey asks, nervously.

"About 5 minutes since you last asked…"

"How can you be so calm?!"

"I'm not calm…!" Lucy protests, her voice a little higher than usual, "But I'm trying to keep a lid on it… at least one of us is!"

"Sorry…" Abbey sighs. She stands from the sofa and starts pacing from the far wall to the balcony and back again, over and over.

"You know that rug is pretty expensive, I don't think Alex and Tom would appreciate you wearing a hole in it…"

"What's taking them so long?"

"Abs, it's only just gone midnight, I'm sure they'll be back soon…"

"I need another drink…" Abbey grabs her glass from the coffee table and makes her way to the kitchen. She opens the fridge and pulls out a bottle of wine, filling her glass to the top while battling with her shaking hands. She can barely function she is so worried and there is no way can she sit still and wait patiently like Lucy. Normally her 'what will be, will be' attitude is endearing, but it certainly isn't helping her right now.

"Any word…?" Sophie looks even paler than usual.

"No, nothing yet…" Alex had filled Abbey in on the details of the raid the night before, albeit reluctantly, as he obviously knew how much she would worry. It seemed like a relatively solid, well thought out plan at the time but now with the clock ticking away she isn't quite as convinced as she had been.

"I don't know if that's a good thing or a bad thing…" Sophie smiles, meekly.

"Me neither…"

"Gemma's been texting me every ten minutes for the last hour, she's driving me crazy…"

"You should try sitting with Lucy…" Abbey laughs, "She's in a Zen like state and it's annoying as hell!"

"She's as nervous as us; she just doesn't like to show it…" Sophie shrugs.

"God, I can't take much more of this…" Abbey pulls her phone out of her pocket and is checking it for the millionth time when the front door clicks open and the lads stride in.

"Oh thank god…" Sophie gasps, as she rushes over to Darren.

"Now then…" Liam greets them cheerfully, "God I could murder a beer!" He kisses Abbey's forehead as he moves past her to the fridge and Nathan follows, running his hands through his hair, exhaustedly.

"Lucy?"

"She's in the living room…" Abbey replies, without looking away from Alex. He is staring back at her with a slight smile playing on his lips as he saunters forward, his mask well and truly in place.

"For you…" He produces the flowers from behind his back and holds them out to her.

"Are you OK?" She whispers.

"Fine. It went fine, we're all OK…" Abbey reluctantly takes the flowers and Alex pulls her into a hug, embracing her tightly, surprised by how much he has genuinely missed her, "It's alright now, I promise,

199

it's over…" Whether it's his comforting words or the effect of being in his arms, Abbey isn't sure, but she relaxes instantly, so grateful and relieved that they are all back in one piece.

"You're squashing my roses…" She mumbles into Alex's chest and he releases her, smiling, "Thank you, they're beautiful…"

"You're welcome…" He croons, lifting her chin and tilting her head back while holding her gaze and everything else around them seems to fade into the background.

"Are we doing this now?" Tom asks, interrupting the moment.

"Yeah. Let's get it sorted…" Alex leans down and kisses Abbey tenderly, "We won't be long. We have to count up…"

"OK…" She answers quietly, unable to think of anything else to say.

Alex leaves the room and she stares blankly after him, still clutching the bouquet of flowers to her chest. The incredibly warped humour of the situation is not lost on her. Plenty of girls have flowers given to them by their boyfriends; it is a perfectly sweet gesture, it's just not usually in the early hours of the morning after he has robbed a seven-eleven at gun point. How can Abbey possibly rationalize that? It is two sides of an extremely disturbing coin.

"I should go help…" Darren gives Sophie a quick kiss and smiles apologetically, as he lets go of her hand and follows them out of the room.

"Well?" She asks, and Liam, who is sitting far too casually at the kitchen table glances up from the spliff he is rolling and frowns at Sophie.

"Well, what?"

"How did it go? Everyone seems to be in a pretty sombre mood…"

"Well, you know, no one really wanted to do the raid so they aren't exactly bouncing of the walls, but it went fine…"

"I wish people would stop saying 'fine'…" Abbey sighs.

"There's nothing else to say. Besides I wasn't there remember, all I can tell you is Nathan's shit at rock, paper, scissors…!"

Despite her worries, Abbey can't stop herself from laughing at Liam's obvious disappointment and she decides that it is probably best to let the subject go. It won't be long until everyone hears all about it anyway when it hits the local news headlines tomorrow. She shudders at the thought.

Liam and Sophie join Nathan and Lucy in the living room and Abbey absentmindedly arranges her roses in a vase, or rather a large water jug, as it is the only thing she can find that will hold them.

It isn't exactly a time consuming task but it is a brief and pleasant distraction for which she is grateful. She needs a few minutes alone and it keeps her occupied enough so that her thoughts do not drift towards the events of the evening, and the dark, disturbing reality of what is now her life.

During the next few days, avoiding that reality becomes altogether impossible. The local news keep running the same story, appealing for witnesses and for anyone with any information concerning the raid to come forward. The headlines in the local paper jump off the page and everyone breathes a sigh of relief when each article states that there are 'still no leads in the case'. Alex is tense, so tense that his cool, calm and collected nature is faltering. The money is still sitting in a black leather holdall underneath his bed and is practically burning a hole in the floor. It is the only evidence that remains linking them to the crime and he is desperate to get rid of it, but it isn't until the following Friday afternoon when he finally gets the call he has been waiting for. He answers after just one ring.

"Marcus..." His tone is clipped.

"Alex, how are you? Feeling nice and flush I hope and ready to offload some of that wealth onto me?"

"I have your money..." There is a brief pause and Alex knows that despite Marcus genuinely wanting the cash, he is disappointed. This was always about hurting him more than the actual debt itself.

"Good. I will be seeing you shortly then. 'The Dog and Bells'. One hour." And with that, he hangs up. Alex holds his face in his hands and exhales sharply, before standing up straight and marching into his bedroom with his cold, matter of fact business like demeanour firmly back in place.

He hates 'The Dog and Bells' pub. Marcus's home from home. It is where he conducts all of his dodgy dealings and is constantly occupied by his burly henchmen, none of whom have a single brain cell to share between them. Despite spending the majority of his time at the strip club Marcus never does any other business there, as it is far too much of an earner. He can't run the risk of it being brought into disrepute and shut down due to his other extra curricula activities.

'The Dog' is his unofficial office, and it is also the place where several years ago, Alex told Marcus he was done with his games and walked away. Marcus has never let it go, and there is no doubt in Alex's mind that he will get an extra little buzz today, getting one over on him in the same place that Alex embarrassed and disrespected him back in the day. Hopefully though, this chapter will soon be over for good.

The pub is exactly how Alex remembers it. In fact he is surprised by how little it has changed in all this time, with the same smoke stained paint and dark, stale carpets. Old fashioned pictures of Leeds hang in various sized frames along the walls and the large bell above the dark panelled bar is still cracked on one side.

Marcus and his cronies occupy their usual spot at the left of the room, where there are several seats, a few slot machines and a worn out pool table. He sits in the middle of a small group, with two women who are young enough to be his daughters flanking him on either side, despite his self-proclaimed 'devotion' to his wife.

"ALEX!" He smiles when he sees him, greeting him like an old friend. It is incredibly unnerving, which is exactly why he does it. A sudden hush falls across the pub as Alex drops the bag on the table in front of Marcus, without saying a word.

"So glad you could make it. Will you have a drink with us?"

"I have somewhere to be..." Alex answers through gritted teeth.

"Well that's a shame isn't it boys. I know a few of my men are keen to catch up with you, to reminisce about old times..." He laughs menacingly and the others join in on cue as his two top dogs, Gazza and Tommo, leer at him from their defensive positions at the edge of the group.

Back when Alex was part of this crowd they were the most feared of Marcus's men. Complete thugs with absolutely no remorse. They got a huge amount of pleasure from intimidating people and inflicting a serious amount of pain and by the looks of things, they haven't changed.

"It's all there..."

"I'm sure it is. But you won't mind waiting patiently while we check, will you?" On command Tommo steps forward and retrieves the bag, zipping it open and hauling out the cash. Three others join him and they flick through the notes, quickly counting it up. Alex and Marcus stare at each other in silence and the animosity between them is almost tangible. Eventually Tommo grunts and nods, confirming that the debt is paid.

"Well Alex, thank you for your cooperation. It has been a pleasure doing business with you..."

"Me and you..." Alex snarls, "We're done. This is over..."

"Your debt is paid. You won't be hearing from me again. But you know how small this city can be son, I'm sure this won't be the last we see of each other..."

Alex turns without hesitation and struts back towards the door, ignoring the angry stares and unspoken threats that are radiating off Marcus's men. They are dying to hurt him, to teach the traitor a lesson, but they are far too loyal - like dumb, obedient pit bulls – to attack without their master's command.

"I'm sure I'll see you soon, kid..." Marcus shouts after him, "I'll be seeing you again real soon..."

Alex clenches his fists tightly and concentrates on counting his steps, controlling his anger and managing to keep it together until he is outside in the cold, mist filled air. He refuses to look back, and with each step, he finally leaves Marcus and his past behind him.

Alex does his best to keep a low profile for the next few weeks, operating below radar as the heat from the raid dies down. The papers are no longer writing about the robbery and there are far more recent, newsworthy stories taking up the pages of the Yorkshire Post. It almost seems to be good to be true; but they might have actually pulled it off. He hasn't heard a thing from Marcus since he squared his debt - which he is more than happy about - and it looks like things are finally starting to settle down and return to normal. The dark cloud that has been hovering over him has finally lifted and it reminds him of the tattoo his uncle had inscribed across his chest, 'Post Nubila Sole'. Latin, for 'after the clouds, sunshine'.

Once Alex had cleared his debt with Marcus there was a fair bit of money left over from the raid and it is money that the group have absolutely no reservations about spending. Darren describes it as 'getting rid of the evidence', while Tom argues that they all deserve a big party, as there is cause for celebration now Alex is no longer under threat. He doesn't argue. They do deserve a good time after everything they have done for him. For their unwavering support and for the massive risk they took. He is more than ready to put it all behind him now and get back to business as usual... making money, living it up and having a good time with his friends.

It is almost 4am on Saturday morning and the 'few drinks down the pub' have escalated - as usual - into a full blown party that is still on-going. Abbey can hear Lucy's ridiculously loud cackle over the beat of the music and she shakes her head, smiling to herself. She has quite a presence for such a small person and the more she drinks the louder she gets. Abbey is debating whether or not she should get dressed and re-join the fun when Alex stirs in bed next to her, rubbing his eyes as he looks up from under his hair.

"Did I fall asleep?"

"You did. I didn't want to disturb you, seen as sleep is something of a novelty…" Alex props himself up on his elbow and leans over Abbey, kissing her softly on the lips.

"I see the party hasn't wound down yet …" He notes, looking at the clock.

The CD player in the front room changes track and the three second pause in between is filled with Liam and Nathan shouting insults at each other from across the room.

"Don't your neighbours ever complain…?" Abbey laughs.

"No. Not so far anyway…" He frowns, raising an eyebrow irritably as there is a loud cheer, more laughter and a round of applause from the living room.

"I was thinking about getting up…" She confesses.

"Oh really? Is there anything I can do to change your mind on that?" He smirks.

"Maybe…"

"Maybe…?" Alex rolls over and lies on top of Abbey, pinning her beneath his body as she giggles. He kisses her passionately and any urge to leave the bedroom vanishes in an instant as she grasps his hair and kisses him back with force.

"It's good to see you smiling again…" She whispers softly as they break apart to catch their breath.

"Well I have a lot to smile about..." He replies, kissing the tip of her nose, "I know things have been pretty tense lately, but it really is over now... I promise..."

"I know..." She smiles up at him, "I'm glad you're OK..."

"What about you?" Alex asks sincerely, before rolling back onto his side and resting his head on his arm.

"I'm fine..." Abbey answers, unconvincingly as she turns to face him.

"Have you spoken to your sister?"

"No."

"You should really call her, Abbey..."

"And say what?" She asks, sadly, "'How's my niece who I haven't even met yet despite the fact she's almost a month old because I'm a terrible fucking person'...?"

"You could just start with 'Hi, How are you?'..." He smiles.

"I still think it's best to keep my distance right now..."

"I get that you need space, but I see how unhappy it's making you, not talking to her. It's just a phone call..."

"It isn't that simple..." Abbey shakes her head, "If I thought that talking to my family would help the situation then I'd go and see them tomorrow, but it won't, I know it won't. They aren't going to talk to me, not properly...."

"How do you know?"

"Because they don't talk about Ryan..." She shrugs. "That's what started all this in the first place. I won't just forget about him and they refuse to acknowledge him. We just go round and round in circles and that will keep happening, until they open up..."

"You're obviously a lot stronger than they are..." He muses.

"How do you mean?"

"By acknowledging your pain and trying to work through it. Hiding from your grief instead of facing it head on is a big mistake. It builds up..."

"I know. That's exactly what happened to my Mum..."

"What is?" Alex asks, intrigued. He waits patiently for Abbey to answer, careful not to pressure her into a conversation that she doesn't want to have.

"When Ryan died, my Mum couldn't handle it..." Abbey sighs, heavily, "She had a complete emotional breakdown. She spent months in bed and would just cry for days. After a few months though, it seemed like she was improving. She was up and about, acting normal again, but it was too normal... too much the other way, you know? That's when we realised how sick she really was. She started suffering from hallucinations and she would see Ryan all the time. And not just see him, I mean she would have full blown conversations with him, like me and you are talking right now.

It was that real to her..."

"Jesus..." Alex frowns, taken aback.

"It was like her mind couldn't cope with the pain anymore, so it just shut down... blocking everything out, like none of it happened. If you tried to tell her that Ryan was gone she would fly into a rage and scream and shout, throw things... it was horrible..." Abbey shudders at the memory and closes her eyes trying to force it out of her mind, and Alex reaches up, tucking a loose strand of hair behind her ear, before brushing her cheek with the back of his hand.

"It must have been rough..." He muses, and Abbey nods.

"She's on medication now and she's doing a lot better, but nobody talks about Ryan, or even mentions his name... because they're scared it might set her off again. I guess I'm the selfish one, for wanting to remember my brother..." She shrugs again.

"I get that your Mum needed protecting... but couldn't you talk to your brother or Anna about it?" Tears spring into Abbey's eyes and Alex instantly regrets his question, as he watches the pain flash across her face. "Oh Abbey..." He wraps his free arm around her waist and pulls her closer, with their faces just inches apart as he kisses her lightly on the forehead.

"You'd think so wouldn't you? But things haven't been great between me and my family since Ryan..."

"They don't blame you?" Alex asks, unable to hide the revulsion in his voice.

"No... it's more like they blame themselves. We all do in a way, because none of us were able to help him. And it's painful for them to be reminded of that... of him..."

"And he was your twin..." The penny drops and Alex closes his eyes, shaking his head with a sad realisation as he understands what Abbey is saying.

"We were alike in so many ways. We were inseparable..." She smiles fondly, before a fresh wave of pain lances through her, "That's why they struggle to talk to me, or even be near me. It's why they distanced themselves. Because when they look at me... they see him..." Alex pulls Abbey into a comforting hug and she shakes her head again, rolling her eyes, "God I'm such a messed up tragic aren't I?!"

"You're a beautiful, messed up tragic..." He corrects her, smiling, "I wish I could help more..."

"You do..." She states, firmly, "Of course you do..."

Alex strokes Abbey's hair affectionately, before gently tilting her head back so that she meets his gaze, and his eyes burn with sincerity as he speaks.

"You're amazing, Abbey. You're so special, and it's a real shame your family don't see that. But I do. I never thought I'd feel this way about anyone..." He smiles, shyly, and Abbey rests her forehead gently against his while holding onto him tightly. He is a life raft, a safe harbour and she is beyond grateful that he is here. She is safe and warm in his arms, protected, cared for and no longer alone.

"Do you still want to join the others?" He grins and her smile returns.

"I am wide awake. But if you're still tired I can leave you to get your beauty sleep...?" She chimes, innocently, mirroring his mischievous tone.

"Are you saying I need beauty sleep Miller?"

"Of course not...!" Abbey laughs, "But if you're tired I can go..."

"I'm awake! I just need a little pick me up that's all..." Alex rolls over and slides open the top drawer of his bedside table, pulling out a brown leather CD case. He quickly unzips it and a small bag of cocaine lands on his chest as he kneels up, throwing the covers back and hooking his arm behind Abbey before pulling her down the bed. She is wearing a pair of black pants and an old, grey Beatles T-shirt, which he pushes up past her waist.

"What are you doing?!" She laughs.

"I told you I need a pick me up... just hold still... this won't hurt...!" Alex jokes, before tapping out a line of cocaine onto Abbey's stomach. She giggles hysterically as he runs his nose across her midriff, sniffing up the white powder and tickling her in the process. She wriggles beneath him as he trails kisses seductively up her body until they are face to face again.

"You do know drugs are bad for you, don't you!?" She frowns in mock disapproval and Alex rolls over onto his back, pulling her on top of him.

"You're the greatest drug..." He smirks, "I'm totally addicted..." And Abbey grins from ear to ear as they get lost together in their own little world.

CHAPTER TEN

FAMILY

"Do we have everything?" Dom asks, as he carefully surveys the hospital room.

"I think so..." Anna replies, strapping Amelia securely into her car seat, smiling down at her as she wriggles and squirms in protest, "Are you ready to go home, Amy?" She coos, "I'll be glad to see the back of this place..."

It has been a couple of weeks since the birth and the day they have been waiting for has finally arrived. They have been given the all clear, and are free to take their baby daughter home. Anna had been discharged after just a few days but due to the traumatic, premature delivery there were various complications with Amelia and she was kept in for observation until she was bigger and much stronger.

"You guys ready to go?" Peter enters the room - car keys in hand - and smiles down at his niece as Dom gently tucks a pale pink blanket around her.

"Yep, we're good..." He answers, distracted.

"I don't think we're missing anything..." Anna adds, as she glances around the room that has effectively been their home for the last fortnight, "Well..." she sighs, "I'm missing a sister but I'm pretty sure she isn't in here..."

"She hasn't been in touch. Not once..." Peter states, bluntly.

"I know... I've called and left messages, but..."

"I don't know why you're bothering Anna. She obviously doesn't care..."

"Jesus Christ, are you listening to yourself?! I mean can you actually hear what you're saying?" Anna snaps, folding her arms across her chest.

"I'll be down stairs..." Dom smiles awkwardly, picking up Amelia's car seat before making a swift exit.

"How can you of all people still be sticking up for her? She hasn't been to see you or even checked that you and Amy are OK...!" Peter argues, incensed.

"She cares, I know she does... but she is in a really bad place right now, and she needs help..."

"She needs to get over herself..."

"God, I can't believe you're being such a bastard about this..."

"Oh what so it's my fault now?" Peters gasps, "She's the one that left Anna, she's the one that walked away..."

"And why do you think she did that Pete?! Do you think that was easy for her?! Do you think it's what she really wants? She's hurting so much that she left home for god sake, she's only 18, how can you be so heartless?"

"She could have stayed and worked it out, but she didn't..."

"And you honestly think we aren't partly to blame for that?" Anna runs her hands through her hair in exasperation and leans against the hospital bed behind her. She stares at Peter and he shakes his head at the floor, unable to meet her gaze.

"She could have come to us if she needed help..." He sighs, unconvincingly.

"You know that isn't true. I've been thinking about it more and more lately..." She swallows hard, struggling with the sensitive subject, "Look, I know we lost a brother too, but it's different for us..."

"Is it? We're all in the same boat Anna, we all love Ryan..."

"Of course we do, but you know what I mean. I'm not trying to make excuses, but he was her twin, Pete, her best friend... I can't imagine how it must feel to lose that..." Anna breaks off mid-sentence, "I just think you're too hard on her sometimes..."

"Maybe you're too soft?"

"Maybe..." She smiles, sadly, "All I know is, I wasn't there for her as much as I could have been. It's just a shame it's taken something like this to make me realise that. I had Dom helping me through it, and you and Mum... well..."

"Well what?" Peter frowns, annoyed, "She needed me Anna, Christ she needed all of us..."

"So did Abbey...." Peter opens his mouth to respond, but hesitates, "When Ryan died..." Anna continues, softly, "Mum turned to you more than any of us because she was so desperate to hold on to that mother and son connection. It brought you closer, I get that... and I'm not blaming you. All I'm asking is that you try and see things from Abbey's perspective. We all had someone... she didn't. Think about how that must feel before you're so quick to judge her..."

Anna can't believe how quickly things have spiralled out of control in the last few months. Abbey has run away and they have no idea where she is. Peter refuses to accept any responsibility and Janet is getting pushed closer and closer to the brink of despair.

They used to be such a strong, loyal, loving family that supported each other no matter what. 'Maybe that's the problem' she contemplates, as she stalks out of the room with Peter following in silence a few steps behind, 'When you lose part of such a tight knit unit, the rest crumbles under the strain'. Despite everything, Anna knows in her heart that Abbey is far from a lost cause. Wherever she is, she must still be struggling with her grief as well as her conscience. If only she would get in touch so that Anna can talk to her properly and tell her that although it might not seem like it now, in time, everything will be alright.

Abbey scrolls through the numbers in her phone and taps on Anna's name in the contacts list. She pauses for a moment, with her thumb hovering over the 'Call' option, before cancelling and locking the screen. 'Maybe tomorrow...' she thinks, knowing full well that she will only follow the same routine again. She has been trying to build up the courage to phone home for months now, but she never quite manages to connect the call before talking herself out of it.

The door to the en suite opens and Alex smiles as he saunters into the bedroom, assessing Abbey's appearance as he fastens his watch.

"You look beautiful..."

"Thank you..." She smiles, shyly. He still has the overwhelming ability to make her feel like a giddy school girl, especially when he is standing in front of her looking so incredibly attractive. His hair is slicked back and styled to perfection, there is a few days' worth of stubble covering his jaw line and his magnetic eyes are as piercing as ever. He's wearing his dark blue Levi's that hang perfectly on his hips, a thin, grey V neck jumper and his black leather jacket.

Abbey drinks him in as he crosses the room towards her and wraps his arms around her waist. He bends his knees slightly so that he is level with her eye line, and she responds by locking her arms around his neck, her heart pounding a thousand beats per second.

"What are you thinking about?" He asks, amused.

"I was actually thinking about how hot my boyfriend is, if you must know!"

"Right back at you, Miller..." Alex smiles, as he nuzzles Abbey's neck and she inhales the crisp scent of his aftershave.

"Oi, you two ready?!" Tom bangs against the bedroom door as he shouts from the hallway and Alex rolls his eyes. He kisses Abbey deeply on the lips, before taking her hand and leading her into the kitchen.

"Wow, you look sexy lady!" Lucy winks as she dances over and hands Abbey a glass of champagne.

The brand new dress that Alex had bought for her certainly makes her feel that way. It is a dark gold, halter neck number that sits just above her knees. It has a delicate gold chain that fastens behind her neck and hangs down the middle of her back and the silky fabric hugs her every curve. She fell in love with it instantly, but completely dismissed the idea of buying it due to the £380 price tag. She argued with Alex all the way to the check-out but he wouldn't listen, insisting that he should be allowed to treat her if he wants. The girl behind the desk who served them had practically turned green with envy, not at the ludicrously expensive slip of clothing, but at the insanely gorgeous Irish man purchasing it.

Wearing the dress knowing that he bought it especially for her makes Abbey feel like a million dollars. In fact, they all scrub up quite well. Usually the weekends consist of a few casual drinks at the pub or the bars on Call Lane, before heading back to the comfort of the flat to party into the early hours of the morning. They rarely go clubbing, as it is busy, expensive and difficult to indulge in their favourites pass time of habitual drug taking.

Abbey has become just as involved in the hard partying lifestyle as the others these days, and all the doubts and worries she had held firmly in her mind when they first met are now well and truly forgotten. It's as if those opinions and morals belonged to a completely different person.

Cocaine is definitely the group drug of choice and Abbey loves how it keeps her awake and alert for hours on end. She really does gain a sense of escapism when she takes it. She feels happy, relaxed and confident, and is able to drink through the night and have a good time, laughing and joking with her friends. Her eyes have been well and truly opened and she has experienced everything from marijuana and cocaine to ecstasy and LSD, although the latter two are far from on a regular basis. It is all part of her new 'live for the moment' attitude, as well as being a vague attempt to switch off, escape her past and forget about all the drama that she has left behind.

Tonight they are celebrating Gemma's birthday, heading out to the opposite end of Leeds for a change and to a huge nightclub called Labyrinth. It is apparently quite popular with the student crowd and is one of the many establishments that Alex deals at regularly. It has a well-known reputation for drugs and illegal all night raves, but is still quite exclusive, hence the smarter dress code that everyone has adopted for the evening.

"Raise your glasses please ladies and gents..." Tom announces at the top of his voice, "To Gem... happy birthday old girl, let's make this a night you'd rather forget!" He laughs, and Gemma nods eagerly in agreement as they hold their drinks aloft. Liam's phone vibrates in his pocket and he swipes the screen to reveal a missed call.

"Taxi's here...!"

"Let's go, let's go!" Darren claps his hands enthusiastically as they all rush around the kitchen, downing their drinks, grabbing their bags and wallets and throwing on their coats. They stagger out of the door one after another and Alex locks up before racing after them down the corridor. He dives into the elevator that Nathan is holding open for him, rugby tackling Tom in the process.

There is an excited buzz in the air and Abbey can already tell that it is going to be a good night. Plenty of alcohol has already been drunk and a fair bit of cocaine shared between them, and she feels tipsy and content, sitting in the back of the taxi listening to the animated conversations and friendly banter around her.

When the minibus pulls up at the entrance to the club Alex pays the driver and slides the door open, stepping down and holding his hand out to Abbey. As she reaches forward Darren grabs hold of it before she has chance and climbs out, pulling Alex into a hug.

"Oh you're such a gentleman..." He flutters his eye lashes and Alex shoves him playfully, laughing as he pulls Abbey into his arms. Gemma and Sophie walk hand in hand, as Lucy and Nathan follow behind, completely engrossed in one another as usual. Liam dives onto Tom's shoulders and he piggy backs him up to the door, passing the thirty or so people in the queue without so much as a glance in their direction.

The large, imposing bouncer standing by the entrance turns and assesses them with caution, instantly breaking into a smile as he sees Alex approach.

"Now then mate, long time no see..." He tilts his head in acknowledgement and Alex shakes his hand.

"How's it going man?"

"Not bad at all. Are you on call tonight?" The bouncer winks, knowingly.

"Nah, I'm taking the night off, out celebrating a birthday..."

"Nice one, have a beer for me yeah?" He turns and shouts to the girl at the cloakroom door, "Tasha... this lot are VIP..."

"OK..." She nods, smiling a little too sweetly at Alex as he leads the way into the club, slapping hands with the bouncer again as he passes. She looks him up and down from head to toe, before her eyes linger seductively on his face and Abbey raises a single eyebrow, willing the girl to look at her, but she doesn't notice her 'hands off bitch' facial expression. At least Alex doesn't seem to notice either, paying absolutely no attention to her obvious advances as he grips tightly onto Abbey's hand and guides her down the spiral staircase.

The club is large and spacious, almost cavernous. It has dark, midnight blue walls and a mirrored glass ceiling, with a huge, fancy looking chandelier hanging high above. The staircase leads into an area that is occupied with a couple of sofas and a cigarette machine. There is a queue on the right hand side of the room that leads to the toilets and straight ahead are three doors, spaced out equally. One has 'R&B' lit up in neon pink above it, the other reads 'Chart' and the third door in the centre says 'Main'.

Alex glances over his shoulder to check that everyone is inside, before pushing his way through the door and into a tunnel like passage with flashing strobe lights. The beat of the music sends dull vibrations through Abbeys chest and she can hear the DJ announce the next track before a heavy bass line kicks in. There are people standing around talking with drinks in hand, and others walking back out of the room towards the exit. More than a few girls look Alex up and down, eyeing him appreciatively, and he nods at a handful of men that greet him as they pass, no doubt some of his clients who he supplies to on the nights he is working.

When they reach the end of the tunnel there is another heavy door which opens up into a massive, circular room. There are two bars - one to the right and one to the left - which have a number of tables and booths situated in front of them. The dance floor is lowered into the ground, and they walk down a handful of steps from the platform level, weaving through the hordes of people dancing around them. Another huge crystal chandelier hangs above the dance floor which again has a mirrored ceiling, and at the very far end, raised up high, is the rather impressive DJ booth with all manner of speakers and lights surrounding it. To the right of the DJ is another set of stairs - slightly higher this time - that lead up and behind the booth towards the back of the club with a small balcony overlooking the dance floor. As they get closer, Abbey notices another bouncer standing at the foot of the stairs and behind him are two posts with a sign hanging between that reads 'VIP' in bold letters. 'Of course' Abbey smiles to herself.

Alex glides through the club like he owns it and people move out of his way without question, staring at him as he heads straight over to the VIP lounge with complete, self-assured confidence.

Every now and then he looks back at Abbey while squeezing her hand tightly, and her stomach flips and her heart lurches as she struggles to believe that this unbelievably desirable man is all hers.

Alex greets the bouncer, but it is a short exchange as the music is far too loud for conversation. On the level behind the DJ booth there is another bar and a smaller seating area. The music is a little quieter back here, but not much. Alex stops in front of the largest booth and gestures for Abbey to sit.

"What do you want babe?"

"Vodka and coke please..." She shouts in his ear and he winks before making his way over to the bar, with Darren, Tom, Nathan and Liam. Gemma grabs the cocktail menu and discusses the options with Lucy, while Sophie practically bounces in her seat.

"I love this song!" She yells, excitedly, "I can't wait to dance!"

Abbey laughs at her enthusiasm and glances over to the bar where the boys are stood waiting for their order. Alex is watching her closely, with a warm smile on his face, and her heart drops through her chest as she catches his eye. All it takes is one look and she turns away, blushing shyly.

It's no wonder he gets so much female attention wherever he goes. Tom, Darren, Liam and Nathan are all incredibly attractive in their own way, but standing there, lit up under the blue and white strobe lights, Alex looks like an Adonis. Or maybe she is just biased? She smiles to herself as she remembers the first time she laid eyes on him in the doorway of the flat. It was like her whole world had dropped through the floor and the attraction she felt struck her like a lightning bolt out of the blue. It's crazy how much things have changed since then. She never would have believed in her wildest dreams that things would turn out like they have and that she would come to know him so well.

To the casual observer on the outside looking in, Alex is coolness personified. Calm, focused, controlled and in charge... he has a dark, mysterious edge to him and a gravitational pull that makes people - men and women alike - want to be near him. But he is so much more than that. Ever since he has let his guard down with Abbey, she has seen the other side of his personality. How sweet and kind he can be. How loving and loyal. He has become so incredibly important to her in the time she has known him. She has fallen, hard, and her feelings are getting deeper by the day. He isn't perfect and the life he leads can sometimes be frightening, but she is no longer the perfect, straight 'A' student she used to be either. Not since Ryan died and her world became a whole lot darker. She was lost for a long time before she found Lucy, Alex and the others, but now she is finally starting to live her life again - albeit a totally different life than before.

The vibe and energy in the club is amazing. The room is absolutely packed and the DJ is really working the crowd. The group have spent the majority of the night in the VIP lounge, with the girls - and Liam -making the occasional trip to the dance floor. Although it is busy the drinks flow freely all night due to the standard special treatment that Alex receives from his friends in high places. There are plenty of trips to the conveniently placed VIP bathrooms for regular 'pick me ups', and as they are out for a messy night, it is more than cocaine being taken.

Abbey has only tried ecstasy once before and she had been in the relative safety of the flat at the time. She loved the rush of happiness and love she felt as the effects kicked in and she couldn't remember ever experiencing such intense and blissful feelings. The hours that followed felt like floating along in a dream and nothing bad or hurtful could touch her. The aftermath, however, was the complete and total opposite. She had come back down to earth hard and was pulled into a deep depression that lasted for almost an entire day. The hollowness she felt had truly scared her and she is unsure if she wants to experience that sensation again.

"Do you trust me?" Alex purrs. He is drunk and high, like Abbey, and he strokes her back gently as she sits beside him in the booth with her legs across his lap.

"Yes..." She whispers.

"Then you have nothing to worry about. I won't let anything happen to you I promise. But it is a totally different feeling, dropping a pill in a place like this... I want to dance in the clouds with you Abbey..." He laughs, playfully. It is so difficult to refuse him when he is being happy, carefree Alex. And the truth is Abbey does trust him... completely.

He reaches into the pocket of his jeans and partially pulls out a small plastic bag. He takes a tiny pink pill between his fingers, pops it into his mouth and swallows, before placing another on the very tip of his tongue. He smirks at Abbey seductively, pulling her forward into a lingering kiss, and as her tongue curls around his, the pill passes into her mouth. She swallows, then reaches for her glass and takes a sip of wine.

Alex waits patiently while she drinks before he leans in to kiss her again. After another minute he stops abruptly and breaks away, feeling a presence beside him. Lucy is staring at them, swaying slightly in her inebriated state. Her arms are folded stiffly across her chest and she has one eyebrow raised while trying to fight the ever constant smile on her face.

"You said 5 minutes..." She moans like a sulky little kid, and Abbey can't keep from laughing. Alex smirks too and releases his arms from around Abbey's waist, leaning back in his seat.

"OK, I'll be right there..."

"You said that last time!" Lucy stamps her foot, "Come on Miller, the dance floor's packed and he's playing some right tunes!" Abbey sighs and kisses Alex lightly on the lips before swinging her legs round and reluctantly standing up. She too sways a little from the head rush and Alex reaches for her, but before he can help Lucy grabs her by the hand and pulls her forward.

"Time to dance!" She shrieks, and Abbey turns and shrugs at Alex apologetically.

"Be careful..." He orders, as he watches Lucy drag her away with a look of irritated fondness on his face.

As Abbey descends the stairs towards the heaving, red hot dance floor she sees Alex join Tom and Nathan at the bar before she loses sight of him through the crowd. Darren and Sophie are dancing sweetly together and Liam is throwing himself about a little too energetically, although he can really move. Gemma is off in a world of her own, dancing in the middle of a circle of guys who can't seem to prise their eyes away from her. 'Who can blame them' Abbey muses, she is absolutely stunning after all, and is moving her incredible figure perfectly in time to the music.

Abbey stares, wishing that she had Gemma's unshakable confidence, but as Lucy grins at her encouragingly she starts to move to the music anyway... twisting and swaying with the people around her as she starts to lose herself to the beat.

The same exhilarating rush that she felt the last time she dropped a pill slowly begins to surface and the effect of the ecstasy totally consumes her. Her body feels light, like it is made of air, and there is a deliciously warm tingle running from the top of her neck all the way down to the base of her spine.

She shuts her eyes dreamily and runs her hands over her shoulders, still dancing as she relishes the delirious high. As she opens her eyes everything around her blurs and all she can hear is the pounding beat of the music and the sound of her own breath in her ears.

She loves this. Loves her friends, loves Alex, loves life. Everything is beautiful, shining, and nothing else matters other than right here right now, getting lost in this song. Alex was right... this is a totally different feeling. It is mind blowing. She lifts her hands and twists them above her head, smiling over at Lucy who is also lost in the moment. The multi coloured strobe lights suddenly take on a life of their own and they twist and dance around her like fireflies, sparkling red, orange, blue and green. She looks up and sees the reflection of the crowd in the mirrored ceiling and it's like she is looking down on everyone, as she dances high up in the sky... dancing in the clouds.

As her scattered thoughts instinctively turn to Alex, he suddenly appears behind her right on cue. His arms snake sensually around her waist and she turns in slow motion to meet his gaze. He moves with her, both of them grinding together in time to the music as they are encased in a bright, rainbow coloured bubble. The lights continue to swarm and dance around them, completely cutting them off from everyone and everything else as their lips meet. Abbey is in a dream - a perfect dream - and she never, ever wants to wake up.

There is a high pitched ringing sensation in her ears and Abbey blinks, disorientated, as she opens her eyes very slowly. All she can see in her vision is a white light shining down on her. It takes a moment for her to adjust to the brightness before she realises she is home, at the flat, in bed. She turns over to see if Alex is lying next to her but she is alone and as she sits up gingerly, a sharp, searing pain shoots through her head.

Her hangover is brutal. It always seems to be much worse when she has dropped the night before, which is perhaps another reason to refrain from doing it again? The memories of last night slowly creep into her mind and she remembers the thrill, the absolute high that she felt, and she knows that no matter how much she is suffering now, it was worth it.

Abbey stretches across the bed and turns Alex's alarm clock towards her, gasping at the time. 1:30pm. She had no idea it was that late in the day. After 15 minutes in the bathroom trying to wake herself up so that she no longer resembles an extra from 'night of the living dead', she wraps herself in one of Alex's zip up tops and ventures into the living room.

Lucy is curled up on the smaller sofa with her legs draped over Nathan. Gemma and Sophie are sitting opposite with their feet on the coffee table, sipping from large mugs of black coffee, and Darren is laid on his back with his eyes shut, his head resting in Sophie's lap.

"Morning..." Abbey smiles in amusement. Clearly they are all feeling just as dreadful as she is and they look up and smile with little enthusiasm, mumbling incoherently in some form of greeting. There is a cough and a moan from behind her and she turns to see Liam sprawled out on the floor, face down next to the sound system.

Abbey taps Darren on the side and he wearily lifts his legs up. She drops onto the sofa as he lowers his feet back into her lap and she glances over towards the balcony at Alex, who is standing in the doorway looking out over the city. He exhales the smoke from his cigarette and winks at Abbey, smiling sweetly. Her hangover disappears for a moment as she remembers last night at the club and more importantly what happened when they got home. She fights the butterflies in her stomach as she smiles back, knowingly.

"Somebody make the pain go away..." Nathan moans, tilting his head back and rubbing his eyes.

"There, there..." Lucy mumbles, dryly, as she reaches up and pats him on the head.

"Thanks..." He smirks, as he kisses her lovingly, and Liam suddenly pushes himself up off the floor and staggers into the sofa, pausing for a moment while he waits for the dizziness to pass. His face is creased and wrinkled from where he has been leaning on his coat.

"Oh and he's alive..." Nathan laughs.

"Fuck me what did I drink last night?!"

"What didn't you drink last night would probably be an easier question to answer!" Gemma giggles.

"I have a vague memory of getting that barmaid to make us our own brand of cocktail...!" Darren reminds him, shaking his head.

"Shit yeah, she was fit..."

"Was she now?!" Sophie muses, as she stops running her hands through Darren's hair.

"I was only acting as wing man babe..." Darren explains, "He needed all the help he could get, trust me..."

"Whatever, she wanted me..." Liam sniffs, as he walks over to join Alex on the balcony. He lights up a cigarette and starts mindlessly tapping a football about. As they all wallow in the pain of their hangovers, Tom staggers in wearing just his boxer shorts and looking rougher than anyone.

"Morning sunshine...!" Alex laughs.

"Fucking hell I feel like shit..." His voice is gruff with sleep and he clears his throat.

"You look like shit..." Alex confirms, smiling.

"What the fuck went on last night?" He asks, half amused, half perplexed, "I had to let some bird out at about half 7 this morning I don't even remember bringing her home!" The others laugh at Tom's obvious confusion and Gemma rolls her eyes at him as he drops onto the sofa beside her, completely lacking in energy.

"What bird?!" Lucy asks, intrigued.

"That blonde lass who was working behind the bar last night...!"

"Oh you fucker!" Liam shouts, and the others burst into hysterical laughter, "I put a lot of time and energy into pulling her, she was having none of it..."

"What can I say mate, she obviously has taste!" Tom smirks.

"And she probably caught sight of your dance moves...!" Abbey quips at Liam, causing the others to howl with laughter again.

"Gutted..." He jokes, holding his head in his hands in mock despair.

There is a brief silence as another wave of tiredness and nausea hits the group and Abbey promises herself she will never drink so much again.

"It's a well nice day today, man..." Liam announces, as he kicks the football up into his hands and leans on the door frame opposite Alex, "we should do something, instead of being stuck inside the flat all day..."

"Stuck inside the flat...?" Alex repeats the words back to him, "Jesus Christ I'm not keeping you all fucking hostage you know, I mean you can go home...!"

Liam laughs but ignores Alex's comment, as he knows, just like everyone else does, that he would never ask any of them to leave. This is their home.

"Like what?" Darren yawns.

"I dunno... a kick about maybe?" The lads scoff at the idea as the girls groan in unison at the mere mention of football.

"What would we do?" Sophie asks.

"Sunbathe..."

"I'm actually liking this plan..." Lucy raises her hand in agreement.

"You're having a fucking laugh aren't you?" Tom groans.

"You'll feel better for it man, trust me! When I played Sunday league I was always battered from the night before, but after a game I felt fine..."

"You played Sunday league?!" Alex tries to hide the amusement in his voice as he frowns at Liam.

"Yeah, but he was pretty shit..." Nathan jokes.

"Was I fuck! I'd run rings around the pair of you..."

"I doubt it..."

"Sounds like a challenge to me Matthews..." Liam grins, goading him.

"Alright you're on...!" He nods.

"Oh what? You're kidding? I can't play football in this fucking state..." Tom drops his head into Gemma's lap, "I'm rough as a bears arse! Which knobhead bought that bottle of Tequila last night?!"

"That'd be you, mate..." Alex laughs, "Don't worry, you can go in goal..." And Tom hangs his arms dramatically across his face, shaking his head at the thought as he pretends to cry.

It is easily the nicest day of the year so far. There isn't a single cloud in the sky and it is hot, really hot. The park is full of families sharing picnics, children riding bikes and teenagers impressing each other with tricks on their skateboards. There is a queue about a mile long at the ice cream van parked by the entrance and the café is heaving. All the tables outside are occupied and Abbey stares over at the arcade, smiling to herself. That's where it all began, the first day she skipped class with Lucy, Nathan and Liam.

It is completely empty at the moment; all the games flash brightly but stand unoccupied as the weather is far too nice to be indoors. Abbey lies back on the grass, feeling grateful towards Liam for having this idea. The mid-afternoon sun warms her to the bones and it feels relaxing and comforting. The pain of this morning is slowly ebbing away as she dozes next to Gemma, who has rolled her t-shirt up above her waist. Sophie sits cross legged beside them in the shade from a nearby tree, shielding her fair skin from the harsh rays, and Lucy is lying on her stomach reading one of her magazines.

"Come on Tom, pick it up...!" Nathan laughs.

They have been playing football for almost an hour now with the occasional break in between. Abbey is uncertain who is winning, she only knows that Alex and Nathan are playing against Darren and Liam, and Tom seems to be on his own in goal. He has thrown up twice already, but is still standing... for now.

The heat had become too much almost instantly and after about 10 minutes, they had all removed their tops. Not that Abbey is paying any attention to the others; but she is certainly enjoying the game more than she expected to thanks to the view from the side lines of Alex running gracefully, with his muscles flexing and sweat glistening on his body. Sitting with her girls on a large picnic blanket, with food and drink and good music on the radio, while watching the boys battle it out on the pitch? She seriously couldn't be more perfectly content if she tried.

There has been quite a lot of play fighting and a fair few disagreements so far, mainly between Liam and Alex, and the banter is off the scale. 'Boys and their competitiveness' she sighs, fondly. There is a loud cheer from Nathan as he scores a goal and Tom leans forward on his knees, coughing and spitting onto the ground in front of him.

"At least you can use your hangover as a reason for being so shit!" Liam laughs.

"He might be shocking in goal Dobson, but we're still kicking your arse..."

"Don't be getting cocky Ireland. It's not over 'til the fat bird sings...!"

The girls laugh as they watch Liam and Alex break out into a play fight in the middle of the field and Tom uses the distraction to rest for a moment, sitting down and leaning forward on his knees.

"Still with us mate?" Sophie shouts over, and he waves half-heartedly while taking deep, steadying breaths.

"Yeah... fine...! Just gonna go find a fat lass... ask her to sing..." He pants, shaking his head with absolute exhaustion as he collapses onto his back with his arms outstretched.

One thing Abbey can't fault about living up North, are the sunsets. The sky over Leeds is painted a beautiful, deep pink with streaks of orange and red illuminating the delicate whispers of cloud. It is late evening but still pleasantly warm, and she closes her eyes as the gentle breeze swirls around her. She loves this time of day - particularly at this time of year - and the view from the flat balcony is breath taking.

Alex places two glasses of red wine on the outdoor table and wraps his arms around Abbey's waist, resting his chin on her shoulder.

"Wow..." He states, taking in the scenery.

"I know. It's hard to believe there isn't more beyond this life, when you see something like that..." She contemplates, out loud. Alex stares at her thoughtfully and she turns to face him, feeling a little embarrassed by her deep and meaningful insight, but he smiles and nods in agreement.

"I certainly hope there's more..." He whispers thoughtfully, "Although I can't think of anywhere I'd rather be than right her, right now..."

"Well, that makes two of us..." Abbey leans forward and as their lips touch, Alex reaches up into her hair, pulling her body tightly against his with a longing intensity. The others, for once, have actually gone home and they are completely alone. Apart from Tom, who is currently comatose in his bedroom, snoring so loudly that the walls are vibrating. It has been a long day. One filled with fun and laughter, completely trouble free, relaxing in the park in the glorious sunshine without a care in the world. It is exactly how it should be for people their age.

Alex begins to laugh as he grudgingly breaks away from Abbey, moving inside and switching on the sound system so that it drowns out Tom's rhythmic snores. He turns up the volume and the soft acoustic melody of Damien Rice starts to play.

"That's better..." He laughs again, "It's a good job I don't need much sleep, living with him all these years would have driven me fucking crazy!"

"He's had a rough day..." Abbey jokes, "Being monstrously hung over and having a football repeatedly kicked in my face, isn't exactly my idea of fun either...!"

"Oh? And what is your idea of fun?!" Alex smiles mischievously, tracing his thumb across Abbey's bottom lip.

"These days...? Anything that involves you..." She answers without thinking, and his expression softens.

"You really feel that way?" He asks, surprised.

"Why wouldn't I?"

"I'm not exactly a catch am I? Teenage runaway, hooligan, criminal..." He shrugs, sadly, "You could do better..."

"That isn't who you are... " She frowns, "Besides, I'm messed up too in case you hadn't noticed! Who isn't...?"

"You're anything but messed up, Abbey. You're beautiful..." He rests his forehead lightly against hers, "and you make me want to be better..."

Alex's whispered confession warms Abbey from the inside out and she smiles as he tilts her chin up to look at him. Without another word, he steps forward and gently places his right hand in her left while sliding his free arm around her waist and they begin to dance, slowly and sweetly from side to side as the sunset lights up the city behind them.

Alex never breaks eye contact and Abbey can see the self-doubt and insecurity that he manages to keep so well hidden play out across his face. He looks so vulnerable, and his guard is completely down as he slows to a stop and they stare at each other for the longest moment.

"I love you..." He whispers with a pained expression and Abbey's breath catches in her throat, "You are the bravest, strongest, most giving person I've ever met. And I'm in love with you...." Her head starts to spin as she stares up into Alex's wide eyed expression, trying to grasp what he has just said. She struggles to find the right words and before she can answer, he speaks again,

"And I'm no good for you. I know I'm no good for you. You deserve more than this, something normal, something safe... more than what I have. But you really do make me want to be a better person, Abbey. You make me want to try and I've never had that before. I feel like you know me... and I... I just..."

Abbey reaches up and holds Alex's head firmly between her hands, forcing him to stop talking and look at her. She doesn't know whether to laugh or cry at his sweet and increasingly insecure outburst but she finally manages to compose herself as she stares deeply into his beautiful eyes with a burning sincerity.

"I love you too..." She whispers.

CHAPTER ELEVEN

CONSEQUENCES

"I understand your frustrations Mrs Miller, but I'm afraid our hands are tied..." The young male police officer perched timidly on the edge of the sofa, clears his throat and shifts uncomfortably in his seat. The young female officer sitting next to him appears slightly less awkward but the overly sympathetic smile on her face is starting to get on Janet's nerves. She places her cup of tea on the coffee table and folds her hands in her lap.

"I know this must be hard..." She smiles, "And that you must be worried. But your daughter appears to be alright and if she is safe by her own admission, I'm afraid we can't force her to return home..."

"I don't know that she's safe. I don't know that she's alright..." Janet snaps, "I don't even know where the hell she is, my own daughter!" Her patience is crumbling fast and all the frustration she has felt during the last six months is threatening to boil over. She is finding it difficult to keep her temper under control and the two officers from West Yorkshire Police who are trying their best to help and reassure her, are currently in her firing line.

Janet blames herself for not going to the authorities sooner and bringing this situation under control. It has gotten so far out of hand and she is genuinely scared that her relationship with Abbey may be damaged beyond repair. She had thought it best to give her the time she claimed she so desperately needed. To let the dust settle and create space between them, in order to give them both a fresh perspective so they can calm down and reassess. But it has been months now, with no progress and no change. Janet, Anna and Peter have all tried in vain to get her to come home. They have asked her repeatedly to stop by the house, so that they can sit down and talk out their differences as a family and hopefully put all of this behind them. But Abbey is hesitant. She is unsure and obviously frightened and Janet feels that she may have underestimated just how much her daughter is suffering. Now it may be too late to fix what is broken, and the thought is truly heart-breaking.

She had called the police out of sheer desperation more than anything else. Hoping that they could find Abbey and convince her that running away and turning her back on her family won't achieve or resolve anything. But here they are, sitting in her living room, politely drinking tea and explaining in a somewhat patronising way, that nothing can be done.

"She is 18 years of age, ma'am, which, although still young, technically makes her an adult and deemed mature enough to make her own decisions..." The male officer speaks again, with a little more authority.

"She's just a child and she's lost. Why won't you help her?" Janet's voice begins to crack under the strain and Anna, who has sat relatively quiet throughout the whole exchange, reaches over and squeezes her hand reassuringly.

"Is there anything you can do?" She pleads, "I just want to know that my sister is OK..."

"We can run her name through the database and flag it on the system. That way if anything comes up we will be alerted straight away, but beyond that I'm afraid we just have to be patient..."

"We understand..." Anna nods, "It's just difficult, the not knowing. This is so out of character for her..."

"I appreciate how concerned you are..." The female officer smiles kindly again, "But as she is over 18, coupled with the fact that she has been in touch since she left home... we can't file this as a missing persons report..."

"We've only had the odd text message..." Janet gasps. "That's it. Anyone can send a text message, someone could have her phone, she could be in danger and you're just sitting here...!"

"Mum... it's OK..." Janet clasps her head in her hands, trembling with anger and crippled by an overwhelming feeling of uselessness, "We saw her at the hospital remember? And she was alright... she's with friends, still in Leeds, I'm sure of it..." Anna croons, softly.

"She should be at home with us..."

"I know..."

"If we hear anything at all, we'll be in touch..." The male officer seems slightly out of his depth and even more uncomfortable since Janet's emotional outburst. 'It can't be easy for them' Anna thinks, 'They are just as helpless as we are'.

"We'll see ourselves out..." They both stand and Anna extends her hand to them before they turn and walk respectfully out of the living room. She sits back down next to Janet and wraps her arms around her, rocking her gently back and forth as the front door clicks shut only to burst open again a few moments later as Peter charges in.

"Oh god, what? What's happened?" He asks, with rising panic in his voice.

"Nothing... everything's fine..." Anna responds calmly, holding her hand up in order to placate him.

"Then what the hell were the police doing here?"

"I called them..." Janet sniffs, "And what a huge waste of time that was..." She stands and collects the empty mugs from the table, before moving wearily into the kitchen.

"Why didn't you tell me this was happening?!" Peter whispers.

"I didn't know, I came to check on Mum and they just turned up..."

"And...?"

"And nothing..." Anna shrugs, "Mum's right it was a complete waste of time. They won't do anything. They won't look for her. Abbey hasn't gone missing she left of her own accord and she is completely entitled to do so... apparently... despite how messed up she is..."

"I'm not sure getting the police involved is the best idea anyway..." Peter muses.

"No... I agree. Abbey might see it as a negative thing, like we're trying to get her in trouble or something..."

"How is she?" He asks, tilting his head towards the door.

"Not great. She's only going to get worse the longer this goes on but what else can we do?"

"I don't know..."

The prospect of Janet having a relapse is a frightening one. Her mental health suffered so much after they lost Ryan and both Peter and Anna are concerned that the added strain placed on her recently could push her to the brink again. It is still an uphill battle; every day is a struggle and only the love and support of her family combined with the medication she is on, will keep her from retreating back into that dark place in her mind.

Lying awake at night, worrying about Abbey and where she is definitely isn't helping her fragile state. It isn't helping any of them. Like Janet, they all believed that this would be a temporary problem. That Abbey would cool off and be home within a week, with her tail between her legs. None of them ever imagined that it would go on for as long as it has.

Anna is becoming increasingly worried and even the anger that Peter had felt towards Abbey and her rebellious behaviour has faltered, replaced instead with a constant anxiety and a steady unease which suggests things are only going to get worse. Abbey is gone and it is starting to seem less and less likely that she will come back. She could be in trouble and they have no way of knowing, no way of contacting her, other than the endless calls and messages to her mobile that go unanswered. They are desperate to help her; to bring her home and get all of this resolved, but it is a feat which seems virtually impossible as they have absolutely no idea where she is.

Abbey takes another sip of red wine, savouring the smooth texture and the beautifully rich taste as she swallows. It is absolutely delicious, and should be, considering the price. As the waiter skilfully clears away her plate she stares across the table at Alex who is smirking at her in that seductive way she loves. It is obvious from his expression that he has more than food on his mind.

"Would you like to see the dessert menu?" The waiter looks at them both, curiously.

"Please..." Abbey smiles in response.

He nods and promptly turns on his heel before striding towards the kitchen, but half way across the restaurant he glances back over his shoulder, frowning at them suspiciously. Abbey would usually take offense at such rude behaviour but she can't really blame him - or anyone else in the restaurant - for their highly transparent curiosity. They don't exactly blend in with the usual clientele of this high end establishment.

They are dining in the extremely opulent 'Il Gusto Elegante', the most exclusive restaurant in Leeds. Stepping through the doors is like stepping back in time to the glamorous 1920's era, with light, art deco style walls and beautiful, luxurious furnishings. Each impeccably laid table displays a stunning candelabra, all of which are lit to create a subtle, romantic mood. A string quartet and a grand piano are situated on a high platform at the far end of the dining area and a mixture of old and modern songs are being played by the house band. It is beautiful, lavish and incredibly expensive.

As the majority of the diners are dressed in their best suits and cocktail gowns, it is no wonder Abbey and Alex are garnering so much attention. Abbey is wearing an off the shoulder, dark green top with black skinny jeans and ankle boots. Had Alex told her how posh this restaurant actually is, she would have at the very least worn a dress.

She feels out of place and incredibly self-conscious and has done since the moment they sat down. Alex on the other hand, is portraying his usual cool, calm and collected demeanour, seemingly unfazed by the ignorant stares and whispers resonating from the other patrons. In fact if Abbey didn't know any better she would say he is enjoying it, leaning back in his chair and casually resting a full glass of wine on his leg. He is wearing his faded blue Levi's, a black shirt and his black leather jacket, which isn't exactly in line with the dress code. He looks like a real bad boy from the wrong side of the tracks - which is exactly what he is - and his cocky arrogance is taunting the 'well to do', upper class snobs around him to no end. Abbey smiles at him, shaking her head slightly, and Alex's mouth twitches up into a sly smile. He knows.

"Here you are..." The waiter passes them both a dessert menu, hovering for a brief moment, before turning his attention to another table nearby.

"So what will it be?" Alex asks, unaffected.

"I don't know, I'm pretty full..." The starter and main course weren't exactly generous in portion size but they were absolutely delicious and surprisingly filling. The Michelin starred gourmet cuisine is like nothing Abbey has ever tasted and she is reluctant to miss out on a third course, but Alex is paying, which she feels guilty about.

"If you want one get one..." He smiles, taking a sip of wine.

"No expense spared?"

"None what so ever Abbey, not when it comes to you..." He laughs, "Besides... it's funny, watching them squirm. They're convinced we're going to make a run for it..."

"Really? How do you know that?"

"Call it intuition... I've had people look down on me my whole life, you get used to it, start seeing the signs..."

"And you don't play up to it at all, do you?" She giggles.

"Like I said... it amuses me..." He smiles back, but his expression hardens slightly and his tone becomes serious, "I remember how people used to treat my Ma after she left my old man. We lived in a rundown house, with no heating, we had no money for food, and people judged her. My Dad was an abusive drunk, but they treated her like she was the failure. She eventually got back on her feet, but when she'd needed help the most, people turned their backs. She wasn't good enough in their eyes. It's that sort of ignorance I enjoy raising my middle finger to from time to time..." He downs his wine and puts his glass back on the table, "I may not earn an honest living, but I have money..." He winks.

"Well, in that case I will have the cheesecake please..." Abbey smiles, trying to keep the conversation light despite the fact she is reeling from the sudden and unexpected glimpse into Alex's past. It explains a lot about him and she wants to know more, she always wants to know more, but she hates to see him brooding and distant so decides to let it go for now as he places their order.

"So, once you've wined and dined me what else have you got planned?" She asks, suppressing the butterflies in her stomach.

"I was thinking we could grab a few more drinks around town then head back to the flat for..."

"For?"

"For... more dessert..." Alex grins, "Unless there's something you'd rather do...?"

"No... that sounds perfect..." She agrees, blushing.

Alex raises his eyebrows teasingly and smirks again as he tops up their glasses with the last of the Rioja. Abbey throws her napkin at him from across the table and they laugh as the elderly couple next to them tut disapprovingly.

"Less of that Miller, we're in a classy establishment here..."

"I thought you said you enjoyed getting a rise out of them...?"

"I suppose I did say that..."

"Well then... what's the problem?" Abbey bats her eyelashes innocently as she runs her foot up the inside of Alex's leg.

"You're certainly getting a 'rise' out of me..." He whispers through gritted teeth, as he instinctively leans across the table, and Abbey does the same, grabbing him by the shirt collar and pulling him forward into a deep, lingering kiss.

"Disgraceful..." He murmurs against her lips, "You'll give that old fella a heart attack if you're not careful...!"

Abbey sits back in her chair, crosses her legs and straightens her top in an overly exaggerated lady like fashion, while smiling sweetly at the gawping couple sitting next to them. They are not the only ones who are staring and Abbey feels a rush of excitement as she takes a delicate sip of wine.

Before she can speak again, Alex begins to laugh under his breath and he shakes his head at the table in disbelief, trying and failing to hide his amusement.

"What?" Abbey asks.

"I was actually thinking about skipping drinks and heading straight back to the flat, now that you've got me all worked up..." Abbey's stomach lurches, "But there may be a slight change of plan..."

"What do you mean?" She frowns, mildly disappointed.

"Two questions..."

"OK..."

"Firstly... how badly are you wanting this cheese cake, because I think we're about to be asked to leave..."

"God, I only kissed you it's hardly a hanging offence...!" Alex laughs loudly, downs his wine and throws his napkin on the table.

"Secondly... how much were you set on it being just the two of us tonight?" His eyes are bright with amusement and she suddenly realises that every time he laughs, his attention is drawn behind her to the street outside. She turns slowly, and there, in the window of the most exclusive, up market restaurant in the entire City are Lucy, Nathan, Liam, Tom, Darren, Sophie and Gemma.

Liam, Darren and Sophie are blowing raspberries on the glass, causing their cheeks to fill with air and widen comically while leaving streaky marks beneath their lips. Gemma is waving enthusiastically, and Lucy and Nathan are flailing about, pulling all sorts of ridiculous faces. Tom is next to them, knocking on the window, pointing, swearing and beckoning them outside.

"Friends of yours...?" The waiter asks as he appears beside them with a plate of cheese cake in each hand.

"I'm afraid so..." Alex confirms, in mock disappointment.

"They don't get out much, not without supervision..." Abbey stammers slightly, and she tries to suppress her laughter as Alex cracks up again.

"I'm afraid I'm going to have to ask you to settle the bill and leave..."

"How much are we talking?" Alex stands menacingly and the restaurant starts to buzz with a mixture of ardent disapproval and anticipation.

"It's £238.75 altogether..." He states, expectantly.

Alex takes his wallet out and drops £300 in twenties onto the table, much to the shock of the waiter and the numerous others who have been watching them non-discreetly all evening. Abbey finishes her wine and quickly puts her jacket on as Alex holds his hand out to her, smiling ominously at the waiter.

"Keep the change..." he states in a mildly threatening manner, before he casually drapes his arm over Abbey's shoulders and guides her through the crowded restaurant. The others approach them outside, still laughing as they greet them, drunkenly.

"Sorry to interrupt your date, but we thought you might want to ditch the first class posers and come and have some proper fun?!" Lucy announces flamboyantly as she steps forward and hugs them both.

"What was all that about?" Tom asks.

"It's nothing... they were just surprised we paid the bill..." Abbey shakes her head, rolling her eyes irritably.

"They giving you hassle?"

"No..." Alex frowns, "Just the usual stuck up arseholes you find in a place like that..." He shrugs, lighting up a cigarette.

"Is that right..." Tom laughs loudly, "So they think they're all important eh? Don't they know who the fuck you are?! No one disses my boy..." He shouts, striding back over to the vast window as the others stare at him in shock. They watch as he bangs on the glass so hard that it shakes and the people still attempting to enjoy their expensive meals inside drop their cutlery as they look up in disgust, "You might be sitting in there with your sharp suits and your designer dresses, flashing your expensive watches with all your family heir looms hanging around your neck. But you 'aint nobody..." He shouts dramatically, raising his arms out to the side in an over exaggerated fashion, as if he is a performer on a stage and this is his audience, "Life isn't measured by how big your house is, by how many cars you own or the size of your fucking bank account... life is measured by moments, real fucking moments, of joy and laughter and pain and confusion. So while you're sat there eating at your fancy restaurant just know that you'll never be as alive as us... you'll never know how alive you can feel, being fucked up, out of your mind, coasting through life without a plan or a clue... filling the dull, meaningless void with real love, real friends, real memories... living each day like it counts. We're the kings and queens... we own the night... we live life with no regrets, and because our minds are open and we're free from the mediocracy of control and repression, we will ALWAYS be far fucking richer than you...!"

The others burst into a huge, rapturous round of applause, cheering and wolf whistling as Tom takes a dramatic bow. People passing by on the street who had stopped to listen are clapping too, and he lights up a cigarette, turning slowly with his arms out stretched, relishing the moment.

There is a sudden flash of blue light at the end of the road and a siren sounds as they all turn and run in the opposite direction. As Tom catches up to them, Alex hooks his arm around his neck and gently pulls him down into an affectionate headlock.

"What the fuck are you on tonight?!" He laughs, messing his hair up before releasing his grip.

"Just high on fucking life mate...!" He replies, pushing him back playfully.

The Locke pub is absolutely packed to the rafters like it usually is on a Friday night, and Abbey fights her way to the bar with Darren as the others find a table in the beer garden. Alex is mobbed as soon as he walks through the door, shaking hands with numerous members of staff and stopping to talk to several people who Abbey recognises as regulars.

There are four hip looking Indie lads setting up their equipment on the stage at the back of the bar and the atmosphere is lively and friendly, with groups of people varying in age, laughing, drinking and enjoying the start of their weekend. The meal had been wonderful, and the alone time with Alex even more so... but this is their scene. This is where they belong. In their down to earth local with the people they love. Abbey is very much at home here and she feels safe, completely accepted as part of the crowd that everybody knows and respects. It is an exhilarating feeling; being a part of a group and having people know her name. Just like they know that she is Alex Matthews girl.

She has caught a few men giving her admiring glances before now, but they would never dream of acting on it, knowing that she is taken and knowing who by. Just like the gang of girls who frequent the pub hoping to catch the attention of Alex and the rest of the lads would never be brave enough to actually approach their table. Instead giggling, whispering and admiring from afar like a flock of infatuated groupies.

They are living the high life - and Tom is right - there is no greater feeling in the world. Kings and Queens he had called them, and it certainly feels that way sometimes. They live by their own rules. They do what they want, when they want and they have the most amazing time, with no worries or responsibilities, especially once the weekend arrives. They party it up, live life to the full and don't have to answer to anyone. Abbey never knew it could be this way. She never knew life could be so exciting, so unpredictable and so much fun. Certain people may disapprove of them but they are usually the same people who radiate jealousy and understandably so. They are well known, well liked, well respected, close knit and from the outside, utterly untouchable. Life is good and Abbey is certain it can't possibly get any better.

But how long can it last? Living a life of excess will surely catch up with them somehow. Being free and not conforming, having a blatant disregard towards the expected 'norms' of society... it must come with a price. Nobody gets to live so freely without any repercussions what so ever, and secretly, Abbey is starting to worry that the bubble will burst. As limitless and invincible as they may feel in their own private world, nothing this good can last forever. Kings and Queens are over-ruled, thrones are lost and nobody is immune to losing everything. It is all so incredibly fleeting, and unbeknownst to them they are about to discover just how easily it can all come crashing down around them.

It really doesn't matter how high they soar because they aren't untouchable, despite what they believe. Even angels fall.

Alex is exhausted. It is 2am and after almost four hours of working the club, he is on the verge of calling it quits and heading home. Last night's festivities had once again continued into the early hours of the morning and even after he had taken himself off to bed, he'd struggled to sleep. His insomnia seems to be getting worse these days.

The pounding music is starting to give him a headache and he can feel his eyes stinging from fatigue. He has made a good profit tonight, with plenty of revellers seeking him out for a decent score. He had received a message from one of his regulars about an hour ago and has arranged to meet him outside the club, away from the CCTV cameras and prying eyes. After this drop, he is done.

"Alright mate..." Alex turns to see his final customer approach.

"Now then, how's it going?"

"Not bad, cheers. You got the stuff?"

"Yeah... not a problem..." Alex makes the exchange, the drugs for a nice wad of cash. Easy money.

"Cheers for coming through man. I'm on a bit of a blow out tonight, really need this..."

"Don't mention it. Have a good one yeah?"

They keep it brief so as not to rouse suspicion, shaking hands before they go their separate ways. Alex prides himself on being careful. He is always vigilant and a constant professional. In his opinion, it doesn't matter how good you are at what you do, if you become blasé you trip up and make careless mistakes.

He will never get too friendly with his clients, and he will never, ever, under any circumstances, become cocky about not getting caught. He knows that anyone could be undercover police and although he has a deal in place with the owner of this bar, he will of course deny all knowledge if the law gets involved. It is his neck on the line and he always conducts himself in a way that protects his interests as well the interests of those around him.

"Are you Alex Matthews?" A tall, dark skinned man in his mid to late thirties appears at the end of the alleyway just as Alex slides his wallet back into the pocket of his jeans.

"Depends who's asking..." He answers, cautiously.

"I was hoping to get a deal?"

"Were you now? And you are?"

"We have a friend in common, or you supply to a friend of mine... he gave me your name. He's inside the club now, I can go find him if you want?"

"I don't know what you're talking about mate, sorry. You must have the wrong guy..."

"Look I'm not police OK?" The man steps forward, blocking Alex's path, preventing him from getting past, "I just want a gram, that's all..."

"Get out of my way..." Alex squares up to him and he bows to the intimidation.

"Please... look I have money..."

"I don't care..."

"Please..." The man scrambles nervously in his pockets as he edges forward, rambling incoherently the whole time. Alex backs away to keep a steady distance between them - not threatened, just wary – and he waits for the opportune moment to make his move. He could have floored him by now and easily fought his way past, but something about the man makes him think twice. He almost feels sorry for him, standing in a damp, secluded alleyway begging a complete stranger for drugs. It is pathetic.

"I'm only gonna ask you politely one more time... move..." Alex threatens; irritated by this unexpected inconvenience when all he wants to do is go home. Suddenly, the man stops and looks up, assessing Alex closely for a brief moment before he begins to back away, "What the fuck is your problem?" Alex asks, but the man says nothing. He simply turns and walks briskly back out onto the street and disappears around the side of the building.

Something isn't right, his behaviour was strange... too strange. Something about the last 5 minutes is seriously off and it doesn't add up. Alex is completely on edge as he stands, running over the confrontation in his mind at lightning speed. 'He didn't threaten, he didn't attack... he didn't go for the money or the drugs, he wasn't in any way offensive or violent, but he was forward... overly forward... he wouldn't stop approaching, wouldn't stop pushing... so much so he physically forced me back...' And then it clicks. The man only stopped once Alex had taken his final step backwards. A step which had plunged him into the shadows and distanced him far enough away from the main road not to be seen, noticed... or heard.

It takes a matter of seconds for Alex to work it out and for the thought to register in his mind, when he suddenly senses movement behind him. He turns, and almost instantly there is a loud nauseating crunch followed by a severe jolt of pain as a fist connects powerfully with his jaw. He drops to his knees and two more punches rain down on him, followed by a sharp kick to the ribs. He is winded, and as he gasps for breath, two sets of hands lift him roughly by the arms and drag him behind the club.

They throw him forward, causing him to land on his knees in the mud-covered, gravel, and he spits a mouthful of blood onto the floor. A pair of polished, brown leather shoes, appear in his eye line and he looks up to see Marcus towering above him.

"Now Alex... didn't I tell you we would be meeting again soon?" He smiles, cheerfully.

"What the fuck are you doing?" He gasps, breathless.

"I thought I would pay you a visit, old friend. I apologise for the back hand tactics. We paid that chap handsomely to distract you and get you where we wanted..." Alex tries to get to his feet but Marcus places a firm hand on his shoulder, pushing him back down.

"What do you want...?"

"There are a lot of things I want Alex... a lot of things... but mostly, I just want to get along..." He sighs, over dramatically. He has two of his henchman flanking him, and two more are standing just behind Alex's right shoulder. There are probably more lurking in the shadows, as Marcus always did prefer intimidation by numbers.

"You have a funny way of showing it..." Alex groans as he sits back on his heels.

"Well the problem is, dear boy, you keep finding yourself in these predicaments because you don't ever seem to consider my feelings. And that is rather hurtful..."

"Fucking hell, you don't even get remotely tired of hearing your own voice do you?" Alex laughs, scathingly and Marcus marches over to him with absolutely no hesitation, back hand slapping him hard across the face. Alex spits another mouthful of blood onto the floor before staring Marcus straight in the eyes. He won't whimper and mule. He won't give Marcus or anyone else the satisfaction.

"You better hold your tongue boy, because I'm still debating whether or not I should cut it out..."

"So what is this so called predicament?" Alex presses. The quicker he gets Marcus talking the sooner this confrontation will be over, although he can't possibly imagine what the hell it is actually about? He hasn't seen or heard from Holt for months now, not since they settled their score. But he has always been a loose cannon, completely random and totally impulsive.

"I'm glad you asked. You see, it's all about chance and consequence, son. The choices we make, the paths we venture down... life works in mysterious ways, but also with a beautiful symmetry. Some people refer to it as karma..."

"Karma? I thought our Karma balanced out when I paid you a nice sum of money?"

"Oh it did... for a while...but that was before something else was brought to my attention that very much re-tipped the scale..." Marcus smiles, and his face is eager and excited, but also angry and full of venom. Alex has no idea why this is happening and once again the situation is totally out of his hands. Marcus has full control.

"And what might that be?" He sighs wearily, already tiring of the drawn out suspense.

"Chris Moorland..."

"What about him...?" Alex snaps.

"Moorland took you on as a business partner after hearing good things about you, Alex. In particular, how well you handle yourself in a difficult situation. How you solve problems, how you make people see that you're not to be messed with. I can appreciate that. But apparently, there was one specific story he heard that impressed him the most..."

"The fight at Labyrinth..." Alex answers without thinking.

"Ah so he told you did he?"

"I don't see how that concerns you..."

"Well, it must be fate, Alex... fate that we keep getting drawn together in this way because it does concern me, very much so..." He clears his throat and begins to pace nonchalantly back and forth as he tells his story, "That group of skinheads you fought that night, well... they'd crossed you, they lied, conned you out of money, damaged your profit and you couldn't let it go. You had a problem, and you dealt with it, made sure it wouldn't happen again. One young lad in particular who was the brains behind the operation, you put him in hospital - with broken ribs, a broken arm and a fractured skull. Now don't get me wrong, I would probably have acted in exactly the same way if somebody messed with my business like that, but unfortunately for you, Alex... you fucked with the wrong boy..." Marcus grabs him by the throat and hauls him to his feet so that their faces are just inches apart, then, with a vicious smile, he steps back and turns towards the shadows where a figure is lurking. Alex follows Marcus' gaze and as the man steps into the light he lets out an audible gasp. The skinhead he fought at the start of the year outside Labyrinth is standing in front of him, hopping from foot to foot with eager anticipation.

"This is Davey..." Marcus announces with pride, "He's my best mate's boy. Unfortunately my good friend is no longer with us god rest his soul but on his death bed I promised him I'd take care of his lad as if he were my own flesh and blood. Now imagine my shock, when I finally got wind of what happened that night and who was responsible for causing him such terrible injuries..."

"I can imagine you were elated..." Alex snarls through gritted teeth, staring at Marcus with absolute seething hatred. He can't believe this. He can't believe that once again something that appeared to be completely unrelated has brought Marcus back into his life and more trouble to his door. Will he ever be rid of him? Or will this vendetta he has against Alex never die? Not until they do?

"Let's just say I wasn't disappointed..." Marcus leers.

"It's just another excuse to come gunning for me and you know it. You said yourself you would have done what I did, that he deserved it, so why are we really here...?"

"Any excuse to wipe the smile off your smug little bastard face..." He spits, "and of course, to keep my promise..." He adds, with fake sincerity. The two lackeys behind Alex step forward and grab hold of his arms as Davey approaches, circling like a lion ready to pounce on its prey. This is going to hurt. Davey doesn't look like he will go easy and seen as Alex put him in hospital and embarrassed him in front of his crew, there is no reason why he should.

Alex tenses as much as he can and takes several fast, deep breaths, mentally preparing himself as Davey strides forward and punches him with all his strength. Alex's mouth fills with blood and the impact causes a flash of bright light in his vision. He has no chance to recover as another punch hits him again from the other side, followed by several to his ribs and stomach. Alex can take him, he already has, and that is exactly why he is being held firmly in place unable to fight back and defend himself. This isn't a rematch; this is revenge, pure and simple. And to Marcus, it is sport.

"That's enough..." Davey stops on command and backs away, smiling at his handy work and Alex drops to his knees. He doesn't make a sound, doesn't gasp, or groan; instead he silently composes himself and remains as still as humanly possible, refusing to writhe in agony or even flinch despite how much pain he is in. He will never show weakness, never.

"Now I think our little exercise has demonstrated exactly what I mean when I say, 'a world of pain'..." Marcus states, "And a world of pain is what you are looking at Alex, if you don't soothe my anger with another down payment of your hard earned cash..."

"You have got to be kidding me..." Alex coughs, spitting up blood, "You want more money, for this?"

"I do not kid, Mr Matthews and I think I have just shown you how deadly serious I am..."

"I paid you everything I owed you and more..."

"Yes, but this little issue of you putting young Davey here in hospital can't just be ignored. So the way I see it, you have two choices. You can either get me more money, let's say another eight grand... or you can let Davey deal out the punishment, and let me assure you, he is more than hoping you will take option number two. As you put him in hospital I think it's only fair that he beats on you until you also require a substantial amount of medical attention..."

"I don't have the money..." Alex coughs.

"No... but you're a resourceful young lad and you managed to get it for me last time, so I have every faith that you won't fail me. I'll give you a couple of weeks of course; I'm not completely unreasonable but if you don't pay up, well, Davey will be very happy about that..." Marcus laughs before whistling sharply and gesturing to his crew, who follow him obediently back through the alleyway and out onto the street, "I'll be in touch..." He shouts over his shoulder, and Alex falls back onto the sodden ground as they disappear out of sight.

He winces at the throbbing ache in his jaw and groans softly as he lets the excruciating pain consume him, kicking his legs out and staring up at the sky as he feels the light, cooling mist of rain on his battered and broken face.

CHAPTER TWELVE

TROUBLE

A dark purple bruise covers almost the entire right hand side of Alex's face and he has a deep gash on his forehead, swelling under his eye, and a scab forming on his lip where it was split open by one of Davey's brutal punches. Every time Abbey looks at him she can feel the panic rising in her chest, but getting upset isn't going to help him. He has enough to worry about without her completely breaking down. She has to be strong.

He sits on the sofa with his phone to his ear, listening intently. Abbey is sat close by his side but she is careful not to touch him as he is in business mode - serious and focused - plus the bruising on his ribs makes him flinch at even the slightest movement. Lucy and Nathan are on the balcony, keeping their distance as the tension starts to build, while Darren, Liam and Tom sit opposite, waiting nervously.

"And when is he back?" Alex sighs, leaning forward and running his hand through his hair, "I see. No, no it's not a problem. I'm aware of that, yeah..." Tom stands up and begins to pace slowly back and forth. It is obvious by Alex's tone that the conversation he is having with one of Moorland's associates down in

London isn't going how they had hoped, "Like I said, not a problem... I'll be in touch. Cheers..." Alex hangs up and throws the phone onto the coffee table.

"Well?" Darren asks.

"He's away... Barbados or somewhere, he doesn't get back for another three weeks..."

"So now what...?" Liam looks at Alex and Tom expectantly, as Nathan and Lucy re- join them from outside.

"Now nothing..." Alex states, flatly, "It isn't your problem. I'll sort something..."

"How? You said yourself you don't have the money and if Moorland isn't around to help you out, what are you gonna do?" Liam presses further, obviously concerned.

"It's not for you to worry about..." The room goes quiet and Abbey stares down at her hands, feeling suddenly nauseous. She knows what it means for Alex if he can't pay Marcus. The beating he took from Davey as a warning will look like child's play compared to what will happen if he doesn't meet the deadline.

"So we just give up?"

"Liam..." Nathan scorns, gently, "Leave it alone mate..."

"Am I missing something? We need money like last time, yeah? So why don't we get it like last time? Do another raid...?"

"No..." Alex snaps, before Liam can finish his sentence, "That's not happening..."

"Why? Mate, you're in shit, serious shit and it's looking like the only way out, again..."

"It isn't that simple..." Alex shakes his head, dismissing the suggestion in a calmer tone but just as resolutely.

"We pulled it off before..." Liam continues, "It all went to plan. If anything we'd be more prepared this time..."

"Do you still have the list of targets your contact gave you?" Darren asks pensively, and Alex and Tom both glare at him.

"It is not happening, end of discussion..." Alex growls.

"So you're just gonna let this jumped up little skinhead put you in hospital then?"

"I won't LET anyone put me in hospital, Daz. I've never let anyone get the fucking better of me in my entire life, but Marcus is relentless. He won't let it go, not when it comes to hurting me, so what the fuck else can I do?!" He shouts, his composed exterior finally cracking as the hopelessness of the situation overwhelms him.

"You can let us help you, like we did before..."

"Liam, you don't get it..." Nathan snaps.

"No you don't fucking get it. It's not up to you and I can speak for myself..." Liam shouts, back, angrily, "I can drive the van on my own. If you don't want to be part of this Nate, then don't be... I mean let's face it you weren't exactly on board last time were you? But I can make up my own fucking mind, we should do this, Alex..."

"My guy said if we ever needed the wheels again all I had to do was call..." Darren adds.

"No... it's too risky. I had no right to ask you before; I'm not putting you in that position again..." Alex stands and paces towards the balcony and Abbey wraps her arms tightly around her waist, feeling scared and uneasy at the confrontational atmosphere.

She hates seeing Alex suffer, almost more than she can stand, and she hates seeing her friends fighting amongst each other. Why did this have to happen? Why can't they all go back to living in their happy, fun, care free little bubble?

"You're not asking us..." Liam points out, solemnly, and Alex's resolve starts to slip. He hates that this is happening. He hates that they are willing to put themselves at risk for him again when it was such a huge sacrifice the first time. But deep down, he knows that this is his only solution. It is the only way - like before - that he can get his hands on such a large sum of money in such a short space of time. Marcus acts as though he is doing Alex a favour by giving him a fortnight to pay up, but he knows all too well that he can't access that sort of cash easily. It is just another way for him to prolong the torture and increase his enjoyment. Another one of his twisted games.

"We go for the second place on the list and we follow the same plan as before..." Darren suggests, "Same time frame, in and out, as quickly as possible..."

"You pulled it off last time..." Liam concludes.

"We were lucky last time..." Tom finally speaks and the others turn towards him in unison. He is clearly unhappy with how the conversation has played out and appears unconvinced that doing another raid is the right move, "That's all it was... luck. And we had the element of surprise. It might have been forgotten about in the papers but the police are still looking for us, the case is still open, don't fucking forget that. The risk is ten times what it was before..."

"It's been months... they won't be on high alert still, not now..."

"But they will be expecting another raid, Daz. They thought our job was done by career criminals, the only reason we managed to get away with it is because it was a one off. No other robberies to link together, no pattern, no further evidence. Another hit will give them way more to work with, it'll bring the police one step closer to our fucking door…"

"But it's only one more raid…" Liam argues, "They might link it together but then that really will be it, there'll be no more to follow up on, no more evidence that'll point to us…"

"Are you sure?" Tom snaps, "Even if we pull it off again, even if nothing goes wrong and we don't fuck up, is this the last one, really?"

"Of course it is…." Liam scoffs, but Darren exhales a long, deep breath with his eyes fixed on the coffee table in front of him, and says nothing.

"That was the line before, remember?" Tom continues, "A one off. Never again. What happens next time Marcus decides he wants to make some easy money? What excuse will he find then to bribe Alex into paying for his life? If this carries on, Marcus won't ever give it up; it'll just be another way for him to make a fucking profit…"

"So we sit back and do nothing?"

"There has to be another way around this…" Nathan cautiously agrees with Tom's viewpoint and Alex turns his attention back to the room after staring silently out of the window; deep in thought while listening to the others argue around him. His face is grave and his eyes are cold as he struggles internally with his predicament. He doesn't want to put his friends in danger; he doesn't want them to risk everything for him. But the fact that two of his friends are willing to make that sacrifice while his so called best friend is backing out; it bothers him. Even though he knows it shouldn't, even though he knows that Tom is right to be wary.

"I want to help you mate, you know I do... I'd die for you brother. But this doesn't feel right to me. It feels like bad fucking news..." Tom stares at Alex, desperately trying to convince him that he cares despite his reluctance to take part in another raid, and Alex maintains the eye contact between them with a blank expression until there is an almost unbearable atmosphere.

"No worries..." Alex finally speaks in a casual manner that is obviously forced, "Like I said, it's my problem..." He shrugs, "and you won't have to die for me brother. Marcus has no interest in destroying anyone else other than me..." He smiles a tense, humourless smile and leaves the room as Liam and Darren look on accusingly. Nathan lights a cigarette and retreats back out onto the balcony with Lucy and Abbey holds her head in her hands. Nothing has been resolved, Alex is still in serious danger and this time it appears he doesn't have the support of his friends, at least not all of them, and not from the one who matters most.

Tom shakes his head in frustration and runs his hands through his hair, pacing back and forth, obviously torn and feeling totally conflicted. He fails to suppress his anger and in one swift movement, punches the wall in front of him. The others look on, totally helpless, as he flings open the living room door and storms out into the hallway.

Everything is falling apart, everything is unravelling around them and they are powerless to stop it. They are unable to do anything, unable to help Alex or agree on a course of action and as they wait, the hours tick by and the showdown with Marcus gets closer.

The following days are uncomfortable and strained. Alex tries in vain to find the money he so desperately needs, but he is met by constant dead ends. Tom wants to help him, but doesn't know how to give his best friend support without putting himself and the others in danger. As he struggles with his guilt and the stress of the situation begins to affect them both, communication between them breaks down. For Abbey, it is like being back at home, amongst all the resentment and the never ending silence filled with unspoken words. She can't stand it.

The thought of once again living in an unhappy, guilt ridden environment truly terrifies her. She has escaped her family drama and as far as she is concerned she has a new family now. Her friends and Alex have become her absolute world and she can't lose them too. She can't just stand back and watch while everything shatters like glass. If anything happens to Alex it will crush her and the others will never forgive themselves, but he simply refuses to raise the point again. He won't beg them to help, as he doesn't want his problems or the repercussions affecting them in any way. Tom knows this, but he still feels as though he is the one letting Alex down. It all rests on his shoulders. Darren and Liam are on board, but he is refusing, trying to be the voice of reason with only Nathan quietly backing him from the side-lines. He is constantly questioning his judgement, second guessing himself and worrying whether or not he is making the right choice... for all of them.

Abbey can sense Tom's doubt and uncertainty and she knows that her only chance to help Alex and ensure his safety is to play on his indecision. The deadline is drawing closer and time is running out. She loves Alex, she can't lose him, and although she can't stand the thought of her friends being in danger she doesn't know what else to do.

Tom exhales the smoke from his cigarette and leans against the balcony, looking out across the Leeds skyline. He is distant and distracted as he battles with his thoughts in the relative silence, with only the soft hum of traffic and the occasional bird song interrupting the stillness of the afternoon. Abbey steps cautiously onto the balcony, still unsure of what she is going to say, and hovers quietly by his side. He doesn't look at her as he takes another drag on his cigarette.

"Are you OK?" She asks, warily.

"I've been better…" He sighs, and Abbey nods, taking a sip of coffee from the mug she is holding, trying to take comfort from its warmth, "You think we should do it, don't you?" Tom's question takes her by surprise but it gives her the opening she needs. It is now or never.

"I don't want you to do it…" She explains, "I don't want any of this to be happening. But if you don't get that money, Tom, then Alex…" She trails off, unable to finish her sentence, flinching at the thought of what the outcome will be if Marcus isn't paid.

"I know… and it fucking kills me. He's my best friend, my brother, and I want to help him. I'd do absolutely anything for that boy, but another raid… something just doesn't sit right with me. I can't explain it; call it gut instinct or whatever you want, I just don't like it…"

"But it's the only way. It was the only way last time and nothing's changed…"

"But it's so fucking dangerous, Abbey. The stakes are higher, the police will be on to us after last time, and there's no guarantee it's even gonna work... we could come away with nothing..."

"At least you'll have tried. At least you'll know that you tried to help..."

"But at what cost...?" Tom looks at her directly for the first time and Abbey sees in his eyes how much it is hurting him, trying to reconcile between his head and his heart, and she almost loses her nerve.

"I don't know what will happen, Tom..." She shrugs, "but I do know what will happen if we stand back and do nothing. Marcus will come after him and no matter what; he'll make him pay..."

"It won't matter much if Alex ends up paying with his freedom anyway... we all could... you too, for assisting an offender..."

"I don't care about that..." Abbey tries to remain resolute, "Not if it keeps him alive..."

"Marcus will just keep coming after him you know? Ever since Alex walked away he's had it in for him, this is the worst it's been but it isn't the first time and it won't be the last. He's a fucking maniac and paying him off won't change that..."

"But it will keep him from hurting Alex...?"

"For now..."

"Then that's all that matters. Please do this Tom. Help him, keep him safe... and then you can figure out a way to get back at Marcus and end this for good..." Abbey reaches over and squeezes his arm, pleading with him as the desperation resonates in her voice. A flicker of doubt crosses Tom's face and his pained expression is all she needs to drive her point home, "He'd do the same for you..." She whispers.

"I know..." He confesses, remorsefully, "We've always had each other's backs, always been there for each other no matter what and I swear that will never fucking change. I can't stand the thought of something happening to him but I can't shake this feeling either, that doing another hit would be a massive mistake..."

"But the alternative, just letting it happen... it will eat away at you Tom..." Abbey continues, softly, careful not to push him too far, "Knowing you could have done something, but didn't... it will never leave you. Trust me, I know from personal experience how horrible it is, living with guilt like that. I wouldn't wish it on anyone..." Tom stares at her as he registers what she is saying and it is clear to Abbey that her insight has struck a nerve. They are all aware of her past and how she lost Ryan, so Tom knows only too well that she is speaking the truth.

"If you were in his shoes, if your places were switched..." She continues, "... then he'd do this for you. I know you're worried that something will go wrong, but if Marcus hurts Alex, seriously hurts him, or worse... imagine how you'll feel then...?"

Tears spring behind Tom's eyes and he quickly looks away, clearing his throat as he takes a final drag on his cigarette before throwing it over the balcony. Abbey feels guilty beyond belief, knowing that she is hurting him and adding to his confusion, but she has to try and help Alex anyway she can. She gently wraps her arm around Tom and rests her forehead against his shoulder, and he responds by leaning into her slightly, before she breaks away and turns back inside.

"Just think about it..." She pleads.

Abbey is unsure at first whether or not talking to Tom has made a difference, or if she has just made the situation a whole lot worse. She is still riddled with worry and anxiety and those feelings don't go away, even when Alex informs her later that night that Tom has had a change of heart and it looks likely they will do the raid after all. Alex isn't happy or relieved, but at least it has offered him some form of hope, despite his reluctance.

Abbey isn't relieved either. The previous terror she felt at the prospect of Alex being attacked has only been replaced with a newer, stronger fear, especially since she has played a direct part in influencing Tom's decision. But Alex and Tom have reached an agreement, Darren, Liam and Nathan have been informed, and all the preparations made. The raid will happen this coming Thursday and hopefully it will all go to plan, just as it did before. But as the reality of the situation starts to sink in for Abbey, so does the lingering sense of dread that Tom had tried to warn her about. Despite her unease, she dismisses the notion that something bad might happen and endeavours to ignore the nagging voice in the back of her mind that keeps telling her how unbelievably wrong this all is.

The rain bounces heavily off the roof of the car as Alex, Tom and Darren sit opposite the seven/eleven, watching closely and waiting for the right moment to make their move. There appears to be one staff member inside, tidying the shelves and sweeping the isles, but the hammering rain makes it difficult to see.

"I'll go check it out..." Darren fastens his coat and pulls his collar up to cover his face, before throwing himself out of the car.

"Be quick..." Alex squints as he watches Darren race across the road and skulk slowly past the shop window. He disappears around the edge of the building and Alex remains alert, assessing his surroundings from the partially concealed car that is parked up across the street. The shop is larger than the last one and is in a much more open, vulnerable position next to a main road. Luckily, as it is late and due to the horrible weather, there is no one on foot nearby and only minimal traffic. After several minutes Darren returns, shaking the water off his hair as he climbs back into the passenger seat.

"Only one guy in there that I could see, half the lights are off and it looks like he's getting ready to leave..."

"We better make a move then..." Alex nods, "Are you ready...?"

"Let's get this over with..." Tom frowns, clearly unhappy, and Darren and Alex exchange a subtle glance as they pull on their balaclavas. Once again they all carry shot guns, but only Alex's is actually loaded with bullets.

Without another word, they simultaneously jump out of the car and rush across the road, crouching low to the ground. The door of the shop is locked but not bolted, and it only takes one attempt for Alex to break it open with his shoulder. The loud crash alerts the shopkeeper and he appears from behind the alcohol aisle, just as Tom cocks his gun and points it in his face.

"Just keep calm and we won't hurt you..." Alex states, "Open the till..." He raises his gun and the man hesitates for a moment, before slowly moving behind the counter and opening the cash register. Alex throws him the empty bag and tells him to fill it, which he does, but there isn't a great deal of money in there, not even half as much as they were expecting. As Darren keeps watch at the window, Tom takes a few steps further into the shop, looking through an open door which leads into a small office at the back. There are bags by the table and he can see a few twenty pound notes on the desk.

"Looks like he was counting up... in here..." Tom gestures, and Alex shoves the shopkeeper hard on the shoulder, forcing him forward. His demeanour bothers Alex. During the first raid the employees were all scared for their lives and therefore fully compliant. This guy is braver and seems almost indifferent to what is going on, which is fairly unsettling. He looks younger and much stronger too.

"The money, where is it?"

"In the corner... by my rucksack..." The shopkeeper answers reluctantly, and he hesitates again by the door, refusing to turn his back on Alex.

"Well get it, hurry the fuck up..."

As he follows the command there is a slight movement at the back of the shop and both Tom and Darren automatically spin around.

"What is it?" Alex shouts, without taking his eyes from the shop keeper.

"I'll check it out..." Darren offers, "Cover the door..." As he creeps down one of the aisles Tom takes his position by the front window.

The rain is still pouring down and there is no sign of life outside, which is good. They are almost done. Once Alex gets the remaining money they can get the hell out of here and go home. Tom stands and waits impatiently, his every nerve on edge, until Darren finally reappears.

"All clear... are we good to..." before Darren can finish his question, the breath is violently knocked out of him and he crashes to the floor, winded and clutching his arm in agony. Another member of staff looms over him, wielding a cricket bat above his head, but before he can strike again Tom strides over and cocks his gun.

"Drop it..." He threatens menacingly, and the man does as he is told, holding his hands aloft, "On the floor... now..." He slowly lowers himself down so that he is resting on his knees and Tom holds his hand out to Darren, "You alright?"

"Yeah... I didn't see him, he came out of nowhere..." He coughs.

"What's going on?" Alex shouts, straining to see while trying to keep the shop keeper in his line of sight.

"Nothing, we're fine..."

Alex is reassured by Tom's response but his relief is short lived as he turns his full attention back to the shopkeeper, who during the brief disruption has picked up an office chair and is now hurling it at him with full force. It crashes into Alex so hard that it knocks him off his feet and the gun flies out of his hands, skimming across the floor.

"ALEX?" Tom shouts him, but he doesn't have time to answer as he scrambles awkwardly to his feet. The adrenaline is pumping, his heart is beating loudly in his ears, and everything from that point on seems to happen at a super heightened speed. The shop keepers rushes forward and grabs hold of the gun. Alex's gun. The gun that is fully loaded. And points it at him with a look of sheer determination. Alex spins around, hardly able to move fast enough and feeling as though he is in one of those dreams where you are running and running but just not moving forward. He hurls himself through the office door as the shopkeeper fires, shattering the woodwork inches above his head.

"Jesus... what the fuck...?" Darren gasps, panicked, as Alex staggers across the shop.

"GET BACK..." He warns them, throwing himself over the counter and landing underneath the window as the shopkeeper fires again, blowing the cash register and the newspaper display to pieces.

Before Darren can react further, the man who attacked him takes advantage of the distraction and charges, tackling him into a set of shelves. They begin to fight, but Tom doesn't help, doesn't even flinch, as the horror of what is unfolding in front of him slowly registers and it freezes him to the spot. Alex pushes himself up off the floor as the shop keeper reloads, but he has nowhere to go and nowhere to hide... he is completely exposed. Running purely on instinct, Tom drops his gun and charges forward.

"Alex... NO..." He chokes out, slamming into him and throwing him backwards. There is another shot, and Alex looks up to see Tom clutching his stomach as blood begins to seep through his fingers and drip onto the floor beneath him.

"No, no, NO..." Alex yells in horror and the shopkeeper stares in wide eyed shock as Tom drops to his knees and falls forward. Alex instinctively leaps over the counter and kicks the gun out of the shopkeeper's hands before he has chance to compose himself, punching him hard in the face, knocking him to the floor and reigning blow after blow down on him until he is unconscious.

Darren grapples with his opponent -desperately trying to fend him off so that he can help Alex and Tom - and as the burly man overpowers him, he lashes out, kicking him in the chest and launching him backwards, buying him enough time to clamber off the floor and gather himself. He almost trips over and looking down he sees the discarded cricket bat at his feet. He quickly picks it up, and as the man charges at him again Darren swings his arm back, connecting the bat with his jaw and knocking him out cold.

"Oh no, no, no, please, no…" Alex sobs quietly, cradling Tom in his arms while trying to stem the bleeding and Darren rushes over, kneeling down beside them.

"Alex we have to move him, now…"

"Go get the car…" He screams, pulling Tom to his chest and rocking him back and forth "God what did I do, what did I do, Tom just hold on mate, please…" Alex begs, with his tears falling freely as Darren races out into the pounding rain and sprints across the road. Tom is still alive, still breathing, but he is losing a lot of blood. It is only moments later when Darren returns and they carry him awkwardly outside, carefully laying him down on the back seat.

"Hurry the fuck up Darren, drive…" Alex shouts as he struggles to keep pressure on the wound.

"Where to?"

"To the fucking hospital, where the fuck do you think?!"

"No..." Tom gasps, "They'll ask... questions..."

"You need to get to the hospital now mate, you need help..." Tom shakes his head and his eyes roll back as he drifts in and out of consciousness.

"He's right..." Darren shouts, panicked, "They'll ask him what happened, and when those guys report the robbery, they'll know Tom was involved..."

"He could die... he's gonna fucking die, just get him to the FUCKING HOSPITAL..." Alex screams and Darren fights back tears as he speeds through the deserted streets and out toward Leeds General Infirmary. Tom grabs hold of Alex's arm and shakes his head again, struggling for breath.

"Just... leave me..."

"What...?" Alex gasps, horrified.

"Outside... leave me... you have to..." Tom chokes, coughing and writhing in pain.

"I can't just fucking leave you, I won't do that..."

"You have to..."

"If they see us, they'll know we're involved..." Darren whispers, explaining Tom's request, "If anyone sees us drop him off, we're done too..."

"God Tom, I'm sorry. I'm so fucking sorry, it should have been me... why didn't you just fucking leave it, why did you have to push me out of the way, you stupid bastard...?"

"I... told you..." Tom smiles despite the fear in his eyes, "I'd die for you, brother..."

"No... God no, please..." Alex sobs heavily as Darren slams on the breaks and comes to a screeching halt outside the A&E department. He climbs out and hastily flings open the back passenger door and they both struggle as they haul Tom out of the car, carrying him over towards the entrance. He drops to the floor just outside the automatic doors as they buckle under his weight.

"Go…" He breathes, barely conscious, "Go…" Alex hesitates, refusing to release his grip on Tom, crying and sobbing as Darren wraps his arms around his waist and tries to pull him away.

"We have to go Alex…"

"NO…"

"We have to go now…" The panic in Darren's voice reaches a fever pitch as he looks up to see a doctor and two nurses running through the hospital towards them. Alex finally relents and they both stagger backwards, causing Darren to trip over as he forces Alex back into the car. He climbs clumsily into the driver's seat and floors the accelerator as two nurses crouch down beside Tom and another rushes over with a gurney.

Darren drives as fast as he can within the speed limit while trying desperately to hold himself together, but his breathing is rapid and his hands are shaking on the wheel. Alex rocks slowly back and forth, staring down at his bloodied clothing, lost in a trance like state and struggling to process what has just happened. His phone starts to ring in his pocket and he blinks hard, unable to function as tears stream down his cheeks and drop into his blood stained hands.

"Answer it…" Darren stares at Alex's vacant expression in the rear view mirror, "ALEX…"

He looks up in response, temporarily snapping back to reality and out of his extreme state of shock as he lifts the phone to his ear, managing to connect the call just before it rings out.

"Head back to the flat..." He whispers after a long moment. Darren can hear Liam's frantic voice on the other end of the line but can't quite make out what he is saying. He sounds panicked, and he has a right to be, "We need to get rid of the car. Just go back to the flat, we'll see you there..."

Liam continues to shout anxiously down the phone, screaming at Alex to tell him what is wrong and what has happened, but he doesn't answer. Instead he cuts him off and hangs up, dropping the phone into his lap as he cries silently, shaking with utter disbelief.

The kitchen door bursts open and Lucy, Sophie, Abbey and Gemma all turn expectantly, their hopeful smiles quickly vanishing as they see the fear and anguish in Liam and Nathan's eyes.

"Are they back yet?" Liam asks.

"What? No. I thought you were waiting for them at the warehouse, you all came back together last time...?" Lucy frowns, alarmed at their apparent urgency and she stares quizzically at Nathan. He says nothing as he slowly crosses the room and pulls her into a gentle embrace.

"What's going on?" Abbey asks, breathless. She can barely speak. Her face flushes and she feels light headed and nauseous as a deep sense of dread washes over her.

"Something went wrong..." Nathan whispers, "We don't know what, they just told us to come back here..."

"Where are they?" Sophie yells, looking frantically between Liam and Nathan, "Where the fuck are they...?!"

"We don't know Soph. They were taking a while so we called Alex... he answered, but..."

"But what...?" Abbey prompts and Liam shakes his head.

"Something was wrong with him..."

"What, what do you mean wrong? Wrong how...?"

"He wouldn't tell me. But he sounded, strange... like he wasn't quite with it. I asked him what had happened but he hung up on me..."

"But he answered..." Gemma points out, "if he answered that means they're OK and they're on their way back here, right?"

"It sounded like they were in the car, yeah..." Liam adds, un- reassured by her optimism.

"We need to ring them..." Sophie hastily retrieves her phone from her bag but before she has chance to dial, Nathan steps forward and grabs it out of her hand, while still holding on tight to a very pale looking Lucy.

"I don't think that's a good idea..."

"They might need help? They could be hurt..." Sophie shouts, snatching it back.

"Alex hung up on us Soph, he told us to come back here and wait..."

"So that's it? We just wait?!"

"I don't know what else we can do...?"

"Oh my god..." She gasps, "Anything could have happened to them. They could have crashed the car or been caught by the police. How the fuck would we know?!" She screams again, trying hard not to cry but unable to stop herself. Gemma pulls her into a hug and she begins to sob as the others look on, all struggling with their own fears and rapidly increasing worry.

Nobody speaks as they sit in a subdued silence around the long glass table adjacent to the kitchen. Another half an hour passes slowly, and the waiting becomes almost intolerable. Abbey feels physically sick. One minute she wants to throw up the next she just wants to scream as loud as she can at the top of her lungs. It is absolute torture, knowing that something is wrong but not knowing exactly what. She is petrified to find out, but desperate for the agony to be over. Just when she feels like she can't stand it any longer, the key turns in the lock and the door opens.

They all rise to their feet in anticipation and Darren walks in, seemingly unscathed but looking pale, tired and incredibly sombre. It is obvious he has been crying. Sophie takes a careful step towards him, hesitating slightly before she reaches up and holds his face between her hands.

"What happened...?" She asks softly, but all he can do is shake his head as his lip begins to tremble. A few moments later, Alex enters the flat in a complete daze and everybody stares at him in absolute horror. He has blood on his hands, on his face and down his neck and although his clothes are black, it is clear to see that they are saturated. Gemma steadies herself against one of the chairs looking like she is about to collapse, and asks the question that no one wants to hear the answer to.

"Where's Tom?" Her breath catches in her throat and Alex stares at her with a haunted expression on his face as a single tear escapes from the corner of his eye, creating a track in the blood on his cheek as it falls.

"I am so sorry Gem..." He whispers, barely audible.

"No..." She cries, shaking her head, "No, don't you dare... don't you fucking dare..."

Alex approaches Gemma and tries to reach out to her but she slaps him hard across the face, lunging at him again before Liam pulls her away and she collapses into his arms.

Alex slumps into one of the chairs and rests his head on the table, trying to block out reality and the sound of Gemma screaming as the others look on in shock. This can't be happening. This can't be real. Everything seems distant and dreamlike as if reality has shifted and they are suddenly trapped in a living nightmare with no escape.

Abbey leans back on the wall and slides down to the floor, clutching her knees to her chest as she tries to fight off the horror and despair, but she can't. This is real. Tom has been shot and the only reason he agreed to do the raid in the first place is because she convinced him.

Now he might be dead... and it is all her fault.

CHAPTER THIRTEEN

PAYBACK

Nearly a week has passed since Tom was injured in the attempted raid and the rain hasn't stopped once. It is very befitting of everyone's sombre, forlorn mood and it shows no signs of waning. Tom is still unconscious in a coma in intensive care and with Sophie by her side for moral support, Gemma finally found the courage to visit him yesterday morning. She hasn't stopped crying since.

Abbey is still struggling with her conscience and the part she has played in all of this. Tom probably wouldn't have changed his mind about the raid if she hadn't pushed him into it; guilt tripped him and emotionally backed him into a corner. But all she could think about was Alex. All she wanted to do was protect him and now he is hurting more than ever. They all are.

The irony of what Abbey said to Tom that afternoon on the balcony certainly isn't lost on her now. She told him the guilt he would feel if something happened to his best friend would never leave him, would eat away at him and now she can see it destroying Alex in the same way.

He has hardly left his room since the bungled robbery, unable to face his friends or look them in the eye, knowing that they blame him - at least partly - for everything that has happened. No one blames Alex more than he blames himself and Abbey is battling to get through to him, but she can't ease his pain, no matter how much she wants to help. All they can do now is hope and pray that Tom pulls through. Thankfully, he has already started to show signs of improvement, but the comfort that brings is tainted by the knowledge of what is waiting for him when he wakes up. The police have already been to the hospital and are keen to ask Tom a number of questions as soon as he is well enough. They know he was at the raid, they know it was him who was shot and almost killed by the night manager. There is no denying it; so even if he does make a full recovery, he is looking at a long stretch in prison.

The flat is dark, empty and eerily quiet and has been for most of the day. Darren and Sophie are staying with Gemma so that they can keep an eye on her and Liam, Nathan and Lucy have kept their distance for the last couple of days in order to give Abbey some space to talk to Alex. They are all worried about him. None of them have ever seen him like this before and he is starting to frighten them. He has completely shut himself off and is letting his anger and self-loathing totally consume him. It isn't healthy, and it certainly isn't helping Tom, or the situation.

Abbey hesitates slightly as she approaches the bed where Alex is sitting. He has his back to her and is staring out of the window at the early evening sky, with a cigarette in his right hand and an overflowing ashtray at his feet. He tilts his head slightly and smiles a weak smile as Abbey perches next to him. His hair is unkempt, his stubble overgrown and his eyes are red raw. He hasn't slept for days and he looks exhausted.

Abbey reaches up and strokes her hand down the side of his face, gently caressing the now faded bruise. He shuts his eyes and leans into her touch, grasping her hand as she moves it away before pulling it into his lap and staring down at their entwined fingers.

"You need to eat something..." Abbey states, softly, and he shakes his head and smiles meekly again.

"Thank you..." He whispers, "For staying with me..."

"Where else would I be?"

"Anywhere but here, like the others..." Alex flinches as he docks out his cigarette and rubs his face with his hands, feeling jaded and utterly defeated. Abbey's heart sinks and she swallows hard. She can't stand to see him like this. She can't bear to see the pain in his eyes and how much he is hurting. She cautiously wraps her arms around him and to her surprise he lifts his feet onto the bed and rests his head in her lap, pulling the sleeves of his hoody down before clutching his arms, tightly to his chest. They stay there for the longest time as Abbey runs her fingers softly through Alex's hair, returning the comfort he had shown her when she turned up on his doorstep, lost and completely distraught. She wishes he would cry. She wants him to scream and shout and react to what he is feeling on the inside. He knows that holding it all in is unhealthy and not to mention dangerous, so why won't he open up?

"They're worried about you. They don't think you're coping..."

"They don't need to waste their time worrying about me..." He frowns.

"Stop it. Don't do this to yourself Alex. They're your family and they love you. I love you. Please don't push everyone away..."

"I don't deserve anyone's pity. This is all my fault, Abbey. What happened to Tom, it's on me, I did that, to my best friend..." Abbey grabs hold of Alex's shoulders and forces him upright, dropping to the floor and twisting her body so that she is kneeling in front of him, her face level with his.

"You didn't cause this to happen, Alex. You didn't know Marcus was going to come after you again and there's no way that you could have known what would happen on that raid..."

"Tom knew..." He argues back, his face twisted in anguish, "He knew it was a risk. He knew something like this was bound to fucking happen..."

"You all decided to do that job..." Abbey maintains her point, but her voice is flat and her tone unconvincing.

"He put himself at risk for me. He did this for me... and I let him. I can't ever take that back. I can't ever make this right. I fucked up, Abbey... I really fucked up..." His voice begins to crack and he fists his hands roughly in his hair, hating himself, unable to escape the truth.

"It isn't just on you..." She breathes, "I talked to him..."

Alex looks up and holds Abbey's gaze, confused and caught off-guard by her sudden confession.

"When?"

"The same day he changed his mind and told you he'd help. I was so scared Alex, scared of losing you.

I could see he was doubting his decision, so I spoke to him about it... and I convinced him to help..." Alex's face displays a varied range of emotion, quickly flitting between shock, hurt and disappointment in a matter of seconds yet his anger fades almost as quickly as it flares and the sorrowful resignation slowly creeps back in.

"It isn't your fault, Abbey..." he sighs, "I reckon he'd have changed his mind anyway. I was the one who let the raid go ahead. I shouldn't have entertained the idea or let myself be talked round. I should have fucking listened to him..."

"You never would have gone ahead with it if you'd known..."

"Doesn't make much of a fucking difference now, does it?" Alex shrugs sadly and Abbey shakes her head, mirroring his expression. Before she can speak again, he stands abruptly and moves over to the wardrobe, lifting his hooded top over his head and grabbing a fresh t-shirt from one of the drawers with a sudden sense of urgency.

"What are you doing?" Abbey asks, taken aback.

"I have to see him..."

"What?! But there might be police at the hospital Alex, they'll be monitoring his visitors..."

"I don't care..." He shakes his head and strides back over, resting his hands firmly on her shoulders, "He's my best friend and he saved my life. I have to see him. I can't just sit around here waiting anymore, I should never have left him in the first place..."

Abbey's legs buckle beneath her and she slumps despairingly back onto the bed as the familiar sensation of panic fights its way through her chest. Alex is careful and far from stupid. If there is even the slightest sign that the police are nearby then he will turn around and come straight home, but that doesn't reassure her much. Everything is such a mess and they are dangerously close to being found out. It is all balancing on a knife edge and one simple mistake could cost them everything. But Alex is grieving, and if seeing Tom helps him in some way and forces him to start dealing with his pain, then she can hardly stop him.

"Be careful..." She whispers timidly, and the fear in her voice causes Alex to turn back as he shrugs into his jacket. He slides his phone into the pocket of his jeans and holds out his hand, pulling Abbey to her feet and into a tight, comforting embrace. He kisses her hair sweetly and runs his nose along the top of her forehead, before tilting her head back and giving her a chaste kiss on the lips.

"I will be. I promise..."

"Do you want me to come with you?" Abbey already knows what the answer will be before the words are out of her mouth.

"No. It's too dangerous; I don't want you involved any more than you are already, not if I can help it..."

"OK..." She shrugs, knowing there is no point in arguing.

"Give Lucy a call; get her and Nathan over here, Liam too. I don't like leaving you on your own..." She nods in agreement and he leans down, kissing her again, "I won't be long..."

As Alex turns to leave all of Abbey's fears, worries and insecurities suddenly engulf her and she reaches up, urgently locking her arms around his neck and pulling him down so that their lips meet again. Alex responds by wrapping his arm around her waist and pulling her close, their bodies pressing together as he runs his other hand greedily through her hair. They eventually break apart, gasping for breath, and Abbey fights back the ridiculous and unwelcome notion that she is never going to see him again. Alex slows his breathing and stares into Abbey's eyes, keeping hold of the tight grip he has on her, while their faces remain inches apart. He hesitates as if he is about to speak, but doesn't. Instead he straightens up and composes himself, leaning forward so that his lips brush lightly against Abbey's mouth once more before he strides with a renewed determination out of the room.

Alex knows how careful he has to be. Visiting hours have been over for a while and the hospital feels almost peaceful as it winds down at the end of the day. There are a few members of the public still milling about in the lobby and he has no problem walking unnoticed over towards the elevators. According to Gemma intensive care is in ward ten, left, right, then left again, out of the lift on the fourth floor.

The neon strip lights ping and flicker above Alex's head as he approaches a set of double doors. Through them is another, long, dark corridor, similar to the one he has just walked down with a sign at the end pointing the way to the 'I.C.U'.

He tries the door to ward ten, but it is locked. He knows there is no point pressing the intercom as visitors are not permitted after 7pm and it looks as though there is no other way in. He glances through the thin, panelled window and he can see an abandoned nurse's station and what looks at first to be an empty waiting room, but there is movement inside and a young couple appear, both of them visibly upset. The woman is crying and grasping a tissue to her face as the man feebly holds his arm around her shoulders, supporting her. They stop and exchange a few words with the only nurse on duty - as far as Alex can tell - before they turn and walk towards him.

He ducks around the corner and presses himself against the wall, hiding in the shadows, waiting for his only chance to get inside. The door swings open and the young couple leave - sobbing quietly - too caught up in their grief to notice Alex lurking in the background. He waits until they are out of earshot then sneaks back round, only just managing to hook his hand through the door before it clicks shut. He creeps forward and spots the nurse sitting at a computer desk in the small office directly behind the reception area. She seems engrossed in an article she is reading on the screen and Alex is able to move to the other end of the ward undetected, sliding through another set of doors and into a dimly lit room with a large glass partition splitting it in two. On the side he has entered there are a number of rather uncomfortable looking seats and a battered old coffee table. On the other, much larger side of the room, are half a dozen beds spaced out equally with all sorts of medical equipment surrounding them.

Three of the cubicles are empty, one has the curtain partially closed around it, and the other two are occupied. Alex stares in hollow disbelief at the patient directly in front of him, momentarily placing his hand on the window as if trying to reach through the glass and prove to himself that what he is seeing is actually real. Tom is half covered by a thin sheet. His chest is bare and he has a large bandage across the middle of his torso. Numerous wires are attached to his chest, arms and neck, and there is a plastic tube angled down his throat which is taped securely in place on his cheek. A large, cylinder shape machine rises and falls in time with his chest and there are regular beeps from the monitor keeping track of his heartbeat.

Alex rests his head against the partition in total despair. This is his fault... and he can't do anything to change it. Nothing will magically make Tom better. If he could switch places with him he would do it in an instant, but that isn't an option. He can't bargain his way out of this. What's done is done and even if this hasn't ended Tom's life it has certainly robbed him of a large part of it. He will most likely spend the whole of his thirties in prison, locked up for a crime he didn't even want to commit. He did this to help Alex and the money they came away with wasn't even close to the amount needed. It was all for nothing.

"Can I help you...?" A startled voice snaps Alex out of his troubled thoughts and he whirls around. A small, dainty nurse who barely looks old enough to be out of high school is standing in the doorway with a pile of neatly folded towels in her arms.

"Sorry..." He frowns, fully aware that he needs to turn on the charm in order to blag his way out of trouble, but he is unable to summon the energy to do so, "I'm just visiting..."

"You shouldn't be here, not at this time..."

"I know..." Alex sighs, thinking quickly on his feet, "I just got here, from Ireland. I thought I'd come by the hospital before trying to find a B&B for the night..." His voice is tired and weary, filled with emotion, and his story hardly sounds convincing. But after momentarily weighing him up, the nurse places the stack of towels on a chair and moves further into the room, closing the distance between them. Alex glances at the clock and realises he has been standing there for almost half an hour. No wonder he has been caught.

"Do you know him well?" The nurse asks, intrigued.

"Yes, he's a good friend..." Alex is reluctant to give anything away but he doesn't want to offend the girl either. He is lucky she hasn't called security.

"Well your friend seems to be in quite a bit of trouble. The police think he was involved in a robbery..."

"They must have it wrong..." Alex swallows hard and shakes his head defensively.

"They seem pretty convinced. You don't think he would get involved in something like that...?"

"No. Not unless he was forced to..."

"Maybe your friend fell in with a bad crowd?" The nurse suggests, and Alex raises an eyebrow as he laughs once without a trace of humour.

"Maybe..." He agrees. There is a passing silence as they both look down at Tom's battered, fragile body and the mass of machines that are keeping him alive, "Is he going to be alright?" Alex asks, turning to face the nurse properly for the first time. She is a little taken aback by the intense and tormented piercing blue eyes that are staring down at her, but once she catches her breath she smiles up at him kindly.

"He has a long recovery ahead of him. It will take a while for him to get back to full strength but it seems promising at this stage. He's still in a coma because his body needs time to heal, but it looks likely that he'll be awake by the middle of next week..."

"Good..." Alex sighs, "That's good..."

"I'm sure he'll pull through..." She smiles, encouragingly, and Alex nods, thankful for her reassurance. With one last glance at his broken best friend he turns to leave, pausing in the doorway as the nurse calls after him, "I'll tell him you stopped by... when he wakes up I mean. What did you say your name was?"

Alex is grateful for her kind words but wary of her inquisitiveness and his walls are instantly raised, with his cold exterior masking the vulnerability that he exhibited just moments ago.

"I didn't..." He frowns, and the nurse stares after him as he disappears out of sight, dodging anymore unwanted questions and hopefully preventing her suspicions from being raised any further.

The rain is still falling outside, but it has slowed to a light mist that swirls around Alex as he crosses the road towards the car park. As he climbs into the driver's seat his phone vibrates in his pocket and he slams the door shut, tapping the message icon as he turns his keys in the ignition. His heart drops through his chest and his blood runs cold when he sees Marcus' name highlighted on the screen.

'Where's my money?'

Alex hurls his phone onto the passenger seat and clenches his fists so tightly they turn white. He leans his head back and screws his eyes shut, breathing deeply through his nose as he tries to bring his temper under control. In a moment of blind fury he punches the steering wheel several times and slams his fist onto the dashboard as his anger and frustration boil over, causing him to lash out, violently. As he slowly regains control and manages to pull himself together, he grabs hold of his phone and types out a message, hitting send without a second thought.

'Tomorrow.'

Alex is ready for a showdown. He is ready to face Marcus and finally give him exactly what he deserves. Seeing Tom tonight, lying there fighting for his life in that hospital bed has changed Alex's perspective entirely and he is enraged beyond compare. It is time for pay back and he is out for blood.

Janet fastens her jacket and smiles kindly at the portly businessman who is holding the door for her, thanking him as she dashes out of the large, glass fronted office building at the edge of Granary Wharf. Why she has to come to these meetings with the director of her firm she will never understand. She dutifully takes notes and neatly types them up on her return, only to file them away where they are never looked at again. A huge waste of time in her opinion, but at least it gets her out and about for the best part of a day.

It is just after lunchtime and her boss and his associate are now off to be wined and dined, leaving Janet to find her own way back to the opposite end of town. She stands, debating whether or not she should head out for something to eat herself or go and catch a bus while the midday traffic is relatively quiet, when she spots a young girl crossing the square towards her. It takes a moment for Janet to understand why she has such a strong feeling of recognition towards this girl, but as the gut-wrenching realisation suddenly dawns, she hurls herself forward without a second thought. Curly blonde hair, brown eyes, pretty... she remembers. This girl was perched on her kitchen counter at the start of the year, the same day she confronted Abbey about her truancy from school. Her name is Lucy, she is sure of it and she will without a doubt know how and where to find her daughter.

Janet battles her way through the throngs of commuters, businessmen and shoppers in the general direction that Lucy was heading but she temporarily loses sight of her. She stops; frantically searching through the crowds, disheartened and almost on the verge of giving up, when she spots her again, turning a corner down one of the little cobbled side streets that lead back towards the City Centre.

Janet follows, keeping a safe distance as she crosses the bridge out onto Neville Street, before walking up towards the train station. It is there that Lucy veers off and takes a left into the circular, paved entrance way of a posh apartment block. Janet watches from the corner of the road as she types a number into a keypad and unlocks the main door, pulling it firmly shut behind her as she enters. This must be it. This must be where Abbey is hiding out. Janet feels a massive surge of relief and for the first time in a very long time, a renewed sense of hope. She scrambles for her mobile in her handbag and makes a quick call to work, explaining rather hurriedly that something urgent has come up and she needs to take an unscheduled afternoon off. As she picks up her pace and practically runs towards the bus stop she dials Peter's mobile and he answers promptly on the second ring...

"I have news about Abbey. Get Anna, I'll meet you at home..."

Lucy is completely oblivious to the fact that she has just been followed, as she is distracted by a million and one things that are playing on her mind. She isn't looking forward to this. She knows something is wrong - she could tell by the tone in Nathan's voice - but as usual he wouldn't explain himself over the phone.

As she approaches the door she can hear raised voices and is greeted in the kitchen by Alex, Darren, Liam and Nathan. They are clearly on their way out and looking like they mean serious business. Abbey and Sophie are standing across the room, visibly upset and apparently reeling from the aftermath of a big argument.

"We've got to go..." Alex picks up his keys and gestures to the lads.

"What's going on?" Lucy asks, and Nathan instantly moves over to stand by her side.

"We're off to pay Marcus a visit..." Alex answers her question but doesn't take his eyes off Abbey, who looks scared and incredibly worried, her expression pleading.

"Marcus? Why...?"

"He wants his money..." Alex quips.

"You don't have his money..."

"I know... but he's going to get something else instead..." The malice and anger that laden Alex's voice, make Lucy recoil, and it suddenly dawns on her what all of this means. She stares up at Nathan but before she can say anything he shakes his head apologetically and let's go of her hand, stepping away.

"This has to end babe, it's gone on for too long..."

"And Tom paid the price..." Darren adds.

"But he'll kill you..." Lucy gasps, horrified and incensed.

"No he won't. I'm tired of playing his fucking games... it's time he got what's coming to him. This ends today..." Alex throws down his authority and everyone knows that he is not to be argued with further. Liam is ready and raring to go and all it takes is a simple nod from Alex and he is out of the flat. Darren follows behind - much to Sophie's dismay - and Nathan and Alex are the last to leave, both of them glancing back at Lucy and Abbey before the door slams shut behind them.

"Why didn't you get here sooner?" Sophie snaps.

"I couldn't have stopped this; they can't be talked round..." Lucy replies, knowingly. She has seen Alex like this before - and her brother - she knows what it means when they behave in this way. Any begging, pleading and screaming is a waste of breath when they are this determined, "What happened? Why now?" She frowns.

"Alex went to see Tom..." Abbey states, flatly, and Lucy instantly understands.

"And now he might get one of the others put in a fucking coma too..." Sophie shouts, her voice shaking as she explodes with anger. Abbey glares at her in disgust, but before she has chance to retaliate Lucy steps in and jumps to Alex's defence.

"This isn't his fault Soph and you know it. Tom's a grown man, he makes his own decisions. He could have said no and stuck to it but he didn't... because Alex needed him and that's what we do. We're family, we're there for each other no matter what, no matter how fucked up things get. Blaming him isn't going to change anything..."

"But this is only going to make things worse..." Sophie sobs, "Your boyfriend, your brother... how can you be so level headed when they're acting like this...?"

"Because someone fucking has to be..." Lucy laughs, throwing her arms up in exasperation before calmly folding them across her chest and taking a breath, "Look... at the end of the day, Tom is one of us, he's Alex's best friend and he almost died. That was Marcus' fault. You can't seriously believe for one second that the lads were just gonna let that go..."

Sophie stares in silence before shaking her head with frustration, completely worn out and utterly defeated. There is no point in arguing and she knows it. Loyalty, brotherhood, friendship... they are the foundations that their group is built upon. The love they have for each other is more important than anything else and when one of them is hurt, they all hurt. Tom was never going to go un-avenged. There was always going to be a fall out; a retaliation. It is just so unexpected and out of the blue that it has all rapidly come to a head today. This is beyond serious, a real game changer and nobody knows where the chips will fall or what the outcome will be.

Alex isn't thinking in the long term. He is tired of constantly trying to plan three steps ahead in an attempt to predict Marcus' behaviour. He is the definition of unpredictable and Alex has learnt that there is absolutely no way to keep track of him. What they are about to do is unbelievably dangerous. Things have finally reached breaking point, but if Alex is honest with himself, it is an unavoidable scenario that has been brewing for a very long time. The hostility and animosity between them has slowly been gathering momentum for years and it has finally become too much to simply ignore. Marcus has gone too far and has goaded him for the final time.

The strip club is open for business all day every day, but as it is relatively early in the afternoon there are only two customers propping up the bar when Alex and the others arrive. It is dark inside, and the atmosphere feels very oppressive. There is a lone girl dancing on a pole in the middle of the vast room, her face resigned and impassive as she goes through the motions with a serious lack of enthusiasm. The bar man breaks away from his animated conversation with an imposing looking bouncer, and they both stand to attention as the four of them approach.

"We're here to see Marcus..." Alex announces and the bouncer squares up to him with a sinister smile.

"He isn't expecting you until later..."

"Well I'm here now..." Alex doesn't wait for him to respond again, too pent up and angry to be wasting time with one of Marcus' lowlife minions. He has no patience for this sort of bullshit today and as a result, he springs forward with absolutely no warning and punches him hard in the face. He collapses to the floor, knocked out cold, and the barman gawps in shock, "I take it he's in his office?" Alex asks, and the kid nods back timidly without saying a word.

Marcus is leaning against his desk with a glass of whiskey in his hand, talking to three of his henchmen - laughing and joking without a care in the world - and it makes Alex's blood boil even more. They all turn at the unexpected interruption and there is a brief flicker of shock and anger on Marcus' face before he quickly composes himself, slipping back into the polite yet threatening demeanour he so often uses in Alex's presence.

"Well this is a surprise..." He smiles broadly as he places his glass down and fastens his suit jacket,

"I take it you couldn't wait to pay me what you owe me, Mr Matthews?"

Alex stands in the middle of the room glaring at Marcus, his seething hatred filling every single pore of his body as he thinks of Tom and everything he has lost. The nasty, vicious little smirk that he has plastered across his face only adds to Alex's rage and the atmosphere in the room shifts. You can cut the tension with a knife as Marcus saunters arrogantly towards the front of his desk with his performing monkey's flanking him on either side, two to the left and one to the right. Alex, Liam, Darren and Nathan mirror their position. At least the fight will be fair at four on four, although the way Alex is feeling right now he could probably take them all out single handed and wipe that self-righteous smile clean of Holt's face.

"Well?" Marcus prompts, his friendly façade slipping.

"I don't have any money for you..." Alex informs him, defiantly.

"Now you see that is disappointing. I take it that's why you've brought reinforcements, because you've failed to get me my cash?"

"I paid a price..." Alex scowls, trying to keep his simmering rage under control as it builds with every passing second.

"Yes, so I heard..." Marcus laughs as he looks across at his cohorts, all of them smiling maliciously with great amusement, "I would say the gangs all here, but then there is one person missing... Tom Warner, am I right? Not exactly one of the greatest thinkers of our time and a cocky little fucker to boot if I remember correctly? He was better than anyone else I know at

298

stealing cars though, I'll give him that. I guess he's been forced into an early retirement mind you, considering his current state?"

Alex sways ever so lightly on the spot, back and forth from foot to foot, his impatience barely containable as he yearns to dish out his revenge. Although only a slight movement, it doesn't go unnoticed by Marcus and he alters his stance in anticipation.

"Like I said... a debt was paid..."

"That's all well and good, but we still have a problem here don't we Alex? Seen as though my deal was with you and not your comatose, soon to be incarcerated friend...?" Marcus' vindictive smirk widens into a full blown satisfied grin as his words have a noticeable effect on Alex. He knows exactly which buttons to press and he is thoroughly enjoying himself.

"You son of a bitch..." Alex spits, "This is all because of you. My best mate is in hospital with the police at his bedside because I was bending my fucking back trying to get you money... and for what? God, you know I'm ashamed to admit it, but I was actually fucking intimidated by you, I mean what a joke..." Alex shakes his head in disbelief and Marcus's face drops.

"Be very careful..." He threatens quietly, but the flood gates are open, the words are flowing and Alex is no longer holding back.

"Why? What the fuck are you gonna do? Don't fucking pretend to me that this is business because we all know what this is really about don't we...?" Alex takes a step forward and Liam, Nathan and Darren close in around him as Marcus' men do the same, shifting defensively, "You're just a sad old man who can't let go. You can't stand the fact that I'm getting the deals you would have got back in the day when you actually had some fucking credibility. You're a laughing stock, and I swear to god, I am not scared of you..."

"You should be..." Marcus snarls through gritted teeth and Alex takes another step closer, staring menacingly into his eyes, completely defiant.

"I surpassed you, Marcus. I out grew you... and all this, constantly attacking me, coming after me any way you can, trying to bring me down... you do it because I'm better than you, and deep down you fucking know it..."

There is no greater revenge for Alex than witnessing Marcus in that moment, standing there speechless and utterly stunned. Not only has he been verbally ridiculed in front of his entourage, but the words ring entirely true. He has been made to look stupid, he has no come back or snappy retort and the feeling is sweeter and more rewarding than any physical punch could ever be.

Alex laughs scornfully and backs away, much to the surprise of the others who are still keyed up and ready for a fight. Although it would give him immense pleasure, Alex isn't about to give Marcus the satisfaction. He has said all he needs to say.

"In future, you stay the fuck out of my way, and I'll keep out of yours..." He isn't naïve enough to think that Marcus will abide by that request for even a second, but he says it anyway, in an offhand attempt to cut all ties for good. Alex is done with this game, he isn't stooping to his level and biting back anymore... it's over.

"You think it's that fucking simple son...?" Marcus shouts, his temper flaring, shattering his perfect routine of the big man on top who is never riled, never

300

angered and never beaten, "You don't just walk away from me..."

Alex continues to stride towards the exit with the others following behind, steadfastly refusing to react in any way to Marcus' angry taunts. They are almost through the door and out of the room when Alex's pace begins to slow and the over powering anger he felt before returns with full force. Marcus is desperate for a reaction, and he plays the only card he knows is guaranteed to work.

"You can point the finger of blame all you want Alex but we both know the reason your best friend was nearly six feet under. You think you're big league, eh? You're just a bunch of fucking kids and it's your stupidity that nearly got Warner killed thinking you could play with the big boys and be any sort of match. Warner's gonna rot in prison because of you Alex... no one else... YOU..."

Alex's intense fury completely over powers him and he turns on the spot mid stride as everything else in the room blacks out. He launches himself forward with tunnel vision and all he can think about and focus on is hurting Marcus. Hurting him the way he is hurting, the way Tom is hurting. It is all that matters now; regardless of the consequences. He needs to pay for what he has done.

Alex's fist connects powerfully with Marcus jaw and he collapses back against his desk, desperately trying to steady himself. His right hand man jumps forward in an attempt to defend him but Alex dodges the attack with ease, unconcerned and almost unaware of anyone else in the room.

Darren tackles the guy to the floor and reigns several punches down on him in quick succession, until he is

3 0 1

struggling for breath and choking on the blood that is gushing from his nose. Liam head butts another of Marcus men before he even has chance to process what is happening and as Nathan takes a punch from the third, he stumbles backwards into the wall next to the pool table. The man charges forward, smiling triumphantly, and Nathan scrambles for one of the pool cues, swinging it back and slamming it hard into the side of the man's head. He falls to the ground and Liam runs forward, kicking him repeatedly until he too is unconscious.

The whole fight lasts less than a minute and as Darren, Liam and Nathan catch their breath, they remain alert, quickly scanning the carnage and making sure that their opponents have stayed down. When they finally turn their attention back to Alex, their mouths drop open and they stare at him in abject horror. He is kneeling over Marcus, pounding on him with all his strength.

Alex's eyes are black and his face is twisted into pure rage as he punches Marcus repeatedly in the face. The left side, then the right side, over and over, again and again, as all the loss, pain and devastation come pouring out of him.

"ALEX, THAT'S ENOUGH..." Darren shouts, throwing himself forward and grabbing hold of his shoulders in an attempt to pull him back, but he is far too strong and the frenzied trance he is in is seemingly unbreakable.

Alex keeps on punching, keeps on thrashing, crying out and yelling as tears start to build and empty sobs escape from his chest. Marcus' face is black and blue and swollen beyond recognition, and Darren begins to panic as Nathan and Liam rush over to help him prise Alex away.

"That's enough man, come on... that's enough..." Nathan cajoles, and he finally relents. They all stagger backwards and Darren instantaneously pulls Alex to his feet and over towards the door as Liam glances down at Marcus, hesitating above him and pleading quietly under his breath.

"Liam, come on..." Nathan shouts, pushing Alex out of the room.

"Is he dead?" Darren's voice is laced with fear as he stops in the doorway and turns back towards Liam, who is frozen and unable to move, waiting anxiously for any sign of life.

"No..." He gasps, finally, "No, he's breathing..." Relief floods through him as Marcus' lips part and a gargled breath escapes from the back of his throat. He is alive, but for how much longer?

Liam turns without further delay and quickly catches up to Darren as they sprint out of the office, down the stairs and through the back exit of the club, to the sound of Marcus' men, coughing, groaning and slowly regaining consciousness behind them.

CHAPTER FOURTEEN

CONFESSIONS

Abbey has absolutely no idea why she is here. Out of all the places she could go to seek comfort and solace, she ends up standing on the steps of Eden Comprehensive, a place that she has hated since the very first time she laid eyes on it. Although it may hold bad memories for her... it is also where she met Lucy, Nathan and Liam, and is the place where she finally started to feel hope for the future again after a year of loneliness and heartache. Perhaps that is why she is here? Because she so desperately needs to be reminded of that sense of hope? She needs to feel that reassurance and know that everything is going to work out, get better, and be OK despite how impossible it may seem.

Ever since Alex took his revenge on Marcus the situation has become even more complicated. Alex is happy. Happy that Marcus finally got what he deserves. They all feel a sense of justification and for now at least, things have seemingly died down between them. Marcus survived the attack, but only barely. Therefore, there will no doubt be repercussions at some point in the future. They all expect that Marcus will plan his revenge but he is in no fit state to take Alex on any time soon.

Despite the relief that respite brings, there is still a horrible sense of gloom within the group. Tom is still in a coma. He hasn't woken up, and it has been over a week since they predicted that he would. If he is unresponsive for much longer the doctors will be forced to re-asses his injuries and decide if there is any likelihood that he will wake up at all. Depending on the results that the various tests and scans reveal – his life support may be switched off.

There is still an obvious divide within the group as a result of everything that has happened. Abbey is still hiding her guilt and Alex's mood swings are truly starting to affect her. For the most part he is still very much the man she loves, but whenever he is reminded of Tom and the fact that he may still die, he lashes out in anger. It is an anger that he feels towards himself but as the closest person to him, Abbey seems to be taking the brunt of his grief. She wouldn't mind so much if she knew a way to help him... but she can't make this any better. She just has to try and be patient.

Lucy is being an absolute rock as usual - as are Nathan and Liam - but Gemma is still furiously blaming Alex and her coldness towards him isn't in any way subtle. Darren is trying his hardest to keep the peace but Sophie is Gemma's best friend and it puts him in an increasingly awkward predicament.

They are all still hurting and grieving massively and everything is a total mess, hence the reason why Abbey needed to escape for the afternoon, to get away and clear head. She had started walking over an hour ago and without consciously thinking about where she was heading, she ended up here.

The school looks smaller somehow, as if her world has expanded immensely since she was the shy, meek, self-conscious new student. It feels like a lifetime ago since she sat in the principal's office on her very first day and as she thinks back to how she felt in that moment, her heart constricts when remembering Mr Harper and the kindness he had shown her.

Surprised by the direction her thoughts have taken, Abbey impulsively throws her cigarette butt to the ground and twists her foot over it before pulling her hood up and climbing the two flights of stairs that lead up to the walkway. It is 4pm and the students are long gone for the day, but the school entrance is unlocked and propped open as the janitor struggles outside with several bags of rubbish in his arms. She waits until he has cornered the building out of sight, before ducking through the doors and into the reception area. It all looks exactly the same. She has changed so much in the last year - everything about her life is different - yet the fact that her old school is exactly how she left it several months ago is oddly comforting to her.

She strolls through the empty corridors, past her old locker and up towards the English rooms, smiling to herself as she remembers Lucy and Liam's prank with the puppets and how happy and carefree they all were back then.

Abbey and Alex's relationship was brand new and she had felt so much excitement and promise. Her heart sinks a little as she considers how much he is struggling now and how much he has come to depend on her. She loves him. She should be back at the flat making sure he is OK. Not here, aimlessly wandering around her old school as if she is miraculously going to find the answers she is searching for. 'What the hell am I doing here?' Abbey thinks to herself, frowning and shaking her head as she slowly comes to her senses.

As she is about to turn back, she hears a slight movement in the classroom next to her followed by a faint cough as someone clears their throat. Unable to fight her curiosity she creeps quietly over to the open door and there, sat at his desk marking a stack of papers, is Mr Harper.

For some bizarre reason that Abbey doesn't fully understand, she feels a huge, overwhelming sense of relief and happiness as she loiters in the doorway watching him. She had instantly noted his good looks on her very first morning at Eden, when he sauntered into Principal Grants office smiling broadly and doing all he could to support and reassure her. He was kind, friendly and caring, and seeing him now in his suit with his top button undone and his tie slung over the back of his chair, his brown hair ruffled and his sleeves casually rolled up to the elbows, he seems so much younger than she originally remembered... and so unbelievably normal.

Suddenly feeling a little scared and strangely uncomfortable, Abbey takes a small step backwards, but Mr Harper catches the movement in the corner of his eye and looks up, blinking hard as he stares at Abbey in wide eyed disbelief. She stands frozen to the spots as he asses her closely and his face is etched with deep concern, causing a lump to form in Abbey's throat.

He turns in his chair very slowly, before leaning forward and resting his arms in his lap. They stare at each other for the longest time and Abbey gets the distinct impression that he is just as happy and relieved to see her.

"Hi…" He whispers cautiously, and Abbey can't find her voice to respond, unsure whether she should be here at all let alone engaging in conversation with her ex-teacher. She takes a step forward, fiddling with the sleeve of her jacket, and smiles meekly, "How are you?" He prompts.

"I'm OK…" She replies in a timid voice, "I'm not really sure why I'm here to be honest; I didn't mean to disturb you…"

"You didn't. Do you want to come in?" He gestures to the chair next to his desk, trying very hard not to spook Abbey by taking the 'softly softly' approach that usually infuriates her. She hates being treated like a child, but right now she doesn't seem to mind. For once, she actually does feel that fragile.

"If you're busy I can go…"

"No, please, here…" He pulls the chair round so that it is directly in front of him and Abbey sits down, looking up from underneath her hair and meeting his gaze properly for the first time.

"Abbey…" He whispers, leaning forward so that they are inches apart, "Are you alright?"

The wall that has been holding back all of Abbey's true emotions suddenly crumbles and that one simple question brings reality crashing into her with full force. She has being pretending for so long, trying to tell herself that everything will be fine and refusing to acknowledge how dangerous, serious and disturbing her world has recently become. She isn't alright. She is so unbelievably far from alright and she has had absolutely no one to confide in.

"No…" She chokes out, shaking her head and biting her lip.

"I didn't think so. You know your family have been really worried about you, they just want you home…"

"I can't go home…" She shakes her head again, more forcefully.

"Why not? Abbey they won't care about where you've been or what's been going on, they just want you back with them…"

"I can't leave my friends…"

"Your family need you…" he urges, softly.

"So do they. I know they aren't perfect, I know they're fucked up. But they took me in when I had nowhere else to go and I can't leave them now it's not fair. They're good people, they are… but everything is so messed up…"

"Ok, it's alright, just calm down and tell me what's been going on…" Mr Harper nods encouragingly and although she is reluctant to open up, Abbey finds that she can't stop herself.

"It was all great at first, better than great, it was amazing… and I was so happy. But then Alex got into some trouble and he needed money fast. It went fine the first time, it worked and they got the money but then the second time it all went wrong and Tom got hurt and now he's in hospital and he might die and everything's changed. It isn't the same anymore, everything's changed and no one knows what to do, I don't know what to do, and I can't keep going on like this. I'm just so scared all the time…" Abbey gasps for breath on the verge of a full blown panic attack as the words come flowing out of her in one continuous, rambling confession. Mr Harper grips her arms and holds her steady, struggling to understand a single word she is saying.

"Shhh… it's OK, it's alright, you're OK…" He pulls Abbey forward and hugs her tightly as she rests her head on his shoulder, rubbing her back while rocking her gently until she eventually calms down. The minutes pass and they remain that way as the silence between them becomes deafening.

Abbey sits up and slowly pulls away, lifting her head so that her cheek brushes against the side of Mr Harper's jaw. She turns slightly and they stare at each other with their faces close and their lips parted. She can feel his breath on her face and the atmosphere between them is charged, full of longing. He reaches up and carefully pushes her hair back, lingering again as he searches her eyes. 'What the hell is happening to me?' Abbey questions herself, quickly snapping out of the intense and surreal moment before pulling away and running her hands through her hair as she rises shakily to her feet.

"God, I'm sorry…" She stutters and Mr Harper stands as well, holding his hand out towards her.

"No…" He gasps, closing his eyes and cursing under his breath, "No I'm sorry Abbey, I truly am that was so out of line, I don't know what I was thinking…"

"I have to go. I should go…" She turns quickly and rushes towards the door but he races after her, gently grabbing hold of her arm and spinning her back round to face him.

"Please, please don't go… I didn't mean to… Christ…" He half laughs while shaking his head and rolling his eyes at the ceiling and Abbey smiles up at him feebly, "Stay. Stay and talk to me… let me help you…"

"Thank you…" Abbey whispers appreciatively, reaching up and gently touching his face with her hand before dropping it back down at her side, "But I really shouldn't have come here..." She turns again and rushes out of the classroom before he has a chance to react.

"Abbey, Abbey wait..." He shouts after her down the empty hallway, but to her relief he doesn't follow.

Abbey spends the entire bus ride back into town in a complete and utter daze. She is so unsure of what just happened - or what could have happened - between her and Harper and she is all the more confused and messed up because of it. She loves Alex. She knows she does. She still gets those crazy butterflies in her stomach whenever she thinks about him despite everything else that is going on in their lives. So what on earth was that all about?

She strides with determination down past the train station and towards the dark arches in order to get back to the flat as soon as possible. She wants to see Alex; to hold him, kiss him, and remind herself that he is who she wants, no one else... and certainly not the head of sixth form at Eden Comprehensive High School.

As she turns onto the road and approaches the flat complex she suddenly becomes aware of a set of footsteps behind her. Could it be Harper? Could he have followed her? Impossible. He was nowhere in sight when she boarded the bus and he wouldn't have a clue where she lives. Then another, much scarier realization dawns on her and her stomach drops. Could it be Marcus? Surely not, seen as all reports indicate that he is house bound and will be for quite a while, but that doesn't mean he can't send one of his cronies to reap his revenge on Alex. That is entirely possible and doesn't seem far-fetched at all.

Abbey picks up her pace and is almost home, only a few yards away, but as she keeps her head down and charges forward the footsteps behind her quicken also, getting louder as the gap between them closes. Should she scream? Should she fight? Should she try and run? Panic and fear start to take over and she scolds herself, trying hard to keep a level head so that she actually has a chance to get out of this. She finally reaches the gate but before she has chance to open it, a hand grabs hold of her jacket and tugs her backwards. She turns, ready to fight the bastard off any way she can, but as she looks into the face of her would be attacker she becomes as still as a statue and her mouth falls open with shock.

"Hello Abbey..." He states, rather formally, and she tries to force her brain and mouth to function again. She doesn't know how much more she can take today.

"Pete..." She finally gasps, and he smiles sadly at her obvious surprise, "What the hell are you doing here?"

"Mum... she saw your friend, the blonde one and followed her here. Anna said that you'd mentioned a flat in Leeds, so I knew it was only a matter of time until you showed up too..." Peter shrugs almost apologetically, and Abbey frowns. She isn't used to seeing her brother so reserved.

"Why?" She blurts out without thinking and Peter's face shows a brief flash of pain.

"What do you mean why? Why did I wait for you once I knew where you were? Because I've been going out of my fucking mind worrying about you, of course I waited..."

"Sorry, I just... I'm surprised that's all..."

"It's good to see you..." He confesses, and Abbey softens slightly, "Can we go somewhere? To talk..."

"You can't force me to come home…" Abbey snaps, considering for a moment that this might be an ambush and that her mum and Anna could be waiting round the corner in a van ready to kidnap her. Her paranoia seems to know no bounds these days. Something she has no doubt picked up from Alex. 'Alex…' Abbey sighs inwardly. She wants to see him so badly but she can't just turn away from her brother, can she? Besides, if he carries on loitering outside the flat and the lads see him he could end up in some serious trouble.

"Fine…" She relents, "We can talk, but I haven't got long…"

"OK, good, that's fine…" Peter shoves his hands in his pockets and waits for Abbey to lead the way. She can't get over how agreeable he is being. It is something she certainly isn't used to.

She doesn't want to venture too far so decides to take him down the road to The Locke. Alex had told everyone to be vigilant and to stay away from the usual haunts in case they were being staked out, but Abbey dismisses it as his over active imagination and that infamous paranoia coming into play. Perhaps if she had taken his warnings more seriously and her head wasn't spinning from the events of the afternoon, she would have noticed the dark blue van parked up at the end of the road with Gazza and Tommo sat in the front, waiting patiently, but as she is still reeling from the shock of being confronted by her brother and her bizarre encounter with Harper, she doesn't spot them.

Peter holds the door open for Abbey and they enter the pub as Tommo sits bolt upright, suddenly alert and on edge. He picks up his mobile and dials a number from memory.

"It's me. We've spotted the girl; she's at The Locke. Yeah, Ok... will do, no problem..." He hangs up and Gazza turns towards him expectantly, "Marcus says to wait and to follow her when she leaves..."

The pub is warm and inviting and Abbey sits at a table in the corner of the bar as Peter buys them both a drink. Steve the landlord smiles and nods hello with pity in his eyes and Abbey smiles back at him kindly. Of course all the locals now know that something has happened to Tom and that he is in a serious condition in hospital. They just don't know exactly what happened to put him there.

Peter places Abbey's vodka and coke in front of her and she takes a large sip, feeling as though she needs a substantial amount of alcohol after the day she has had.

"So you're a big drinker now?" Peter raises an eyebrow as he takes a smaller sip of his half a lager.

"Not particularly..." Abbey lies, irritated at the assumption, even though it is right.

"So how are you?"

"Fine thanks, you...?"

"I've been better..." He admits.

This is unbelievably awkward and Abbey really doesn't want to be here. Peter is annoying her as usual but seeing him also makes her realize how long it has actually been since she has spoken to her own family. She does miss them, in spite of everything, but she really doesn't have the strength to deal with all of those hurtful and conflicting emotions right now, not on top of everything else that has been thrown at her today.

"I'm sorry..." Peter blurts out unexpectedly - and Abbey stares at him, taken aback by the words she never thought she would hear her brother say in a million years, "I'm sorry about everything Abbey. I screwed up. We all did. It's taken me a hell of a long time to realize that. To see things from your side and to understand why you acted the way you did. I appreciate now how hard it was for you... is for you... and I'm sorry I didn't see it sooner..."

"What's brought this on?" Abbey gasps, still not completely trusting what she is hearing.

"Losing my little sister as well as my little brother..." He answers honestly, before taking another swig of his drink and looking Abbey straight in the eyes, "There were a lot of things I needed to work through. You weren't wrong, when you asked me why I couldn't say Ryan's name. It hurt too much..." Abbey flinches at the mention of her beloved twin brother and sighs sadly, shaking her head.

"You were so stubborn, so convinced that you were handling it and you wouldn't listen to me, or talk to me, about anything..." Abbey reminds him, angrily.

"I know..." He agrees, "I thought by looking after Mum, I was dealing with my grief but I wasn't... I wasn't helping her or myself. I just didn't want to face it. I know that now..."

"Well, I'm glad..." Abbey nods, "I'm glad you're finally dealing with it properly. It's important to grieve and move on..."

"We're all doing a lot better... when it comes to Ryan I mean. I guess losing a second sibling really shocks things into perspective and forces you to admit your mistakes..."

"You haven't lost me..." Abbey whispers, unconvincingly.

"I hope not. Not anymore anyway…" Peter reaches across the table and tries to hold Abbey's hand but she pulls it away. She is unsure whether she is ready to let her brother back in to such an extent and it would also be extremely bad news if one of the locals saw her holding hands with a mystery man and reported it back to Alex. Maybe she shouldn't have brought him here after all? She will have to tell Alex now anyway in case they have already been spotted by someone they know.

"Will you come home…?" Peter asks, abruptly.

"It isn't that simple…" Abbey shakes her head and sips nervously at her drink.

"Why not…?"

"Because I have a life here now…"

"I miss you, Abbey. We all do, so much. You haven't even met Amelia yet and she's getting so big now, she's growing and changing, everyday…"

"Is this why you came here?" Abbey snaps, "To guilt trip me? To make me feel bad?"

"No…" Peter holds his hands up defensively, "No, Abbey, that isn't why I'm here. I'm not playing games with you and I'm tired of arguing. Things really have changed, I've changed, and I mean it when I say I want you to come home…"

"Me too…" She sighs sadly.

"You want to come home?" The hope in Peter's voice causes guilt to lance through Abbey and she immediately regrets her choice of words.

"No… I mean, I've changed too…"

"Well…" Peter sighs, unrelenting, "seen as we've both changed, hopefully for the better… maybe we can formally introduce ourselves and start again from scratch as the brand new, well-adjusted people we are today…?" He holds his hand out to Abbey across the table and she breaks into a smile despite herself, gripping it lightly in hers before shaking it firmly as they both nod in agreement. She sits back in her chair, laughing to herself, and Peter's expression becomes serious once more.

"Please think about it Abbey. We want you to come home… I want you to come home, where you belong…"

Abbey has no idea what to say. She can't agree to that but she doesn't want to dismiss the notion entirely either. Did she always believe deep down that one day she would go back home? Maybe.

But the truth is right now, she has no idea where she belongs and she has never been more confused. Before she can find the right words to respond, the loud buzz of her mobile breaks the tension and interrupts her train of thought.

'One Missed Call: Alex'

"Something wrong…?" Peter asks, curiously.

"No. But I have to go… you should go, I mean…"

"OK. If that's what you want…"

"It is… I'm sorry…"

"But you'll think about what I said…?" They both stand and Peter grabs his jacket from the back of the chair, hooking it over his arm.

"I will. I promise…"

"Thank you for talking to me today, I'm sorry I ambushed you in the street. I just really needed to see you…"

"No I understand, and I'm glad we talked…" Abbey actually means what she says and as Peter steps forward to hug her, she lets him, returning it briefly before pulling away. He nods once, and with a grateful glance back he leaves the pub.

Abbey drops back into her chair, feeling exhausted and emotionally drained. When she woke up this morning she never expected that she would have such an eventful day. She only went for a walk to clear her head. God, that was hours ago. Alex must be out of his mind. And right on cue, her phone rings again.

Peter stands outside in the doorway of the pub feeling cheerfully optimistic. That went better than he had hoped and talking to his sister, seeing first hand that she is safe and well, has temporarily put his mind at ease. He can relax now, knowing that she is OK, and hopefully once she has had time to think things through and process the idea that their relationship can and will improve, she will be in touch.

As he throws his jacket on and zips it up against the cold, he is totally unaware of Gazza and Tommo still sitting in the blue van parked up across the street. Tommo dials through to Marcus again as they lurk in the shadows, watching him closely.

"Yeah, the lad has come out but Alex's girl is still inside. What do you want us to do?" He listens quietly as Marcus gives his command on the other end of the line, "Ok... not a problem. We'll bring him to you..." He hangs up the phone and starts the engine.

"What did he say?" Gazza asks.

"He says the girl might have slipped out the back so we're to follow him..."

"And?"

"And force him to take a little joy ride with us..." They smile at each other knowingly as Tommo swings the van around and they curb crawl towards the end of the street where Peter is walking alone.

Alex had been fairly pissed off when Abbey finally answered her phone and she knows full well that he has every reason to be. Disappearing for an entire day at a time like this probably isn't the best move she has ever made and she feels terrible for making him worry.

As she opens the front door to the flat, everyone is there, sitting around the large glass table in the dining area next to the kitchen, talking amongst themselves. Even Gemma is present which is unusual as she hasn't been around in a while due to her less than favourable opinion of Alex. But he has summoned them all together for a reason and he clearly has something to say that they all need to hear.

The others smile at Abbey in greeting as she crosses the kitchen towards them but Alex doesn't look up from his seat at the head of the table. She is standing right next to him when he finally acknowledges her presence and despite his obvious anger, her heart leaps and her stomach flips as their eyes meet. In that instant she feels whole again and all the confusion and craziness from earlier that afternoon just seems to dissipate. She belongs here with Alex; there is no doubt in her mind and as she smiles at him lovingly his bad mood falters and he smirks back, shaking his head with mild irritation.

"Have you had a nice day?" He whispers sarcastically, and Abbey frowns slightly as she leans down to kiss him.

"I'll fill you in later…" She replies, and he tilts his head to the side with intrigue, momentarily studying Abbey's face until he is satisfied that he has no reason to be alarmed.

Abbey has every intention of telling him about Peter showing up outside, but the whole Harper situation will be forgotten about, put down to a severe momentary lapse in judgement and sanity.

"So what's this all about Al?" Lucy asks, no longer able to suppress her curiosity, and Abbey moves over to sit in the empty seat beside her.

She too is curious as to what Alex has to say. He definitely has his business face on - serious and calculated - and all eyes are on him as he leans back in his chair, exhaling slowly.

"Moorland's been in touch... " He announces, "I wasn't going to bother him with all the Marcus bullshit seen as it's more or less sorted for now, but the guy that I spoke to a couple of weeks ago must have told him I'd called and he rang me last night..."

"And...?" Darren presses.

"And... I filled him in. I didn't exactly tell him everything but I explained how Marcus had demanded money from me and how the first time round, as good business, I paid him back. Then I told him how he came after me again... and what it eventually resulted in..."

"What did he think to that?" Liam asks.

"We talked... and he agreed with me, with all of us, that knowing what Marcus is like he isn't going to let this lie. He will come after me again when he's back to full strength, which could be fairly soon..."

"So he'll help?" Abbey tries to sound as calm and collected as the others, but she knows that Moorland is Alex's best shot at ending this cat and mouse game with Marcus once and for all. If he isn't willing to help, god knows what will happen? It might never be over.

"He will. The fact that I sorted it out the first time round... paid Marcus and dealt with the problem myself... he was impressed with that. Not ringing him straight off the bat was obviously the right move..." He sounds relieved, and as the lads all nod in agreement Abbey senses that Gemma is rolling her eyes, but she can't be sure. She doesn't like to look directly at her these days as the hostility she feels towards Alex understandably gets channelled towards her on occasion too. Whether it is on purpose or not, she isn't sure.

"That's good news, mate..." Nathan sighs, "Has he got some sort of plan or...?"

"Yeah, he has..." Alex's tone shifts slightly and everyone instantly tenses. This is obviously the reason he has brought them all here - to explain the details - and judging by his demeanour it doesn't seem like good news at all.

"It isn't long term, you have to remember that...."

"What isn't?" Sophie frowns, "Just tell us..."

"It's been a few weeks since I put Marcus in a bad way and if I'm right, it won't be long until he comes after me again. Because he knows you all... and what you mean to me..." Gemma shifts awkwardly in her seat and Alex looks directly at her as he speaks again, "What you *all* mean to me... it isn't safe. And I'm sorry for that. Moorland has a man up North that has a few connections in common with Marcus. He's keeping his ear to the ground, waiting for any information to come to light and when Marcus is ready to make his move, Moorland will know... and he'll be here waiting for him..."

"That doesn't sound too bad..." Lucy smiles, reassured.

"Moorland's coming here..." Alex confirms, "Which means, we can't be..."

"What are you saying?" Her smile fades and Nathan holds her hand under the table.

"Moorland has offered to sort this out for me. But if I'm here when Marcus makes his move... if any of us are... it could get seriously out of hand. He thinks it would be better for everyone, if we keep out of the way until it's over. So we all have to lay low for a while. I mean seriously below radar... that means no Locke, no park, none of the bars I deal at.... and no flat. Marcus and whoever he has doing his dirty work, they know how close we all are, they'll be expecting us to be together, so, to make it safer..."

"We can't be together until it's over..." Darren finishes his sentence in an incredibly bleak tone of voice and the room falls silent as they all try to process what that means.

"I'm not leaving Lucy..." Nathan scoffs as the realisation registers and Alex raises his hand to calm him before he loses his temper.

"And what about Gem? I'm not leaving her on her own..." Sophie snaps.

"That's not what I'm asking..." Alex shakes his head, "Nathan... you, Lucy and Liam, you should stick together but don't go to any of the usual places, not at all... I fucking mean it. You need to find somewhere away from here to lie low for a while..."

"My cousin has a place in Wakefield? It shouldn't be a problem..." Liam offers reluctantly, and Alex nods, happy with the suggestion.

"And you three should be alright at Gemma's, seen as it's well out of town. There's no reason for them to know where you live, especially since you haven't been around in a while. Is that alright with you, Gem?" She stares at Alex icily, but her disgust isn't quite as apparent as usual and she nods once.

"How long for?" Darren asks quietly, as he stares across the table at Lucy and she meets his worried gaze. They have been completely inseparable since their early teens but now it is far too dangerous for them to stay together. Nathan won't leave Lucy, and Darren can't leave Sophie. If they join up that would leave Liam and Gemma on their own and the group would be too big to go into hiding. It just isn't plausible. They are divided, and will be until Moorland decides that it is safe enough. Alex knows what he is asking and what it is costing them but his resolve doesn't slip. He knows that if they stick together they are more likely to be found and he will not lose any one else. This has to be done.

"Until I get the call..." He answers, solemnly.

"When is this happening?" Sophie whispers.

"Pretty much now guys. I'm sorry..." Alex shakes his head at the table and nobody speaks for the longest time. They are family and they have always stayed together no matter what. Recent difficult events may have caused anger and upset within the group but being actually, physically separated is another thing entirely and the idea upsets them all.

"Where will you go?" Gemma asks, and everyone looks at Alex expectantly, especially Abbey, who in the shock of the moment hadn't even stopped to think about the two of them.

"We need to get away, out of Leeds, maybe even out of England... the further the better..." He stares at Abbey, trying to read her reaction, but she keeps it hidden. She needs to hold it together right now, for him and for the others. She is determined to handle this the best possible way she can. She has to be strong for Alex... she owes him that.

Saying goodbye to everyone is horrible, especially when it comes to Lucy, Nathan and Liam. Abbey has no idea when she will see them again and the uncertainty breaks her heart. Her chest feels empty and hollow as her friends leave one by one and she struggles to wrap her head around what is happening. Just when she had been thoroughly convinced that they had hit rock bottom, this happens. 'But it is necessary...' Abbey reminds herself, 'this is going to make things right again...'

When she and Alex are finally alone he wraps his arms tightly around her waist and rests his head against her shoulder.

"We should pack..." He suggests and she nods sadly as she turns to face him.

"So, where are we going?" She asks, and he smiles down at her wistfully.

"Home..."

Chapter Fifteen

The Getaway

Peter's breathing is rapid and panicked. His hands are bound tightly behind his back and the bag that has been placed over his head is making him feel increasingly claustrophobic. His heart is beating fast and loud as he tries in vain to listen to his surroundings in an attempt to figure out where he is and what the hell is going on.

He had been walking, just walking, on his own through the bottom end of town after he had left Abbey at the pub. He was almost nearing the back of the train station when there was a screech of tyres behind him - then everything went black. The sharp pain in the back of his head confirms that he has obviously been hit and temporarily knocked out. When he came to, this is the state he found himself in.

He can hear nothing but the roar of the engine echoing through the empty hollowness of the van. They have been driving for about ten minutes now, at least that's how long he has been awake. He has no idea how much of the journey he has been unconscious for. He might not even be in Leeds anymore and the notion terrifies him. Who the hell are these people? And what do they want?

Eventually the van slows down onto crunching gravel and comes to a sudden stop. The driver and passenger doors open and slam simultaneously before the transit door slides back, causing daylight to flood inside. Peter still can't see a thing, but he can sense the change in light and he is grateful that it is still day time. He feels two pairs of hands grab him roughly by the arms and heave him forward, throwing him to the ground as the van slams shut behind him once more. He is dragged forward several feet into a cold, damp building and as he sits there leaning forward on his knees, he wracks his brain, trying to think of every possible scenario and how he can survive this in one piece.

If these guys are robbers surely they would have just taken his watch and wallet and left him knocked out cold in the middle of the street? And if they are a group of psychopaths, wouldn't they have waited until the cover of darkness to kidnap someone and butcher them for fun? The truth is, he has absolutely no idea what the hell is going on, but he has the rather distinct impression that he is about to find out.

A set of footsteps - quiet and distant at first - get closer and closer until Peter can sense someone standing right in front of him. There is a tug on the rope around his neck and the bag slides up over his head, freeing him. The fresh air fills his lungs and he relishes the sensation, before blinking hard and looking up at the imposing figure looming above.

He is fairly short and stocky, older, grey haired and mean looking, and to Peter's surprise he is dressed quite smartly in a well-tailored, navy blue suit. His face is twisted into an angry, bitter expression and it is almost completely covered in injuries. He has several cuts and healing scabs, there is bruising around both eyes and his bottom lip is drooped slightly in what looks to be a permanent state. Whoever this guy is, he took one hell of a beating from somebody.

"Do you know who I am?" He asks, bluntly and Peter blinks, only just managing to shake his head in response.

"No. No I don't. Why am I here?"

"You're here, due to a random chain of events that none of us could have predicted..." Marcus sighs almost wearily, before turning on his heel and back hand slapping Peter so hard across the face he almost spins 360 degrees. He hits the cold concrete and gasps for breath as pain spreads from his ear down to the back of his neck.

"What the hell do you want?" Peter coughs, and Marcus simply nods once. On command the two sets of hands pull him back up into a kneeling position.

"How do you know Alex Matthews?" He asks, and Peter frowns up at him confused, trying hard to focus his blurred vision while still reeling from the unexpected punch.

"I don't know who that is..."

"Is that so? I find that rather hard to believe..."

"It's true..." Peter pleads, "I've never heard of an Alex Matthews..." Before he can elaborate further Marcus swings his arm back again, this time punching him hard on the side of the jaw. There is a rush of warmth in Peter's mouth and he leans forward, resting his damp head on the cold ground while spitting out the torrent of blood that is gushing from the wound inside his now swollen cheek.

"I'll ask you again, how do you know Alex Matthews?" Peter rocks back on his heels and looks the brutish stranger in the expensive suit, square in the eyes.

"I promise you... I don't know who you think I am, but I have no idea who you are or who Alex Matthews is..." He closes his eyes and braces himself for another bout of pain but nothing comes. As he slowly glances round he can see that the man is now talking to two others - no doubt the lackeys who picked him up and brought him here - over in the far corner of the vast room.

But what is he doing here at all? Who the hell is this Matthews guy and why do they think he has something, anything, to do with him? The excruciating pain is starting to affect Peter and he can feel his eyelids drooping. He is on the verge of blacking out, but he can't lose consciousness again, not here; god knows what they will do to him. The length of rope binding his wrists together is slicing and cutting into his skin and it burns every time he flinches. The first punch has left him with a sharp, throbbing pain in the side of his head and the sensation of blood in his mouth is making him feel nauseous. After what seems like the longest time, the thug approaches him again, more than likely to start the second round of violent questioning.

"You say you don't know Matthews, but you obviously know his girl... how the fuck can that be?"

"His girl...?" Peter coughs and spits up another mouthful of blood. The anger and irritation in Marcus's face flares and he grabs Peter by the throat, squeezing his hand tightly around it so that he can't breathe, "I am trying to decide whether you are incredibly brave or seriously fucking stupid right about now son... but if I can give you once piece of advice? Do NOT fuck with me..."

As he releases his grip Peter drops back onto the floor and inhales deeply, struggling for breath as his crushed throat slowly opens back up. He is slipping, slipping away to a quiet place, but he can hear the three of them talking again and a distant voice stands out, clearer than the others.

"It was definitely him, boss. He went into the pub with her... then he came out on his own..."

Peter runs the words through his fractured mind, over and over again. The pub...? 'In with her then out on his own...' He is talking about this afternoon with Abbey. That's where all of this started, where they must have followed him from. God this has something to do with his sister, his baby sister.

"No..." Peter gasps, faintly, and once again he is hoisted to his knees.

"No...? No, what...?"

"What do you want with her...?" He asks without thinking.

"Oh so you've decided to co-operate have you?" Marcus's response sounds overly cheerful but his friendly demeanour is quickly counteracted by a sharp punch to the stomach, followed by a right hook to the left side of Peter's jaw, "It's not her I'm all that bothered about to be honest..." He continues, as if he hasn't just winded a man and fractured his face, "It's more her arrogant little fuck of a boyfriend that I'm keen to get my hands on..."

"Her boyfriend... I don't... I don't know..."

"Jesus Christ..." Marcus stands up straight and fastens his suit jacket, staring down at Peter with nothing but anger and contempt, "You've brought me a real fix here fella's, great fucking work...!"

"She's my sister..." Peter gasps, his voice becoming weaker as he drifts in and out of lucidity.

"You're sister?"

"Yes..."

"Well, your sister has recently become involved with a young man that I happen to want dead. He crossed me, more than once... he did this to my fucking face and NO ONE gets away with crossing Marcus Holt..."

"Please... please don't hurt her..." Peter struggles to keep his eyes open as his speech begins to slur. He can't hold on much longer.

"And give me one good reason why I shouldn't?" Marcus laughs, maliciously.

"What... do you want...?" Peter is slipping further down into the blackness, barely able to control his thoughts let alone engage in conversation with this total psychopath.

"I tell you what. I promise I won't hurt your sister. I will keep her out of this, as long as you tell me what I want to know..."

Peter tries to form his mouth around the word 'what' but it comes out as a quiet cough and Marcus slaps him hard around the face. It hurts, but it is nothing compared to the previous blows, he is simply trying to keep him awake so that they can finish their bargaining.

"I am only going to ask you this once. If you answer me honestly, my boy's will drop you off where they found you and all this will be over..." Marcus raises his eyebrows and Peter manages to nod despite the searing pain and high pitched ringing in his ears, "Now, it is common knowledge that Matthew's and his crew frequent The Locke, the pub you and your sister were in this afternoon... but they haven't been around in a while and I so desperately need to see young Alex and have several harsh words with him. So, you're going to tell me the truth, and you are going to tell me right now, do you understand....?"

"Yes..." Peter whispers the word so quietly it is barely audible and Marcus leans in closer, his whiskey soaked breath stinging Peter's eyes as he pronounces each word through gritted teeth.

"Where does Matthew's live?"

Peter lies on his bed staring vacantly at the ceiling, unable to move even a fraction due to the unbearable pain shooting through every limb. He feels like he has been hit by a freight train and although he is utterly exhausted, he can't fall asleep.

After he had answered Marcus' brutal interrogation the best he could, his two men had dropped him back - as promised - right where they picked him up from earlier that day, simply throwing him into a ditch at the side of the road. He managed to stagger into a more populated area closer to the city centre and it was there that two passers-by called an ambulance, kindly sitting with him until it arrived. He was treated and released within a few hours and once Anna had stopped screaming and crying at the sight of him, she just about managed to drive him home and help him into bed.

She kept asking who had done this to him but he couldn't bring himself to tell her the truth, claiming instead that he had been jumped by a gang of youths. The whole family are seriously worried about Abbey and have been ever since she left home. Now it appears that things are far more serious and fucked up than any of them could ever have imagined. How can she possibly be involved with these people? Who are these friends she is staying with and who is this so called boyfriend with such frightening enemies? None of it adds up or makes any sense.

Peter had of course tried ringing Abbey, over and over again, but as usual it went straight through to her voicemail. He doesn't know what else to do now or how to help his sister and he is terrified that the information he gave to this thug Marcus will somehow put her in more danger than she appears to be in already.

Ever since Abbey ran away from home Peter had been desperate to find out where she was living, but for the first time today he was truly grateful that he had never managed to discover her exact address, as Marcus no doubt would have beat it out of him eventually. All he could tell them was the name of the apartment block and the street it is on and he feels unbelievably guilty for giving even that much away. He feels as though he has betrayed his own sister and put her life on the line. Marcus had promised that he would leave her out of it but he doesn't exactly seem like a man of his word or someone who can be trusted. Either way, it is too late now. All Peter can do is pray to god that if and when Marcus finally discovers where Abbey and this Alex Matthews are living, she is somewhere far, far away - out of danger where she can't be harmed.

Unbeknownst to Peter, Abbey is further away than he ever could have imagined; far from the flat, from Leeds and from the threat of Marcus Holt. She sits quietly, staring out of the small, circular plane window down at the Irish Sea below. The seatbelt signs ping and light up as the stewardess announces cheerfully over the tannoy that they will be landing at Belfast City Airport within the next half an hour. Alex clips his seatbelt together and reaches for Abbey's hand, taking it gently in his, and she smiles at him as he squeezes it reassuringly. He hasn't spoken much during the flight, no doubt preoccupied with what is happening back at home with Marcus and Moorland. He isn't used to being in the dark and it isn't something he handles well.

Once the decision to split up the group had been made, the plan was instigated with lightning speed. After saying a tearful goodbye to the others, Abbey and Alex had packed their cases, locked up the flat and driven straight to Leeds and Bradford Airport. Alex had managed to book a last minute flight online and they made it with only minutes to spare, rushing through the departure lounge as though they were fleeing for their lives. 'I suppose in a way we are...' Abbey muses to herself, as the coast line of Northern Ireland looms ever closer. She has barely had time to think, to breathe, to process... and now here she is, sitting on a plane as it turns and slowly descends into Alex's homeland. First Harper, then her brother... and now an unscheduled getaway. It really has been the most insane 24 hours of her life.

Once they have collected their luggage from the arrivals gate, they make their way over to the car hire business at the far side of the building. The man behind the counter takes Alex's details and asks him how long he requires the vehicle for, which completely throws him. He has no idea how long this will take or how quickly Marcus will make his move and as a result, they could be in Ireland for quite some time. In the end they settle for two weeks, in the knowledge that if they need to extend the lease they can do so over the phone.

The incredibly polite and helpful manager walks them to the underground garage and shows them to the shiny new Volvo that will be theirs for the duration of the trip. As Alex settles into the driver's seat and starts the engine, a huge, unexpected smile slowly spreads across his face. It's as though Abbey can physically see all the anger, tension and worry draining away and he is suddenly the much younger, happier, care free Alex that she adores. It's a side of him that she hasn't seen in so long.

"Let's go..." He grins, as they exit the garage onto the main road and drive out into the early evening sun.

The journey to Ballycastle takes just over an hour and Abbey savours every second of the scenery as they head out of the bustling City of Belfast and up to the very tip of County Antrim. She has never been to Ireland before - and the scenery is breath-taking.

As they drive through the little coastal town where Alex was born, she imagines an adorable little boy with dark, chocolate brown hair and bright blue eyes, skipping through the market stalls and laughing with his mother. It is hard to picture Alex in the innocence of childhood; somehow the two don't quite mix.

"How are you feeling?" She asks impulsively, saddened by the direction her thoughts have taken.

"I'm fine. Are you OK?" He replies, concerned.

"Yeah, I just... I only ask because it must be strange for you, being back here after all this time. It must bring back a lot of memories..."

"Yeah, I suppose it does..." Alex sighs after a long pause, and Abbey can see a brief flash of sadness in his eyes before the walls close around him once more. She isn't going to get anything out of him, at least not right now.

"So where are we staying?" She asks, curiously, and Alex's mouth twitches up into her favourite smirk.

"Just a little further..."

They carry on driving down towards the sea front and round past the little Marina, where dozens of boats of all colours and sizes, bob gently on the waves. The coastline is absolutely stunning and as they cross a small bridge and veer left, Alex points towards the horizon.

"That's Fair Head..." He announces, and Abbey follows his gaze to a huge cliff face in the distance, rising high out of the bay, with dark jagged rocks cascading down into the ocean. The beach sweeps round in an elegant curve beneath it, back towards the Marina which is now much smaller, below them in the distance. It is a beautiful and dramatic sight.

As Abbey stares out across the ocean she suddenly becomes aware that they are driving quite far out of town. The road they are on is quiet, scenic and very secluded. She is about to ask how much further, when they round another bend and a pretty little cottage comes into view. It is built with white stone and is surrounded by flowers and rose bushes. Alex pulls the car up onto a grass verge beside it and turns off the engine, smiling sweetly.

"Home sweet home..." He sings, and despite everything that has happened in recent months, Abbey can't help but return his smile with enthusiasm.

For the first time since the trip was planned, she actually feels excited about being here. Up until now she viewed it purely as a getaway, as a place where they can hide from danger until the worst is over and they are summoned back to Leeds by Moorland. But now that they have actually arrived she feels a total sense of release. They are far, far away from all their problems. Nothing and no one can touch them here and it makes Abbey feel almost elated. For now, it is just her and Alex, the two of them existing together in their perfect little bubble. She misses the others terribly; they are both still deeply worried about Tom, and no matter how far she runs she can never truly escape her family problems. But here, surrounded by the outstanding beauty of the North Antrim Coast, she finds it much easier to let her worries slip away for a while.

The little cottage is gorgeous. The open plan living room is warm and inviting, with an authentic log fire and a bay window that looks out for miles across the North Sea. There are two sofas and a coffee table arranged neatly on a huge cream rug that covers a large section of the laminate floor in the centre of the room. In the far right hand corner is a door that leads into the quaint little kitchen, with its slate tiled floor and country style, cream units.

Upstairs is the bathroom and a large, double bedroom, with the decor very much following the same style as the rest of the house. Another bay window proudly displays the views outside and a huge, white, four poster bed takes up most of the floor space. Abbey is instantly charmed by the cottage and all its sweet little homely touches. Locally made ornaments and trinkets are set out proudly on display, along with large vases of fresh flowers, and various framed quotes of Irish poets and authors adorn almost every wall. It is perfect.

After what feels like a never ending day of packing, travelling and unpacking, Abbey is beyond tired. She stifles a yawn and is barely able to keep her eyes open as the time approaches 10:00pm. It has been such an exhausting few weeks and now that they are nestled away in the total peace and quiet of the Irish countryside, she can feel the lethargy taking over. Her mind has finally slowed down. It is no longer working overtime, trying to digest and process everything that she has been through and as a result, she feels as though she could sleep forever.

"Tired?" Alex whispers in her ear, startling her slightly. She is staring blankly out of the window into the darkness, nursing a glass of red wine in her hand as the log fire crackles and pops behind her.

"Yes..." She admits, "Exhausted, actually..."

"It's been a long day... week... year..." Alex smiles forlornly and she nods in agreement, "I'm sorry it's been such a struggle, Abbey..." He croons softly, placing her glass of wine on the windowsill and pulling her gently into his arms, "But it will get better..."

"I know. I think this trip will be good for us. It'll give us a break from everything, we can get some perspective back... and we get to spend some time together..."

"Well, I'm definitely on board with the last part..."

Abbey reaches up on her tiptoes and kisses Alex softly but as she pulls away he holds her firmly in place, kissing her back ardently and leaving them both breathless.

"So, how tired are you exactly?" He grins against her mouth, and before she even has time to respond she is in his arms and half way up the stairs.

The following morning the sun shines brightly in the cloudless sky, piercing through the soft white curtains that are draped across the bedroom window. As Abbey stretches out lazily, her hand nudges something by her side and she rolls up onto her elbow in surprise, staring open mouthed at Alex who is still sleeping soundly next to her. His breathing is heavy and his eyelids flicker softly as he dreams. 'What time is it...?' She wonders to herself, instantly turning and glancing at the little vintage alarm clock sitting on the bedside table. 9:45am. Alex is still asleep and it is 9:45am. That is a definite first. Perhaps he got up in the night? She was dead to the world; it isn't as if she would have noticed? But it doesn't look like he has moved and he seems so peaceful and rested. Still amazed, Abbey carefully leans down and gives him a gentle kiss on the head before climbing out of bed and tiptoeing downstairs, trying her hardest not to disturb him.

It looks like another beautiful day outside and as Abbey stares up at the clear blue sky, her thoughts suddenly turn to home. It hardly seems fair that they get to be somewhere so beautiful when the others are separated, cut off, and no doubt struggling with the situation. She quickly reaches for her phone and types out a message, sending it to Lucy and Sophie. She tells them that they have arrived at their destination safely and both she and Alex are missing them all like crazy. It is the one thing she hates most about all this, being away from the rest of the group, and she hopes that they are keeping themselves safe and coping the best they can. Although deep down she is sure that they will be fine, it is still worrying, being so far away from them.

Eager for a distraction, Abbey mindlessly fills the kettle and sets out two mugs, placing a spoonful of coffee in each. They had only managed to grab a few things to eat and drink as they rushed out of the flat so will have to go shopping later and stock up, especially if they are going to be holed up here for weeks.

Her stomach grumbles loudly at the welcome thought of food just as Alex shuffles into the kitchen, yawning and scratching the back of his head. He is only wearing his boxers and Abbey takes a moment to appreciate the sight.

"Good morning..." She smiles and he winks as he leans down to kiss her, "You slept well?"

"I did..." He states, surprised, "A little too well... It's weird. I'm not used to getting a full night; I can't remember the last time I managed that..."

"Well, this is how normal people function Mr Insomniac, better get used to it..."

"I doubt one night will have cured me for good but I do feel better..." Abbey's stomach rumbles loudly again and Alex smiles as he snakes his arms around her waist, nuzzling the side of her neck.

"Sorry..." She blushes, "I'm starving!"

"In that case how about we rustle up some breakfast and eat it in bed... spend the day curled up in that four poster...?"

"Hmmm, I like the way you think..." Abbey laughs as she prises herself out of his grip and slides across the room, opening the fridge to display it's lack of contents, "But rustle up breakfast with what, exactly?"

"Oh yeah..." He frowns, scratching his head again.

"Sleep really doesn't agree with you does it?" She laughs and he shrugs as his hair flops down over his eyes.

"Go get a shower so you feel more human, then we can go stock up on food and explore the town..."

"Is that the plan for today then?" He asks, pouting in mock disappointment.

"Yes, yes it is... now go...!" Abbey turns him in the doorway and slaps his bum as he walks back through to the living room, grumbling something under his breath.

"That's sexual harassment you know..." He shouts as he rounds the corner to the stairs, and Abbey smiles to herself as she pours out the coffee, nervously checking her phone at the same time.

No replies.

If Abbey was asked to describe Ballycastle using just one word, it would have to be idyllic. It holds so much character, with its charming little houses and their perfectly manicured gardens, the picturesque marina and the friendly hustle and bustle of the Town Square.

After raiding the local supermarket and buying enough to feed a small army, Abbey and Alex spend the rest of the day strolling around, taking in the sights and familiarising themselves with the layout. It is all brand new to Abbey, but for Alex it is simply a case of reacquainting himself with his childhood home. She isn't overly sure what effect - if any - it is having on him, as she never quite knows what Alex is thinking. He seems happy enough though, smiling and laughing, telling her tales of where he used to hang out with his friends, showing her his old school, and gasping out loud at various store fronts that have - rather unsurprisingly - changed in the last ten years. There is only a brief moment when his good mood falters and it occurs as they walk past the end of the street where Alex used to live with his Mum. Whether they happened across it by accident or on purpose she is unsure, but they do not venture down it. It clearly holds too many painful memories that Alex doesn't wish to confront.

It is a completely different way of life in this little seaside town. Peaceful, quiet and relaxing, the pace is much slower here and it is in stark contrast to the manic chaos that they have left behind them in Leeds. It is something that Abbey could quite easily get accustomed to and she finds herself secretly hoping that this issue with Marcus will take at least a bit of time to get resolved, so that she can hide away in this welcome tranquillity for a while longer.

The view from the patio of their lovely little cottage is even more striking at sunset. The clouds are illuminated by the low lying sun and the ocean shimmers below. The ragged cliff edges frame the scene perfectly and behind them the huge, majestic Knocklayde mountain bears down on them, covered in an abundance of deep purple heather. The birds sing in the trees above and Abbey sighs with utter contentment as she rests between Alex's legs - her back to his front - on a wooden sun lounger that they discovered propped up against the far side of the house. The outdoor fire pit is crackling beside them as they lay wrapped up in a large woollen blanket.

"Penny for your thoughts..." Alex asks, turning slightly to kiss the side of Abbey's head.

"I was just thinking about how easy it seems here..." She answers, a little reluctantly, "Like the further away we get from home, the further we are from all our problems. It's nice..."

"It is..." He agrees, "But you know we can't just run away from everything. It doesn't work like that..."

"I know. I know we can't stay here forever..."

"Would you want to?" Alex asks, his voice rising in pitch as he is unable to hide his surprise.

"Live like this you mean? Me and you, with nothing and no one else to worry about... yeah, maybe I would..."

"There's a big part of me that wants that too... but..."

"It's OK..." Abbey shrugs, tilting her head to look at him, "You don't have to say it. It isn't just about you and me, I get that. We have the others back home... responsibilities and obligations..."

"Doesn't mean I wouldn't hide away with you forever if I could, Abbey Miller..."

"I know..." She smiles, taking hold of his free hand and locking their fingers, "Can I ask you something?"

"Anything..."

"Is it hard for you, being back here... truthfully?" There is a long pause and Abbey holds her breath as she waits for Alex to answer.

"In a way... yeah..." He finally replies, "The last time I set foot in this town I was a completely different person... young and very naïve. I guess coming back here and the nostalgia of it all just brings it home..."

"Brings what home...?"

"I don't know..." He sighs, wearily, "How much I've fucked up in my life I guess..." Abbey's heart constricts and she turns in her seat so that she is lying on her side, resting her head on Alex's shoulder. He stares down at her with eyes older than his years and she lifts his hand up to her mouth, kissing it gently.

"You can't think like that. No one knows how their life is going to play out or what will get thrown at them. You had a pretty rough start..."

"I suppose... It doesn't stop me from wondering what my Ma would think about all this. What she'd think of me... if she'd be proud..."

"I'm sure she is..." Abbey whispers sincerely, but Alex shrugs and shakes his head, seemingly unconvinced.

"You know we used to go for walks all the time. My Ma loved to walk..." His expression becomes almost childlike as he recalls a distant memory and Abbey pulls the blanket tightly around them, before curling up in his arms, "She used to take me to the top of Fair Head and we'd look out across the Ocean. On a clear day you can see right across to the coast of Scotland. She used to say that we were on top of the world... right at the very top... and no one could touch us..."

"She sounds great, you're Mum..."

"She was. She was an amazing woman. She lived a hard life, struggled and fought like hell... but she finally found her peace here. It just never felt like enough for me. It was only one tiny part of the world and I wanted to see it all..."

"And now...?"

"And now, I think I understand her more..." He admits, "I think the reason my Mum loved it here so much is because of how isolated it can be. She adored small town life because it was so removed from all the drama and bullshit she'd managed to escape. With the exception of my dead beat Dad her life was pretty happy towards the end. Maybe that's why she appreciated it so much... maybe you have to go through real struggle to realize that the quiet life ain't so bad..."

"How did she die?" Abbey asks, unable to hide her intrigue any longer.

"A car crash..." Alex answers bluntly, but his eyes suddenly darken and Abbey can tell from his expression that there is clearly much more to the story. Her curiosity is burning, but something about his demeanour stops her from asking any further questions.

They lay there for several minutes in a reflective silence, listening to the rhythmic crash of the waves below them in the distance. Alex could never have predicted that his life would follow the path that it has. All those years ago, walking along the beach hand in hand with his mum, he had his whole future ahead of him. So much promise. Abbey can relate. Two years ago, if someone had told her how much her world was going to change she would never have believed them. She had it all planned out; her path, her future, it had all seemed so certain... and then everything unravelled in the blink of an eye.

If Alex's mum hadn't died when he was so young he never would have moved to Dublin with his uncle. He might never have lived in London and as a result he never would have crossed paths with Tom. It could have turned out so very different for all of them, if just one of those things had played out any other way. Just like if Ryan hadn't taken his own life on that miserable night two years ago, Abbey wouldn't be hiding out in Ireland with this beautiful, complicated, troubled man that she has fallen head over heels in love with. In fact she wouldn't have the faintest idea that Alex even existed.

A sudden pang of sadness shoots through her chest at the thought and she quickly dispels it. It is scary how much he has come to mean to her and she can't even begin to imagine her life without him. Especially now that they are so far away from home, cut off from their friends and everything they know. It feels like it is just the two of them against the world and for the moment at least, being here together is all that matters.

CHAPTER SIXTEEN

A DIFFERENT KIND OF LIFE

Abbey can't recall the last time she felt this relaxed, calm and content. She has been in Ireland with Alex for almost two weeks now and it has done her the world of good. She feels refreshed, happy, and for once she can actually see the light at the end of the tunnel. Removed from all the drama that has surrounded her ever since Ryan died, she finally has a clearer perspective of where she is heading and what she wants from her future. She still has a long way to go to get her life back on track but one thing she knows for certain, is that Alex will be a part of it.

The past fortnight has brought out the side of Alex that he works so hard to keep hidden, sometimes even from the closest people to him. Back in Leeds he is the man in charge, respected and revered, the no nonsense drug dealer who is always in control. But away from all that, he is just Alex Matthew's, the boy from County Antrim who has a ridiculous sense of humour and a spontaneous sense of fun. There is no business talk, no frown lines or worry etched across his face. The care free side - the true side of Alex's character - is the dominant one here and it has made

Abbey fall even more in love with him than she ever thought possible.

This trip has brought them so much closer and even after such a short amount of time, Ballycastle is starting to feel more and more like home.

"ALEX... DON'T YOU DARE..." Abbey squeals, trying to control her laughter and fake her anger more convincingly.

"Or what? What exactly are you going to do about it Miller...?" Abbey can't see Alex's face but she can sense the mischievous smile behind his voice and she knows damn well that he won't hesitate to drop her into the Ocean if she mouths off again.

She is currently hanging over his right shoulder, grabbing onto the back pockets of his jeans for support while he swings her dangerously close to the freezing cold water of the North Sea. She can't contain her laughter, despite the fact that she really doesn't want to be drenched in the crashing waves. She squeals again as he slaps her on the backside and wades further in, drenching his boots and the bottom of his Levi's. Abbey glances up and spots a couple walking their dog, smiling in amusement at the pair of them. They must look like any other young couple in love, messing about and play fighting on the beach, giving away no clue as to why they are really here. No one has the faintest idea about the kind of life they lead back home.

"You're in luck... I'm feeling charitable!" Alex announces, "Plus my feet are fucking freezing..." He laughs, running back towards the beach and placing Abbey's feet firmly back on the sand. He keeps his arm around her waist, kissing her sweetly as she punches him playfully on the arm and he jogs backwards, holding his hands up apologetically before turning around and admiring the setting sun in the burnt orange sky. It is their favourite time of day. Abbey has never witnessed sunsets like the ones in Ballycastle and the view from the beach is truly breath-taking.

She stares fondly at Alex as he stands facing out to sea with his hands in his pockets. He takes a deep breath of fresh air and exhales slowly, as a slight smile plays on his lips. Being back in Ireland has done him the world of good too. He has never been happier or felt freer and Abbey hopes more than anything that this newly acquired inner peace will last once they return home, despite knowing in her heart that it most probably won't.

Her phone vibrates loudly in her pocket and pulls her abruptly out of her thoughts. It is a message from Lucy. She has been texting much more frequently in the last few days. It is obvious that she is beginning to struggle with the separation and desperately wants things to return to normal. It can't be easy for her - or any of them back home - and Abbey feels a crushing sense of guilt at the fact that she is so happy here and that part of her secretly never wants it to be over.

Towards the end of the first week Darren had phoned Alex to let him know that Tom is awake and out of intensive care. He is still in trouble, still looking at a lengthy prison sentence, but he is alive... and the relief that both she and Alex felt in that moment was truly overwhelming. It was as though a huge weight had been lifted and it was then that the change truly happened in both of them; when they finally felt as though things might turn out OK after all. But it is far too easy to feel that way here, away from everything, surrounded by the solitude of the beautiful Irish coast. Abbey wishes things could stay like this forever but no matter what, reality is never far behind.

"What's wrong?" The alarm in Alex's voice startles her.

"Nothing... it's just Lucy texting again, saying she misses us..." She smiles casually and rolls her eyes, making light of the situation. She hasn't told Alex how much Lucy is struggling. She doesn't want to say anything that might affect his good mood and bring him down. He deserves a break from all the drama and from having to look after everyone all the time.

"What's happened? Is she OK?"

"She's fine Alex, nothing's happened..." Abbey whispers soothingly, and he relaxes slightly as he turns and saunters over towards a group of rocks that are nestled into the sand. He perches on the edge of the largest one and runs his hands through his hair, resting his elbows on his knees as Abbey sits down next to him. She gently reaches up and strokes his back as he shakes his head apologetically.

"They're fine Alex. You need to stop panicking; they can take care of themselves..." Abbey's voice is soft and calming and Alex seems to relax further, but it is clear that something is still troubling him. Abbey recognizes the look on his face and she knows all too well what it means. If he wants to talk he will, but it is best not to push him or try and force the conversation. Sure enough after a minute or two, he reluctantly speaks again.

"I just keep thinking..." He sighs, "Tom waking up, getting better... It feels too good to be true. I'm worried that because he's OK someone else will get hurt or something else will happen to fuck things up... and everything will fall apart for real this time. It's weird, but no matter how hard I try I just can't shake this fucking feeling..."

"It's not always bad news Alex..."

"Yeah...?" He laughs, cynically, "It is in my experience..."

"I know you feel responsible for them, but..."

"I am responsible for them..." He interrupts, "They're my family Abbey. It's my job to look out for them. We look out for each other and I feel like this whole fucking mess is my fault. They're all suffering because of my choices; because of the things I've done... how the hell is that fair?"

"They know the drill. Isn't that what you guys are always telling me? That you're all in it together? Why do you think that suddenly doesn't apply when things get tough? They all understand that this had to be done Alex and it's only a temporary situation..." Abbey tries to sound enthusiastic and reassuring, but it doesn't help that a huge part of her wishes that this actually was a permanent solution.

"I just can't believe how fucked up everything is now and it's all because of the life I lead, the things I've done... and for what? What the hell is it worth?"

"It will all work out... I promise..." Abbey smiles half-heartedly as she rests her head on Alex's shoulder unsure of what else to say, and he sighs again wearily, unable to shift his forlorn mood.

"I need to fix this Abs... I need to do better. I can't keep living like this. Constantly on edge, waiting for more trouble to kick off, always looking over my shoulder. It's time to make a change..."

"What kind of change...?"

"A change so that I can live my life like a normal fucking person. Cut back on my dealing; cut ties with the bars and clubs, then maybe I can speak to Moorland and eventually I'll be able to sack it off all together? I can get a real job. I was a bar manager in Dublin for a year, maybe I'll start that up again, I don't know. I'm just done with it... I'm through with surviving. I want to live. I want a normal life with no bullshit or danger. I want to be back with my friends and I want a future... with you..."

"The small town life...?" Abbey whispers as she smiles up at him with tears in her eyes. It is a revelation to hear Alex talk this way and to know that he not only wants this to be over but wants to move forward, to start fresh with a clean slate. Surely if they both feel like this then it doesn't matter what part of the world they are in? They can take their quiet, small town life back home to the City with them?

"Something like that..." He smiles shyly, "You're the first person to make me think I can have that kind of life Abbey... like I can be more than this... like I'm worth more..."

"God, you are Alex... you are worth so much more than what you see of yourself. You're a good man, I know you are... and I love you..."

"I love you too..." He sighs, his voice filled with longing and relief as he leans forward and kisses Abbey softly on the lips, "That's why you deserve so much more than this. You deserve better. I keep talking about how important friends and family are and I feel like I've kept you from yours..."

"That's not true..." Abbey frowns defensively, a little surprised at the way the conversation has turned,

"The choices I've made regarding my family I've made by myself..."

"But I haven't exactly helped. I haven't tried to convince you to get back in touch with them and sort things out. Because I'm fucking selfish when it comes to us and I'm sorry..."

"Don't be. I'll deal with my family my own way Alex, you don't get to feel responsible for that too..."

"OK, I guess not. But your brother reached out to you, maybe it's time to try and fix what's broken? Being back here, with all the memories... I can't tell you how much I miss my Ma. I'd give anything to be able to speak to her again. Despite all the mistakes she's made, your mum is still your mum Abbey... try not to forget that..."

"OK Jeremy Kyle, I'll do my best..." Abbey quips as she rolls her eyes insolently and Alex bursts into laughter. His mood instantly lifts and he is back to happy, smiling care free Alex just like that. The man is still so unpredictable... emotional roulette.

"Watch it or you'll be in the sea good and proper this time..." He jokes, standing up and holding his hand out to Abbey. He pulls her to her feet and throws his arm around her shoulders as he kisses her forehead. The sun has almost set and the chill breeze whips off the waves, dancing around them as they walk entwined with one another, sheltering from the cold.

Abbey is quiet, running over the conversation in her mind and trying to understand what it all means. From what she can gather, there is hope. Hope for the future, for their future. That's how it feels. Both she and Alex appear to be on the same page and she is excited about the prospect of a simpler life and a brand new start. For the first time in two weeks, Abbey doesn't feel quite so dismayed at the idea of going home and that is definitely, a good sign.

There is a loud bang as Marcus breaks through a panel of glass in the communal door of Alex's apartment block and it shatters noisily to the floor. He waits for a moment, listening out for the slightest sound or movement but no one stirs. He carefully reaches through and unhooks the latch, pushing his way into the lobby followed closely by three of his henchmen.

It had taken Marcus a while to find out exactly which flat Alex calls home, but after trying and failing numerous times he'd had the ingenious idea of dressing one of his men as the local postman.

It may sound ridiculous, but it got results. Tommo had waited around the side of the building for the actual post to be delivered, then managed to sneak his way inside and carefully check every single one of the pigeon holes situated at the bottom of the stairs.

His fake uniform successfully fooled the several occupants who had walked passed him in the hall; all of them completely oblivious to the fact that he was actually stealing post instead of delivering it. Just as he was losing hope of finding anything, there sticking out in plain sight, was a bill, addressed to Mr A Matthews of flat number 38 - 9th floor. It was the information that Marcus had been waiting for and he was eager to make his move as quickly as possible. He had devised a plan, run it by his men, and now here he is, breaking and entering at 3:00am and bristling with excitement at the confrontation to come.

The four of them - all dressed in black clothing - slide silently into the lift and Tommo presses the button for the ninth floor. A minute later the doors ping open and none of them speak as they make their way stealthily down the hall. They check the numbers on each door as they pass, quickly reaching the end of the corridor and flat number 38.

A bitter smile spreads across Marcus' face and he pauses to savour the moment before nodding to Tommo and Gazza. They step forward without hesitation and pull a large sledgehammer out of the duffel bag that the other lackey has been carrying for them. He dutifully keeps watch as they prepare to break down the door, waiting for Marcus' command.

"WAKEY WAKEY ALEX, RISE AND SHINE..." Marcus shouts with glee, and with one swing they destroy the latch and break the door handle clean off. As they charge into the kitchen Marcus' excitement instantly disappears and his face drops as he stands rooted to the spot. The other three flank him on either side while staring silently in open mouthed shock.

"Well, well... Marcus Holt. It's certainly been a while..." Sat at the glass table like a civilized host greeting a guest at a party, Chris Moorland slowly crosses his legs and rests his hands in his lap. He has a polite smile on his face, but it is simply there to mask his true intent, "I think we have a lot to talk about don't you?" He asks, with a hint of menace.

The other seven seats situated around the glass table are taken up by Moorlands men, all of whom sit in a stony silence with absolutely no emotion showing on their faces. They are completely impassive.

"Moorland…" Marcus just about manages to regain his composure but his voice sounds shaky and uncertain, "to what do we owe this pleasure?" He asks.

"I think you know the answer to that Marcus…"

"I'm unsure as to why you're here, Christopher. Surely any dispute I have with young Alex is between the two of us. It doesn't really concern you…" A wide, genuine smile spreads across Moorland's face and he gestures to the man who is sitting in the seat across from him. He instantly vacates the chair and circles the table so that he is standing behind Moorlands right shoulder.

"Why don't you sit down?" Moorland invites politely and Marcus cautiously makes his way over, pulling the seat further back and away from the table. Tommo and Gazza remain loyally by his side but they are starting to look increasingly uncomfortable, "And you… shut the door will you? We don't want to disturb the neighbours if we can help it, do we?" He smiles a sinister smile and the lackey looks awkwardly to Marcus who simply nods in agreement. As the door clicks shut Moorland turns his full attention to Holt and ignoring everyone else in the room, they stare at each other for the longest time. Moorland is the first to speak.

"You're messing with my interest's old friend…" He claims in a threatening whisper.

"I'm here to get my revenge, revenge I clearly deserve…" Marcus instantly snaps back, gesturing towards his face.

"As far as I'm aware, you were the one who dug your own grave… or, scarred your own face, shall we say? You came after him, he got you the money, which to be honest I certainly wouldn't have done… but young

Alex clearly felt as though he owed you in some way. You both agreed the debt was paid and then you went back on your word, you pushed your luck… this was the result…" He waves his hand casually, as if they are sat chatting about the weather.

"My dispute with Alex goes back a damn sight longer than you know…"

"He filled me in…" Moorland shrugs, "Told me how he left you, how he'd had enough of your unpredictable ways. It's a free country Marcus; he's entitled to do that…"

"And if he did the same to you? Cut you off, ended your business relationship without warning? How would that sit with you?"

"I certainly wouldn't turn it into a personal vendetta if that's what you mean?"

"Of course you wouldn't…" Marcus scoffs sarcastically, and Moorland tilts his head and raises an eyebrow. His patience is limited and it is wearing thinner by the minute. Marcus Holt is without doubt the complete polar opposite of him. The way he conducts himself and the way he handles his business. His approach couldn't be more different. They have known each other for years and have inevitably crossed paths before, but he has made a point of staying away from this wannabe gangster and his amateur ways as much as possible. This whole debacle is proof that he is clearly no professional and Moorland is highly irritated that he has had to travel all the way from London to deal with him. It is a waste of his time and an extreme inconvenience.

"This ends now…" Moorland states and Marcus immediately goes on the defensive as his self-assured confidence returns.

"It ends, when I say it does…" He grins.

"No. It ends now, Marcus. If I were you I would accept that and disappear quietly, because I am less than thrilled about having to leave my home and my family to travel up here and deal with you. I'm annoyed at the fact it's 3 o'clock in the morning and I'm sat in this kitchen conversing with a fucking mediocre halfwit who isn't even worth my time when I could be in bed with my wife…"

"Mediocre halfwit…?" Marcus snarls as he rises to his feet, and Moorland stands too as the rest of his men rise in unison beside him, preparing themselves for a possible fight but still displaying no emotion what so ever. The tension in the room is palpable and the forced civility that has been displayed so far is teetering on a knife edge.

"That's right…" Moorland confirms as he walks around the table, standing face to face with Marcus. He towers over him, his presence powerful and domineering.

"And what if I refuse to disappear quietly…?" Marcus smirks with slightly less authority than before, and Moorland leans forward so that the two of them are standing just inches apart, staring angrily as his lip curls back.

"I'll make you…" He whispers and Marcus doesn't respond. He simply takes a subtle step backwards to widen the gap between them and swallows hard, "You're a little fish in a tiny fucking pond, my friend. You don't even come close to being in my league and you know it. Alex Matthews is one of my investments… if anything happens to him, my business suffers and that is not something I will tolerate, do you understand me?" Marcus nods slowly and Moorland's demeanour quickly slips back into mock friendliness as he ushers them through the kitchen, "Well then, I'm glad we all understand each other. It's late, I'm sure you fella's ought to be getting home...?"

Moorland smiles as he opens the front door and gestures politely out into the hallway. The lackey can't get out of there quick enough and he is followed closely by Tommo and Gazza, who are trying hard to keep their tough guy images intact whilst being completely out of their depth. Marcus is the last to approach the door and his anger is visibly raging below the surface, yet he is unable to act. He knows - although it pains him to admit it - that Moorland is right. He is far more powerful and connected and he is definitely the wrong man to cross. His revenge will have to wait until the day Alex no longer has Moorland's protection, which could be years down the line, but he will bide his time. He will not forget this.

"If I have to come up here again because of you there'll be no pleasantries or friendly conversation around the dinner table. I am only going to warn you once. Stay away from Matthew's. Do you hear me?"

"Loud and clear..." Marcus snarls through gritted teeth before striding furiously out of the flat, his face twisted in anger and his fists clenched at his side.

To Alex's own amazement, he has managed to stop obsessing about what is taking place over 200 miles away in Leeds. When he and Abbey arrived in Ireland it was all he could think about and focus on, yet now, after a relaxing couple of weeks and receiving the unbelievably good news about Tom's improvement, he has decided to take a more laid back approach. 'What will be, will be'. There is little he can do about it now anyway, tucked away with Abbey in this tiny little corner of the world.

He has always had an extremely hard time putting his trust in other people, especially when trusting them to sort out his problems, but this time, he had been left with no other choice. He knows that Moorland will do right by him, but his friends are the only people he believes in enough to rely on completely; his friends and Abbey. She is the one person he has opened up to more than anyone else in his life. She has helped him, fixed him almost, although he is still perfectly flawed on many varying levels and probably always will be. But he feels different with her, like he isn't battling through this shitty life alone anymore. She picks him up when he spirals down, calls him on his bullshit and makes him laugh when he needs it the most.

Like now, as he leans in the doorway of the tiny little kitchen watching her dance around in her underwear and a faded T-Shirt that is full of holes, he feels completely at ease. She looks so good. And whatever it is she is cooking, smells amazing. It is simple moments like this, these little snap shots in time, that make him yearn for this kind of life. He wants out of the world he has lived in for so long. He wants, for once, to walk a decent path instead of constantly straddling right and wrong. He wants it all and he wants it with Abbey.

Yet if he is totally honest with himself, he isn't sure if he will ever be able to fully break away from the drug dealing and petty crime that over the years have become commonplace. Anything outside of that world feels completely unknown to him.

"Anything I can do?" He asks, as he opens the fridge door and pulls out another beer. Abbey turns, not quite startled but clearly not expecting him to be standing so close.

"No thanks. I think I have everything under control...!" She smiles, skipping over to him in time to the music and planting a tender kiss on the corner of his mouth. Alex takes a swig of beer as she turns back to the stove and he watches fondly as she sways back and forth, singing under her breath more than a little out of tune. Smiling, she tilts her head round and raises her eyebrows.

"Are you making sure I don't burn anything?" She enquires, sarcastically.

"No... mainly I'm just enjoying the view..."

"Is that right? Well dinner is almost ready..." Alex takes the hint and slaps Abbey's backside as he walks back into the living room and over to the two seater dining table that sits in front of the bay window. It is another perfectly clear night. The moon reflects beautifully across the ocean which is calm in the stillness and the sky is littered with stars.

"Shall I open a red or are you sticking with beer?" Abbey shouts from the kitchen.

"Red is good..." He yells back, unsure whether she has heard him over the music until she dances through the door with the bottle in one hand and two glasses in the other. She wiggles her hips and uses them to push Alex out of the way so she can place them down on the table and he grabs hold of her waist, kissing her neck.

"It's really not fair of you to flaunt a vision like that arse you know?"

"I am not flaunting... I'm dancing! And you get to see this arse on a regular basis so it shouldn't really be affecting you in such a red blooded way...!" Alex laughs at her feministic statement and kisses her seductively below the ear.

"The day you don't affect me in that way Miller, it will be a fair few degrees colder in hell. It's out of my control..." As he begins to slide his hand underneath her t-shirt Abbey slaps it away and wriggles in his arms.

"Well you'll have to control it right now because the food is ready..."

"Forget the food..." Alex murmurs as he nuzzles her neck.

"ALEX!" Abbey giggles, trying her hardest to squirm free, "It's still on the stove, it's gonna catch on bloody fire in a minute...!" As she breaks out of his grasp and darts back into the kitchen he shakes his head in amusement.

"I suppose we don't want you setting off the smoke alarm again, do we?"

"I did not set the smoke alarm off, it was the log fire!"

"If you say so..." He smirks.

"I'll have you know the smoke alarm loves my cooking..." Abbey states defiantly, "It always cheers me on!" Alex laughs loudly at Abbey's joke which has an element of truth to it, but before he has chance to sit down at the table his phone rings and he jogs over to where it is plugged in on charge, picking it up and swiping the screen.

"Hello?"

Abbey serves up the food and carries it proudly through to the living room, but her smile quickly fades as she notices the concern etched on Alex's face. He is leaning against the fireplace with his phone to his ear, listening intently. His anxious body language speaks volumes and it is there in his eyes, that look that she had almost forgotten about, the one she hasn't seen since they left home. He is in full on business mode and the serious, defensive, in control Alex is back without question.

"OK... so what now?" He asks.

Abbey can guess who is on the other end of the line and her heart sinks as she drops dejectedly into one of the chairs, suffering from a sudden loss of appetite. It is the call she has been dreading. She knew it was bound to happen eventually but she isn't ready to give all this up and return home to face reality. She doesn't want to leave, "OK. Thank you... and I'm sorry about all this. I never meant for it to get so out of hand, I really appreciate you stepping in.... will do... thanks..." Alex hangs up the phone and turns to face Abbey. The flickering orange glow from the fire lights the contours on his face, plunging him half into shadow, almost as if the darker side of his personality is already clawing its way back to the surface.

"Moorland?" Abbey asks, meekly.

"Yeah... apparently it's all sorted..." His answering tone is just as quiet as he stares down at his feet.

"So I guess the holiday's over..." Abbey tries to muster a smile but she can feel the tears forming behind her eyes as she desperately tries to swallow back the lump in her throat, "I should probably start packing..." She stands and Alex frowns at her, taking three steps forward as he holds his hand out tentatively.

"Aren't you going to eat your food?"

"I'm not so hungry now..." Abbey can hear the tone in her voice changing into one of sadness and disappointment. She knows this isn't Alex's fault and that they had to go home eventually but she is struggling to hide her true feelings.

"I'm sorry; I wish we could stay, but..."

"I know..." She sighs, closing the gap between them and wrapping her arms loosely around Alex's waist. He bends his knees so that they are both at eye level and tilts her chin up, forcing her to look at him.

"Things will be different. All the bullshit with Marcus, it's over now and once were back home things will be a lot easier. I promise..." Abbey smiles and nods in agreement as Alex pulls her into a tight embrace. She wants so badly to believe his words but she isn't reassured. After the conversation several days ago on the beach she is well aware that they want the same things and she genuinely believed him when he confessed to craving a normal life, with no more crime or drug dealing or wannabe gangster thugs threatening them at every turn. But now that the notion of going back to Leeds is an actual reality she can feel the dread creeping back in and the dark clouds descending. Something tells her that the life they both long for isn't going to be quite as easy to maintain away from their perfect little bubble in Ireland.

The journey home turns out to be worse than Abbey could have predicted. Alex is lost to her again... locked away deep in his thoughts, with those all too familiar frown lines permanently fixed on his face. She can tell that he is already planning three steps ahead, plotting his next move, ready to get back into the swing of things. Business as usual. She can feel the young, care free side of him slipping further and further out of her grasp as the distance between them and their beautiful little cottage grows.

At the airport they sign off the papers for the hire car and head straight to the departure lounge. The plane is delayed by half an hour due to bad weather, prolonging the inevitable and torturing Abbey even further. When they do finally take off, the flight feels like it is over in no time at all and they are soon descending into Leeds and Bradford Airport. Home at last.

It is a little after 8:00pm when they finally arrive back at the flat. As they round the corner to the front door Alex's pace slows and Abbey peers around his shoulder, trying to see what has caught his attention and made him approach more cautiously. The front door handle is completely smashed in, with several splinters of wood sticking out of the frame work and scattered across the floor.

Abbey is about to say something but stops herself as she hears a low murmur from inside the kitchen. She feels a rush of panic and grabs hold of Alex's arm. Surely they haven't returned home to a trap? Is Marcus in there waiting for them? But as she strains harder to listen, her breathing steadies when she recognizes the familiar voice. Alex opens the door and as they step inside, Lucy, Liam and Nathan all turn in unison. They are sitting around the glass table where Moorland and his men were gathered just two nights earlier and after a brief pause as the realisation sinks in, Lucy dives out of her seat and launches herself across the room. She throws her arms around both Alex and Abbey, almost knocking them over with the force of her hug.

Abbey's mood instantly lifts as she is overcome with happiness and relief. She had been focusing so hard on her and Alex's relationship - revelling in the fact that they were so far away from home and all of their troubles - that she had buried her feelings for her friends and pushed everything else to the back of her mind. It is only now, as Lucy is hanging off her neck refusing to let go, that she realizes just how much she has missed them.

"Hey Luc..." Abbey just about manages to choke out, and she finally takes a step back as Nathan and Liam look on, amused but also seemingly relieved.

"Don't you two ever, ever leave like that again OK?" She practically yells, and Alex gently drapes his arm over her shoulders, kissing her on the top of the head.

"We won't..." He smiles, and Abbey and Alex hug Liam and Nathan in turn as Gemma appears in the hallway, lingering sheepishly by the door.

"Are you OK?" She asks.

"Yeah, we're fine..." Alex replies hesitantly, "How are you?"

"Better. Better now you guys are back..." She smiles timidly and he crosses the room, pulling her into a comforting embrace which she returns. Things seem to be looking up already.

"So where did you guys get to?" Liam asks.

"Ireland..." Abbey replies, smiling at Alex as they both think back to their perfect little escape, "We hired a cottage by the sea, went for walks on the beach, ate in every night... it was nice..."

"Sounds like a riot..." Liam laughs mockingly and Abbey punches him on the shoulder in protest.

"It was a nice change of pace..." Alex agrees and Liam pulls an 'I never had you down for the quiet life' kind of expression. If only he knew what Alex had confessed to her while they were over there? Maybe in time they will see the difference in him for themselves, if he sticks to his word and actually makes those changes. That remains to be seen.

"Well, you obviously had a better time of it than we did. Liam's cousin, god bless him for putting us up, but seriously, to say he isn't the cleanliest of guys would be a major understatement…!" Lucy screws up her nose as if visualising an unwanted memory and shakes her head in disgust.

"After three weeks it was starting to get a bit much…" Nathan nods in agreement, "We were getting a little stir crazy…"

"Yeah I can imagine…" Alex sighs, "I really am sorry for having to ask you to do this…"

"Well, it's over now…" Lucy practically sings and Abbey can't refrain from hugging her again. She has missed her bubbly, infectious optimism more than she can say.

"And everything can go back to normal…" Abbey adds cheerfully, but instead of being met with reassuring smiles and agreement from the others, Lucy, Liam, Nathan and Gemma all look down at the feet, shifting nervously.

"Almost…" Gemma whispers sadly and Alex stares at each of them in turn.

"What is it?" He asks, but before any of them can answer the battered front door creaks open and Darren and Sophie appear. Abbey instantly rushes over to Sophie and hugs her tightly as Alex shakes hands with Darren, pulling him forward and slapping him affectionately on the shoulder.

"You alright brother…?" Darren asks, as he takes a step back.

"Yeah… we're good. It's good to see you man…"

"You too…" He smiles, but he is visibly apprehensive and despite being happy to see Alex and Abbey home safe, something is clearly troubling him. Alex slowly scans the room again and everyone appears to be avoiding his gaze on purpose, everyone apart from Abbey, who is equally mystified.

"Will someone please tell me what the fuck is going on…?" He demands, and Darren reluctantly steps forward.

"It's Tom…" He replies, sombrely, "He's looking at nine and a half years…"

CHAPTER SEVENTEEN

VISIONS

The transport entrance to Armley Prison is an eerie and unnerving sight. The large green door sits underneath a stone archway that is positioned in the middle of two castle style turrets and the faded brick work and iron clad windows have a dark, medieval look to them. Just off to the side there is a slightly less intimidating entrance which leads into the lobby of the main building.

Alex zips his jacket right up to the collar and thrusts his hands in his pockets in an attempt to block out the cold that is sending a chill right through him. He doesn't know whether he feels this way due to the miserable weather or because of the empty dread that this place instils in him.

It is 5:30pm on a Wednesday evening and as he listens to the pounding rain hammering down on the roof above, he stares vacantly at the sign standing a few feet to the right that declares this as the 'Visitor's Entrance'. The irony isn't lost on him. He is entering Armley Gaol of his own free will when he should really be wearing the light grey prisoners garb and pacing irritably in his cell. Alex cannot stand the idea of being locked up. Losing his freedom is his worst nightmare and he knows all too well that he wouldn't be able to handle it. He can't think of anything worse and his stomach twists with a nervous guilt as he waits in line to see his best friend for the first time in over two months.

Tom is in this position because of him. He got a nine year sentence because he refused to admit that he was working alongside anyone else during the robbery, insisting that he acted alone. In short, he didn't give Alex or Darren up to the police, which would no doubt have bought him favour with the judge. He took the full responsibility and even if he gets out in half the time on good behaviour, it is still five years of his life that he will never get back.

As Alex reaches the front of the queue he empties his pockets into one of the small, metal lockers and stands with his legs apart and his arms raised. A female prison warden carefully pats him down, first the right side then the left. She checks his documentation against his name on the list and waves him through without a single word. Why is it that people in positions of authority such as prison guards or airport security, always have a way of treating you like a suspect? They look at you as though you've done something wrong even when you are following orders and towing the line.

If only she knew the truth.

Alex enters a large, open plan room alongside the other visitors and discreetly picks a table over by the window. It is very basic, with stark white walls and a linoleum floor that squeaks under foot. The numerous benches are set out in orderly rows, each with four chairs arranged neatly around them and there are two hefty looking security guards lurking vigilantly in the background. As the door that leads from the prison block slides open, the inmates file quietly into the room in a regimented fashion. Tom is the last to appear and Alex instantly stands, half raising his hand to catch his attention.

He struggles with a conflicting range of emotion as he watches Tom slowly cross the room, feeling happy, relieved and extremely thankful that he is walking, talking, alive and still breathing; but at the same time, seeing him so uniformed in the standard grey prison sweats and t-shirt makes his heart sink. It is a painful vision and it makes the situation - and his guilt - all the more real.

They smile feebly at one another in an awkward silence as Alex tries to think of something to say, but every form of greeting that runs through his mind seems far too casual and informal. Eventually, at exactly the same moment, they both take a step forward and pull each other into a desperate hug. When they finally break apart they each take a seat and Tom rubs his face with his hands.

"You look like shit..." He jokes and Alex smiles despite himself. God he's missed him.

"It's not a patch on how I feel mate..." He answers solemnly and Tom shakes his head at the floor.

"We don't need to have this conversation Al. I'm not angry; I don't feel betrayed. You'd have done the same for me if it was the other way round... I know that..." Alex nods earnestly in response. It's true. Despite how much losing his freedom would destroy Alex he would still go down for Tom if he had to. He would die for him; and he knows that same level of loyalty works both ways. Tom would die for him as well. He almost did.

"How are you holding up...?" Alex asks.

"I'm alright. I had my last hospital visit yesterday and they say I'm fighting fit, so that's good. I don't think I'll be doing back flips anytime soon but I'm healed..." Alex nods again and Tom smiles at his lost, guilt ridden expression, "It really doesn't matter how many times I tell you this isn't your fault... does it?" He laughs quietly under his breath.

"Why did you do it you silly bastard...?" Alex sighs in frustration, "Why the fuck did you have to push me out the way?"

"Keep your voice down..." Tom warns, as he glances subtly over his shoulder, checking for the guards that are pacing the room. Thankfully, they are out of earshot.

"Don't think I'm not fucking pissed off with you for making that call..." Alex snaps, leaning forward and glaring at him irritably. A look of amusement slowly begins to spread across Tom's face and he throws his hands up in the air in mock indignation.

"Fuck me! You're welcome you ungrateful prick..." He states - and once again he somehow manages to snap Alex out of his anger. They both end up laughing despite the fact that there is nothing even remotely funny about the situation they find themselves in. It might seem crazy but it is incredibly therapeutic, and Alex wishes more than anything that they were sat outside in The Locke beer garden having this conversation over a cold pint, instead of here in this horrible stale room that smells like crap food and disinfectant. He'd give anything to change this.

"How are the others doing?" Tom asks, once they eventually calm down.

"Now that you're not banging on death's door anymore they seem to be doing alright. I hear Gem's been to see you?"

"Yeah..." Tom laughs, rolling his eyes, "Silly cow had to go and wait until I was banged up to finally admit how she feels, didn't she? I've loved her for years and she tells me now..."

"She's worth the wait..." Alex notes, instantly flinching at his own words as they take on a dual meaning.

"That she is..." Tom smiles again, but this time there is a hint of sadness in his eyes.

True to form, Tom always knows what Alex is thinking usually before Alex even knows himself, and as the clock ticks down on the hour they have together, they are both fully aware of how this conversation is going to end.

"And all the shit with Marcus?" There is more than a hint of venom in Tom's voice as he pronounces his name, "It's over...?"

"It seems to be. Moorland came up and they had words. Marcus is an arrogant prick and he 'ain't exactly the sharpest tool in the drawer but even he isn't stupid enough to cross Moorland. He knows that's a fight he can't win..."

"Pays to have friends in high places..."

"Maybe..." Alex shrugs, "I guess we'll see if it's made a difference. Either way I'm through with running..."

"Just be careful..." Tom warns, "I can't watch your back from inside a prison cell..."

"You just look after yourself mate. I need you out of here in one piece..."

"I'll do my best..." Tom jokes, dryly and the hollowness that Alex feels in the pit of his stomach rises up, consuming him. He wants to grab Tom and break him out of this shit hole. He wants him back home at the flat, listening to his terrible trance music, moaning about his hang over and snoring so loudly that it gives Alex a headache. In all the time they've been friends, they have been inseparable. Now they are going to spend at least the next 5 years apart.

The conversation becomes much lighter for the remainder of the visit as they talk about their friends, reminisce about the past and laugh about the good times; remembering the days before everything got so complicated and messed up. Alex savours every moment. It feels so good, just sitting with his best friend, talking and laughing together, especially seen as the last time he saw him he was unconscious in a hospital bed. Despite the agony and hopelessness that Alex feels at Tom being locked up, he is beyond grateful that he is still here. He has absolutely no idea what the hell he would have done if he had been killed.

"Ten minutes please..." One of the guards bellows loudly - and Alex glances at the clock above the door. Why does time always move so fast when you don't want it to end? He takes a deep breath as Tom stares down at his hands on the table, before leaning back in his chair with a half-smile on his face. He already knows what Alex is about to say and that Alex really doesn't want to say it, but he has no choice... not really.

"I'm gonna be alright mate. I'll keep my head down and my mouth shut. I'll be on my best behaviour, a fucking model prisoner. You won't need to check in on me anyway..." Tom is trying to appear upbeat and unfazed but Alex knows him better than that. This is killing both of them.

"I wouldn't be checking in for fuck sake. I want to come and see you, because I miss my best mate, there's no other reason to it than that... but I'm... you know it's not..." Alex stutters and sighs in frustration as he struggles to find the right words and the guilt gnaws away at him as he knows he has to unwillingly betray Tom again.

This visit is the first... and the last. Alex's name is now noted down on prison records and the more he comes to see Tom the more suspicion he will raise. His name will flag up on the visitor's sheet and the police will be on the lookout for anyone that Tom speaks to regularly. They know damn well that he wasn't acting alone. They've seen the CCTV footage from the night of the raid and they've heard the eye witness accounts from the store owner and the two nurses that saw them drop Tom at the hospital. It was also a massive risk for Alex to go and see him in intensive care and he was spotted there too. It could all stack up against him and he needs to be on the outside, for Abbey and for the others, to keep the group together. They both know that... and that is why this all too brief hour has to be the last time they will see each other until Tom is released.

"Five minutes now please..." There is a sudden buzz in the room as the 30 or so friends and relatives begin to say their cheerful goodbyes, none of which are as final as Alex and Tom's. He wishes this was a more private moment and that he had chance to say everything he wants to say but there is no more time. Any minute now he has to walk out of those doors and leave his best friend behind.

"I'll miss you man..." Tom whispers, no longer able to mask his sadness and pretend that he is fine and Alex doesn't respond, too busy biting back the threatening tears.

"Start making a move please...?" The guard asks as he passes their table and Alex waits until he is out of earshot before he speaks again.

"I am so, so sorry mate..." He states slowly and sincerely, while looking directly into Tom's eyes. This time there is no sarcastic response or light hearted joke. He simply nods knowingly in return.

The room is clearing fast and they both rise to their feet, tucking their chairs neatly back under the table before moving round to face each other. There is nothing left to say, just an understanding between them that this is necessary... and that it can't be changed. They embrace again, with even more desperation than before.

"I love you brother..." Alex whispers and Tom pulls away, gripping both of his shoulders tightly.

"Just be safe, mate... and be fucking happy for Christ sake..." He laughs, and Alex forces a smile, "Stay out of trouble yeah? And look after Gem for me?"

"I will..." He nods, as Tom backs away from him under the watchful gaze of the security guards, pausing once more at the door with his hands in his pockets and that typical cockney grin plastered across his face.

"I'll see you on the other side mate..." He nods - and with that he disappears out of view as the bell signals loudly and the door slides shut, locking forcefully behind him.

Abbey has never seen Alex so quiet and withdrawn. Ever since he went to see Tom in prison he has barely spoken a word to anyone. She knows how much he is struggling but as frustrating as it is, she is unable to help him in any way. Nothing can change what has happened.

Their beautiful little cottage in Ballycastle feels like a vague and distant memory and just as she suspected, things have almost completely returned to normal since their arrival back in Leeds. As far as she is aware, Alex hasn't ended any of his arrangements with the clubs he runs drugs at and he seems more involved with Moorland than ever, no doubt partly due to the fact that he feels indebted to him for sorting out his problem with Marcus. It is beyond disappointing, as Abbey now knows what kind of life they could have together if they left all this behind and started again. She got a taste of it in Ireland and she wants more.

Although saddened that he hasn't yet made any changes or followed through on his promise, Abbey is aware that it isn't just Alex who needs to confront some of the issues in his life. The advice he had given her that day on the beach regarding her family has remained firmly in the back of her mind. How would she feel, if like Alex, she no longer had the opportunity to speak to her mum again? What would that do to her? Maybe he is right... maybe it is time to reach out and try and rebuild some bridges. After all, you never know which moment is going to be your last or how many chances you might get.

The idea of texting Janet out of the blue after all this time is an incredibly daunting one, so Abbey decides it will be much easier to reach out to Peter first. After they had spoken over that brief drink at The Locke she had admittedly felt a fleeting notion of hope. He appeared much calmer, much more understanding, and he actually listened to her for the first time since god knows when.

It does seem like he has changed and is genuinely ready to sort things out and after thinking about everything long and hard, Abbey realises she wants that too. Her family are her family after all, despite how dysfunctional they may be.

After sending a message apologising for not being in touch and explaining that she had been away, Abbey asks Peter if he wants to meet up again and his response is quick.

'We definitely need to talk. What time and where? Not The Locke...'

OK. Not exactly the reply she was expecting. He seems overly tense and she has no idea what he could possibly have against The Locke, but she needs to be reasonable and meet him half way.

'Tomorrow? We can meet at The Coffee shop by the train station? X'

'That's fine. I'll see you there at 12pm.'

Perhaps she had imagined how well their last meeting went? Was the difference she had noted in her brother nothing more than wishful thinking? These texts certainly aren't as receptive as she was hoping they would be, but it is difficult to accurately read emotion through a message and she really needs to stop being so paranoid. She won't know for sure until she sees him face to face.

Her nerves start to kick in and she is suddenly anxious about the impending meeting. Luckily she has a pleasant distraction in the form of Lucy; and spending time with her best friend again definitely makes being back home much easier to handle. They always seem to be surrounded by unavoidable drama, yet it is easily forgotten and pushed to one side with Lucy.

She is an eternal optimist, always the joker, making everyone laugh and cheering them up. It is exactly what she needs.

"So it's two table spoons of this stuff, right...?" Lucy frowns, rubbing her face with the back of her hand and leaving a smudge of sauce underneath her eye.

"I don't know..." Abbey giggles, "This is your concoction, not mine!"

"Fat lot of use you are Miller, you're supposed to be my able bodied assistant..."

"I am not taking any responsibility for poisoning our friends..." She laughs, and Lucy wrinkles her nose in disapproval.

"I just want a nice family meal around the dinner table, is that too much to ask...?" She pouts, and Abbey reluctantly jumps down from the kitchen unit where she had been perching away from all the mess. Lucy passes her the recipe book and she dutifully scans through the instructions.

"Yep, two table spoons... then some crushed garlic and some black olives..." Lucy grins enthusiastically and Abbey rolls her eyes at her child like excitement. Darren clearly isn't the only one in the family who gets pleasure out of cooking. Whether Lucy's cuisine will be quite as successful remains to be seen - it is definitely questionable at this point - but Abbey knows the real reason why she is doing all this.

Lucy had really struggled being separated from everyone. She and Darren were on their own for so long after their parents abandoned them and as a result this is the only family she has ever known. Losing that even for a few weeks, has really shaken her up. The thought of no longer having that love and stability there is a notion that terrifies her and it brings all the fears and insecurities that she felt as a child rushing back to the surface. This group dinner is a way for her to mark the occasion and officially bring everyone together again.

"OK... I think that's it. Now it just has to cook for an hour..." Lucy grins triumphantly, as if making an Italian chicken dish is the greatest achievement known to man. She then proceeds to fly around the kitchen in a blur, loading the dishwasher and wiping down the sides as she chats in her usual animated tone about anything and everything. Abbey has missed her so much and it certainly feels good to belly laugh again.

"Do you want a line?" Lucy asks, as she empties her pocket of a note and half a bag of cocaine.

"No thanks, I'm good for now..." Abbey frowns slightly; she can't recall ever seeing Lucy do drugs through the day before but it is nearing 5pm; perhaps she's just over excited about the night ahead?

As Lucy sets out four lines and takes them one after the other Abbey finishes tidying up, drying her hands and dusting herself off as Darren, Sophie, Liam and Nathan file into the kitchen with bags of food and drink.

"My god am I seeing what I think I'm seeing?!" Darren scoffs, "My little sister in an apron?!"

"Shut up Daz...!" She yells, whipping it off, screwing it up and throwing it at him, "You're not allowed to make fun. I tried really hard didn't I Abs?"

"She definitely tried..." Abbey grins and the others laugh affectionately.

Darren ruffles Lucy's hair as he and Sophie make their way through to the living room and Liam takes a seat at the table.

"Did you actually manage to get any of the meal into the oven?" Nathan laughs sweetly, as he approaches Lucy and wraps his arms around her waist.

"What do you mean?" She asks, confused, and he smiles again, kissing the tip of her nose, "You have a little bit of sauce just here..." He points to the smudge underneath her eye.

"Oh..." Lucy giggles as she pulls her sleeve down and rubs it vigorously across her face, "Gone...?"

"That bit has..." Nathan grins, "But the sauce down your other cheek, on the side of your neck and in your hair is all still there..." Lucy smacks him playfully in the stomach and sticks her tongue out.

"Very funny! I've only just finished my masterpiece I haven't had time to clean up yet...!" She skips across the room and down the hall towards the bathroom, shouting about how they will all be eating their words later when they are begging for second helpings. Abbey shakes her head in amusement and places the recipe book back on the shelf before helping herself to a beer out of the fridge.

"Abbey...?" Nathan says her name so quietly, that for a brief second she is unsure whether or not he even spoke.

"What's up?" She smiles and he glances over at Liam who quickly stands, quietly closing the kitchen door so that the three of them are alone, "What's going on?" She asks again, suddenly alarmed.

"It's nothing too serious..." Nathan begins, but his tone along with the worry that is radiating from him, says otherwise, "I just need to talk to you about Luc..."

"What about her?" Abbey frowns, confused.

"When you guys were away, you know she took it pretty hard, us all being split up...?" Abbey nods. She had spoken to Lucy about it numerous times since they got back and she is well aware of how difficult she found it, "She was pretty lonely and worried I think, that things weren't going to be the same again. So to make herself feel better, I suppose for comfort, she started doing way more drugs than usual. I tried to reassure her but she still kept using more regularly..."

"Earlier, just before you guys got here she racked up some lines. I thought it was strange but I didn't think it was anything to worry about..." Abbey confesses, and Nathan and Liam exchange a glance.

"It probably isn't anything to worry about..." Liam adds, shrugging it off and moving over to stand with them, "But it won't hurt to keep an eye on her, you know?"

"Yeah sure..." Abbey nods, placing her hand on Nathan's shoulder, "I'm sure it's fine mate, you now Luc she's always OK... and she's smart..."

"I'm probably worrying more than I need to but she's been taking more and more, constantly, throughout the day. I told myself that once you guys were home it would stop but it hasn't. I'm just scared it's gonna get out of control..."

"It won't..." Abbey reassures him sternly, "We won't let that happen..." Nathan nods gratefully but his accompanying smile doesn't quite reach his eyes. He is genuinely scared for her, which makes Abbey question whether she should be scared too. Was she really so naive to think that she could come home from her blissful trip to Ireland with Alex and everything with the others would be totally fine? Did she really imagine that none of this would affect them at all? Things are never that simple and she feels as though she has let her friends down with her ignorance, but at least now she knows how bad things have been, especially for Lucy and she is determined to make it right.

The group dinner goes down surprisingly well and despite the obvious discomfort caused by the empty seat at the end of the table where Tom should have been sat, everyone is in relatively high spirits. The set up afterwards is just the same as always, with the lads gathered around the TV screen battling it out on the Xbox while Abbey, Lucy, Sophie and Gemma sit together, chatting drunkenly on the sofa. There is the usual level of alcohol and drug taking and Abbey cautiously notes what and how much of it Lucy is participating in. Nathan was right. She seems to be racking up lines every ten minutes or so, even smoking more weed than usual, and she is positive that she saw her drop ecstasy at one point in the evening too. She usually saves the harder stuff for when they go out clubbing, especially pills as they are much more of a social drug, but not this time. She is taking almost anything she can get her hands on. Abbey had hoped that Nathan was over reacting but it quickly becomes clear that he has a right to be concerned.

As Abbey walks hastily through the train station on her way to meet her brother she runs the events of the previous night over and over in her mind, quickly reaching the conclusion that this issue with Lucy is something that needs to be discussed. An intervention would be incredibly confronting and a little dramatic, so she decides that it is probably best if she has a conversation with her alone first, just to test the water.

Lucy has always been there for Abbey throughout her constant family dramas and she is clearly struggling herself now due to all the upheaval in the last couple of months. It is time for Abbey to return the favour and be there for her, if and when she needs the support.

The thing that is troubling Abbey the most is whether or not she should discuss this with Alex beforehand? When they were away in Ireland, she was fully aware that Lucy wasn't coping but she kept it from him, knowing that it would only make him worry and bring him down. If she keeps this from him now too, will he be angry? Will he take it out on her and accuse her of leaving him in the dark regarding one of his best friends?

It is difficult to know what to do for the best, especially since Alex has been so preoccupied lately, going out almost every night until the early hours of the morning and falling back into his old, familiar routine like he's never been away. Abbey is no longer waiting for him to make the changes he promised he would in order to give them both a happier, more stable life. Although the problem with Marcus seems to have been resolved, it seemingly isn't quite as easy for Alex to cut ties with his other clients and contacts, particularly the ones that he has known for years.

Abbey can't say she is all that surprised. This is his job, his domain, what he has always known - and the reality is he may never change; but she knew what she was taking on when they got together and she knows what kind of person Alex is deep down. She loves him and if she has to accept his chosen profession as part of the package, then she will. Things are finally starting to settle back into some form of normality and if Abbey is completely honest, the one thing that has never altered amongst all the recent turmoil is their relationship. The trust and comfort they have in each other and the love they share is as strong as it has ever been. He may have his faults, but Alex is a good person who loves and cares for her and that is worth so much, especially considering the lack of stability that she has suffered in her home life.

It almost feels like enough, if only Abbey could forget about the open and honest conversations that they shared in Ballycastle. That way she could focus on what they have together, instead of constantly dreaming about what they could have. But that idea, that happy notion of no more crime, violence, drugs or threats, it is an ideal world that she can't seem to let go of and it is all the more difficult to dismiss knowing that deep down, there is a big part of Alex that wants that life too.

As Abbey approaches the door to the coffee shop she feels like her head is about to explode. There is so much going on, so much to think about, and she finds herself secretly wishing that she was back on that beach in County Antrim, gazing calmly out to sea without a care in the world.

A lot of things need fixing - mainly Lucy - who is clearly abandoning her smart and sensible outlook when it comes to taking drugs. Abbey has a horrible feeling it will only escalate if no one confronts her about it, but trying to figure out what to say and how to approach her is giving her a splitting headache. Perhaps she should talk to Alex after all? Or maybe it would be better to keep this between her and Nathan for now? If there is a serious problem though, shouldn't they tell Darren? 'God... why is everything so fucking complicated these days...' Abbey frowns, shaking her head in a feeble attempt to clear her thoughts. She can't afford to be distracted by this now. Another thing that needs fixing and has done for a while is her fractured relationship with her family.

There had definitely been a slight break through with Peter before she and Alex had to run for the hills and she is keen to develop it further. She wants to work at this and at least try to get their relationship back on track. She needs to focus.

Abbey takes a deep, steadying breath and enters the coffee house. It is relatively quiet, with a single waitress cleaning up behind the counter and only three tables occupied by customers. Two businessmen sit by the window talking fervently over a newspaper and a laptop, a small group of mothers with their young children in prams gossip over skinny lattés at a table by the till and sitting alone at the back of the shop is Peter. Abbey approaches slowly and as he looks up from his coffee her blood runs cold. He is covered in faded bruises, there is a healed gash on his lip and his left hand is bandaged.

"Oh my god..." Abbey gasps as she carefully sits down in the seat opposite, "Pete what happened...?"

He stares quietly for the longest moment as if trying to work something out from her reaction, before he finally answers in a low voice.

"I met an acquaintance of yours..."

"What?" Abbey glares in horror, praying to god that he isn't about to say what she thinks he is.

"A really friendly guy, called himself Marcus..." Abbey's blood runs even colder still. How the hell has this happened? How has Peter got himself involved in this? Why would Marcus want to hurt her brother? She can't believe that this is real; her two separate worlds are colliding despite how impossible it may seem.

"I don't understand..." She whispers meekly. Something about the way Peter is staring makes her tread very carefully into the conversation.

"Neither do I..." He states, "There's a lot I don't understand..."

Abbey swallows hard, trying to figure out a way to calm and reassure her brother while protecting her friends but she has no clue how to get out of this. Peter should never have crossed paths with Marcus or found out about any of the trouble he has caused. She never dreamt in a million years that this could happen.

"He's..." Abbey begins nervously, trying to find the right words, "He's someone that a friend of mine knows... from his past..."

"And that would be your boyfriend I take it? Alex Matthews?" Peter snaps, his voice remaining calm but trembling under the strain.

"How did you...?" Abbey retaliates before thinking, immediately regretting giving so much away with just three simple words.

"He shared quite a lot, it was pretty enlightening..." Peter leans forward, resting his elbows on the table and clenching his fists against his forehead, "Not only do you have a boyfriend that I knew nothing about, but I find out he has people after him that want him dead..."

"He said that...?" Abbey gasps, "When? When did this happen?"

"Why?" Peter's anger starts to crack through the surface as his lip trembles with genuine alarm, "What can you do Abbey? Do you think you can protect your boyfriend? Do you think you can protect yourself? I've met this guy remember, he beat the shit out of me just to get to you and this Alex guy..."

"It's sorted now, it's over..." Abbey states under her breath, urging Peter to calm down and lower his voice as the waitress glances cautiously over the counter, eyeing them suspiciously.

"Over...?" Peter laughs darkly in exasperation, "This isn't a game Abbey, for god sake you're in serious danger. You need to come home, this has gone on long enough..."

"I told you, I can't just come home..."

"Yes you can..." He barks and there is a sudden hush across the coffee shop. He takes a sip of his drink with a trembling hand and composes himself before speaking again, "I had no idea things were this bad. I'm not going to let you go back to this dead beat loser who has a target on his back. It isn't fucking happening..."

"How dare you..." Abbey smarts, "That dead beat loser happens to love me and for your information I love him too..."

"Oh for god sake..." Peter scoffs, but Abbey ignores him. He has that all too familiar look on his face, patronizing and disdainful, as if Abbey is just some stupid little kid who doesn't have a clue about anything.

"He was there for me when you weren't..." She glares, "He's looked after me, taken care of me. He's been my rock through all of the bullshit that's happened between us... he was there when my family abandoned me..." Abbey shuts her eyes and lifts her hand to her face, only just managing to stop herself from screaming out loud out of sheer frustration. A few minutes pass in a stony silence and Peter stares guiltily at the table, "I'm

so sorry that you got caught up in this, I really am..."
She adds, "but you have to believe me when I say that
it's sorted. It really is over..."

"And you think that's enough for me?" Peter gasps,
incensed, "You seriously think that I'm just gonna
accept that and walk away?"

"You don't have a choice..."

"Abbey, please..." He begs and she holds her head in
her hands, saddened and disappointed by the way their
meeting has gone. She had truly believed that they would
talk things out today. That they would clear the air so
they could move forward and try and make things right
again. It had gone worse than she ever imagined and as a
result she now finds herself in an impossible position.

Peter has learnt the truth about Alex. He has discovered the part of his life that should have remained hidden
and now he knows that he is dangerous in some way.

Abbey had been clinging on to a vague hope that
maybe she could reconnect with her family while keeping Alex close but that dream has just been shattered.
There is no way that Peter will be accepting of him, not
now, and he has already voiced his scathing opinion of
her friends. No, it is obvious that this can only work
one way. If she wants to make amends with her family
she will have to leave Alex and the others behind. It will
have to be a choice, one or the other... not both.

"I have to go..." Abbey whispers, rising from her
seat, completely overcome with a sense of despair.

"Please Abbey, I'm begging you just come home with
me now... please..."

Peter grabs hold of her wrist to stop her from leaving
but she quickly prises his hand away. The waitress
standing behind the counter folds her arms, glowering

at Peter disapprovingly as if she is preparing to step in at any moment.

"Let go of me..."

"I'll call the police... I'll tell them everything Abbey, I swear. If I can't protect you by getting you to come home then I'll call them..."

"All that will do is make things ten times worse. It will put me in danger and you as well. I know you don't want that. Please just leave it alone..."

"I don't want to lose you..." Peter chokes out, his eyes brimming with tears as his demeanour switches from anger to raw pain in a split second. Abbey is completely torn in two. She had been hanging on to the hope of a reconciliation even more than she had realized and it now seems totally implausible that she will ever be able to keep her family and her friends in her life at the same time.

It has broken her, she feels the lowest she has felt in a long time and as a result, she no longer has the energy to lie.

"I think you just did..." She whispers tearfully, before bolting through the exit with the image of her brother's devastated expression printed firmly in her mind.

The disappointment Abbey feels is almost unbearable. Deep down she had truly believed that one day, she would be in touch with her family again. That they would be back on good terms and she would be able to have it all... her family, her boyfriend and her best friends. Now that is clearly never going to happen.

After arriving home to an empty flat feeling completely dejected, she desperately wants to talk to Lucy and tell her about what happened but she stops herself from picking up the phone. Lucy clearly has her own problems to deal with right now and Abbey has offloaded to her enough in the past. She doesn't want to make the situation any worse for her by throwing her own dramas into the mix.

As Alex and the others all appear to be out, there is nothing for Abbey to do other than sit in the deafening silence and think about all the things that have once again spiralled way out of her control.

The choice to make peace with her family has been taken away from her by Marcus. Now there is no way she can keep all the people she loves in her life without having to make a sacrifice, but how the hell can she possibly choose? She loves her friends and can't imagine her life without Alex, but can she really turn her back on Janet, Peter and Anna for good? Not to mention the fact that her best friend and the strongest person she knows is currently on the verge of having a drugs related breakdown. It wouldn't be right to walk away from her now.

It is a hell of a lot to deal with and it all feels that much worse because of the life she got a taste of in Ireland. The simple life she and Alex had called it. The reason it felt so good to get away is because life is always such a struggle here, or at least it has been ever since Marcus made his ransom and Tom got injured in the raid. She had arrived home feeling totally refreshed and was ready to strive for better, but the positivity faded fast and they have quickly fallen back into old habits. 'Can we really keep on living like this?' Abbey muses sadly.

It has been a slow day and as night finally dawns she is more than happy to see her bed after an exhausting and emotional afternoon. It takes a while for her to fall asleep and even when she does; she is unable to switch off her doubts and worries completely.

It is a little after 2:00am when Abbey's eyes suddenly flicker open, and she lies still, waiting for her breathing to slow down and return to normal as the dream that woke her in a panic already starts to drift from her memory. She is too warm and feels strangely claustrophobic, quickly kicking off the covers as she rolls over and is greeted by an empty bed. Needless to say Alex's issues with sleep definitely weren't cured in Ballycastle.

Wide awake and unable to switch off her thoughts, Abbey decides to get up and search for her insomniac boyfriend. Maybe now would be a good time to discuss the day's events with him and break the news about Lucy? In the relative stillness of the early morning when everything feels a little calmer? She creeps barefoot over to the living room, but apart from the street lights that line the road below glowing dimly through the balcony door, it is in total blackness.

As she turns toward the kitchen she stops off at the bathroom, thinking how she should probably go to the toilet now if she is about to be embroiled in a long, in depth and emotional conversation with Alex about all manner of things.

After washing and drying her hands she stops for a moment, staring at Tom's toothbrush that is still sitting in the glass beaker on the shelf. It just doesn't feel real that he won't be around anymore, not for a long time at least. She wonders where they will all be in five years' time and what Tom will be greeted with when he walks out of prison.

Abbey reaches up and carefully closes the door of the little vanity cupboard that sits on the wall above the sink. For a very brief moment she is certain that she must have fallen asleep on her feet, as in the reflection of the mirror she can see the faint outline of someone standing in the corner behind her. As panic begins to rise in her chest the shadowy figure takes a small step into the light and Abbey swings around in sheer horror, screaming loudly as she comes face to face... with Ryan.

She drops to the floor in shock and disbelief, kicking her legs frantically as she scrambles backwards and pushes herself up against the wall. Ryan takes another slow step forward - holding his hand out as if trying to reach her - and she screams again, covering her head with her arms.

As a pair of hands grab hold of her wrists she thrashes furiously, trying to break free and wake herself up from this terrifying nightmare.

"ABBEY... Jesus Christ, ABBEY IT'S ME. Babe, it's alright it's me... you're OK..." Alex pulls her forward without hesitation and she curls up tightly in his arms, shaking and sobbing uncontrollably.

"He was here Alex, he was here..." She cries.

"Who was here? Abbey, is there someone else in the flat? ABBEY...?!"

"It was Ryan. I saw him Alex; I swear to god I saw him... Ryan was here I swear..." Her breathing is ragged and she trembles with terror as Alex tightens his grip around her, concerned, confused and struggling to understand what the hell is going on.

"It's OK, shhhh... I've got you, it's OK..." He whispers in her ear, as they rock gently back and forth, entwined together on the cold tiles of the bathroom floor.

Chapter Eighteen

Little Black Hearts

Those desperate hands stretching out towards her and that cold, vacant stare. Abbey is finding it impossible to shake the image of her brother out of her mind. It had seemed so real. Like he really was standing right in front of her, trying to reach her, to tell her something perhaps? But it can't have been Ryan; there is absolutely no way that what Abbey saw was real. She is a rational person. She doesn't believe in ghosts and ghouls or anything remotely paranormal. Therefore the only explanation she has for what happened three nights ago in the early hours of the morning, is that she has finally, completely lost it.

Alex had displayed an array of emotion while holding Abbey in his arms as she cowered on the bathroom floor. She had been so afraid to look up for fear of what she might see, that they ended up sitting there for the best part of an hour before he finally carried her back to bed. He was scared, upset and confused, and a little angry when Abbey struggled to explain to him exactly what was happening, as she didn't understand it herself. He was frustrated that he couldn't help, again, not coping well in a situation that was way out of his control.

Once she had managed to calm down and regain a grip on reality, Abbey spoke to Alex and tried her best to explain to him what she had seen. She cringed at her own words as she spoke them aloud, knowing how ridiculous and crazy she sounded. As always, Alex was as caring and supportive as he could possibly be but he couldn't hide the look of genuine concern in his eyes.

Abbey is fully aware that he has every right to be worried. Who the hell can blame him for that? It isn't every day your girlfriend starts screaming her head off in the middle of the night after receiving a visit from her dead twin brother. God knows what he must have thought?

She has spent the last few days rehashing the terrifying moment over and over, still shivering with fright at the memory of Ryan silently raising his hand to her, completely void of emotion. Abbey has no idea what the hell it says about her frame of mind but she has part rationalised it into three possible explanations.

1. She had just woken up. It could have been her subconscious projecting the vision while she was still awake? Especially seen as it was a bad dream that had woken her with a start in the first place? It's possible... although as soon as she had climbed out of bed to find Alex she hadn't felt tired or drowsy in the slightest.

2. The vast array of drugs that she has been taking over the past year have finally started messing with her brain. It could be the case. But she hadn't taken anything on that particular night that would cause her to have such a disturbing hallucination?

Or 3. The stress and anguish she feels due to everything that has happened lately has seriously started to affect her. Although Abbey doesn't want it to be true, deep down, she knows that this explanation is probably the most likely. Her family - particularly her mum - don't exactly have the best track record in coping when things get tough.

In all honesty, the combination of all three most likely culminated in Abbey seeing Ryan. She must be far more fragile than she first realised after everything she has been through and coupled with her post sleep state and the fact she has been tampering with mind altering substances on a fairly regular basis... well, it was a recipe for disaster. Or rather a recipe for disturbing visions. At least that is the conclusion Abbey has reached, as it is the only explanation she can accept without scaring herself further. The alternative is far too awful to consider; the idea that she is slowly turning into her mother.

On a slightly more positive note, Alex's priorities seem to have shifted considerably after Abbey's little 'episode'. He is incredibly attentive, constantly checking in and making sure that she's OK after her momentary breakdown. It is perhaps the only good thing to come out of such a traumatising experience and Alex seems to have finally realised that ever since their trip to Ireland he has been throwing himself back into 'work' with perhaps a little too much determination. It was important for him to get back on track and reclaim some control and power in his life - plus he was keen to prove himself to Moorland after all of his help - but after disclosing this to Abbey she had taken the opportunity to remind him that family should always come first. The group is fractured and it is important that they all stick together right now. They need him and so does she.

He had been extremely receptive to her advice and was surprisingly quick to act on it; switching off his phone through the day and spending much more time at the flat than before. After this unexpected turn around - and considering that perhaps communication really is the key - Abbey had finally confessed to Alex about Lucy. He was of course angry and concerned at first. But Abbey assured him that things were improving now that Nathan had managed to talk to her directly about their concerns. It had been an uncomfortable conversation by all accounts and Lucy was highly defensive about what she was being accused of, but she eventually agreed that perhaps she had started to get a little carried away with it all and promised that she would take more care in the future.

The drugs had been a coping mechanism, she took them to block out the things that were hurting her but now, as far as Abbey is concerned, she doesn't need to strive for that numbing effect anymore. Not when she can turn to her, or Nathan or any one of the others instead. She just needed reminding that her friends are here for her to talk to and confide in no matter what and now that they all appear to be on the same page, Abbey truly feels like things will work out.

Needless to say the revelation about Lucy, along with Abbey's frightening melt down, seems to have shocked Alex into focus. He understands better than anyone how tough it has been lately and even though things appear to be improving, it's about time they forgot about all the bullshit and got back to what they do best. And that's drink, laugh and party in style. It's time they started a new chapter and before they can do that, they all need to blow off some serious steam.

By 8pm on Saturday night enough alcohol has been drunk to sink a small ship. Alex has gone all out, supplying booze, food and limitless drugs. The music is turned up full and they are all in high spirits, looking forward to the night ahead. He has even turned his phone off again - refusing to deal with anyone work related in his down time - and has organised guest list entry to one of the best clubs in town. He has missed this. Abbey can tell. He is laughing and joking with the lads like a typical 28 year old and his relaxed, care free demeanour is firmly back in place... at least for now. Truth be told, Abbey has missed it too. She remembers so clearly how much of an escape this was when she first met her friends and became part of the group. They saved her. They gave her hope and support when she needed it most and it meant the world. Things may not have stayed quite so simple and complications arose, but that's life. And it is to be doubly expected when you live a life like they do.

Tom is missed by all of them. It feels strange not to hear his loud, cockney accent bellowing across the room, cracking jokes and telling his hilarious stories. But he would want this. He would want them to be happy and to rebuild the bond that has been damaged lately, by their on-going problems and the resulting separation. It feels good to be back together in this way and Abbey is comforted, knowing that if they can make it through all the bullshit that the last few months has thrown at them, then their friendship really is strong enough to survive anything.

Alex stands by the CD player, scanning through a stack of albums while trading insults and banter with Nathan from across the room and Liam skilfully divides a small pile of cocaine into several lines, laughing as Darren dives over the sofa onto Gemma and Sophie, breaking up their conversation. Abbey watches them all fondly, feeling a slight pang of concern as she is reminded that someone else other than Tom is missing out on the fun.

Lucy told Nathan that she needed to be on her own for a little while, whatever that means, but it has been half an hour since she left the room and she still hasn't re-joined the party. It is strange behaviour for Lucy as she hates missing out and is terrible in her own company. She gets bored instantly with no one there to mindlessly chatter to.

Abbey stands discreetly and moves over towards the door, glancing back just in time to see Nathan flash a brief and appreciative smile. He is obviously anxious but is trying hard not to make a fuss, as it would inadvertently cause Lucy to feel even guiltier about making him worry.

After checking her and Alex's room and finding no sign of Lucy in there, Abbey knocks lightly on Tom's bedroom door before pushing it open, pausing on the threshold as she smiles quizzically at her best friend. Lucy is laid on Tom's bed with her head hanging off the end of the mattress. Her wild, blonde hair dangles loose with the tips almost touching the floor and she tilts her head back further as she smiles in greeting.

"What are you doing?" Abbey laughs in amusement.

"Just thinking…"

"About what exactly…?"

"You know… stuff. I'm trying to get a bit of perspective…"

"By hanging upside down…?!" Abbey quips.

"Everything's been pretty messed up recently. I figured maybe if I change the way I've been looking at it all, it might start making sense...?"

"So... let me get this straight..." Abbey smirks as she moves further into the room, "Because, in a manner of speaking, all the changes that have happened lately have turned your world "upside down", you thought that if you literally turned yourself upside down, things would be the right way up and would make sense...?!" She frowns at her own explanation.

"Exactly..." Lucy states nonchalantly and Abbey moves over to the other side of the bed, fighting back her laughter as she lies down beside her. She fans her hair out from underneath her shoulders and drops her head back so that it is hanging off the mattress in the same position as Lucy's. They both turn to look at one another, laying there in silence for a brief moment.

"You're really weird..." Abbey states affectionately and Lucy breaks into a huge grin.

"It's taken you all this time to figure that out...?" She laughs.

"No... I just thought it should be said..." They smile at each other and Abbey rolls her eyes, before staring back up at the ceiling, "Do you want to tell me why you're really in here...?" She presses, cautiously and Lucy sighs in response.

"It just feels weird... without Tom..."

"I know. I keep looking for him and then remembering..."

"Do you think he's OK?" She asks in a pained whisper.

"I really hope so. He can look after himself Luc, you know that..."

"It isn't fair though. He should be here…"

"I know…" Abbey completely agrees but she shifts uncomfortably, unsure whether Lucy's opinion of it being unfair is also her way of implying that it should be Alex in prison instead.

"It's just not the same…" She adds, sadly.

"It'll take time, but we're all trying. Everyone's here tonight, having a laugh together and we're missing you in there. Having fun again doesn't mean you're abandoning Tom. Do you really think he'd want you moping about in here instead of enjoying yourself?"

"I suppose not…" Lucy smiles, "It used to be me giving you the pep talks didn't it?!"

"Yeah it did…" Abbey laughs, "And those pep talks worked…! What is it you used to say? 'Live for now, party like it's your last'… You should take your own advice!"

"It's pretty hard to get in the party spirit when things have been so shit lately…"

"That's all the more reason to try! We need to get back to how it was and start having a laugh again…! God knows we deserve it!"

"I think I like this new optimistic Abbey…!"

"Well, it's my new outlook on life, you know? The way I see it, if you want something to be different then make it different because no one's gonna do it for you. If you're stupidly positive then eventually things are bound to get better, right…?"

"Are you on drugs…?" Lucy jokes and they both burst out laughing.

"Yes, Yes I am, but that isn't the point…!" Abbey states in mock defiance, "Things will get better, Luc.

We all have each other and that's what counts. Tom isn't gone forever..."

"True..." She nods in agreement, turning to look directly at Abbey again, "But what about you... seriously? Alex mentioned what happened last week Abs, that's full on..."

"Yeah, I guess it is..." She shrugs.

"You saw your brother? I mean actually, physically saw him?"

"I don't know what the hell that was about if I'm honest, but it scared the shit out of me. For more than one reason..."

"How do you mean...?" Lucy asks, and Abbey gestures dramatically with her hands as if the answer should be obvious.

"You mean apart from seeing dead people in my bathroom? It scared me because my first thought was..." She trails off, almost not wanting to say the words out loud, "It's feels like what happened to my Mum, is happening to me..."

"You don't know that..."

"My Mum *saw* Ryan, Lucy. All the time! She spoke with him, like I'm talking to you right now, I mean it's insane. I always thought she was completely crazy but now I'm doing the same thing..."

"You didn't talk to him. You saw him for a few seconds, Abbey..."

"But he was so real... like I could actually reach out and touch him. I honestly don't know what would have happened if I hadn't screamed the place down and made Alex come running..."

"I bet that really shit him up..." Lucy muses, trying to fight back a smile.

"Not half as much as it shit him up hearing that his girlfriend clearly needs committing..." They both laugh darkly in the knowledge that all jokes aside, it is definitely something that Abbey needs to keep a close eye on, "Seriously though... what if it is happening to me? What if I am losing it like my Mum did?"

"You've had a lot to deal with Abs... we all have. When people are under pressure and stressed out their minds react in different ways. Maybe it all just got on top of you and this was your heads way of saying you can't cope anymore? It doesn't mean you're going crazy...!"

"I hope not! You're crazy enough for the both of us...!" She smirks and Lucy nudges her playfully in the ribs.

"You'll be fine. Like you said, you've got us lot to make sure of that..."

"So do you..." Abbey interrupts, "And you know that talking to your friends is better than burying yourself in drugs..."

"Is this the part where you tell me off?"

"No. I'm not your mother. But you were the one who told me you had to be smart with drugs and not push your limits... remember?"

"I know. It's hard to explain... Everything just got too much for me to handle and I needed that escape, then the more I did, the more I needed bigger and bigger hits to get it..."

"But you're not doing that anymore right?" Abbey scolds, "You're partying on the same level as the rest of us, not getting silly with it?"

Lucy smiles but says nothing as she lifts her hand and makes a cross shape over her chest in the sign of a promise. Abbey wishes that Lucy would give her some proper reassurance and swear to her that she's learnt her lesson, but when are things ever that simple? If Lucy was struggling enough to get to this point with drugs then there's no way she can just flick a switch and suddenly be fine. Besides, if she was feeling better then she wouldn't have spent half the night on her own hiding in Tom's bedroom, but what more can Abbey do?

"It feels like it's just one thing after another these days..." Lucy sighs.

"Tell me about it. There always seems to be something... so much for your good luck charm Blake!" Abbey smirks, automatically reaching for the chain around her neck and twirling the amber pendant between her fingers.

"I told you, it's the thought that counts...!" She laughs, "I swear to god, luck just doesn't exist... at least not the good kind anyway!"

"I don't know, sometimes it does. I found you lot when I needed you..."

"That was more by chance I reckon. But I guess it worked out well. You got with Alex and you landed me as an amazing best friend, you really can't fault that!" Abbey smiles and raises her forearm so that her elbow is resting on the mattress beneath her. She tilts it towards Lucy and she mirrors her action so that their arms twist together and they lock hands.

"I could do a lot worse...!" Abbey smiles, "But I do get what you mean. It must be really nice, being one of those people that just coast through life, getting whatever they want! Some people have all the luck...!"

"You know what I think Miller?"

"What?"

"I think..." Lucy announces, with underlying amusement in her voice, "That our guardian angels must drink as much as we do...!" Both Abbey and Lucy burst into a fit of laughter and continue giggling for a good five minutes. The sensation of hanging upside down is causing the blood to rush to their heads which only prolongs their amusement. Eventually Abbey sits up and clears her throat, struggling for breath as she leans forward, feeling more than a little light headed.

"Well, watching over us two must be one hell of a job, you definitely wouldn't do it hung over...!"

"Very true...!" Lucy agrees, as she rolls onto her side.

"Will you come back to the party now please...?"

"Sure. I'll be through in a bit..." Lucy nods, and Abbey frowns at her impatiently. Why can't she just come through now, pour herself a drink and have a pick me up or two? She will feel so much better for it instead of staying in here and making her bad mood worse by dwelling on things that can't be changed.

"Don't be too long OK...?" Abbey requests, but there is a hint of authority behind her voice and Lucy nods obediently.

"Yes boss...!" She laughs, "And thanks, Abbey. I love you to bits; you know that right?"

"Of course I do..." She smiles back in return, lingering for a moment by the open door, "Things will work out Luc, I'm sure of it..."

"I know. We'll be fine..."

"Love you too weirdo...!"

Abbey wants her happy, fun loving Lucy back so badly. This dark mood she seems to have spiralled into has been going on for far too long. Ever since Nathan confronted her about her escalating drug use she has withdrawn into her shell and Abbey is unsure of how to reach her. Maybe she just needs more time? After all, she knows how much they all love her and when she is ready to deal with this properly they will be there for her without question.

As Abbey re-joins the party Lucy lays back on Tom's bed - the right way round with her head on the pillow - and glances at the clock on the wall. She knows that Abbey is right and that she is wallowing in self-pity but she just can't seem to get motivated. She has no energy what so ever and isn't in the mood for getting drunk at all. Restlessly, she sits up again; swinging her legs round and perching on the edge of the mattress as she slides open the top drawer of Tom's bedside table. There are various papers stuffed in there along with a phone charger, a couple of lighters, half a pack of cigarettes and some old photos. Lucy flicks through them with a heavy heart. They are a few years old, taken on various drunken nights out during happier times. One from Tom's birthday two years ago of him swigging tequila out of the bottle and sticking a defiant finger up to the photographer almost makes her laugh out loud. He is such an idiot. God she misses him.

As Lucy tries to muster up the energy to join the others in the living room, something catches her eye. It is a green plastic carrier bag wrapped up small and stuffed right at the back of the drawer, almost as if it has been hidden. She gently pulls it out and unravels the contents from inside. There are several pills, each with tiny little black hearts stamped in the centre. Lucy recalls Tom telling her about these. They are a particularly strong brand of ecstasy - mixed with various other ingredients - which Tom claimed would 'put a massive smile on anyone's face and blow their fucking mind'.

Lucy hesitates for a second, turning the little pills over and over in the palm of her hand. Maybe these are exactly what she needs? She wants to lighten up and get herself back into a positive frame of mind but she has been hitting the usual stuff so hard lately that the effects aren't as strong or as satisfying as they used to be. This stuff though, is meant to be dynamite. She could take a couple, just to get her in the partying mood? One last blow out... one final night of getting that ultimate high and then she will kick it into touch and go back to being sensible. No more risks. She sits for a couple of minutes, internally debating with herself, before grabbing her bottle of beer and placing one of the pills on her tongue. 'Why the hell not...?'

All Abbey can do is shrug at Nathan as he looks up at her expectantly. She tried, but Lucy can be extremely stubborn sometimes. He knows that more than anyone and smiles a 'what can you do?' sort of smile before going back to his conversation with Sophie. Abbey joins Alex and Darren on the balcony and Alex passes her the joint they are smoking.

"How's she doing...?" Darren asks.

"She's OK... she said she'll be out soon..."

"What's bothering her?"

"Tom... among other things, but she'll be alright..."

Alex frowns as a brief flash of pain shoots across his face. It is still difficult for him to speak about Tom without feeling a wave of crippling guilt. Sensing his discomfort and determined not to spoil the mood of the night, Abbey leans forward and kisses him unexpectedly, instantly breaking him out of his despairing train of thought.

"What have I missed...?" She asks cheerfully, and both Alex and Darren roll their eyes.

"Mainly a load of fucking bickering..." Darren shouts, just loud enough for the others to hear.

"Oh come on it'll be funny..." Gemma whines over the music, "We always have to sit and watch you lot play bloody FIFA!"

"What am I not getting?" Abbey asks, confused.

"Gem has brought some games for us to play..." Liam laughs, throwing a cushion at her from across the room, "But it isn't fucking happening...!"

Darren and Abbey move back inside as Alex finishes the joint, and Sophie hands Abbey the two computer games. One is 'Karaoke Sing Star' the other 'Just Dance'.

"I don't give a fuck... I'm up for it..." Alex announces; much to Gemma's approval. They high five as he passes her on the sofa and Abbey knows that he is only doing it to make her happy. Things are a lot better between them now and he wants to keep it that way.

"Oh man, seriously...?" Liam shakes his head at the coffee table and quickly starts racking up some more lines, no doubt to gear himself up for an all singing all dancing competition.

"What's the matter, afraid I'll show you up...?"

"Like you could Matthews...!" Liam taunts, pointing to himself proudly, "You know what they say... voice of an angel..."

"Face like an arse..." Darren finishes, and the others laugh in unison as Liam raises his middle finger.

"I'm better at singing, but I reckon I'd be alright at the dancing one too to be fair..." Alex states casually, and Abbey, who had been idly listening to the conversation whilst reading the back of one of the games, lets out a short, quiet laugh. It happens before she can even think about it and as the others look on expectantly, bristling with amusement, Alex raises an eyebrow.

"Something to say, Abigail...?" He accentuates her full name and she wrinkles her nose at him. He knows how much she hates that. She tries to fight the smile that is spreading across her face but fails miserably.

"No... it's just... well, you know babe..."

"Know what?" He too is trying hard to keep a straight face as he edges slowly towards her, sauntering a little too nonchalantly.

"Well... I've seen you dancing, and..." Before Abbey can finish her sentence the others burst out laughing and Alex grabs her around the waist, swinging her round and throwing her onto the sofa. He kneels over her, tickling her manically while pinning her arms at her sides and she half screams, half laughs as she begs him to stop.

"And? And what...?"

"And you're better at singing that's all I was going to say, you have a lovely voice...!"

"Oh really, It didn't sound like you were going to say that...!"

"I was I promise! ALEX!" She screams and he quickly relents, sitting up and pulling her across his lap so that she is cradled in his arms.

"The cheek of it Miller..." He tuts jokingly, and she smiles at him, fluttering her eyelashes sweetly.

"Alex is in; Me and Soph are in... Darren, Nathan...?" They both hold their hands up in defeat and Gemma lets out a little squeal of excitement as she dashes over to the TV unit, "It's going to be so funny...!"

She claps, "And I think we'll go with the dance game... sorry Al...!"

"That's fine! I still reckon I've got some pretty decent moves, despite my girl's brutally honest opinion... " Abbey giggles apologetically as Alex pulls her forward again, kissing her neck, head and mouth, "It's good to see that smile..." He whispers and she reaches up, gently running her fingers through his hair.

The others have resumed their bickering and they launch into an animated debate about who should be on which team, leaving Alex and Abbey encased in their own little bubble for a welcome moment.

"It's good to see yours too. You've really missed this haven't you?" She asks, quietly.

"I honestly didn't appreciate how much. I've been so distracted lately... so busy trying to get things back in order that I've been distancing myself without even fucking realising it. I'm sorry..."

"It's OK..."

"No, really..." Alex insists, taking Abbey's hand in his, "I know I said a lot of things in Ireland and I want you to know that I haven't forgotten. About how things are and how we want them to be... about me and you..."

"I know... It'll take time, but that's OK. We'll get there, all of us... " Abbey smiles and Alex kisses her forcefully on the lips before pulling away and holding her face between his hands.

"I love you..."

"I know. I love you too..." She replies, and as their lips meet softly again a flying cushion courtesy of Darren hits them both in the side of the face.

"Come on Al, you were the one who fucking agreed to this...!" Alex stands with Abbey in his arms and gently places her back down before rolling up his sleeves and taking his position in front of the TV screen.

"Watch and learn children… watch and learn…" He states as he jogs on the spot confidently, and Abbey shakes her head in amusement, "Lucy can't miss this…" She laughs, as Sophie picks up her glass and skips towards the door.

"I need a refill, I'll get her…"

Alex - although Abbey hates to admit it - is actually pretty good. 'Is there anything this man can't do?' She wonders to herself as the others form a semi-circle around him, cheering him on, or in Liam's case, shouting insults at him in an attempt to put him off. Gemma is right, it is hilarious, and although they were reluctant to play at first the boy's competitive sides are already starting to come out. Typical!

Sophie stumbles through the door with two bottles of wine tucked carefully in her arms along with a six pack of beer in her hands. She places the drinks down on the table and uses the distraction of the game to slide over to Abbey.

"Did Lucy say anything about going home?"

"What? No. Why?" Abbey frowns as her heart sinks with disappointment, "She hasn't left has she?"

"I can't find her…"

"She was in Tom's room…"

"I know but she isn't in there I checked, she's not in the bathroom either…"

"Is she in our en suite?"

"I didn't look, but I doubt it…"

"I'll go…" Abbey hops over the sofa without anyone noticing and heads straight for Tom's bedroom across the hall. Sophie is right; there is no sign of her. She quickly sticks her head around the bathroom door before checking in her and Alex's room. It is in total darkness apart from the dim glow that is radiating from the en suite but the light is only on because Abbey left it earlier by mistake. 'Where the hell is she?' Sophie joins Abbey outside the bedroom and instantly reads the panic on her face.

"Was she alright when you spoke to her earlier?" She asks, with a sudden sense of urgency.

"Yeah, I thought she was... I don't know... Are you sure she isn't in the kitchen?" Without another word Sophie races down the hallway to check again, leaving Abbey standing with her hands on her hips, questioning whether she missed any obvious signs.

The laughter and music coming from inside the living room appear distant and detached in comparison to the dread that is suddenly coursing through her. Obviously Lucy wasn't completely OK but she didn't think she was upset enough to pull a disappearing act? She should tell the others. Maybe Lucy didn't want to bring everyone down, so she took herself off home and has text Nathan to let him know? That must be it. It has to be... this is so unlike her.

Before Abbey can break the news to the others she hears a faint, muffled noise from inside Tom's bedroom and freezes on the spot. She can't still be in there can she? She wasn't on the bed when she looked in a minute ago, she is certain of it. Abbey slowly opens the door and stands half in half out of the room, suddenly terrified of what she might see. There is definite movement. It is quiet and muffled, but constant, like a steady, dull thud.

Abbey takes a few steps forward and something catches her eye. There is a green bag on the floor by the foot of the bed with several pills scattered around it. As she strides over to take a closer look her heart stops and her breath catches in her throat. She can hardly move, hardly speak, as her blood runs ice cold and her eyes fill with horrified tears. Lucy is on the floor, her eyes are rolled back and her body is rigid as she shakes violently back and forth. The dull thud is the sound of her elbow repeatedly hitting the edge of the radiator as she rocks from side to side. Everything is happening in slow motion like time is standing still, and after what seems like forever, Abbey eventually finds her voice, takes a huge, deep breath... and screams.

"ALEX... NATHAN..." She sounds unrecognizable even to herself as her voice twists into an animal like wail and the fear and panic take over. She drops to her knees and grabs hold of Lucy's head, trying to turn her onto her side so that she doesn't choke. Her jaw is locked and her lips are turning blue.

"Oh god no, Lucy please..." She begs between broken sobs. She can hear the loud, thundering sound of approaching footsteps before the door flies open and the others burst in. Nathan throws himself across the room and immediately pushes Abbey out of the way. Grabbing hold of Lucy and lifting her head, he turns her onto her side and reaches into her mouth in an attempt to clear her air way. Darren is right next to him with a look of sheer horror on his face.

"What the hell did she take?" He gasps.

"I don't know; she didn't have anything on her when we were talking but these were on the floor..." Abbey hands Darren the bag of pills and Alex snatches it away. She hadn't even noticed him standing there but he is right beside them, looking down at Lucy with his face pale and his eyes wide as Gemma and Sophie sob quietly in the doorway and a shell-shocked Liam tries his best to calm them down.

"We need to call a fucking ambulance now...!" Nathan screams and Darren backs away, shaking his head and holding his hands over his tear stained face in utter disbelief. Alex sees that he is going into shock and quickly steps forward, snapping into action and taking charge like he always does. There is no time to panic and lose focus now.

"We can't..."

"What...?!" Nathan gasps.

"There's no time for that, we have to move her. Liam, bring the van around..." Alex drops to his knees and grabs hold of Lucy's shoulders as he tries in vain to keep her still.

"But..." Liam is about to protest when Alex's head snaps up and the look on his face instantly stops him from arguing.

"NOW..." He shouts and Liam does as he is told without question. Alex's eyes are so dark they are almost black and he has never looked more frightened, or more dangerous. Nathan's breathing is heavy and broken as he pins Lucy's legs to the floor, trying his best to keep it together despite the tears that are now streaming down his face.

"Oh please, please baby, please..." He prays, over and over with quiet desperation, as the others look on helplessly.

CHAPTER NINETEEN

WHO'LL STOP THE RAIN?

A single drop of rain runs slowly down the window, picking up speed and growing in size as it merges with other droplets that are dotted across the glass. Abbey absentmindedly traces her finger along its path, watching as it glides disjointedly all the way down to the bottom and pools in the corner of the wooden frame. The streetlights outside shimmer through the downpour - blurring the view into an almost abstract pattern - as she silently prays for her best friend.

By the time they had gotten Lucy into the van she had stopped fitting. Her breathing was shallow and her lips pale. They had raced to the hospital and made it to the emergency room in less than five minutes but it still felt like a lifetime. Liam had barely touched the breaks before Alex had kicked open the door and thrown himself out; followed immediately by Nathan, who stepped down with Lucy in his arms and sprinted through the automatic doors, screaming frantically for anyone to help. A doctor who had been filling in charts at the reception desk was the first one to run over to them.

"What happened?" He asked, while checking for Lucy's pulse.

"She took something... we don't know what..." Nathan's tone had been fraught and panicked but he was telling the truth, they really don't know what is in those pills or how many she has swallowed.

"How long has she been like this...?"

"We found her about 10 minutes ago..."

Two nurses had then appeared with a gurney and Nathan stepped forward without hesitation, gently laying Lucy's limp and lifeless body onto the hard green mattress. He had run alongside them as they wheeled her through the hospital ward, until a nurse held out her arm and blocked him from entering through a set of double doors that were clearly labelled 'staff only'. Abbey can't get the image of Nathan's face out of her mind as he was forced to let go of Lucy's hand and watch her disappear down the corridor away from him. His pain was almost unbearable.

"You can wait in the family room..." The nurse had offered kindly, "We will come through and update you as soon as we can..." And that's exactly where they have been waiting for almost an hour and a half now. It is becoming insufferable, the not knowing, and Abbey isn't sure how much more of this she can take as she hugs her chest and watches the rain lash against the window.

Darren is sitting quietly against the far wall, resting his head on Sophie's shoulder as she gently rubs his back and Gemma and Liam are sitting on either side of Nathan, who is staring blankly at a scuff mark on the carpet in front of his feet. He hasn't looked up, spoken or even blinked for the last thirty minutes. God knows how he must be feeling. If Abbey were in his place and it was Alex they were waiting to hear about, well, she can barely handle the thought. It is heart-breaking enough waiting on the fate of her best friend.

Alex is pacing. Up and down, back and forth. It is a typical response for him; it's how he almost always reacts to a stressful situation that is completely out of his hands. Power, authority, control... that's what he knows, but once again he finds himself in a situation that he is incapable of changing or making any better. So all he can do is wait, like the rest of them. He sits down in a chair over in the corner and anxiously runs his hands through his hair for the hundredth time.

"They must know something by now..." Liam sighs, breaking the silent tension that is coursing through the room.

"I'm sure they'll tell us when they do..." Gemma smiles meekly and Alex shakes his head in exasperation, leaning back in his seat and raising a weary hand to his face.

"Not necessarily..." He mumbles, almost to himself and Nathan finally looks up, staring at him with subdued anger in his eyes.

"What do you mean?" Darren asks, confused.

"With something like this they're gonna have questions. They might not tell us how she's doing or let us see her until we've spoken to the doctors... and the police..."

"Can they do that?" Sophie gasps, "I mean Darren's her brother, they have to tell him don't they?"

"They'll tell him... but they might try and get more information out of us first..."

"Then we'll give it to them..." Nathan states under his breath in a defiant tone. Alex stares at him for a moment, but decides not to retaliate. Everything could implode so easily right now. Tensions and emotions are running high and it isn't the time or place to get into a debate about what they are going to do if they are asked uncomfortable questions they can't answer.

"Let's hope it doesn't come to that..." Sophie whispers, turning her head towards Darren and running her nose through his hair, "She'll be fine babe..."

"She should have known better..." He despairs, "She's smarter than this what the fuck was she thinking?"

"This isn't her fault..." Nathan snaps.

"Well whose fault is it then...?" He shouts back, "I couldn't reach her, for three weeks, I couldn't see her and you promised me she'd be fine..."

"You're putting this on me...?" Nathan gasps in revulsion, "I tried, I WAS there for her, but she kept on pushing me away..."

"Then you should have tried harder..."

"She hid it, Daz. She hid it from me. But as soon as I found out I did try, I begged her to talk to me but she was hurting too much. About Tom, about not seeing you, about the group splitting up, your parents... EVERYTHING. I fucking tried..."

"You should have taken better care of her..."

"Yeah, well so should you..."

"I couldn't see her..." Darren yells again, furiously.

"And that isn't on me..." Nathan's answering tone is much quieter but it is still laced with suppressed rage, "That isn't on me..."

Abbey closes her eyes and rests her head against the window frame, refusing to turn around, refusing to be drawn in. She can't stand this. It is all falling apart again, it is all unravelling... and this isn't helping anyone, especially not Lucy.

"You think I wanted this?" Alex asks, his voice almost inaudible, "Do you seriously think I wanted any of this to fucking happen?"

"It's happened anyway hasn't it..." Nathan shrugs, "All of it... first Tom, now Lucy..."

"Alright, I think we all just need to calm the fuck down..." Liam interjects, but Alex stares at Nathan, no longer listening to anyone else as his scathing accusation breaks his heart.

"I didn't ask for this. It was out of my control, all of it, and I handled it the best way I could..."

"You handled it by doing things your way, by doing what was right for you, no one else, and this is what it's brought on..." Nathan shouts - and Alex slams his hands down, throwing himself forward into the path of Liam who has jumped up to block him, pushing him back.

"You son of a bitch..." He spits, and Nathan stands, squaring up to him as Gemma grabs hold of his arm, "I can't control what happens in my life but I do what I can to make it right, like I've always done... not just for me but for my friends, my family, the people I love. You think you're the only one here that loves that girl? You think this isn't fucking killing me too? I couldn't have known... I couldn't have known about Tom or Lucy or what any of this would lead to, but don't you think I'd change this if I could? I'd go back in time right now and fucking beg Marcus to kill me if it would make even part of this mess right again but I can't. I did what I did to survive... to try and keep us all together, to make things right and keep us safe, but it just kept getting deeper and deeper..." Alex gasps. His breathing is fast and ragged, his fists are clenched and his arms are tensed at his sides as he spills his heart out in a devastating confession. Nathan slumps despairingly back into his seat and holds his head in his hands as the others look on, crying silently. Liam is still gripping Alex's shoulders. At first it was to prevent him and Nathan from coming to blows but now he is holding him steady, supporting him, as he begins to lose hope and give up.

"Come on man… it's alright…" Liam consoles, and Alex takes a step back, falling against the wall and leaning forward on his knees. Abbey stands quietly in her spot by the window looking at each of her friends in turn before resting her worried gaze on Alex. He looks so helpless… and so young.

"She's everything to me…" Nathan whispers, "She's my whole life…"

Alex runs his hand across his face and looks up, not at Nathan, but at Abbey. Their eyes meet and he stares at her intensely with so much longing, fear and love in his expression that it is almost her undoing.

"I know…" He states, sincerely, without breaking their eye contact and Abbey moves slowly across the room, cautiously sitting down beside him as she places her hand in his.

It is hard to believe that only a short time ago they were actually on the verge of being happy again. Sitting here in this little room with the worn floor and the ripped seats brings about a horrid sense of despair. Abbey finds it quite shocking that this is the room where people wait for quite possibly the worst news of their lives. There isn't anything remotely warm or comforting about it.

Needless to say after nearly two hours, the walls have begun to close in around them and they are all feeling incredibly restless. The suspense is killing them and Darren sighs loudly with exasperation as he springs to his feet and strides across the room, no doubt to ask the nurse yet again what is taking so long and if there is any news? But before he can reach the door a young, blonde haired doctor enters, looking tired, drawn and very weary.

"Are you here for Lucy Blake?" Darren takes a small step forward in response to his question and the others stand expectantly.

"Yeah, I'm her brother..." He holds out his hand and the doctor shakes it once, before letting go.

"I'm Doctor Walters..." Abbey stares at his other hand which is holding his scrub cap and she makes note of how tightly he seems to be gripping it. Why is he so tense?

"How is she doing?" Nathan asks, and the Doctor frowns at Darren.

"Are you all family...?"

"As good as..." Alex responds, but he doesn't seem to accept that as a reasonable answer.

"Perhaps we should speak outside for a moment?" He gestures towards the door and circles his other arm around Darren but he doesn't move.

"They are family. Anything you have to say to me you can say in front of them..."

"Please, just tell us how she's doing... please..." Nathan begs impatiently, unable to stand it any longer, "Can I see her?" He asks, and Doctor Walters looks away fleetingly, shaking his head at the floor.

"I'm afraid not..." He replies.

"Why? When can I see her?" Nathan is becoming more and more frantic and as Abbey pays closer attention to the way the Doctor is stood, his body language and the sorrowful look on his face, she begins to feel physically sick.

"Lucy took a massive overdose of an extremely potent brand of ecstasy..." He begins slowly, now talking directly to Darren, "She also had traces of cocaine, alcohol and marijuana in her blood stream. Her body was unable to handle the amount of conflicting toxins that she had ingested and as a result, she went into shock. The seizures were brought on by her body fighting back and ultimately the stress this caused meant her heart and lungs shut down... and she stopped breathing..."

The room suddenly becomes darker, quieter, as though someone has pressed pause on life and everything beyond this hospital simply fades away into nothing.

Alex is gripping Abbey's hand painfully tight but she can barely feel it. She is numb to everything... everything apart from the doctor and what he is saying. She has to fight to concentrate as her heart beats loudly in her ears and everything sounds like it is being played on a time delay. Every word he speaks takes a few seconds to register properly, almost as if her subconscious is trying to block it out, to mute it, because from the very moment he entered the room part of her already knew exactly what he was going to say.

Sophie stands next to Darren, holding onto his shoulders supportively and Liam and Gemma flank Nathan. They don't touch him, but remain close by his side as he rocks silently from foot to foot with agonizing anticipation, urging the Doctor to tell them good news and reassure them that she's going to be fine. But the dark, heavy cloud that seems to have descended over them tells Abbey that she isn't the only one who's hope is rapidly draining away.

"We had three doctors working on her for well over an hour…" Dr Walters' voice has dropped to a sombre whisper as he stares sorrowfully into Darren's eyes, "We tried everything… we did everything we possibly could. But I'm afraid it wasn't enough to re-start her heart. I'm very sorry… but she died, half an hour ago…"

And everything stops. 'She died, half an hour ago'. The words echo around Abbey's head, obliterating her thoughts and completely destroying everything happy and joyful inside of her. She is holding her breath, only realising when she begins to feel faint and her legs buckle beneath her. She drops into the nearest chair and places her hand to her chest. Alex has already gone down. He is slumped on the floor with his back against the wall and his knees pulled up towards him. He is grasping at his hair and his shoulders are heaving as if he is sobbing uncontrollably, but Abbey can't hear him… or anyone. Everything is silent and moving very, very slowly.

Nathan is on his knees with his arms wrapped around his waist, leaning forward as if he is buckling with actual physical pain. Liam and Gemma both hug him tightly as they cry heartbroken tears of their own and Darren simply stares at the Doctor, unable to process anything. He cannot accept what he is hearing and simply frowns, shaking his head as if there has been some terrible misunderstanding. Sophie rests against his arm in despair and his breathing gradually turns into frantic, grief stricken gasps as the reality slowly sinks in.

"I am so very sorry for your loss…" Doctor Walters continues sincerely, "I appreciate that this is a terrible time, but the police will be with you shortly, to ask a few routine questions..." And with one more rueful smile, he leaves the room, shattering their whole world in his wake.

"No... She can't leave me. She can't fucking leave me..." Nathan sobs hysterically, his hands and voice shaking with raw, crippling anguish as Alex quickly staggers over to him and Darren collapses into Sophie's arms.

"Get up mate... come on..." He gestures to Liam and Gemma backs away as they both pull Nathan to his feet. He stumbles slightly, his face soaked through with tears, but he manages to remain upright.

"She can't leave me..." He sobs again.

"We have to go..." Alex states and the others look on, scared and confused as Nathan shoves him away forcefully.

"No! I want to see her... I need to be with her..."

"There isn't time Nate... you heard what he said. The police are on their way, if they catch up with us now it's over. We're done. We need to get out of here..."

"Darren can't leave..." Sophie reasons, "He has to stay, to speak to the doctors and sort things out; to prove he's her next of kin. It'll look wrong if he just disappears..." Alex runs his hands through his hair and paces the room for a minute; momentarily leaning against the window as he thinks things over, before reluctantly approaching Darren.

"I am so fucking sorry mate, but you and Soph are gonna have to deal with this right now. If we're here, they'll ask for my name and address; if they ask for my address they'll come round and check things out. We could all get done for possession... they might even think we had something to do with Lucy..." Darren looks up, heartbroken and distant, as if he isn't quite seeing Alex kneeling in front of him. Sophie rubs his arm tenderly, as Alex gently grabs hold of his face, "Daz... do you understand what I'm saying? This can't be linked back to mine. If they start looking in to it god knows what they'll find... not just the drugs, or the dealing... but the raid. They might piece it together somehow and there's no way we can risk that. I need to know if you can handle this brother?" Darren simply nods once and swallows hard, composing himself for a moment as he stares numbly at Alex.

"I'll say I found her at ours... that you guys had only just got there when we brought her outside..."

"That won't work..." Sophie sighs, tearfully, "You told the Doctor in the lobby that it had been ten minutes since we found her, it takes at least twenty to get here from ours..."

"We were all in shock..." Alex argues, "A mistake like that can easily be made in a panic, we just have to hope they don't ask too many questions. Lucy took the drugs without us realising or knowing about it, we found her afterwards, that's all true... you won't be lying, Daz, not about that... only about where she was when it happened..." Darren simply nods again while staring at the wall in front of him, completely blank and extremely pale.

"For god sake, how the hell can you even think about this right now?" Gemma snaps and Alex turns towards her with a frustrated and resigned expression fixed firmly on his face.

"Because somebody has to..." He frowns, knowing that once again, he has to be the one to step up and take control of the situation. To keep the others out of trouble and shield them from the police, any possible interrogations and any further heartache. He knows that none of them can take much more. Darren will speak to the doctors and then he can come home, where they can all grieve openly together. But right now, Alex has to be the one to put his emotions aside and thinks three steps ahead. Despite the fact that he wants to crumble and break down just as much as the rest of them.

"You better go... they'll be here in a minute..." Darren confirms, distractedly, and Alex nods in agreement as he and Liam lift a broken Nathan to is feet again before dragging him forward.

"Let's go..." Alex orders, and Abbey and Gemma follow hurriedly behind. They reach the end of the corridor and approach the main elevator, which is thankfully empty when it arrives. Alex is fairly certain they haven't been seen by anyone who matters but the faster they get out of here the better. As he quickly punches the button for the ground floor, two police officers appear in view and discreetly enter the waiting room, at the very same moment the lift doors slide shut.

The following days all merge into a constant, confusing blur and Abbey is only able to pin point certain moments that stand out in her memory for all the wrong reasons. Like when Darren went missing for nearly twelve hours and Sophie was utterly beside herself. The day that Nathan drank himself into oblivion and trashed the flat in a blind, grief filled rage. And the moment she lay silently on the bed, burying her face into a pillow as Tom made his monthly call to Alex and he had to break the devastating news. That was by far the worst. Every other passing hour seems totally irrelevant in comparison. The time in between has no form, meaning or purpose and she hardly knows what day it is, let alone what time. All she does know; is the date they're all dreading, keeps edging ever closer.

The questioning that Darren had endured at the hands of the police turned out to be fairly tame and they thankfully seemed to accept most of what he told them about the events of that night. The fact that he was in shock and had only just found out his little sister had died meant they went easy on him, plus Sophie had been there to back up his story. Only time will tell if anything more will come from the enquiry, but as far as they are all aware, it is simply being recorded as an accidental overdose and a tragic misadventure.

Once Lucy's body was finally released, Darren had set about the heart-breaking task of arranging her funeral. A few family members have been invited but it will mainly be friends gathering at the graveyard this coming Tuesday to lay her to rest. Perhaps most upsetting of all is the fact that Darren doesn't know how or where to contact their parents. Not that Lucy would want him to. She had accepted a long time ago that she would never share a conventional, loving relationship with her mum and dad, and after they walked out on her and Darren at such a young age without a second thought for their safety or welfare, the general consensus is that they simply don't deserve to be told.

'Strange…' Abbey muses, sadly, 'to think that they are out there somewhere, completely oblivious to the fact that their only daughter is no longer alive…'

It makes Abbey wonder how long it would take for the news to reach her family if something terrible happened. It isn't a welcome thought and she quickly dispels it. She has been thinking about them a lot lately. What with all the pain and loss she is suffering at the moment it is only natural that she would reassess her life and begin to appreciate things more. Even though Abbey has never been so cut of and isolated from her family, she is incredibly grateful that she does - at least in a sense - still have them.

When Tuesday finally arrives the weather is dull and overcast, yet every so often there is a slight break in the cloud and the sun shines through, brightening up the day. It doesn't reflect Abbey's mood at all and she hopes that the clouds don't clear completely, as it hardly seems right to have an afternoon of beautiful weather accompanying such a sombre occasion.

She sits, perched on the edge of the bed wearing a black shirt, a black pencil skirt and her nude heels. She has a matching jacket slung over her arm and her amber pendant - which is now even more precious to her than before - is hanging daintily around her neck. Alex is standing in front of the mirror in the en suite and he skilfully fastens his cufflinks before quickly adjusting his light grey tie. He too is wearing all black and against his dark, brown hair and few days' worth of stubble, his bright, piercing blue eyes stand out even more. He looks a lot paler than usual too and Abbey can see the cracks beginning to show in his resolve. He always keeps everything bottled up and manages to hold it together despite his true emotions raging beneath the surface. He always has to be the strong one, never breaking down, but he doesn't fool her.

"I still can't believe this is real..." Abbey whispers, "How could we let this happen...?"

"Nobody *let* this happen, Abbey..." Alex answers without taking his eyes from the mirror as he struggles to get his tie perfectly straight, "Lucy made a mistake, there's nothing we could have done to prevent that..."

"Yes there is..." Abbey gasps, but Alex doesn't respond. He twists and tugs at his tie again several times until he loses his temper and pulls it clean off, tossing it to one side as he leans against the sink.

"What do you want me to say to you?" He sighs deeply.

"I want you to admit that things aren't alright. Of course we could have prevented this; we could have done *everything* different. It wasn't an accident Alex... accidents are something you have no control over, this was a choice..."

"A choice that Lucy made for herself..."

"Exactly..." Abbey despairs, rising to her feet and standing in the door way of the bathroom, "She knew it was a risk. She knew it was dangerous, but she did it anyway. You all go on and on about how it's OK as long as you know you're limits but it's bullshit, Alex... she was the smartest out of all of us and she still lost control..."

"And you tried to help her. You spoke to her, repeatedly, we all did, but you can't force someone into thinking differently Abbey, it doesn't work like that. It doesn't matter how many times we tried to tell her otherwise, Lucy was always going to do whatever the fuck Lucy wanted to do..."

"And that is what scares me..." She confesses, meekly.

Alex frowns with frustration as he picks up his tie, flinging it around his neck and fastening it angrily. This time he doesn't stop to perfect it. Instead he strides across the bedroom and over to the wardrobe, taking out his suit jacket and shrugging it on abruptly.

"I can't actually believe how self-righteous you're being right now..." He snaps, fixing his collar, "Taking drugs is perfectly fine when it fucking suits you, isn't it? When you needed a distraction you didn't question anything, in fact you were more than happy to get as trashed as the rest of us! You've spent the last god knows how long doing more drugs than most and now you want to preach about how wrong and immoral it is?!"

"Because it isn't the same anymore, Alex..." Abbey shouts, completely confounded, "It isn't about getting high and having fun... Lucy is dead and Tom is rotting in prison because of the life we lead, does that not register with you?!" They stand across the room from one another staring in a stony silence and Alex rubs his face, before stepping forward and holding out his hands in placation.

"Look... it should never have happened. And I wish more than anything that we could have helped her, you know I do. But Lucy took drugs because she wanted to... we take drugs because we want to. And yeah there's a certain amount of danger involved, of course there is but we know that and she knew that too. She knew the score Abbey, it was her decision, her choice... no one else's..."

"And that makes it better does it?" Abbey blinks, fighting back tears. Alex is upset too, but he is trying his hardest to keep it all in and remain detached. He can't ever fall apart... not in front of the group. It would make him far too vulnerable and he needs to keep focused in order to get himself and the others through the coming afternoon. He hates fighting with Abbey - more than anything - and even though he knows how angry and confused she is, he just can't deal with it right now. He needs to bring this argument to an end.

"People take risks every day..." He states, resolutely, "The fear of that should never stop you from living the way you want to live..."

"My god..." Abbey gasps again, shaking her head despairingly, "You know that is almost exactly what Lucy said to me when she sold me this life..." There is another, long, drawn out moment as Abbey's words hang in the air, but before either of them can speak again there is a knock on the door and Gemma peers round.

"Sorry to interrupt guys, but we're ready to go..."

"We'll be right there..." Alex answers without breaking away from Abbey's despondent gaze and Gemma nods, smiling a bleak, fleeting smile as she quickly escapes the awkwardness.

"Listen..." Alex sighs, taking another step forward and reaching for Abbey but to his surprise, she pulls away.

"You can stand there and make all the promises you want..." She states, solemnly, "But it won't bring Lucy back. Jesus, Alex... who's next?" And with that she turns away, grabbing her bag and her jacket from the bed in one swift movement before marching out of the room without so much as another glance in his direction.

Not sticking to the promises he made in Ireland is one thing but being in complete denial about how tragic everything has become is something else entirely. It's as if he doesn't want to admit that Lucy is gone which is understandable, but his 'these things happen' attitude is beyond belief. He is obviously putting his barriers up and seriously bottling his grief and that never, ever ends well with Alex.

The funeral is even more heart-breaking and far more difficult than any of them could ever have predicted. The turnout is huge, with mourners practically spilling out of the doors of the church. It is a testament to how popular and loved Lucy was and it makes it even more tragic to think that she will be missed by so many.

Beautiful white orchids adorn the coffin and the poignant order of service contains numerous photographs of Lucy with the important people in her life. Abbey tenderly traces her finger over a picture of the two of them, hugging and smiling in front of the camera, both completely oblivious that the photo is even being taken. They look so happy - and as the vicar speaks of her infectious character and her lust for life, a gut wrenching sadness consumes Abbey once more. The last time she was sat at a funeral, she was saying goodbye to her twin brother, the one person in the world who understood her better than anyone. It feels as though she is repeating the experience over, and for the second time in her life she finds herself struggling with an almost unbearable sense of loss.

After the thirty minute service concludes to Credence Clearwater Revival's 'Who'll Stop the Rain?' Lucy's body is interred in the adjoining cemetery, in a beautiful plot beneath a blossom tree. Despite almost two weeks of grieving while trying to adjust and cope with her death, it is without doubt the harrowing moment when reality truly hits home. As the vicar recites the committal prayer and the coffin is lowered, it is all so incredibly final. She is gone... and they are never going to see her again.

One by one, the mourners tearfully lay their flowers and pay their respects, until Abbey, Alex, Darren, Sophie, Gemma, Liam and Nathan are the only ones left at the graveside. None of them move - almost as if they can't physically bring themselves to leave - knowing that when they do, it will all be over and they will have to let her go.

Without saying a word, Nathan steps forward, gently throwing a single white rose onto the coffin before dropping to his knees. His face is crumpled in agony and his shoulders slump forward in utter despair as if he has absolutely nothing left inside him. No joy, no hope, and no purpose. There isn't anything any of them can do other than stand quietly at his side, lost in their own grief as they wait for him to say his devastating goodbye.

Once Nathan's thick, heavy sobs have stilled slightly and his pain has almost exhausted him, he walks arm in arm with Darren back towards the car and Sophie and Gemma follow behind. Liam takes a deep, steadying breath as he stands for a moment longer, staring down at the coffin with heart-wrenching disbelief. He looks as though he is about to say something, but doesn't. Instead he takes a step back and looks up at a patch of blue in the sky above, smirking as he raises his hand in a loving salute.

Abbey clings tightly to the amber pendant around her neck, placing it against her lips and kissing it softly as she begins to back away beside Liam. It is only then that she properly acknowledges Alex for the first time since leaving the church. The damn has burst. The cracks have opened and tears fall freely down his face as he stands at the foot of the grave with his hands held respectfully in front of him. He is still battling his emotions, but he can't contain them anymore. He can't hold it in. He finally has to admit that Lucy has really gone. Abbey places her hand gently on his shoulder and he exhales sharply, rubbing his fingers in his eyes in an attempt to stop the tears. He shakes his head with a sorrowful resignation and as he grasps Abbey's hand he reaches into his pocket, pulling out a slightly dog-eared picture of the group. They are all smiling at the camera, ready for a night out, young, happy and completely carefree. Lucy is in the centre of the shot next to Alex and he has his arm draped affectionately over her shoulder.

He releases his grip and they watch as the photo flutters down into the grave, landing face up amongst the bed of scattered roses.

"I'll see you later, kid…" He smiles, sadly, "Take the party up there, show 'em how it's done…" And after one final, reflective pause, they turn and follow the others back to the car and onto 'The Locke' for the wake.

After her fifth double vodka and coke Abbey loses count of how much she has had. She wants to drink herself into a stupor so that her memory becomes blank and she can block out the world around her, but it doesn't seem to be working. Instead it drags her down further into the depths of her pain and she can't seem to claw her way back out.

The many friends that have joined them at the pub for a drink in Lucy's honour seem in relatively high spirits for a wake. There are tears, but there is also laughter, and a lot of reminiscing about the good times and the fond memories they shared. Perhaps it is exactly how it should be at a funeral? Remembering the happier days and being thankful that you had someone so special in your life, even it was for far too short a time. But Abbey, Alex, Gemma, Sophie and Darren have distanced themselves from the rest of the congregation and have absolutely no desire to join in. None of them feel like talking, choosing instead to sit alone and drink continuously in a feeble attempt to numb the pain. Nathan had barely lasted half an hour before it all got too much for him and Liam had to take him home, and judging by the state he was in when he left, Liam will most likely be staying with him for the rest of the night as well.

They are all scared for Nathan, but it is incredibly hard to take care of someone else while you're battling with your own pain. Abbey understands that now and for the first time ever she truly appreciates how difficult it must have been for her mum and her brother. She hated them for not reaching out to her enough after Ryan died. They didn't try to help her or take the time to understand what she was going through but they couldn't, because they were too busy struggling with their own grief and trying to find their own way through the hurt. It wasn't easy for any of them.

As the pub begins to close up and Sophie and Gemma carry an almost comatose Darren to a waiting taxi, Abbey and Alex head back to the flat alone. Still reeling from their heated exchange earlier, the atmosphere between them is slightly awkward as they walk quietly side by side. Abbey hasn't been this drunk in a long time but she has no intention of stopping for the night. She had felt irrationally jealous of Darren as he sat slumped in the passenger seat of that car, teetering on the brink of unconsciousness. She wishes she could close her eyes and switch off her thoughts as well, but ever since Lucy's death she seems to have inherited Alex's sleep deficiency. Too many harrowing memories keep racing through her mind and she just wants them all to stop. That is why she plans to follow Darren's example and is determined to carry on drinking until her brain completely shuts down.

They arrive back home to a dark, empty flat and Alex retreats into the bedroom almost immediately, which Abbey is grateful for. She wants to be on her own to cry and sob and let herself feel without anyone holding her back. There is a fresh bottle of vodka in the fridge but no mixers. Usually that would bother her but tonight she is on a mission to get blind drunk and pouring it straight will no doubt enable her to achieve that goal a lot faster.

As Abbey relentlessly downs numerous shots - only stopping for another line of coke or to drop another pill - she can gradually feel herself slipping. She honestly doesn't know where the hell she can go from here. Things can't get any worse and she feels utterly trapped. Her family fell apart and now her friends are suffering too, and once again she feels as though she is completely on her own. She is drifting, with no direction and no hope, and the two people she wants to talk to more than anything in the world are lost to her forever. 'How did it ever get to be like this?'

Painfully vivid images flash through Abbey's mind in quick succession. Lucy's lifeless body, Ryan, Alex, her mum, her brother's battered and swollen face, Nathan at the hospital... one vision after another in a persistent, dream like assault. It is all too much and as the intoxicating effects of the cocaine and ecstasy spread through her body, she begins to lose her grip on reality, spiralling even further down into the deep black hole of depression. She wants this pain to be over. She doesn't want to feel, or think, or be anymore. She isn't strong enough to cope with this.

Completely removed from reality and unable to rationalize anything; all Abbey can focus on is the peace of mind that she so desperately longs for. All she wants is to see Ryan and Lucy again, and as she struggles to distinguish between what is real and what is a product of her imagination, she suddenly finds herself staggering outside onto the balcony.

Very hesitantly, she places her hands on top of the steel barrier, feeling the smooth, cold metal beneath her fingertips before slowly tightening her grip and pulling herself upwards. She carefully throws hers legs over the side before leaning forward and gently tilting her head back, breathing in the cold night air as she marvels at the stars and the sense of freedom they bring her. Utterly immersed in her drug induced haze and the welcome feeling of weightlessness, she doesn't hear the balcony door slide open or notice a shocked and terrified Alex appear behind her, with his eyes wide and his arms outstretched in horror.

Chapter Twenty

Starting Over

"Abbey…" Alex whispers, breathlessly, "What the hell are you doing…?"

It takes a brief moment for Abbey's mind to pull into focus as she turns her head towards the distant and echoing sound of Alex's voice. Her vision is blurred and her heart is beating fast, despite the strange sense of calm that has clouded over her.

"Is this real…?" She whispers back, while looking down at the road nine floors beneath her.

"What?"

"Is this real…?" She asks again - and Alex edges cautiously towards her with his hands outstretched in an appeasing fashion, as if he is approaching a startled animal he doesn't want to frighten.

"You know this is real Abbey. I need you to give me your hand and climb back over the railing…"

"I don't… I don't understand…" She shakes her head and sways slightly from the dizzying sensation, causing Alex to hold his breath and lean forward apprehensively. The balcony is wet from the earlier rain and Abbey is drunk and totally out of it. She could fall to her death at any moment.

"If you slip, you'll fall... and we're a long way up babe. I need you to give me your hand so I can pull you back over..."

"It's a lie you know..." Abbey murmurs so quietly it is barely a whisper and Alex almost doesn't catch what she is saying.

"I'm not lying to you..." He answers impatiently, trying to remain calm while desperately urging her to grab hold of his hand.

"No, not you... I mean this, all of this. It's a lie..."

"I don't know what you're talking about..." Alex stresses, helplessly. He is trying hard not to make any sudden movements that might alarm her, while speaking slowly in a low, reassuring voice, as if trying to reason with a child.

"This... all of this..." She continues, dazed and distracted, "You take a hit and it makes you feel free. It makes you feel like you can do anything. You feel like everything is fine, better than fine... but it's a trick. You don't know what's real or what isn't... the good or the bad... it lies to you, this feeling... It's a lie..."

"Abbey... you're tripping. *Please* come back inside..." Alex begs, knowing full well that she is too far gone to be reasoned with.

"Is this real...?" She asks quietly once more, while gazing dreamily at the ground, "If I let go now... would I fly...?" Abbey flexes her fingers in the tiniest, most subtle way imaginable but it is all Alex needs to jolt him into action. He leaps forward and wraps both arms tightly around Abbey's waist, hauling her over the railing and dragging her aggressively back into the living room. He finally let's go as he throws her down onto one of the sofa's and the impact shocks her out of her drug induced haze. She gasps as the reality of what she has just done comes sharply into focus, but before she can scream, panic, or cry, Alex grabs her shoulders and spins her round to face him, standing above her while shaking her wildly.

"What the fuck are you doing Abbey, for Christ sake?" He shouts, terrifyingly loud, "Do you really think that's the answer? Do you really think that's the way out? You of all people, after what you went through with your brother... you'd seriously put your family through that again... you'd seriously do that to me? I've lost Lucy and I've lost Tom and everyone's hanging on by a fucking thread... I'm only just hanging in there and you go and do something so fucking stupid, Abbey? Why? I can't lose you, do you understand me.... I can't fucking lose you too..." Alex's anger begins to subside towards the end of his furious rant and he drops to his knees in front of the sofa, crying with frustration, anger and grief. He pulls Abbey down onto the floor next to him and wraps his arms around her neck, holding her close and gripping her in an unbreakable embrace. She holds him back tightly as she sobs into his chest and they sit there together for the longest time, crying for Lucy and for Tom, for the hopelessness they feel, and for the life they dreamt of living together, which they know they can never have.

It is the final straw for Abbey. Sinking to a new low and letting the pain overcome her so much that she ends up in the same frame of mind - the same hollow, empty space - as Ryan did years before. Alex was right to say what he said. After everything she and her family went through and she almost follows the exact same path. It is the wakeup call she needed. For so long she has been torn in two, between her real family and her life with her friends, and despite how much she loves them, how much she loves Alex, she has never truly been able to let go of her family. She never wanted to choose between them but now she feels as though the choice has been made for her due to the escalating circumstances and the dangerous situation she has found herself in. It isn't easy; in fact it is almost impossible for Abbey to consider life away from all she has known for the past year. The friends she has grown to love; good people, just a little messed up, like her. And Alex, who is still by far the most important thing in her world.

Her heart sinks in her chest as she accepts what she has to do. It is far too complicated now and things have gone way beyond her control. What happened on the balcony is testament to that. Even though she loves Alex and always will, she knows she has to get out.

Spending the next few days agonising over her decision doesn't help, but she can't deny that it feels more and more like the right thing to do. Whether or not she tells Alex though, is something she can't decide on - and the uncertainty is killing her. He saved her life, helped her in more ways than he will ever know, and now he's the one that is struggling and she is planning on running away. He deserves more than that, he deserves better. But it is becoming clearer by the day that Abbey isn't the one that can give him what he needs. Not when her staying means she could lose herself completely and end up sharing the same fate as Ryan and Lucy. It is too big a risk.

If she tells Alex he will beg her to stay, he will plead with her, and because of her feelings for him, because of how much she loves him, she knows all too well that she will give in. She won't be able to remain steadfast and determined because whenever she sees Alex hurting, she goes to him without question. She won't be able to stand causing him pain, seeing that look of hurt and betrayal in his eyes, so perhaps it is best that she slips out quietly, saving them both the pain of a heart-breaking goodbye? It is selfish. Abbey knows it. She is taking the easier option, the coward's way out... but it is the only way she can stomach the thought of walking away from him. Her Alex. Her beautiful, messed up, complicated boy. If only things were different, but there is no hope in wishing - and as she unwillingly acknowledges the fact that she may never see him again, her devastated tears keep falling.

Once Abbey's plan is in place, all she can do is wait. It feels like the ultimate betrayal and she just wants it to be over. Her bag is packed in the bottom of the wardrobe and a handwritten note explaining her actions is stowed away in the back pocket of her jeans. 'A note... after everything we've been through together... it all ends with a pathetic note...' she scolds herself. It is pitiful, she is piti-ful, but as her stomach turns with disgust at her own actions, she reminds herself that it is the only way. It's what she has to do and she knows she can't back out now.

Due to Alex's insomnia, sneaking out in the middle of the night is easier said than done. But at 3:00am on a Thursday morning, he finally falls into a deep, heavy sleep and Abbey's window of opportunity opens. She lies on her side for the longest time, staring at him longingly. He looks peaceful and rested... and so much younger. He is so incredibly lost and she prays to god above anything else that he eventually gets through this and finds his way.

She takes in every inch of his perfect face, committing it to memory while fighting the urge to reach out and touch him, knowing how easily he can wake. She doesn't want to go. A huge part of her wants to stay in this moment forever and she has to physically force herself to get up, to climb out of bed and throw on her jeans and hooded top. Moving as slowly and as quietly as she can, she pulls out her bag and slides the wardrobe door shut before creeping back over to the bedside table and laying the note face up. She looks down at Alex again, lifting her hand to her face while holding in a gut wrenching sob, wishing that she could kiss him one last time. As the unbearable ache in her heart almost consumes her, she musters all the strength she possibly can and quickly turns on her heel, striding out of the bedroom, down the hall, out of the kitchen and into the waiting lift.

As she presses the button for the ground floor, she completely breaks down, dropping her bag at her feet and leaning forward, resting on the mirrored wall as she wails inconsolably. It is over. It is done. She has really left him. As the doors slide open a few moments later, she races through the lobby and outside into the early morning stillness, reaching for her mobile and calling a taxi, which arrives in less than five minutes.

"Are you alright love...?" The driver asks as Abbey bundles herself clumsily into the back seat.

"I'm fine..." She mutters, unconvincingly.

"Where to...?"

"Meanwood please..." She sighs, rubbing her hands across her tired face, "I'm going home..."

With hardly any traffic on the roads, the taxi pulls up outside Abbey's house quicker than she would like.

She thought she would have time to calm down, to figure out what she is going to say and do when she sees her family for the first time in months. But her time is up. She pays the driver and climbs reluctantly out of the car, standing aimlessly at the bottom of the driveway as she stares up at the house. It seems smaller somehow and unnervingly alien... not how home should feel at all. Unsure of what to do, she approaches the door with caution, grasping her key in her hand. It doesn't feel right, as though it is rude and totally out of line to just let herself in after all this time. So instead, she takes a deep, calming breath and knocks once, loudly.

After a few seconds the landing light turns on and she sees a figure approaching the door. Is this a mistake? What if she has burnt her bridges and they don't want her back? Why the hell would they? Abbey's instincts are telling her to turn and run but she can't. He nerves are paralysing and she is frozen, rooted to the spot as the latch slides back and the key turns in the lock.

Peter opens the door and stares impassively for what feels like the longest time, frowning drowsily as he stands there in nothing but his grey joggers with his mouth hanging open as if he can hardly believe what he is seeing. Abbey can't find her voice but she doesn't need to. Peter lurches forward without a word and grabs her by the arm, pulling her forcefully into the house and into an all-consuming embrace. He grips her so tightly she can hardly breathe, but she returns his hug, just as fiercely.

A few seconds pass - and as Abbey wonders with apprehension whether her mum has slept through the commotion - she hears a short, quiet gasp, followed by footsteps racing down the stairs. Without looking up she feels Janet throw her arms forcefully around them both, encasing her in love and comforting her, as she is overcome with an enormous sense of relief.

Dr. Morris turns the last page of the bound, A4 document she is reading and removes her glasses with a satisfied smile. Abbey sits across from her in the large, comfortable leather arm chair just as she has done twice a week for the last three months. The office is small, warm and cluttered... and in the short time that Abbey has been at Trinity and All Saints rehab centre, it has become reassuringly familiar. It is a far cry from how she first felt when she walked through those doors, completely devoid of hope with no idea what the future might hold. She can appreciate now, sitting here at the end of her treatment, just how far she has come - and it is all thanks to this woman. Although part of her is glad that her time here is over, the idea of leaving these safe and comforting surroundings is more than a little terrifying.

"So..." Dr. Morris smiles, "How do you feel...?"

"I don't know..." Abbey replies, honestly, "Happy, I think? Grateful, but nervous too... I know the hardest part isn't over..."

"No. But you've come a hell of a long way Abbey; you should give yourself credit for that..."

"I guess..."

"You have..." She reiterates, holding the bound document aloft to stress her point further, "This is everything, right here. Everything you've lived, everything you've been through, everything you've survived. It's a hell of a lot for anyone to deal with, let alone someone as young as yourself... but you got through it. You came here and you dealt with your demons. You didn't think you could write down your story at first, you struggled with it... but here we are. Our last session together and you've managed it. I'm proud of you..."

"Thank you..." Abbey grins, sincerely.

"It's pretty powerful stuff..." She notes, flicking back through the pages, "How did you feel, writing it all down?"

"Good. Well... not so much at first... and it was difficult at times, but that was the point wasn't it? To force me to look back, to process it all..."

"And have you...?"

"I'm getting there..." Abbey nods, "It'll take more than a couple of months in this place to get me fully back on track but it's definitely helped, writing it all down, working through it... so thank you..."

"It's why I'm here..." Dr. Morris smiles, appreciatively, "Now comes the challenging part..."

"And by that you mean the rest of my life...?" Abbey jokes.

"Yes. One that is positive, fulfilling and drug free. I have every confidence in you, Abbey. I know you can move on from this. You're an extremely bright and capable girl who took a wrong turn but this isn't the end of your story, there's plenty more to come..."

"Do you really think people can go back to the life they had before all this...?" Abbey asks, still not entirely convinced.

"I do. I know you can have a happy and stable life again. It won't be completely the same but I think you already know that. You've changed and you've grown and now is the time to move forward, without letting your past hold you back. What happens next is entirely up to you…"

Abbey wishes she had the same faith in herself as Dr. Morris seems to have in her, but the idea of heading back out into the real world is an unbelievably daunting one. She can't stay here forever though, and no matter how much a part of her wants to hide away for the rest of her days, she has to face the music eventually.

Abbey zips up her suitcase and wheels it over towards the door, turning back and pausing for a moment as she says goodbye to the room that has been her home for the last ninety days. It is time to close this chapter and move onto the next, and she can do it, she knows she can, with her own determination and with the support of her family… who are currently waiting for her downstairs in the lobby. Abbey exits the lift and Janet rushes straight over to her, hugging her proudly as Peter takes her suitcase out of her hands.

"Alright Mum, let her at least get to the car before you start smothering her…!"

"I'm just so happy to see you…" Janet beams and Abbey can't help but laugh at her enthusiasm, "Have you got everything…?"

"Yep…" Abbey nods, "I'm good to go…"

"Then let's get you home…"

Abbey hugs Peter in greeting before following him out of Trinity and All Saints main reception area. She walks hand in hand with Janet towards the car park where Anna is waiting next to Dom with an excitable Amelia wriggling in her arms. Abbey smiles brightly at her welcoming committee, greeting them all warmly before they climb into the waiting cars and set off on the long drive back home to Leeds.

A grieving twin, a teenage runaway, a drug addict; Abbey has been all of those things, but as they head slowly down the long, winding driveway with the rehab facility shrinking smaller into the distance, she can feel all of those personas gradually slipping away. She closes her eyes and sighs deeply, feeling a welcome sense of release while at the same time mentally preparing herself for what is to come. Abbey is ready to start a fresh, to move forward like Dr. Morris had said, and she is more determined than ever to turn her life around and make the most of this second chance.

During the time Abbey spent in rehab she did a lot of thinking, a lot of soul searching, and as a result her relationship with her family couldn't be in a better place. She had been scared and worried at first, fearing that the damage caused by her actions would be permanent and things would never be the same between them again, but it was a worry that turned out to be unfounded. Family is family after all, and they were just as keen to work through their problems as she had been. There was a lot of talking, some of it heated, some of it more than a little unpleasant, but it was necessary for them to discuss their differences under the watchful eye of Dr. Morris, whose idea of family therapy sessions once a fortnight turned out to be the best thing about the entire process. Finally discussing their feelings together means a huge weight has been lifted and it really does feel like they have wiped the slate clean. It is a new beginning... for all of them.

The one thing that Abbey is genuinely terrified about is her impending return to school. She is to start her final year of sixth form all over again, only this time she won't be the 'new girl'... she will be the girl that everyone is talking about.

The girl who went off the rails and ended up in rehab.

The girl who got expelled for fighting and has only been allowed back in under strict supervision.

The girl who not only lost her twin brother, but her best friend too.

She will no doubt be the topic of discussion for quite a while to come and those personas that she tried so hard to shed will be lurking in the background and on the lips of all the gossip mongers, but it is to be expected. If it were somebody else in Abbey's shoes, she knows she would probably be talking about them too. It is human nature after all. She will just have to deal with it the best she can.

Prior to her first day back, Janet accompanies Abbey to a meeting with Principal Grant and she is hugely grateful for her support. He is still as irritating as ever, but due to the way her previous enrolment at Eden Comprehensive ended he seems to be even more dismissive of her than the last time she was sitting in his office. Abbey accepts that he has a reason to feel the way he does, but his no nonsense lecture about how if it were up to him she would never have been allowed back into 'his school' in the first place... isn't exactly the pep talk she was hoping for.

At least the obvious disdain he feels towards Abbey means he wants as little to do with her as humanly possible, which suits her just fine, and after Janet graciously reminds him that it wasn't his decision and that Abbey has been accepted back in whether he likes it or not, he turns a vivid shade of purple before abruptly escorting them out. As a parting shot, he reminds Abbey for the tenth time that he will be 'watching her closely' and tells her that from now on it will be Mr Harper helping her get back on track, and he sincerely hopes that she 'makes the most of her education, instead of squandering it'. 'Prick'.

"Well that was delightful..." Janet remarks sarcastically as they wander back through to reception, "He's a shitty little man isn't he..." Abbey bursts out laughing and shakes her head at her mother's unexpected assessment.

"Good to see that's another thing we agree on these days Mum..."

"Yes well, if he gives you any trouble you tell me. I'm not having him persecuting you, it's not fair..."

"I promise you'll be the first to know. Thanks for fighting my corner..." Abbey smiles and Janet tucks a loose strand of hair behind her ear before giving her a gentle hug.

"Of course, what are Mum's for?" She grins, before glancing hurriedly at her watch, "I have to get to my meeting... are you alright to see this Mr Harper on your own?" Abbey's heart lurches and she swallows hard as the thought of seeing him again fills her with a range of crazy, conflicting emotions. Nerves, fear, regret, guilt and much to her annoyance... excitement. She has butterflies battering her stomach and she is unsure whether it is a good thing or not. It is definitely a complication she could do without, especially when she needs to be focused in order to get her grades back up to scratch.

"Yeah, it's fine, don't worry... I'll see you at home..."

Abbey slowly makes her way through the familiar corridors and over towards Mr Harper's office. She knew he was still acting head of sixth form, so as soon as she was accepted back into Eden Comprehensive this meeting became pretty much inevitable... she just hadn't really thought about it until now. She had tried to push it to the back of her mind instead of adding it to her list of things to worry about.

She rounds the corner by her old locker and peers through the thin glass window in the door. Mr Harper is sitting at his desk, resting his chin on his hand as he scans the computer screen in front of him. He has a slight frown on his face, his hair is in disarray and the top two buttons of his shirt are undone in a casual manner. As Abbey appraises his appearance she vividly recalls the last time she was here, when they almost kissed. Her stomach lurches and she quickly clears her head, trying to focus on the fact that he is her teacher and not, under any circumstances, her boyfriend. 'Don't think about it, don't think about it, don't think about it...' she chants over and over in her mind as she taps lightly on the door before entering.

Mr Harper instantly rises from his seat with a surprised expression on his face, but despite his evident shock, there is a slight smile playing at the corner of his mouth that reveals he is genuinely happy to see her.

"Hi..." Abbey nods, shyly.

"Abbey... come in, take a seat..." She hangs her bag on the back of the chair opposite Mr Harper's desk and perches lightly on the edge, struggling to look him directly in the eye, "How are you?" He asks.

"I'm well thanks..." She smiles, "Better..."

"I'm really glad..." He states, sincerely, "It's good to see you..." Abbey wants to tell him that it is good to see him too, but she stops herself, as if speaking her mind might somehow betray her true feelings.

"Abbey...?" Mr Harper's tone forces her to look up and their eyes meet properly for the first time. He pulls his chair round to the other side of the desk and sits down in front of her, careful to leave a significant distance between them, "I want to start by apologising, about what happened the last time we spoke. I crossed a line. I want to assure you that it won't happen again..." Much to her surprise, Abbey's heart sinks a little and she hopes the disappointment doesn't show on her face.

"It's OK... you were just trying to help. It was my fault, I was a mess..."

"You've been through a lot; it's good to see you're feeling better though. You look really well..." He adds his last statement with a slight reluctance and there is a brief moment where neither of them speak. It is clear to Abbey that they are both thinking about the almost kiss and she can feel the tension between them building.

It is confusing the hell out of her to say the least. It is obvious that she is drawn to him, but this strange chemistry between them seems to be more than based on physical attraction alone. It isn't something she is looking for or something she particularly wants to feel... but she can't seem to help it. She has just come out of a serious and complicated relationship. A relationship with someone she really, truly loved. Surely, it is too soon to be moving on? In truth, she still loves Alex, even now. The fact that she is reduced to tears whenever she so much as thinks about him makes that fact fairly obvious. She misses him like crazy. Perhaps that is why she is drawn to Harper in this way? She is trying to replace something that she has lost, or at least the idea of something? But then that doesn't explain away their previous encounter which happened when Alex was still very much a part of her life? 'Confusing as hell...' Abbey confirms to herself, rolling her eyes a little.

"What...?" Mr Harper smirks, trying to read her expression.

"Nothing..." She muses, " It's just, I'm not all that sorry, about what happened before... or what nearly happened..." The rational part of Abbey's conscience is screaming at her to shut up. She has no idea why she is saying this, but Harper has the ability to bring out the truth in her. To make her open up and confess her feelings, no matter how awkward it might be. He shifts slightly in his chair but doesn't lean back or widen the distance between them.

"I'm your teacher, Abbey..." He states, running his hand round the back of his neck, "I have a duty of care..."

"I know that..." She nods in agreement, "But I'm not a kid..."

"I know. In that case, how about we compromise with friendship?" He grins suddenly as a memory rushes to the forefront of his mind, "Or is that too lame for you? I remember you saying that once... 'I'm your teacher but I'm also'..."

"Your friend..." Abbey laughs out loud as she recalls their very first conversation and they smile at one another, sweetly, "Were you really going to say head of sixth form?"

"I was..." he holds his hand to his chest with sincerity, "you jumped in with your corny assumption before I could finish..."

"Yeah, well, I wasn't much for the touchy, feely crap back then. I had a lot of people trying to reach out to me and it was getting pretty exhausting..."

"I can imagine. People always mean well, but it can be suffocating..." Abbey recalls Harper's story of what happened to his brother and her heart swells with sympathy. She had forgotten just how alike their past experiences are and how much she can relate to him. Perhaps that is another reason why she feels such a close connection?

"So, are you ready to finish what you started with you're A-Levels...?" He asks, cheerfully.

"Both ready and willing..." Abbey nods.

"Good stuff. We'll get your timetable sorted and a schedule of your lessons... it might be difficult at first, getting back into the swing of things, but any problems or issues and we'll sort them together..."

"Thank you... Mr Harper..." Abbey smiles widely, amused at using such a formal address for a man she is supposedly 'friends' with and whom she very nearly kissed. It is clear that he sees the funny side too, smiling in response as he moves back over to his side of the desk.

"Matt..."

"Hmm...?"

"It's Matt, Matt Harper..."

"Oh, OK..." Abbey grins, "I'm glad you told me that... it'd feel even weirder calling you Sir..."

"Matt's fine..." He laughs, gathering together the various books and paperwork that will guide Abbey through her final year of school... again.

It's strange to think that someone so young can have such a demanding job role, one that is so full of responsibility. She had discovered through a bit of calculated snooping that Matt Harper has only recently turned 27. That is almost two years younger than Alex, and he couldn't be more different or live a more contrary life to the one she very recently turned her back on. It just goes to show that everyone has their own story, and everyone copes with the hand they are dealt in different and varied ways.

"It's good to have you back…" Matt smiles, and Abbey nods, agreeing with him wholeheartedly. It is beyond strange to think that she would ever be happy to be back in this place, but she really, truly is.

Living a normal, structured, teenage life is something Abbey hasn't experienced in a long time and as the months go by, she can feel the trauma of her recent past fading into the background. She will never forget, but her focus and drive to move forward has clearly started to pay off, at home with her family as well as with her achievements in school.

There isn't a day goes by where she doesn't think of her friends and the 'family' she left behind. She constantly wonders how Nathan is coping; she can't turn a single corner or walk down a single hallway at Eden without being reminded of him, Liam and Lucy. The walls and corridors are steeped in memories and although painful, it is a link to her friends that she is grateful for, as she still feels connected to them in some way.

Her phone never rang. There were no messages or missed calls after she left. Alex must have been so furious? Or perhaps he secretly wanted her to leave? Abbey will never really know. But her love for him hasn't faded. She still worries constantly, still hopes and prays that he is alright and staying out of trouble. She hopes that Darren is grieving and dealing with the loss of his sister. She hopes that Sophie is helping him and that Gemma is standing by them all, not distancing herself like before with Tom. They will always be in her heart and she is eternally grateful to them for bringing her back to life when she needed it the most. It is just so unfortunate and so incredibly sad, that it all came full circle and she had to walk away in order to survive.

Working on her relationship with her family has been an on-going process ever since she left rehab and moved home. Nothing is perfect, nothing can be 100% fine every single day, and in true sibling form Abbey and Peter have clashed more than once. But it is the normal, stereotypical squabbling that you would find in any home. Where they bicker and argue until Janet steps in and orders them both to be quiet. Nine times out of ten they end up laughing together, instead of hating each other and responding with the silent treatment for several days. It is a healthy, stable relationship and Abbey is thriving as a result. All that time she spent being angry at them, all that time she wasted staying away from home and ostracising her own family; it means she is all the more determined now to make it up to them, for her own sake as well as theirs.

She has managed to regain that loving connection with Janet and Peter that had been missing for so long and becoming a first time Aunt has brought her even closer to her sister than before. She absolutely dotes on Amelia. Watching her change, grow and learn is something she completely missed out on in the first few months of her life and it is one of her biggest regrets. She looks at her niece, who is so young and innocent with her whole life ahead of her and Abbey wants nothing more than to protect her, guide her and ensure that she never has to suffer by taking the wrong path like she did. Seeing life from a child's eyes has given Abbey a brand new perspective on almost everything and for the first time in a very long time, she feels like she knows who she is, what she wants and where she is going. She has her family back, she has more than one positive goal to work towards and her future looks bright. Yet despite everything going so well and Abbey feeling genuinely happy again, she still knows that things can change in a heartbeat.

Life is unpredictable, you have to learn to take the rough with the smooth and it is important never to get complacent. She made a promise to herself that she will never again take anything for granted as one of the biggest lessons Abbey has learnt throughout all of her struggle, is that so much of what happens is beyond anyone's control.

A seemingly insignificant moment, a reaction, a simple decision... something so small can set your life on an entirely different course and turn your whole world upside down. Other people's choices can have serious consequences too; consequences that can ripple back onto you without warning or expectation. Even choices made by the person you love; that were made months ago, at a different time, during a different life... can still come back to haunt you.

CHAPTER TWENTY ONE

FINAL GOODBYES

As the final school bell sounds marking the end of the day and the end of term, there is a loud cheer and a round of applause from the sixth form common room and the surrounding classes.

It is over. The last nine months have absolutely flown by and Abbey's A-Level course is officially done. She had sat her final exam at the start of the week but the handful of remaining classes were spent finalising her last bit of course work and saying goodbye to her friends.

If someone had told her a year ago that she would be finishing out the school year, gaining her qualifications and deciding on University courses, she would have called them crazy. It felt like an unachievable dream… but it is one that she has now accomplished, and she couldn't be happier.

As she leaves the common room for the final time, waving to her friends and nodding excitedly as they confirm their plans for the evening, she practically skips down the hallway towards Matt Harper's office. It is bitter sweet, knowing that finally graduating from Eden will mean she won't get to see him every day. He had kept his promise and they have developed a firm friendship over the course of the last few terms. He had become less and less like a teacher and more like an equal as they got to know each other properly on mutual ground and she will miss him terribly, even though she is certain that she will see him again.

Abbey taps lightly on the door and enters without waiting for a reply, hesitating in the entrance when she sees Mr Macintyre, the head of year 11, sitting in the seat opposite Matt.

"Oh sorry… I can come back?"

"No… no it's fine, we were just finishing up…" Due to the fact that Mr Macintyre is twisted in his seat closely assessing Abbey, he doesn't notice Matt shaking his head and widening his eyes in a pleading fashion.

"Oh right…" He eventually responds, a little surprised at the apparently abrupt ending to his conversation, "I'll see you anon then Matt. Enjoy your summer…"

"You too…" He replies, shaking his hand politely.

"What was all that about…?" Abbey asks once he is out of ear shot.

"That was you saving me from an already 40 minute conversation about his caravanning plans and his favourite fishing spots…"

"Oh right…" She laughs, "I was going to say, you looked riveted…"

"I wouldn't exactly label it the most exciting conversation I've ever had…"

"Well, maybe not yet but that'll be you in a couple of year's gramps, with your thick rimmed reading glasses and your tweed jacket…" Abbey laughs out loud at the ridiculous mental image and Matt smiles in response, shaking his head with his arms folded as he stands up straight from his leaning position by the window.

"What am I going to do without your constant abuse and inappropriate sarcasm...?" He asks, moving towards her.

"Learn to fish...?" She smiles again, and to her surprise he steps forward and places his arms tightly around her shoulders, hugging her affectionately.

"Well done you. You did it..."

"I did, didn't I?" She grins, trying to regain control of her fluttering heartbeat after the unexpected contact between them, "And here is my final piece of coursework, all finished as promised... T's crossed, I's dotted..." Abbey hands him the folder she is carrying and he circles his desk, placing it neatly in the top drawer.

"So you'll be celebrating tonight no doubt?"

"That's the plan yeah; we're headed to a few spots in Town I think..."

"That's good. And have you thought anymore about your University courses yet?"

"You just can't wait to get rid of me can you?" Abbey jokes, and he stares directly at her, smiling shyly.

"That couldn't be further from the truth Abbey; I think you know that..." His voice is wistful and it causes the butterflies in Abbey's stomach to momentarily reawaken.

"You'll have another charity case to work on next year I'm sure..." She laughs.

"You were never that..."

"I know, I'm just joking around..." He seems to be in a bad mood today and Abbey dares to entertain the notion that it is because she is leaving.

"You definitely deserve a break after all your hard work but you should really be considering your options and thinking about what you want to do next..." He confirms.

"I am; I'm just not decided yet. It's harder than I thought it would be..."

"It's a big decision; but I could help you with it if you want? We can always sit down and go through it together?"

"That would be great..."

"How about Saturday...?" He asks, trying hard to appear aloof and casual, "We could go for a drink...?"

"Are you asking me out, Sir...?" She smirks mischievously and he saunters back over towards her so that they are standing face to face.

"Yes, Miss Miller, I am..." He answers softly.

"OK..." She stammers, "Well, Saturday is good for me..."

"I have my sister's delightful children in the afternoon, but I'm free after that. Shall we say about 7:30pm?"

"Where...?"

"We could try that new bar in Headingly, the one on Otley Road...?"

"Sounds good..." The overwhelming tension is building between them and the hairs on the back of Abbey's neck are bristling with delight. The spark has always been there, but this time he seems to be responding to it, far less cautiously than usual. They stare at each other momentarily and Abbey has an irresistible urge to lean forward and kiss him, but before she has chance to act on impulse, he reaches up and gently cups her face in his hand, stroking his thumb lightly across her cheek.

"You're officially still my pupil…" He whispers, "But on Saturday you won't be…" The promise in his voice sends a rush of excitement pulsing through Abbey and she beams up at him knowingly.

"In that case, I will see you on Saturday evening… Mr Harper…" She smiles sweetly and he takes a step back, nodding in response.

"I'll text you…"

"OK…" Abbey turns and slips back out into the hallway as if she has some naughty little secret, which in a sense, she does. Stealing one last glance through the window, Matt winks at her and smiles a sweet, alluring smile, which causes her to blush. Suddenly her plans for tonight appear far less exciting and she is eager for the weekend to arrive.

Abbey wasn't overly sure how Janet would take the news of her going out on a 'date' with her teacher, but rather surprisingly, she handled it quite well. Matt may be seven years her senior but Abbey is incredibly mature for her age, she always has been, and even more so now after everything she has been through and her recent life experiences. He is a stable, honest, decent guy, who has a respectable job and a responsible outlook on life. Plus he earns his money legally and doesn't partake in any crime or drug taking at all. Therefore in Janet's eyes, he ticks all the boxes.

Peter isn't quite as thrilled about her potential new relationship and as she sits in the kitchen with her family on Saturday afternoon, there a heated group debate about her love life, much to her utter dismay.

"I'm just saying it's a bit weird that's all…" Peter holds his hands up in defence before rinsing his mug in the sink, "Surely you see where I'm coming from…?" Dom shrugs and smiles indifferently as he sits at the breakfast bar with Amelia in his lap, and Anna passes her another piece of apple before resting her hands on her hips.

"God you are so archaic…" She argues, "People form relationships in all sorts of ways these days and you're acting like he's fifty or something… he's not that much older than Abbey…"

"Yeah but he's her teacher…" Peter exaggerates, "Surely there are rules about that sort of thing…?"

"She's 19, Pete… nothing happened while she was still in school because of that reason but she's an adult now, no longer a pupil, no longer enrolled at the school he works at…" Abbey smarts a little at Anna's first comment. It isn't technically true that nothing has happened between them before now. When they shared a moment together last year she hadn't finished sixth form but then she wasn't actually attending classes at the time either? She honestly isn't sure if that counts or not?

"Can we please stop talking about this now?" Abbey begs, and Dom laughs sympathetically.

"I'm just saying, I find it a bit odd…"

"We get it Pete…" Anna snaps, "But I've seen the grin on my little sister's face this year and I am more than happy for her to see a guy who makes her feel that way… aren't you?"

"I suppose so…" He admits reluctantly, "But I'll be watching him…" He frowns.

"Seriously…?" Abbey shakes her head with irritation and looks down at her drink, only glancing back up as

Peter rests his hand on her shoulder and kisses the top of her head.

"Hey, I trust you OK? I just don't want you getting hurt..."

"I know..." She smiles, "But you have to give him a chance first!"

"Fine..." He grumbles, rolling his eyes as he picks up his jacket from one of the bar stools, "I have to check on an order that's been delivered for a job next week..."

"I'll see you tomorrow then..." Abbey smirks, "I'd appreciate it if you didn't follow us around tonight in a trench coat and dark glasses..."

"Don't be ridiculous..." Peter scoffs, "I don't own a trench coat!"

"Of course not, silly me..."

"Have fun... but be careful, please..." He adds, seriously.

"I will, I promise..." And seemingly satisfied with Abbey's reassurance, Peter leaves, shrugging into his jacket as he playfully punches Anna on the arm in passing.

"Can you believe him?" She sighs, as Janet appears from the garden in her sun hat and shades, dusting the mud from her hands.

"He's only being protective. As annoying as it may be you can do a lot worse than having a protective big brother..."

Abbey remembers back to when Peter used to drive her up the wall with his interfering. How she always used to see it as him being patronising and arrogant when really all he was doing was worrying about her. Funny how a clear head and being in a good place emotionally can enable you to see things as they really are, instead of seeing the worst. She kind of enjoys the fact that Peter has her back these days. She would look out for him in the same way too.

"So…" Anna smiles as she stands behind Abbey's seat and locks her arms around her neck, "Have you thought about what you're going to wear?"

"Yep, I have… Actually, I better go start getting ready…"

"It's only 3:30pm…!" Anna exclaims, as Abbey wriggles out of her grasp.

"I know, but I officially need to get out of this conversation…"

"You can escape now…" Dom laughs, "but you know she'll be bombarding you with questions tomorrow…" Anna shrugs and nods in agreement as Abbey grimaces at the thought. She will no doubt get the third degree from both of her siblings, her brother in law and her mum. But it doesn't frustrate her half as much as she lets on. They only do it because they care, and having them all take an active interest in her life, no matter how cringe worthy it might be, is an amazing feeling.

She appreciates how lucky she is.

Abbey somehow manages to get herself ready and changed in just under an hour which is a new personal best, but now she has another three to kill until she meets Matt with nothing to do but wait. After pacing nervously for several minutes, constantly checking and re-checking her hair and make-up, she reluctantly ventures back downstairs.

"Swit Swoo, very nice…" Anna beams as Abbey walks into the kitchen. She is wearing a black crop top with a thick, chunky gold necklace, her dark blue jeans, black ankle boots and her dark brown leather jacket. She picks up her keys from the kitchen work top and throws her bag over her shoulder, bending down to kiss Amelia before giving Dom a quick peck on the cheek.

"Are you going already?" Janet asks looking at the clock above the door.

"I can't wait around here for two hours, I'll go insane…"

"Don't be nervous sweetheart; you'll have a lovely time…" She smiles encouragingly.

"I know, I just don't want to sit here clock watching. I have few jobs I need to sort…"

"Do you want me to come with you?"

"No, don't be daft its fine. I'll text you when I get to the bar and when I'm on my way home, OK?"

"OK darling… have fun…" Abbey hugs Janet, squeezing her hand reassuringly as she turns to leave and Anna high fives her sister as she passes, grinning from ear to ear.

"Enjoy…" She chimes, and Abbey rolls her eyes as she smiles and waves at Amelia again before ducking out of the kitchen and setting off towards the bus stop at the end of the road.

Abbey's errands included posting several references for potential summer jobs as well as returning a handful of books to the library opposite school, but it had taken far less time than she expected it to. As she walks back outside into the pleasant evening sun, she ambles quietly along the street, thinking of her future, about what she is to do next and how this could be an exciting new beginning in more ways than one.

Without realising it she has soon ended up on the outskirts of the park and with plenty of time still to waste, she wanders down past the cricket green, through the play area and over towards the arcades. It looks exactly the same as it did and all the bittersweet memories come flooding back from the endless days she spent there with Lucy, Nathan and Liam. They were happier times, when she was so unbelievably grateful for their friendship and she feels a pang of sadness thinking back to how it all ended. She misses Lucy so much and wonders what she would think about all of this. Would she be proud of her for finishing school? Or would she be angry at her for walking away from Alex and their friends? It is something she will never know.

Abbey sits down at one of the tables in front of the arcade and watches a group of teenagers over at the skate park, practicing tricks on their boards and BMX's. The sun is low in the sky and there is a soft, gentle breeze rustling the trees above her head. She feels calm and content and although still saddened, thinking about the friends she has lost, she reminisces fondly of the afternoons they spent together, gossiping, joking around and laughing more than Abbey could ever remember laughing before in her life. Despite being in such a good place now, she really does miss them.

There is a loud clatter as one of the teenagers tries and fails to land a jump from the biggest ramp at the skate park and he tumbles to the ground in a heap. Abbey watches closely as he remains there for a few seconds before slowly getting up and dusting himself off. He appears to be uninjured, but his fall draws Abbey's attention long enough so that she fails to hear the scrape of a chair pulling up beside her.

"Hello stranger..." The familiar voice makes her jump and she stills slightly before turning slowly in her chair.

"Liam..." She gasps.

"How's it going?" Abbey's eyes tear up as she stares at her old friend and she swallows hard, composing herself. Instead of answering his question she instinctively leans towards him and they hug for a long, lingering moment.

"It's so good to see you, how are you?" She asks, running her hands underneath her eyes to prevent her tears from spilling over. He smiles at her reaction and lights up a cigarette, offering her one, but she politely declines. Just like she had done on the very first day they met.

"I'm good thanks..." He nods, snapping his lighter shut, "What are you doing here?"

"Oh I was just passing..."She shrugs, casually.

"I come here too sometimes..." He smiles, ignoring her far too flippant response, "Just to remember, you know? The way it used to be..."

"Feels like a million years ago..."

"It might as well be..." He sighs, "I heard you're on the straight and narrow now? That you did a stint in rehab?"

"Yeah I did, last year..."

"3 months?" Abbey nods and Liam shakes his head, looking impressed, "Good for you... really. I admire you for it. Same old story for me though I'm afraid, some of us haven't got that sort of will power. Plus I like chasing the high a little too much..."

"That's sort of what rehab is for Liam..." She smiles and he laughs in return.

"Yeah I guess so…"

"And everyone else…?" Abbey asks, cautiously. Trying hard not to single out one person in particular, "How are they?"

"Getting by, same old same you know…" He takes a long drag on his cigarette and exhales slowly, "He misses you, even now…"

Abbey's heart lurches and she has to bite down hard on her lip to stop herself from crying again, "He was fucking unbearable after you left… impossible to be around. Threw himself into work as usual to keep focused. Truth is, it hasn't really been the same since Tom and Lucy. I don't know how the fuck you're ever meant to get over something like that…" He frowns, and there is real deep rooted sadness in his eyes as he speaks Lucy's name.

"How's Nathan doing? And Darren?" Abbey asks, and Liam shrugs, leaning forward and resting his elbows on his knees.

"As well as can be expected I suppose. We get through… what else can you do?"

"Liam… I just want you to know, I never wanted to… I never meant to leave like I did, I just…"

"It's alright, Abbey. Alex told us what happened. I get it…"

"I'm still sorry…" She sighs and he smiles sympathetically, "Will you tell them that? And tell them all I said hi…?"

"Why don't you tell them yourself…? I'm on my way to meet them now…"

"I can't tonight…" Abbey replies quickly, panicked by the suggestion.

"Why not?"

"I'm meeting someone in a couple of hours…"

"A couple of hours is plenty of time to show your face and say hello…" Liam stares at her expectantly and Abbey finds herself toying with the idea for a moment despite her better judgement; completely torn down the middle, not knowing what to do for the best. Even though she knows she really shouldn't open that door and risk her recovery, she wishes more than anything that she could have said a proper goodbye to her friends and this might be the only chance she gets to explain her actions.

"I doubt Alex would want to see me…" She confesses.

"I don't know about that. Anyway he's working tonight, chances are he won't even get there until later and you'll have gone by then…" Liam is trying his best to persuade her, but she is still unsure, "Come on Abs… just come for one drink. We were your friends once remember? We were your family. Or does that not mean anything to you these days?"

Denny's Bar at the bottom of Merrion Street in Leeds has been one of Alex's main dealing spots for the last few years. He started doing business there way before he and Abbey met and according to Liam, he still works it on a regular basis. However, he has assured her that he won't be there until later tonight, which leaves Abbey relieved and disappointed all at the same time, and after a good ten minutes of Liam guilt tripping her into joining them she agrees to come for a drink.

They walk down a dark, narrow flight of stairs and into a long passage with posters of rock and indie bands covering every inch of the wall from floor to ceiling. There are several low hanging seventies style light shades illuminating the way and as they reach the end of the corridor it opens up into a large spacious room. The bar is situated at the top end and there are booths running down either side, slightly raised up from the rest of the seating area and the dance floor. The door they have just entered through is next to a montage of various musicians with a huge neon sign reading 'Denny's' suspended in the middle. Just across from them at the very back of the room, tucked away in a booth that is private and secluded, are a small group of people, four of whom she instantly recognises. As she follows cautiously behind Liam feeling almost sick with nerves, she hears a loud and pronounced, 'OH...MY... GOD...'. Gemma's obvious shock catches the attention of everyone gathered at the table and they all turn to follow her astonished gaze.

"Look who I bumped in to..." Liam announces proudly.

"Oh my gosh, Abbey I can't believe you're here..." Gemma throws her arms around her in a huge, welcoming hug as Sophie edges out from her seat at the table. She too greets Abbey warmly and their ability to instantly banish her nerves and make her feel completely at home still amazes her, just as it had done back when they first met almost two years ago.

"Bloody hell lass, It's fucking good to see you..." Darren shouts, as he lifts her up and swings her round.

"It's good to see you guys too..." She giggles; catching Nathan's eye as he carefully places her back down, "Hi Nate..." She smiles nervously, and his sweet and sad expression causes a lump to form in her throat. He climbs quietly out of the booth and steps forward, hugging her tightly - almost as if he is reluctant to let go - and tears pool in her eyes again. He is a lot thinner than she remembered and he looks so tired and worn out. It is obvious that he is still struggling with the physical and emotional effects of losing the love of his life. Perhaps he always will?

After her initial anxiety wears off Abbey can't believe how good it feels to see them all again, after spending months on end worrying about them and wondering how they are coping.

"What are you drinking Abs?" Darren asks excitedly, "This is cause for celebration! Or... do you still drink...?" He adds, apologetically.

"Yeah, I do... a glass of wine would be great?"

"No worries..." As he jumps down from the booth and strides across the dance floor Abbey takes a seat at the table with the others. She is introduced to the three people she has never seen before, who are apparently acquaintances of Alex. The two men are pleasant enough but the woman that is with them is frosty and unresponsive. Abbey quickly reaches the conclusion that she either thinks of her as the heinous bitch that broke Alex's heart, or, she is threatened because she wants Alex for herself and the ex-girlfriend turning up wasn't part of her plan. She isn't overly sure which it is but the second possibility makes Abbey's blood boil and her jealousy washes over her in a disarming wave. She has no right to feel this way, she has no claim to Alex what so ever after what she did, but when has jealousy ever been a rational emotion?

After ten minutes in the presence of her friends it feels like she has never been away. They talk and laugh openly together, reminiscing about the times they shared and all the crazy nights they partied their troubles away.

Darren and Sophie are still head over heels in love and it is a relief for Abbey to see that some things never change. Gemma informs her that Tom is doing well and is keeping his head down in prison, focusing on his release while studying a few courses to hopefully gain more qualifications for when he is back on the outside. It could be as little as three years until he is free now, instead of the initial five they originally thought.

Nathan had suffered a really difficult time in the months after Lucy died and he is apparently still battling to get his head straight. It was always going to be unbelievably tough for him to move on and the others seem to position themselves around him in a protective manner, constantly checking where he is and making sure that he is OK. Abbey doesn't press for details but it is fairly obvious due to the way they are acting that he must have gone quiet badly off the rails. They all seem to be keeping a close and watchful eye on him. He assures Abbey that he is doing much better now though and he seems to be in good spirits tonight, laughing and joining in with the banter full conversation.

Unsurprisingly, it isn't long until Abbey's departure becomes the topic of discussion and she grasps the opportunity to explain her actions, informing them of the various reasons behind why she left in such a cold, abrupt manner. She had been deeply worried that they would be angry and judgemental but to her great relief it soon becomes apparent that she needn't have felt that way at all. They understand. They know how painful it had become for the whole group and they admit that they always suspected deep down that she would eventually return to her family. Regardless of how much she appreciates their understanding, she is still highly apologetic and makes sure that they all appreciate just how much she has missed them.

It feels like a huge weight has been lifted by putting her cards on the table and talking so openly with them and she has gained a real sense of closure by seeing them tonight. Her guilt has lessened greatly and she is enjoying being back in the fold more than she ever thought she would. But drug taking is still a very obvious part of their lives and Abbey is hyper aware of various substances being continuously passed around the table. She manages to keep herself focused on whoever she is talking to, resisting the urge to look around while ignoring her morbid curiosity. She misses being in that frame of mind like crazy. That absolute high from taking drugs is a sensation like nothing else and she would be lying to herself if she said she didn't still crave it. But she has come so far recently and her life is firmly back on track again, exactly how it should be. She has absolutely no desire to spiral into old habits and throw all of her hard work away. As the night rolls on and the alcohol flows, more and more drugs will be offered around and handed out in a far less subtle manner. She knows that she can't stay here much longer with such a strong temptation in front of her, but it's OK, she has somewhere else she needs to be anyway.

"So are you glad you came?" Liam asks, swigging his pint and throwing his free arm over Abbey's shoulder.

"I am..." She admits, "It's been good to catch up with everyone, to say a proper goodbye..."

"A final goodbye..." There is only a hint of a question in Liam's tone as he already knows the answer. She can't come back to the group... not now. Her life is different, she is different, and although they mean so much to her and she will always love them, her friends live in a completely different world, one that she can no longer be a part of. There is no going back.

"I'm really glad you came too, mate. And I know you're little Miss responsible and everything these days, but we had some fucking good times didn't we? Me, You, Nate and Lucy…? I hope you remember that, I hope you remember the laughs we had, instead of all the bullshit…"

"I will, of course I will…" She smiles and Liam winks at her affectionately.

Abbey pulls out her phone to check the time. It is 6:57pm. She has been here for well over an hour now and has had two glasses of wine, not enough to get her drunk but enough to take the edge off her nerves for her impending date. She had almost forgotten about meeting Matt due to the unexpected turn of events and how her evening has played out, but there is a missed call highlighted on her phone along with a flashing voicemail notification at the top of her screen.

She presses her finger to her ear in an attempt to drown out any background noise and walks slowly away from the booth, through a set of partly opened curtains and into a little area that leads on to the toilets.

'Hi it's Matt, I hope you get this before you set off. I'm running a bit late but I will get there as soon as I can. It'll probably be about 7:45pm, not much after, I'm really sorry. I've been looking forward to seeing you all day, Abbey… all week actually. Give me a ring if you need to, but I'll see you soon anyway. OK… Bye.'

Abbey grins from ear to ear as she saves the message and hangs up. It's time to make a move but she will finish her drink first before she sets off. It should only take twenty minutes or so to get to Headingley from here and she doesn't want to arrive too early or appear too keen.

Saying a final goodbye to her friends will be difficult, but it is better than never having the opportunity at all. She wonders idly if she should leave a message for Alex with Gemma or Sophie but what could she possibly say to him through someone else? It wouldn't seem right and she has no idea how to even begin to explain herself anyway. Her heart sinks and she feels an overwhelming sense of anguish that the one person she won't get to see is the most important person of all, but she has to accept the inevitable. With a deep, resigned breath, Abbey locks her phone and slides it into her pocket but before she has chance to turn around and head back through to the bar, a quiet, tormented voice speaks softly behind her in an achingly familiar Irish accent.

"I didn't believe them when they said you were here…" Abbey's whole body locks into place and her heart lurches in her chest as she lets out a sharp, quiet gasp. She is almost paralysed, unable to turn around and face him as she genuinely doesn't know what it will do to her. A warm shiver runs slowly down her spine and all her nerves stand on end. She clearly still has the same reaction to his voice and his presence as she always did, "Aren't you going to look at me…?"

Abbey's tears instantly threaten, but she just about manages to compose herself before taking three small steps, turning on the spot.

Alex is standing inside the curtains just out of view from the others. They are completely alone, and in the heart-breaking moment their eyes meet Abbey wants nothing more than to run into his arms. Her memory didn't do him justice; and seeing him standing there with his guarded stance and his reluctant expression, she feels an overwhelming need to comfort him.

She doesn't know what to say, how to speak, or how to act. The gap between them feels far too wide, strained, and uncomfortable but his body language prevents her from moving any closer. As the silence stretches on they stare at each other across the empty space, searching for answers to unspoken questions. Abbey can barely stand the painful sense of longing that is almost crippling her and the heavy ache in her heart is more than she can handle. She longs to touch him, to kiss him, to hold him again, and all the love that she has been burying for so long comes rushing back to the surface.

"Alex..." She gasps, only just managing to force out his name in a whisper.

"You know I didn't understand it..." He continues softly, looking down at the floor, "When I woke up that morning and you were gone. I didn't understand how you could leave me like that..."

"Alex, I..." Abbey tries to speak but her words get caught in her throat and he glances up, his eyes glistening under the dim light that is hanging above them, casting eerie shadows over their unexpected reunion.

"I was so angry..." He continues, "Angry at you for leaving, angry at myself for not doing more and I missed you..." He takes a step forward, reiterating his point by stretching out his hand towards her before quickly snapping it back down at his side, remembering himself, "I missed you so fucking much..."

"I missed you too..." Abbey sobs, stepping forward so that the gap between them grows smaller still,

"I never wanted to leave you Alex, you have to know that... but I had to get out. I needed to get myself better, to fix what was broken. It was never you I was walking away from...."

"You just disappeared..." He whispers solemnly.

"Please don't be angry with me..." Abbey looks away, remorsefully. What a stupid thing to say. Of course he should be angry, he has every right to be, but the thought of him hating her is almost too painful to endure and she wishes more than anything that she could make him understand why she had to leave.

"I'm not angry..." He shakes his head and Abbey's mouth snaps shut in surprise, "Not anymore. It took me a long time to realise it, but I know you only did what you had to. Things got so dangerous, so out of control. You realised it before I did and you knew something had to change. When you left, it finally made me see how bad things really were and it made me step up..."

"I never wanted to hurt you, Alex; I really hope you believe that..."

"I know..." He nods, and he lets out a short quiet laugh that is littered with sadness as he smiles at Abbey longingly, "We really had something didn't we...?"

"Yeah we did..." She agrees, smiling back at him through her tears, "And I still... You know, I... I never stopped..." Abbey stutters as she nervously runs her hands through her hair, struggling to find the right words. She knows exactly how she feels about Alex, how she will always feel, but saying it out loud won't change a thing and that crushing realisation devastates them both.

"I know you had to get out. You tried to tell me but I wouldn't listen, I didn't want to hear it. But I get it now..."

"I'm still sorry…"

"You don't owe me an apology Abbey; you don't owe me anything…" He frowns angrily and a look of self-loathing flashes across his face.

"That's not true…" She disagrees, stepping forward and instinctively placing her hand on Alex's arm. How can he possibly think that? She owes him so much, she owes him everything and he is still so unbelievably important to her. They shared a life together and feelings that intense don't just go away, "You know that's not true…" She states firmly again, desperately trying to convince him, and he closes his eyes looking lost and tormented as he lifts his hand and runs it softly through her hair, causing her heart to skip several beats.

"I wish I could have been more for you…" He sighs, resting his head gently against hers.

"I wish I could have stayed…" Abbey responds, and he smiles down at her with a sorrowful acceptance.

"You couldn't. You never really belonged here Abbey. You mean the fucking world to all of us… but you were never meant for this life. You deserve so much better, I always told you that. You were lost… it just so happened we were the ones who found you…"

"I'm so glad you did… despite everything…" She confesses, and her lip begins to tremble as she knows she has no choice but to say goodbye to the one person she loves more than anyone else in the world, "Promise me you'll look after yourself?" She pleads.

"I will…" He nods, choking back tears as he takes a deep and calming breath, "You'll always be my girl you know? Always…" And all Abbey can do is nod back in response as she struggles to bring her crying under control. She knew that this would be painful, but she wasn't prepared for it to be quite so excruciating.

"I love you..." She whispers and Alex drops his shoulders in despair as those three little words break through the last of his resolve and he gives in to the agony of the moment.

They are so close that Abbey can smell his aftershave and feel the warmth of his breath on her face and neck as he stares down at her. Will this be too painful? Will this hurt too much? She isn't sure... but she can only agonize about it for a fraction of a second, as he leans in closer still and gently tilts her head back.

"I love you too..." He whispers, before pulling her into a forceful, passionate kiss. Abbey instinctively wraps her arms around his neck and they press their bodies together tightly, grasping and pulling at each other with desperation and grief, completely lost in the moment. Kissing each other, not 'as though' it is their very last kiss... but with the painful understanding that it is.

When they finally break apart they stand locked together for a minute or two, unwilling to step back and completely release their hold on one another.

"I have to go..." Abbey whispers, sadly and Alex finally removes his arm from around her waist, causing a hollow emptiness to twist in the pit of her stomach. As he takes hold of her hand, that ever familiar charge of electricity surges through her and she wonders if she will ever feel this strongly about anyone again?

Saying goodbye to her friends only adds to the sadness and sense of loss that she is feeling but she remains incredibly grateful to Liam for bringing her here tonight and for giving her the chance to see them again. She embraces each of them in turn, hugging them tightly as they exchange their emotional farewells. She will never forget them, or the love and friendship they showed her at the loneliest time of her life. They saved her in so many ways.

Alex stands quietly on the side lines, too busy savouring his last few minutes with Abbey to notice the stranger lurking in the shadows by the edge of the bar. He has his hood pulled up with a baseball cap partially obscuring his face and after assessing the scene closely, he turns and sprints through the emergency exit, out onto the street and over to a black 4x4 that is parked up at the side of the road.

"They're all in there. Matthews, his friends... and his girlfriend too..." The lackey struggles to catch his breath as he dutifully informs Marcus Holt of Alex's movements.

"Excellent..." Marcus grins, viciously, and he twists his hands around the steering wheel as he stares at the main entrance to the bar, waiting to make his move.

Abbey and Alex climb the last of the narrow stairs and exit Denny's onto the street outside. It is still relatively quiet and would seem as though the Saturday night revellers have yet to descend onto Leeds city centre, or at least onto Merrion Street.

Abbey faces Alex with a heavy heart and reaches up on her tip toes, kissing him lightly on the lips once more as he smiles down at her.

"I'll see you around Irish..." She jokes sadly, and Alex shoves his hands in his pockets, shaking his head with a vague smile on his face.

"No you won't..." He replies, and they stare at each other longingly once again, as the realisation dawns that this is really it. It really is over.

Abbey begins to back away into the middle of the empty road, knowing that she has to eventually turn around and leave Alex behind her for the final time. Neither of them seem willing to break their gaze, but Alex finally relents, smiling with genuine affection as he looks down at the ground and edges back into the doorway of Denny's, completely unaware that several yards up the street, Marcus Holt is sitting patiently behind the wheel of his car.

He turns the keys in the ignition and as the engine roars to life, he shifts forward in his seat with bitterness and venom in his eyes.

"Right..." He growls, "Let's get this little fucker where it really hurts..." And without any hesitation what so ever, he slams the car into gear, pulls out of the parking space and floors the accelerator.

There is a loud screeching of tyres followed by a loud metallic thud and Abbey catches the look of sheer horror on Alex's face before he is suddenly out of sight. All she can see is white, then the buildings and the sky above her. They are spinning, round and round, spiralling wildly out of control. No. It is her. She is the one that is spinning.

She feels limp and weightless as she flies through the air and her world slows down so much it almost collapses into freeze frame before she slams into the cold, hard concrete. Searing pain spreads through her every limb and she can feel a pool of warmth encasing her head and forming around her right hand. She can hear someone frantically calling her name. Is it Alex? She searches for him desperately but her vision is becoming blurred. If only she can see him, then it will be alright. Everything will be alright.

There is screaming and shouting, and so much commotion surrounding her but Abbey can't feel anything. She is falling, falling into darkness, when Alex suddenly appears above her, shouting her name and gently stroking her face, looking panicked and terrified. She wants to tell him not to worry, that she is OK and that she loves him... but she is slipping further and further away, unable to hold on any longer. She takes one last look into those beautiful eyes – bluer than the bluest sky - before the taste of blood catches in her throat, the numbness pulls her under and everything around her fades to black.

Epilogue

Gone

Janet reaches absentmindedly into the overflowing wash basket, carefully pulling out a single garment at a time before folding it neatly. She drops each item on top of the growing pile of clean laundry and mindlessly continues the cycle while staring distractedly at the wall above Abbey's bed.

It is early evening and the sun sits low in the sky. Every so often Janet glances over at Abbey who is standing in the window in the corner; staring down at the empty street below and watching the weeping willows sway gracefully in the breeze.

"I just don't understand…" Janet sighs, quietly, "I don't understand why you would go there? I mean what was the point? You were doing so well, you'd turned a page, you'd moved on… and then you go to that bar, back to those kids…" She drops the t-shirt she is holding and lifts her hand to her face, quickly composing herself before hastily re-folding it, "They may have been your friends once, Abbey, but you have to leave them behind now. You shouldn't have been there in the first place, you shouldn't have been anywhere near that street or that speeding car…" Abbey slowly turns around to face her mum but she doesn't speak. She simply stares at her with wide, beseeching eyes as Janet continues her tireless rant, "Why did you have to go to that bar with those people? What on earth were you trying to prove? It just doesn't make any sense to me..." Her voice rises in pitch as she becomes more and more irate but Abbey still doesn't respond, "You were doing so well darling. Everything you'd come through and everything you'd achieved. God I was so proud of you. I was so proud..." Abbey takes a small step forward and tilts her head to one side, raising her shoulders ever so slightly in an apologetic gesture, but Janet struggles to look at her, unable to contain her sorrow and disappointment as she throws her head back and sighs again deeply.

"Mum...?" Anna stands a few feet away on the landing, watching Janet with fraught concern.

She waits patiently for her to respond, and after a lengthy pause Janet blinks hard as if trying to remember something important. She turns slowly towards Anna and away from the empty window, with a lost and vacant expression on her pale and tear stained face, "Who were you talking to...?"